November Rain

November Rain

DONALD HARSTAD

CROOKED
LANE

Copyright © 2013 by Donald Harstad

All rights reserved.

Published in the United States by Crooked Lane Books, an imprint of The Quick Brown Fox & Company LLC.

Crooked Lane Books and its logo are trademarks of The Quick Brown Fox & Company LLC.

The Library of Congress Cataloging-in-Publication Data is available upon request.

978-1-61129-049-3

Cover design by Lori Palmer

Printed in the United States.

www.crookedlanebooks.com

Crooked Lane Books
2 Park Avenue, 10th Floor
New York, NY 10016

Second Edition: September 2015

10 9 8 7 6 5 4 3 2 1

ACKNOWLEDGMENTS

I would like to thank several young women who provided insight and information for several characters in this book. Courtney Zaph Bently, Kelly Zaph Carnes, and Molly Zaph, who provided great insights into the thinking of the young women in the book.

Victoria Baillie McCorkindale, a nurse who worked at St. Thomas Hospital in London, and who I met at a party in Elkader, Iowa. Victoria gave a description of the workings of the hospital that proved invaluable, and a delightful rhythm of speech that was of great use in one character in particular.

I would also like to thank Bob Mecoy, my agent, for his tireless efforts, persistence, and sense of humor.

To My Wife, Mary
Who has never stopped believing in me.

Prologue

M y name's Carl Houseman, and I'm a Deputy Sheriff in Nation County, Iowa. It's a pretty big county, as Iowa goes, covering about 750 square miles. Our total population is about 19,000, and our largest town has nearly 2,000 people. Among other things, that means that when our daughter Jane went to college, there were more people in her dorm than there were in her hometown.

I'm 56; about six feet four and about 275 lbs., give or take. I have less hair than I did last year and a whole lot more than I'll have in a year or two. It's harder to tell it's thinning, since it's all gray now. I'm what those who don't want to irritate me refer to as "experienced." Under Iowa law, in fact, I'm so experienced I'm eligible to retire. Under Iowa's Public Employee's Retirement System, I can't afford to.

This is the story of the Schiller case. It doesn't have a case number, because it didn't happen anywhere near our jurisdiction. That's the same reason that the official case file is out of my reach. Nonetheless, I got assigned to it. Reluctantly, just for the record.

Washington, DC

Excerpt from an Intelligence Briefing entitled: "Task, Collect, Process and Use" presented by special agent Volont of the F.B.I. to a joint task group on April 19, 2002.

One of the weaknesses of a typical terrorist organization is their inability to act in a timely fashion. This is the window of opportunity that can enable us to discover the intent to act and to intervene decisively before the act is committed.

This is the area where our response has been the least effective. We feel that the primary reason for that lack of effectiveness is twofold: insufficient resources to enable us to differentiate between accurate and inaccurate information; and a failure of interpretation after reliable information has been received and identified as such.

Chapter 1

Tuesday, October 28, 2003
Pond Square Park
Highgate, London, UK

Emma Schiller left the Gatehouse Pub, and walked quickly toward her flat on the southwest side of Pond Square Park. She'd been drinking, was embarrassed, hurt and very angry at one Martin Granger, and wasn't quite ready to see her roommates.

She walked to the south edge of the little park, scrunching the tiny rocks under her feet, and sat on a bench near the public restroom. The lighting was adequate, although she thought it was too yellow. There was very little activity in the village, and except for the make of the cars parked in the square, she could have been home in Maitland, Iowa.

"Well, it's a good thing you're not," she said, quietly, to herself. In Maitland, they probably just wouldn't understand. The problem had started with Martin Granger, a young teacher she'd met at the Pub more than a month ago. They'd struck up a conversation, enjoyed each other's company, and she had wound up sleeping with him at his flat four nights later. Emma had no regrets about sex with Martin. None whatsoever. Emma's attitude toward sexual relationships had been, for at least the last fifteen of her thirty-four years, very much focused on the here and now. She would have termed any sexual relationship that lasted more than six months as having gone on too long. She very nearly always managed to end them on her terms, and in her way. She was happy to have brief relationships, and was absolutely convinced that she would never have one that lasted as long as a year. She certainly didn't want or need something long-term.

"The little prick," she said softly.

Martin had caused her to violate one of her very few hard and fast rules about relationships. Never sleep with a married man, or one who was engaged. Everybody else was fair game. A simple rule, and in her entire life she'd never found herself seriously attracted to anyone who had been married. She was determined to never be the other woman in a relationship.

Tonight, Martin had informed her that he was engaged, that the wedding would be quite soon, and that he was sorry, but that things would have to stop. Worse, he'd done it after she'd joined him and some of his friends at their table, and had actually asked the little creep to escort her home. The implication of her request had been very clear to him, and to his friends. He had acted embarrassed, and the inflections of his voice had made it appear as if she'd already known of his fiancé.

"The bastard," she said. She had, in fact, asked him if he were encumbered in any way before she'd ended up in his bed the first time. She'd never forget his answer.

"Hardly. I'm not the sort who has long relationships."

She'd thought they were birds of a feather. She took a deep breath. So much for that idea. And to top it all off, she'd come to the Pub tonight with her roommates, and had insisted that they leave and not wait up for her. Both Jane and Vicky had asked her if she were "sure you'll be all right?" She'd been irritated. Neither of them had any romantic action at all. Why interfere with her?

The statement that had topped it all was that one of the other men at Martin's table had said something she hadn't entirely caught, but involved the words "slutty," and "American."

She'd put him back very firmly in his place, when she'd grabbed his collar and said, "Fuck off, you pencil necked little schoolboy." Well, she thought that maybe she had. It had felt very good to say it, but the recollection was beginning to sour.

She leaned forward, and put her head in her hands. "Aw, shit," she muttered, and took a deep breath. "Forget him. Hell, forget *them*. You're just embarrassed."

She thought that was good advice, straightened up, and almost started to get to her feet when she became aware that there was somebody standing very close in front of her. Her first thought, before she raised her head back up, was that it was Martin.

"Piss off," she said, loudly, as she stood.

It was not Martin. Instead, in the yellowish light, she found herself staring at a fairly tall man with sharp features.

"Oh.," she said, with an embarrassed giggle. "Oh, I'm so sorry, I thought . . ."

The first blow was to the left side of her face, and nearly knocked her off her feet.

"What?!" she yelled, as she caught herself with her right and on the seat of the bench. Her first instinct was to kick out, and she did, but he jumped back, and she missed. She became aware of a hand trying to grab her from the rear, and she lunged to her left, pulling the shoulder of her sweatshirt from his grasp.

Emma had always been something of a fighter, and even surprised and a little drunk, her reactions were very good. She lunged directly at the man who had hit her, screaming as loudly as she could. He grabbed her, but she frantically twisted her five foot one inch frame, at the same time as she struck out with a flurry of blows to his face. They both went to the ground, and she managed to stand before he did. In three steps, she'd left him behind, and was just filling her lungs to scream when a third man she hadn't seen stepped from a shadowy area near a tree, put his shoulder down, and ran right into her. His shoulder hit her in the chest and abdomen, driving her upward and back, completely off her feet, and knocking her breath away. She hit the gravel with a thump that knocked the remaining wind from her, with his body crashing down on hers an instant later. She flailed her arms, but was picked up by her legs and arms by what she thought were two people, and the third delivered a kick that caught her in the kidneys.

She came around a few seconds later, confused and in a lot of pain, but was able to realize that she was already in a car. She was trying to fight, get her breath, and vomit all at the same time. Someone was pounding on her back saying "Lie still! Lie still!"

Another was trying to put some tape over her mouth, and the one pounding on her back stopped for an instant, and said something in a language she didn't understand. The tape disappeared, replaced by a rough hand pressing her face into the crack of the seat. As she vomited up her last Guinness, she tried to move her head, afraid that she would drown.

Every time she raised her head, somebody would strike her in the middle of her back, and say, "No!"

She started to get her breath back, gasping, spitting, and gagging. She had a dim awareness of looking at the back of a driver's seat, before some hands grabbed her ankles, held them tightly together, and bent her legs, bringing her feet up toward the back of her head. Then, whoever that was, leaned heavily, pinning her even more firmly to the seat.

The hand on her neck relented, and her face was turned toward the front of the car. Tape was slapped over her mouth, wound part way to the back of her head, tangling in her hair. She jerked her head back, and was rewarded with another blow to the face. Stunned, she was dimly aware that a roll of tape was being wound around her head, over and over. Then her wrists, behind her back, were tightly bound. Then her ankles. Then they seemed to pass something between her ankles and her wrists, tightly bringing them together behind her back.

Then, and only then, did the pressure ease and the blows stop.

"American whore." It was said in a low tone, but very clearly. Then the same voice said, "Call him. Tell him you have her."

"Right. Yes. Is she alive?"

"Don't be so foolish. Call him and tell him you have her."

What Emma Schiller couldn't know, and surely couldn't have cared about at that moment, was that these things happening to her were the result of months of planning.

Chapter 2

January 11, 2003
Ashburnham Road
London, UK
22:35 Greenwich Mean Time

It had begun months before, on a cold night in London, with what was effectively a committee meeting. The organizational meeting of the steering committee of the London Movement for the Freedom of Khaled al Fawwaz and Ibrahim Eidarous, as it was originally known, brought together three people with similar interests; two men and a woman. Dr. Robert Northwood was a professor of English, a man known only by the name of Imad was an electrical engineer, and Hanadi Tamish was a solicitor. The three had initially met at a rally for the liberation of Palestine, and had continued their relationship ever since. Tonight, at the professor's flat on Ashburnham Road, they met to formalize their interests.

Unbeknownst to both the professor and the solicitor, the electrical engineer Imad, who had graduated from University College with an MSc in Broadband Communications was also a 1988 graduate of an al-Qaeda training camp. That particular credit he had never shared with the administration of UCL. It is important to note that, while he had attended the camp, he was not a member of al-Qaeda. He had not, as the Americans would say, made the cut; and as a consequence, had not been permitted to take an oath of loyalty to Osama bin Laden. He had been informed, though, that his subsequent actions and activities would be closely watched. Anything that furthered the broader goals of that organization would be considered in his favor.

The solicitor Hanadi insisted upon the keeping of "proper minutes." That was agreeable, especially since she had just volunteered to be the group's secretary.

The question of chairman was the first real order of business. The professor of English, much to his feigned surprise, was the unanimous choice.

The post of Treasurer went to the engineer, because the posts of secretary and chairman were already occupied.

Finished with those mundane tasks, the three discussed their agreement to work together to obtain release of political prisoners held in the UK; especially Khaled al Fawwaz and Ibrahim Eidarous. That their release would be the ultimate goal of the group was agreed upon unanimously, and so recorded. It is of interest that both Professor Northwood and the solicitor Hanadi were thinking exclusively of an activist organization, and nothing more. Both envisioned pamphlets, protests, and letters to the media. Imad the engineer had no such reservations, but kept his thoughts on that matter to himself.

The adoption of their group name required no thought at all, and was also a unanimous decision.

There remained the question of who would design the website for the group, and it was a task happily given to Imad, since he had extensive computer training and experience, and one of his fellow workers was skilled at computer art, and could design a logo. This was entered into the minutes as a consensus of the group, with the provision that the logo be approved by unanimous vote at a later meeting.

During this original meeting, the subject of religion was obliquely addressed. Although they were fully aware that Professor Northwood was the only non-Muslim present, Hanadi said that it was her opinion that a unity of purpose was the primary requirement for the members, and that politics was the principle tool for their joint endeavor. Not only that, but she offered that religious diversity within the group was very likely beneficial, and would serve to underscore the universality of their cause. Northwood and Imad agreed.

Imad then brought up two questions that occupied much of the time in that first meeting. First, he stated his opinion that they would require "soldiers" to do much of the unimportant work for the organization, as the three of them were professional people and had serious work-related obligations. Recruitment was discussed, and eventually turned into a task to be handled by the engineer, who was going on holiday beginning the next week and would have the free time to interview prospects. Hanadi then objected to the word "soldier," and even though Imad strongly disagreed, he kept it to himself and it was changed to "worker" by consensus.

The second question put forth by Imad regarded the utility of an "operations" manager. He was quick to state that it would in no way effect the true chairmanship. It would, however, facilitate the super-vision and direction of whatever workers they would be able to recruit.

"Organizer," said Hanadi. "It would be more of an organizational function."

"Not unlike a Chief of Staff," said Professor Northwood. The idea had a certain appeal. There was very little discussion regarding this, since Hanadi said she was certain that it would be a very time con-suming task, and she did not have the time to devote to it. Conse-quently, the Imad also became the Chief of Staff.

The engineer Imad, therefore, had gotten himself in the position of financial officer, Chief of Staff, and field general all in one. The pre-conception by Northwood and Hanadi regarding the activist nature of the group allowed for unbalanced responsibilities. Given the na-ture of the group as they saw it, it couldn't possibly make a significant difference.

The professor had sincere and honest concerns about the nature of the people being held at Belmarsh prison. He also sympathized with some of the ideology of Osama bin Laden, particularly where the pres-ence of Western troops in the Middle East was concerned. Although not an anti-Semite, he also opposed the Israeli actions in Palestine, and their handling of the entire Palestinian matter. Professionally, the pro-fessor also felt that a position within a group that opposed political repression would enhance his reputation among his peers. The Univer-sity could hardly object to faculty members participating in an activist organization of high ethical and moral standards; and the inquiry by a private organization into the welfare and status of political prisoners in Belmarsh would certainly qualify. The fact that he was the non-Muslim among them also appealed to his ecumenical sensibilities. The fact that he had been elected their chairman appealed to a somewhat more pedestrian side of his nature. He was, as he enjoyed telling his friends, a man of four passions: English literature, politics, women and the his-tory of the London Underground. Or, as he would sometimes put it, his profession, his beliefs, and his two hobbies.

Lately, Northwood found himself wishing to expand his relation-ship with Hanadi. He found the solicitor attractive both intellectually and physically, and she seemed to like him, as well. The fact that she was some twenty years younger bothered him not in the least. He still managed select relationships with his female graduate students, and had a very high regard for himself in that area. Idly, he wondered if she would be interested in his guided tour of the Underground.

The activist tactics he envisioned at that initial meeting incorporated no violent acts whatsoever. He was a firm believer in the power of the written word.

Hanadi herself was very sincere about the release of the prisoners, and had every intention of participating in their legal activities toward that end. She was a strong believer in the rule of law, and the effecting of change through legal avenues. She was employed by an old firm in London, whose four senior partners were QC's and heavily involved in the legal battles of the left. Their approval was tacit, and she was very concerned with impressing them, as she held the motivations of the firm in the highest regard. She was also a devout Muslim, and sincerely felt that the religion of Fawwaz and Eidarous was at least one of the reasons they were being held, if not the principal one. She also had family members in Palestine and her parents were living in Lebanon. She maintained close contacts with them, and traveled to see them at least twice a year. They, too, would have enormous approval of her if she were to obtain the prisoner's release; and substantial approval would be voiced even were she to try and ultimately fail. To Hanadi, her family's approval and recognition of her was of equal importance to, and perhaps the result of, her religion. She had been known in law school as one of the most sincere and passionate believers in the law, never developing the somewhat cynical attitude of many of her contemporaries.

She, too, had no intention of committing any violent actions. The thought of doing anything illegal at all would have run counter to her nature. She did have family members who, perhaps, felt differently, but she herself was a firm and solid believer in the rule of both Islamic and secular laws.

Imad was concerned with three goals from the outset: obtaining the power behind the scenes, which he had achieved by becoming the treasurer, chief of staff, and field commander; recruiting one or more non-Muslim participants, which he had accomplished by voting the professor into the chairmanship; and most importantly, establishing a cover organization for his more active operations. This third goal was well on its way, and needed only the recruitment of his soldiers. His motivation regarding the prisoners in Belmarsh Prison was their utility to his cause. He was a terrorist, although one without portfolio at this time. He, too, had relatives in other countries: Saudi Arabia, the United States, the United Kingdom, France, Germany and Egypt. Most were uncles and cousins, and several would have been hard put to recognize him in a crowded room. All of them would offer their help if asked.

He was committed to violence from the very beginning. He believed in the effectiveness of explosives and automatic weapons.

The last subject for the evening was introduced by the new chairman. "Do you suppose we need code names?"

The tone of his voice told Imad that code names would appeal strongly to Northwood. Imad was careful not to scoff. He, after all, was *already* operating under an alias. "I think code names would be fine," he said, fully aware that his 'cell members' would very likely be using their own email addresses and their own telephone numbers to communicate messages with their 'code names,' rendering them pointless in any practical sense. He was also aware, although he would have been hard put to elucidate it, that his acquiescence to a rather childish behavior would make him even more effective within this little cell when the time came.

Hanadi liked the idea of the code name, considered that it could ad a unique flavor to their proceedings, and also agreed. She, herself, fully intended to acquire a new email account under an assumed name.

"I'd like to use Marwan," said Northwood, quite seriously. "As a tribute to the 9/11 hijackers." Marwan al Shehhi had been the hijacker who had piloted United Airlines Flight 175 to its doom, and Northwood liked the sound of Marwan.

To himself, Imad felt that the martyred al Shehhi would not have approved. But if this token Englishman wanted to do this thing, he would not object.

Hanadi considered for a moment. "I would choose Ayat," she said. "For personal reasons." Ayat Akhras had been an 18 year old girl who had blown herself up at a bus stop in Jerusalem. She had been a friend of one of Hanadi's cousins, and Hanadi had met her on her last return to her paternal home. She had been shocked and very saddened by this event, but found to her surprise that she admired the commitment of the young woman.

Neither Northwood nor Imad knew this information, although Imad knew instantly who Ayat Akhras had been. He and Northwood did not press her regarding her personal reasons. Hanadi had let it be known in many ways that she was a very private person.

There remained Imad. "I shall keep Imad," he said. He smiled. "Also for personal reasons."

Robert Northwood found that slightly irritating. His "man of mystery" façade had been trumped by an actually mysterious man. He did hope that Hanadi, or Ayat as she would now be known in their circles, would ignore that.

The meeting adjourned after an agreement was reached to meet weekly, in varied locations. It was an informal, friendly and innocuous beginning; constructed by two amateurs and a professional. It is of interest that this was the last time that the group would meet on such relaxed terms.

July 5, 2003
A Compound near Wana, Pakistan

The house was small, but clean and well kept. The chief occupant was known, even in the village, as 'the Man in the House.' His name was not spoken, although there was absolutely no doubting who he was, and no doubting the loyalty of each and every villager. Their caution was for the sole purpose of preventing any chance of the name of the man to be overheard by any visitor to their village in the mountains. He never stayed more than a week, and this was his fourth visit in a year.

There were three al-Qaeda–linked compounds in the hills near the village; a training facility that had been a small farm and which dealt exclusively with the design and packaging of explosives; the small safe house that contained 'the man' and his small group; and the furthest from the village and on the only road into the place, was an isolated series of small huts that contained the security group who protected the residents of the small safe house. The village, in turn, was near the town of Shakai, about 25 kilometers west of Wana, the largest town in South Waziristan. South Waziristan was part of a Federally administered Tribal area on the Pakistani/Afghan border. The actual border was a mater of some conjecture, and was described in various intelligence documents as "permeable."

The tall man, who had made the long, arduous and at times extremely dangerous trek from Kabul, closely pressed by US Forces, had enjoyed relative peace for the last year. Although the invasion of Afghanistan by the US in October of 2001 had not been anticipated, by February of 2002, the man and his followers had been able to consider themselves relatively secure. The American aircraft surely were not about to drop their bombs on Pakistani soil, or even an area that might be Pakistani. As for their Special Operations troops, he was always concerned, but not worried. The local tribesmen were very alert, and he had friends in the Pakistani Military Intelligence service.

He was seated on the floor, at a small table, signing and recording documents that were to be taken out this afternoon by courier. He glanced up at his visiting brother-in-law.

"This . . ." He glanced again at the paper before him, making certain that he had the title correct, ". . . London Islamic Reform Movement for the freedom of Khaled al Fawwaz and Ibrahim Eidarous?" He looked back up. "Is there truly a need for this Movement?"

"Not a need," said his brother-in-law, who had read the correspondence from London over an hour ago. "A use, I think. They are led by one of some reliability, who has had training. Imad Imadhi."

"The engineer?" The man remembered him as having great potential use for the organization, but he had not been considered sufficiently reliable to be accepted into the fold.

"Yes. There are also members of the educated class, who are either born in Britain, or who are at least citizens. They are requiring some little funding, which could be provided by assets on hand in London. All that is required is that they undertake an operation. If they succeed, it is a benefit. If they fail, and their identities revealed, it is also a benefit because they will shock the British."

The man thought. "I remember Imad. Yes. An electrical engineer is a very useful thing to be. And a native born Englishman linked to our goals will be upsetting, I'm sure." He smiled. "So. Then they should undertake this action they propose. It is one in keeping with their name. Allah willing, they will succeed."

Both men were silent for a few moments. "There are the five in Belmarsh Prison. Attention could be drawn to their plight by this. They have no need to coordinate with other cells. It is a stand-alone operation. It is a way for Imad to prove his worth."

The tall man considered, and then said, "It needs to divide, if possible."

"They say they propose a hostage," said his brother-in-law.

"Their demand should be high. The immediate release of the five. They are to be taken to the Egyptian Embassy." He smiled thinly. "Let that be the Egyptian's dilemma."

"Excellent." The brother-in-law smiled. "Should we suggest an American hostage? Any additional strain between the Americans and the British . . ."

"Notify Hjaer that there will be a diversionary operation. Give him the adopted name of the group. When he hears of them, he will know that we have given them our guidance, that they act for us, and that he will not need to concern himself with their activities."

Hjaer was their senior operative in London. Hjaer was a very busy man.

Each document was completed, signed, and given to a courier, one Hamid Rama, a bona fide member of The Harkat-ul-Mujahideen. In the course of his long and dusty journey, he walked the fifteen or so kilometers to Wana, arriving late in the evening. From there the next day, he rode in the back of an old Volkswagen pick-up that was headed to Bannu. Those 138 road kilometers took an entire day, as they had two flat tires on the journey. From there, he traveled another 350 kilometers by bus to Muridke, an Arab financed suburb of Lahore where he and his fellow terrorists had many, many friends. He had now traveled more than 500 kilometers from Wanna. At Muridke, he handed the small packet to another courier, who began his own 1,000 kilometer route to Karachi. The shipment of the parcel from the small village on the Afghan border would take eight days. Once in Karachi, the message was transcribed and posted on an Arabic language website which would only exist for ten days. At the same time, an innocuous email was sent to an address in London, with the childishly cryptic sentence: "I intend to purchase the goats on the 23rd." That was the date when the recipient should check the website. The original document was then placed on an ageing steamship, and would arrive in Australia in about a month. From there, it would be sent via the Royal Mail to its recipient in London. It would be received as confirmation not only of an operation, but of a deep and binding confidence. It was a confidence that was not to be betrayed.

Chapter 3

Tuesday, October 28, 2003
Ashburnham Road
London, UK

At the time Emma Schiller was sitting with her friends at the Gate-house Pub, Robert Hastings Northwood, known to his terrorist cell members as "Marwan," was in his flat on Ashburnham Road, looking out the window, and wishing he were alone. He glanced at the VCR above his television. The blue numerals of the clock said 9:55 PM.

"She should be at the tube station about now," he said, shifting his gaze back to the street below. He was in his forties, thin, and of medium height. He had close, curly black hair and there were those who assumed him to be Jewish at first glance. That amused him no end, and he encouraged it.

His new partner in this wild enterprise, who was sitting in the overstuffed chair in Marwan's flat, nodded. "Then we should have our call in ten or fifteen minutes, no?"

"We should, yes."

"Good."

This new partner, known to Marwan only as "Mr. Kazan," was a squat individual, in his sixties, dark complexioned with a full head of grey hair, and a bushy salt and pepper moustache. His only truly remarkable feature was a pair of uncommonly large ears. Marwan had met him on two prior occasions, the first of which had been only the previous week, when Mr. Kazan had been introduced to the committee by the engineer Imad as being his 'mentor,' and who would now assume leadership of their committee.

Northwood/Marwan had protested, and had been told very clearly that it would be in his best interests to adapt quickly. That had been very much a surprise, and would have had him fleeing for his life if he hadn't been so profoundly surprised, and if Hanadi hadn't been there. He trusted Imad to an extent, but he wanted desperately to impress Hanadi, and she seemed to accept the change in leadership with no objections at all. Besides, this Kazan fellow was obviously too old to be of a personal interest to Hanadi. What could be the harm? As his sister had once told him, he sometimes let his thinking be done by the wrong organ.

Marwan/Northwood had originally proposed this plan, if it could be termed such, a few weeks ago. It had started out as mere conversation, something with which to pass the time until Hanadi joined them. He had said to Imad, while they were having coffee in a restaurant across the street from Hanadi's law firm, that the way to attract the attention of the establishment to the seriousness of a group seemed to require the taking of a hostage. He proposed this in an ironic way, but the distinction seemed lost on his companion.

Imad seemed very receptive to the concept, and expanded the scenario, saying that it should be an American hostage. "That could serve a useful purpose. Let everyone know it's the Americans who are . . . responsible, in a general sense. Nobody here would take it *personally*, if it was an American. If it was an American, so what?"

"Of course," said Northwood, hurriedly, "we wouldn't want to go to jail for years. So it should be a staged affair."

"Staged?"

"The hostage would agree to be taken, and would then reveal it as a more of a dramatization than an actual crime."

"We should ask Hanadi about that," said Imad. "But keep going. I like this."

"Well, I suppose we could videotape the hostage . . . with some suitable slogan in the background. Muss up his hair, you know . . . make him appear distressed. Read a statement. Off camera," he added hastily. "Demand the release of several of the Belmarsh prisoners. Then, next day or two, expose it as a hoax. No harm done. A teleplay, in a way. Theatrical, you know." He mused for a moment. "Art, really," he said, distracted by the thought.

"Who would you take as a hostage? Do you know some Americans?"

"What? Oh, indeed. Of course. I have a good half dozen in my classes right now. Graduate students. Doctoral candidates. Not kids. In their late twenties or early thirties."

"How would an American agree to do this? They can't have much interest in our people at Belmarsh."

"I can be most convincing," Northwood had said. He would cringe at that memory in retrospect.

Imad gave him a skeptical look. "Would you have someone in mind?"

Succumbing to what he would later refer to as the Henry Higgins syndrome, Northwood glanced around the room, and his eye fell on Emma Schiller at a table some distance away.

"I could persuade her," he said.

Imad followed Northwood's gaze. "Which one?"

"The smallish young woman in the corner, with the blond man. She's wearing a red sweater," said Northwood, looking back toward Imad.

"You think so?"

"I do. That's an American named Miss Schiller. Emma Schiller. She's just one of my students, and a randy little thing at that. I could," he'd said, with great confidence, "persuade her to do many things." He gave Imad a knowing look. "It would be a pleasure."

"Truly?"

"Oh, certainly. Without a doubt." A night at his flat, he thought. Perhaps a trip to his sisters' in the lake country, for deep political discussions while naked under the down comforter. "Easiest thing in the world," he said. A man, after all, needed to play to his strengths.

Robert Northwood had not discussed that "plan" with Imad again, until after the introduction of Mr. Kazan into the group. When Imad had outlined the hostage plan in front of Mr. Kazan, Northwood had started to backpedal. He'd never actually thought of *doing* it. And they certainly weren't talking about using the down comforter approach.

The implications were not pleasant.

Imad then outlined a somewhat different plan, in which the girl Emma would be taken before she agreed to cooperate.

"I'm sure you can persuade her later," he'd said, with a strange, tight smile. "We have the greatest confidence in you."

"Absolutely not." Northwood explained that, without her pre-cooperation, the entire hoax concept would be jeopardized.

"Nonsense," had been interjected by Mr. Kazan. "Our method will add realism."

"Your method," said Northwood, "will add ten years. Piss off."

Imad looked astonished. Mr. Kazan, however, merely smiled and said, "It is always good to know the true nature of your associates, Mr. Northwood. Thank you for your frankness."

Early the next morning, Professor Robert Northwood had been awakened in his own bed by three men dressed in dark clothing, and wearing ski masks. One was sitting on either side of his bed, very effectively trapping him under his covers. The third stood near his head, looking at him with very intense eyes. Every light in his bedroom was on.

"You are the Professor Northwood?" asked the third one, in a flat voice.

Northwood thought he was going to vomit, but managed to say that he was.

"Mr. Kazan wishes us to tell you this," the man said, slowly and with the distinct appearance of a student reciting from memory. "The plan will go the way he decides. You need not be on tape. You will persuade the woman. He further wishes you to confirm to us that you agree to this."

Northwood, absolutely terrified, was simply unable to speak. The man apparently took this to mean that he was hesitating to agree to the conditions.

"Do not be a fool. You can have many happy years."

There was no display of weapons. None was needed. Robert Northwood would say later that he had never seen anyone so convincing in his entire life.

"Tell Mr. Ka, ka, ka, Kazan," Northwood got out, "I agree."

The man leaned forward and kissed him on his forehead.

"Good night. Sleep well, Professor."

With that, and without another word, the three calmly and deliberately turned out the various lights, and very quietly left the room.

Since that night, Northwood had lost eight pounds from his spare frame, had slept fitfully at best, and had gone to his chemist and obtained several packets of anti-diarrheal medication, which he took daily. He had also obtained an old cudgel, intending to keep it near his bed, but had thought better of it. He strongly suspected that they would simply use it to beat him to death.

Professor Northwood now secretly hoped that all this was only being done to test his sincerity and that of his cell members, and that the whole enterprise would be abandoned as soon as they showed they could perform the tasks successfully. How he hoped that was to be the case.

There had been huge changes in the London Movement for the Freedom of Khaled al Fawwaz and Ibrahim Eidarous since its formation a few months ago. Things had become so much more intense and serious. The first major event had been a sudden change in Hanadi/Ayat. She had become much more withdrawn, more anti-western in her conversation, and had been developing a near obsession with her duty to her family. He had no idea why. His chances of becoming involved with her seemed to have evaporated. He knew from bitter experience that any relationship with a woman that committed to a cause was doomed. He would be nothing more than a distraction. It was, he thought, a shame.

Imad had also changed, and had become more dogmatic and less purely political in his approach. They had printed one article in a local paper, which had been received as well as could have been expected, and which had prompted the Northwood to believe that they would continue until they had generated enough interest to stage a protest outside Belmarsh Prison. It was not to be. Both Imad and Ayat had begun to make increasingly anti-British and anti-US statements, concentrating on the state of the war in Iraq. At the same time, anti-Jewish feelings, coupled with enormously strong pro-Palestinian sentiments were being expressed by Hanadi/Ayat, in particular. Northwood/Marwan had no idea what had prompted these changes, and if his opinion of himself had been a little more realistic, he would have realized that he had completely lost control of the London Movement for the Freedom of Khaled al Fawwaz and Ibrahim Eidarous. More to the point, the Movement had taken on an urgency that bewildered him. Regardless, he refused to acknowledge his own bewilderment, preferring to believe that he had some control over matters.

It was that belief in his control that had prompted him to suggest taking a hostage, of sorts, and using that person to demand the release of the prisoners. Staged, of course. He had not actually believed that the proposed course of action would be undertaken. That was the moment that he'd completely lost control of the group, the moment that Northwood/Marwan had failed.

Now, trying not to stare at the other man in his flat, he once again tried to decide just who this Mr. Kazan really was. He new absolutely nothing about the man, other than he had been introduced to him by Imad. He seemed rather educated, Northwood thought, although certainly not of his own intellectual stature. He appeared to be of Arabic extraction, although Northwood/Marwan could not be positive. He'd sought him out in the telephone book, to no avail.

Interestingly, it never occurred to him that, while he was not using his real name, Mr. Kazan might have been doing the same.

Another aspect of this evening that made him edgy was that the two times they'd met previously, Mr. Kazan had been accompanied by a bodyguard. Yet, on this night, Mr. Kazan had apparently come to Marwan's flat on his own. He caught himself surreptitiously checking the bedroom door, as if Mr. Kazan's bodyguard would have been able to let himself in through the third floor window. He was painfully aware that this selfsame bodyguard could very likely have been one of the intruders in his bedroom. This was not the way he'd envisioned things the night they'd organized their movement. Not at all. Yet to acknowledge his growing fear would also have been to acknowledge his failure. Unacceptable.

They waited in silence.

They waited twenty-two minutes, with the only sound between them being the lighting of a cigarette by Mr. Kazan and then the very faint, bell-like ring produced as he periodically knocked the ashes into the Waterford bowl he had commandeered as an ashtray.

When Marwan's cell phone rang, the noise was startling. He unfolded the instrument and placed it to his ear.

"Yes?" He listened for a few moments. "Yes, exactly at 8:40." He listened again, and then spoke sharply. "You will wait all night if necessary. Is that clear?"

He closed the phone. "She seems to be late."

"Yes," said Mr. Kazan, calmly. He inhaled deeply. "You have their number?"

"Yes."

Mr. Kazan looked at the VCR. It was 10:18 PM. "You will call them at midnight, and suspend the operation."

Northwood/Marwan started to feel relief. God is good, he thought. This is merely a test, after all.

"Of course," said Mr. Kazan, as he leaned forward and put out his cigarette in the expensive bowl, "that is if you have not received a positive contact by then."

That was a jarring note, canceling Northwood/Marwan's relief. In a bizarre moment, he found himself concerned that the heat from Kazan's cigarette might crack the Waterford bowl. He was surprised at the shallowness of his thinking under stress. "Certainly. One must never lose hope. Until then, may I offer you something? To eat or drink?"

"No," replied Mr. Kazan.

"I have some excellent coffee," he said, forcing a smile. "Mazbuta? And with cardamom . . ."

"Then drink some," said Mr. Kazan, abruptly. He settled back in the chair, and stared out the window.

Northwood/Marwan knew that from Mr. Kazan's vantage point

at this time of night, all he could possibly be seeing was the illumi-
nated night haze, or the reflection of the room itself in the window
glass. Nonetheless, Mr. Kazan's gaze was that of a man watching something of great interest. It didn't dawn on Northwood/Marwan that
Mr. Kazan might be watching *him* in the reflection.

"I shall," he said, moving into the modern kitchen and hating the
feeling that he was being intimidated and ordered about in his own
flat. He told himself that he would not have let this happen had Imad
not divulged to him that he had been summoned home to help fight
the infidels and that in his absence Marwan would be wise to tread
lightly around Mr. Kazan. He remembered Imad's exact phrase: "He is
of another generation." Somehow, over the last several months, he'd
never thought that Imad might be returning to the Middle East, and
especially not to do battle against British or American troops. A man
could very easily be killed doing that. Nor, he thought ruefully, had he
expected to find himself in the middle of a real terrorist operation.
Especially one of his own invention. He, too, could get killed, and
right here in London. Except, he reminded himself, for the fact that
this was merely a test. He was very certain of that, and very certain
of his intellectual superiority over this Kazan fellow. Pass the test, he
thought, maintain your membership for a couple of months, and then
resign.

The fact that Imad had lied to him, and was not leaving London,
was one of several things that never occurred to him.

As he poured the powdered coffee beans into the pot, and put two
cups of bottled water into the microwave, he remembered how impressed Imad had been that he made coffee in the traditional way. He'd
never told anyone that he'd learned to do that only to impress Imad
and his friends.

Now, he was regretting, not his infatuation for Hanadi, but the
method he'd chosen to approach her. Perhaps she might have been as
interested if he had remained . . . That line of thinking could get him
killed, in his present circumstances. He had always been able to maneuver his way through situations, but only by staying alert and focused.

Glancing into the living room, he couldn't help thinking that Mr.
Kazan reminded him of an old sentinel staring out over the great
wastes of some desert. Alert, but stone bored. Ageing, alert, bored and
boring, and a thoroughgoing bastard, he thought. Just some great
lump of a poisonous toad. "Suspend the operation," indeed. How
much more vague could he have been?

"If we hear nothing by midnight, will we simply postpone, then, or call it off altogether?" He spoke more loudly in order to overcome the sound of the microwave. Even so, he thought his voice betrayed no tension at all, as far as he could tell. It was an effort to keep it that way.

"When the time comes . . . ," said Mr. Kazan, and picked up a book from the coffee table. He hadn't bothered to raise his voice, and Marwan had to strain to catch what he said.

"Of course." The toad was obviously playing this game out to the very end. Or, maybe the toad didn't know what to do. Now out of the line of sight of Mr. Kazan's back, he looked at his watch. 10:24. Nearly ninety minutes to go. He found himself praying that midnight would come, and the operation would be cancelled. It *had* to be cancelled. This was, after all, merely a test. The alarm on the microwave went off, and he poured the water into the pot. If Imad had been present to be impressed, he would have boiled it on the stove.

He knew he never should have suggested this plan to his Imad in the first place, and cursed himself for being an ingratiating bastard. He'd dreamt it up just to impress and amuse him, late one night as they sat up discussing political things. He'd never remotely imagined that it would not only be implemented, but *commanded* by the likes of Mr. Kazan.

Nonsense, he said to himself. It's just a test. Don't let them get at you this way.

He returned to the living room, and sat stiffly on the couch with his demi tasse. He raised it to head level, and said "Fi sehtuk." He knew he'd made a mistake as soon as he said it.

"Keep to your English," snapped Mr. Kazan, taking his eyes off the vast empty space that was the London night sky, and glaring at his host.

"Your health," said Marwan, refusing to be further intimidated. He took a sip, and smacked his lips in a defiant gesture he somehow felt was lost on Mr. Kazan.

Mr. Kazan held up the book he'd been leafing through. It was entitled *The London Beneath Your Feet*. "This is a very interesting book," he said. He put it down.

"It's a hobby, of sorts," said Northwood. "The tube, the sewers, the cable ducting."

"I saw," said Mr. Kazan, lighting another cigarette.

"I'm writing a book on this subject, myself," said Northwood/Marwan.

"So Imad tells me," said Mr. Kazan.

"I have old plans . . . would you care to see them?"

"No."

Small talk, thought Northwood, was utterly wasted on Mr. Kazan. He glanced at his watch. It was 10:40. He took another sip of coffee, savoring the taste, and nearly spilled it when his cell phone rang. He experienced a dreadful sinking feeling in the pit of his stomach. He'd been hoping that they'd miss her altogether.

Carefully, he put down the little cup, and opened the phone after the third ring. "Yes?" He listened for a moment, put his hand over the phone, and said, "They have her." That sounded squeaky, so he cleared his throat, and said, "Sorry, it's the coffee . . . they have her, now," in a much calmer voice.

Mr. Kazan regarded him closely. He nodded. "Good."

"We continue?"

Mr. Kazan sighed. "Yes."

"You're serious?"

Mr. Kazan just stared at him.

Northwood/Marwan spoke into the phone. "Proceed," he managed. He heard an acknowledgment, and closed his phone. He felt fear again, fear for his own life, and fear of the future. This had gone dreadfully wrong. He was secretly astounded that Anton and Hamza had been able to actually capture the girl. They were so, well, inept and amateurish. He chose to ignore his own amateur standing because to do otherwise would rob him of any illusion of control. The survivor in him, more the realist, began scrambling. He took another sip of coffee, and noticed that his hand was steady. Did that really mean anything? He'd always heard that a steady hand implied strong nerves.

There was silence in the flat. It dragged on for several seconds, and Northwood/Marwan very nearly committed suicide by confiding to Mr. Kazan that he thought it all a rather silly plan, and that they should just try to stop now before things got out of hand. Otherwise he would have to go to the police. Fortunately for him, Mr. Kazan spoke before he could form the right words.

"I am wondering that you indicate such indecision. Imad has a high regard for you. I will tell you that I attribute it to the newness of the situation. That is how I shall say it in my report."

"Thank you," said Marwan. It was all he could think to say.

"It would be good if you made your family proud," said Mr. Kazan, softly. "I shall inform Ayat that the operation is under way." He lowered his voice. "See to it that nothing happens to her. She is of inestimable value." He raised his voice. "I am ready."

There was an immediate knock on the door, and it opened, revealing the familiar bodyguard who had accompanied Mr. Kazan on the two previous occasions. He must have been standing just outside all the while. Marwan was somewhat taken aback, having locked the door himself after Mr. Kazan had entered.

Mr. Kazan stood. "I will contact you tomorrow, in the evening." He looked very intently at Marwan. "Follow your procedures to the letter."

With that, he walked to the door and left. The bodyguard leaned back into the room, smiled at Marwan, and made a show of locking the door before he pulled it closed behind him.

Marwan sat abruptly on the couch. "Emma . . . Emma, it is for a good purpose," he said. "But I am truly sorry." He took a deep breath, held it, and released. Exactly what had Mr. Kazan meant by his last statement? Procedures? What procedures? It wasn't as if they had a bloody manual. If the old bastard hadn't been so intimidating, he would have asked him. And what was that about his bloody family? Could the old bastard actually *know* some of them? Nothing seemed impossible.

Hanadi would know. He'd just follow her lead. It would be a simple matter of a kidnapping, a statement, and then the release of the hostage. It would go smoothly, and without undue risk to anyone, including Emma Schiller. After all, he was in charge, and he would arrange things that way.

Chapter 4

Monday, November 10, 2003
Maitland, Nation County, IA, USA
13:32 Central Standard Time

On Monday, November 10, 2003, I was in my office at the Nation County Sheriff's Department, taking advantage of a really slow couple of weeks to get caught up on my paperwork. I'd already finished my last two residential burglary reports, and was getting ready to tackle eleven incidents of mailbox vandalism, all along a five mile stretch of the same gravel road, when my intercom line buzzed.

I answered it with, "Yo." I mean, it was the intercom. The call couldn't be from the public.

It was Norma, our new secretary. "Carl, the Sheriff would like to see you in his office."

That was a little unusual. Not that he wanted to see me, but the fact that he had Norma call, and that she had referred to him by his title instead of just calling him Lamar. Lamar Ridgeway, the Sheriff, normally just walked down the hall to my office, or just stuck his head out of his office and shouted. His office was only fifty feet away.

"Okay. Just a sec," I said, curious. "Gotta save my work . . . ." I'd picked up the faint hiss that told me her phone was on speaker mode, and that she wasn't talking into a handset. That usually meant that Lamar had the door between their offices open, so he could hear my response. That also meant that any possible guests of his could hear every word I said. Her desk was just outside his door.

As I clicked on the 'save' icon, I decided Lamar probably had an important guest, and wanted to impress 'em by not shouting to me through his open door and having Norma use his title. I'm not the Department's investigator for nothing. My experience had also taught me that when Lamar seemed to be on his best, civilized, behavior it was not always a good thing.

Lamar has the only nice office in the Department. By that, I mean the curtains and the carpet sort of go together; he has a high backed leather captain's chair, and a big desk that's the only one in the office that's not US Government surplus, and is made of real wood. Not only that, he has our complete inventory of furniture manufactured since 1975, including three matching guest chairs and a matching couch. He used to have a coffee table, but he'd replaced it with an old 48 inch cable reel from the County Shop. He'd done that just so he could tell people that he didn't believe in wasting anything bought with taxpayer's money.

I came around the corner, Norma gave a warning grimace, and I saw that his office was packed with people. Not surprisingly, I knew every one of 'em.

Norman Gunderson, high school superintendent; Allen Jones, president of Northland Savings Bank; and his competitor, Willy Morton of Farmers Union bank were in the chairs. Olivia Young of the law firm Wilkins, Hughes and Young, was seated on the couch; along with Mike Ludwig, owner of Ludwig's Super Market. The Reverend Samuel Thiese and Father Virgil Lahre were standing just inside the door. Seated on Lamar's brand-new two-drawer file cabinet was Kayla Eder, current editor of the *Nation County Journal*. They were all community leaders, and only Olivia and Kayla were ever here, for any reason. Something was definitely up, and I suspected I wasn't going to like it. The last people a cop wants to see in his office are a bunch of community leaders acting in accord. It almost always means that good police methods are about to be replaced with favors and concessions.

I just said, "Hi, everybody."

"Carl, we got a question for you. . . . ," said Lamar. He looked sort of pleased.

"Sure. . . ." That was a god start. I like questions.

"We're having a meeting about Janine Schiller's daughter Emma," said Lamar.

"Sure." A little red flag started up the pole. Emma, along with our daughter, Jane Houseman, and another young woman named Vicky Burman were old friends, and the three were together in London, taking a semester of very special graduate level courses they'd all wanted to do for years. Their whole project had been made affordable by the fact that a girlfriend of theirs who worked for the US Embassy in

London had taken a temporary transfer, and let them house-sit her flat. They were all very happy with the arrangements. Well, they had been, until some nine days ago. On October 28th, Emma Schiller had gone missing in London.

Jane had been sending me email every day, and was becoming extremely worried. She'd been giving me some inside information on the matter, and had told me that Emma had a tendency to, frankly, go to a party, pick somebody up, and head off to the nearest bed with them. That had surprised me. As Jane had said, "Sometimes she's been known to stretch out a good night into a good week." I'd told Lamar about that aspect of the case as soon as I'd heard it. His response had been classic Lamar: "Really? Shit, she sounds like a guy." At that time, he and I sort of assumed that she would turn up shortly. I think most people had thought the same. That was on the fourth day she'd been gone. Since then, as time passed, the feeling that she was the victim of foul play had gotten stronger. By now, I'd reached the stage where I honestly figured she was dead.

Jane, being a cop's daughter, had reported the matter to the Metropolitan Police in London after Emma had failed to come home after class on Wednesday. She'd told me that the police over there were taking the case seriously, and seemed to her to be working it diligently. Unfortunately, they hadn't been able to find any trace of Emma.

Emma's disappearance had gotten lots of local publicity back in Iowa, and everybody here in Maitland, our county seat, seemed to have one of those yellow ribbons tied around something or other. The story had been on Cedar Rapids, Dubuque, and Waterloo television stations two or three times apiece so far, and on CNN at least once. The fact that Janine was a widow with two daughters, and that her husband had been killed in the same wreck that had cost her the use of her legs, just fueled the human interest aspects of the situation. There was a "Find Emma" fund drive that didn't seem to me to have much direction other than possibly sending her mother Janine to London. Since Janine was confined to a wheelchair, that could get very expensive, and probably wouldn't accomplish much. Anyway, Janine Schiller had been getting lots of sympathy and support, but there was only so much one could do.

"Like I was saying, we're all pretty damned worried," said Lamar, in the self-conscious and deliberate tone of voice he used when speaking in public. "I've started our own inquiry through Scotland Yard," he said to the assembly in his office, "but haven't heard back yet." He looked around, apparently trying to give the impression that we checked with 'The Yard' on a weekly basis.

Actually, I'd been the one to check with the Metropolitan Police. I'd contacted them via police teletype, two days ago. I'm the investigator, and it was part of my job to cooperate with other departments. Cooperating with New Scotland Yard had never been anticipated in that job description, but that just made it more interesting. Lamar's involvement had been to receive my verbal report, which had simply been that I'd tell him when we heard back. The fact that the agency in question had been called *New* Scotland Yard for more than a hundred years was consistently overlooked by Lamar. Ah, well. Bosses are like that.

"Carl," he continued, addressing me, "these folks have come to me because the fund drive is doing well, and they'd like to hire somebody to go over there and check things out."

"Really?" To me, that meant they were going to hire a private detective. That hadn't occurred to me. I wondered who they had in mind.

"Yes. They sort of wanted to hire Lloyd Boyd," he said slowly and distinctly.

Lloyd Boyd, aka Loidy Boidy, was a private detective in Dubuque. He did mostly injury cases for insurance companies, and made a pretty good living going into neighborhoods and bars where the attorneys who hired him wouldn't venture, and obtaining what was basically speculative information from uninformed people who had the time to talk with him. That and the occasional photograph of somebody with a fake back injury lifting an engine block. He'd been a cop in Illinois years back, and been fired for misconduct of some sort.

The Lloyd Boyd connection told me that Lamar wanted me to dissuade them, or at least, to help him do so. Piece of cake. And I could be totally honest, to boot.

"He's an idiot," I said, looking around the room. "Honest to God, really, don't hire Lloyd."

"That's what I told 'em," said Lamar, looking smug.

"We've dealt with him before," I said, looking at the office full of people. "He's pretty worthless, in my opinion. And about as unconscientious as anybody I've ever met. I know you could do better than him. A whole lot better. There are some really good private detectives out there. Cedar Rapids has a really good one, and I even have Mike's number. I'll vouch for him any day of the week."

"I told 'em that, too," said Lamar. He now looked really, really pleased. Well, we were heading into an election year, and it sure wouldn't hurt his chances if this group in his office was impressed with his performance. I don't want to give the impression that Lamar is some political toady or anything like that. But he's got political smarts, and backers like these would be a big help. He also enjoys getting reelected because it means that the County continues paying his medical insurance.

"I wonder, though," I said, committing an error by volunteering information, "if this might not be a little unwise. I mean, if I were working for the Metropolitan Police, and some American private detective turned up . . . even a good one . . . I think I'd just tell him to butt out before he'd be able to screw up the case."

Lamar's face split into a wide grin. "That's exactly what I said you'd say."

It's always nice to make Lamar happy, but I was getting a little suspicious. My little red flag started climbing further up the pole. The terms 'cat,' and 'canary' flickered in the back of my mind.

"Well, regardless, I think that Emma's been missing way too long," interjected Reverend Thiese. "In my opinion somebody needs to do something, and pretty quickly, too. And now that the fund has got some money . . ."

It was all I could do not to say "No shit, Sherlock?" It had been almost two weeks. If Emma was at risk, time was getting very short. Like I said, if she were really at risk, the chances of finding her alive were getting pretty slim after this length of time. I thought the excellent possibility that she could be dead was best left unsaid in this group, even though most of them were probably thinking the same thing. On the other hand, I wasn't going to share information about her crowded sex life, even though that seemed to hold out the only hope for her being safe.

"I sure won't argue with that," I said. It was the easy way.

"We've got the people here," said Allen Jones, "who're on just about every important standing committee in town. As of today," he said, "we have more than twenty thousand dollars that we've raised. That's ticket and board money. We can buy the tickets, and send somebody good. We all feel that we owe it to Janine Schiller to give this our best shot."

"I think we do, too," I said. How could I disagree? I hoped Mike the Private Detective would appreciate this, and thought I'd hint to him to bring me something from London for my troubles on his behalf. But I really thought they were going to be hindering the London cops. I said so, again.

"London's a big place," said Father Lahre. "We really don't think we should wait too long to find out just what's happening there. We surely don't want the trail to get cold."

Cold? That was an understatement. I figured the trail was about as cold as Emma by now. I shrugged. "Well, the trail's really about as cold as it gets, to tell you the truth. She was in a pub on a Tuesday night, and just disappeared. She was seen leaving, but so were a bunch of people about that same time. Nobody knows if she was connected with any of them or not. Apparently nobody they've been able to track down saw her after that, and nobody heard anything from her at all. Period." I shrugged. "She just vanished."

"So you think it's an impossible case?" asked Olivia Young.

"Well, no . . . not impossible." I shrugged. "I hate *impossible*. I think it's a very difficult one at this point. As far as we know, there's really no evidence except for the fact that she's gone. But with the Metropolitan Police working the case, there's nobody else in the world that could get to the bottom of this business any faster."

"Well, do they have an AMBER Alert system over there?" asked Mike Ludwig.

In such august company, sarcasm wasn't appropriate. I took a deep breath, and said, "I don't know that they do." I held up my hand. "What I mean to say is, if they do have some sort of system, it might not be called that."

"Well, maybe somebody from over here ought to go over there and show 'em how that sort of thing works," he said.

I looked at Lamar, and he just smiled. For some reason, he was letting me do all the work here.

"Well, in the first place," I said, "you all know our daughter Jane's over there sharing an apartment with Emma. She's the one who reported her missing. Anyway, she tells me that the Metropolitan Police are being very active in pursuing this. There's not much they can do, really. I mean, with no witnesses at all, no suspects, no anything. . . ."

Mike Ludwig just held up his hand, and said, abruptly, "I think that only makes our point. Opportunities may be slipping away."

"Believe me," I said, "those guys over there are good. And they know their town better than anybody else. Knowing that area is the single most important factor in solving the case."

"I'm sure," said Allen Jones, standing. "But what we were thinking of was somebody we could trust, to . . . ah . . . well, keep an eye on things over there for a week or two, until she turns up. Look at it through fresh eyes. Talk to them. You know. Let them know we're really interested."

That's when I made my second error. I bragged. "Well, if it'll help,"

I said, "we had a pretty good contact with a specific officer in the Metropolitan Police. . . . name of . . . Blyth, about two years ago," I said. "We could contact him." An FBI agent I knew actually had the contact, but I'd been in on the conversation with him back in December of 2001. That wasn't all that long ago. Hopefully, in that time Blyth had neither died nor retired.

"That's what I told 'em," said Lamar. "I just couldn't remember his name."

Well, now I at least knew Lamar actually read some of my reports. "I don't know what else can be done . . ." I said.

"We thought we'd send you," said Lamar, right out of the blue.

"What?"

"You. You're an officer. You're a good investigator. And you get along well with foreign people."

"Foreign people? The English? They ain't exactly *foreign*." I looked him square in the eye, and knew the answer before I asked. "Send me? You're kidding?"

"Nope. Not a bit. I'm dead serious, and we're all in agreement that it should be you."

"I can't go over there, Lamar. Honest. I'd have no jurisdiction for one thing."

"Observer. That's what you'd be," said Lamar. "You don't need jurisdiction to observe."

He was sounding well prepared on this. That was a really dangerous sign. My little red flag was snapping in the breeze by now, and straining against the top of the pole. "Well," I said, "we don't have any guarantee they'd let me . . . and besides, I have too much to do here."

Lamar gave me a knowing look. He knew how busy I was right now. "I think we can spare you for a bit."

"And I don't even have a passport," I said. "That alone will take ten days. Either they'll find her, or the trail will be stone cold by the time I get there."

Lamar looked over at Olivia Young. "That's not what Olivia says."

Olivia smiled. "We can get a passport issued for you in Chicago inside twenty-four hours. We did it for a client once. It's easy."

"I don't even have time to have my shots," I said, reaching. "And I could be allergic. . . ." Believe me, even the hives sounded better than what I was hearing.

"You don't need shots to go to the UK," said Olivia.

I was getting a little desperate. "The County Personnel Policy won't allow a leave of absence without thirty days notice, and I can't afford two weeks without pay anyway." That was not only true, it was painfully true.

"I talked with the Board of Supervisors about that 'bout ten minutes ago," said Lamar. "Lucky for everybody concerned, you got two weeks vacation left."

Our vacations were sacred. Absolutely untouchable. It was the one thing the Department never screwed with. I was dumbfounded that he'd said such a thing. "Not my vacation . . . !"

"Naw, don't worry," said my esteemed Sheriff. "I wouldn't do that to ya. We're gonna call it a special assignment."

"What?"

"Well," he said, "since nobody knows what the hell is goin' on, who's to say that her disappearance might not be connected to something back here?"

"Like what?" I asked, startled.

"Oh, in these times," said Lamar, "could be about anything. We can't rule out terrorists. You know that. Or meth labs and sales. . . . We both know we got so many labs here we can't keep track. A real persistent stalker from her high school days. Something like that."

Something along the lines of 'Get real' wasn't really appropriate. I thought for a second. "I think they call that a 'low probability,' Lamar," I said.

"Well, gee," said Lamar with a tone of pleased finality, "we just won't know that until you get over there and look things over, will we."

Okay, let me be honest. Although I was trying very hard to come up with logical and rational arguments against my going, at the same time I was thinking that I'd really like to go, I'd like to see how the Metropolitan Police worked this kind of case, and how cool it would be to visit Jane in London. I also mentally ran through what I had available to wear; and how I'd pack it in my old suitcase. Consequently, each time Lamar shot down an argument, my mind would add an item I'd need in my luggage.

"Well," I said, wondering if anybody had an umbrella I could borrow, "I guess it comes down to being your call."

"It's the only way," he said.

"So, like what? Do I contact a travel agent?" I had a few decent shirts, but only two pair of slacks to my name. Blue jeans? Sure.

"We've already obtained your ticket and accommodations via the Internet," said Norm Gunderson. "Expedia dot com. Confirmed just before I came up here."

Since he was the school superintendent, I thought I might as well try to get my wife, Sue, permission to come along as well. "Can you get a sub for Sue? I'd really like to have her along." Sue was an English teacher, and I thought I might as well ask her boss while I had his attention.

"The school has a rule about applying for leaves of absence, just like the Sheriff's Department," he said. "Thirty days advance notice. I tried to find a way around that, I really did. But we can't classify this as part of her job, like Lamar can with you."

"Sure." Right. Explain that to Sue.

"And I talked with Sue this morning, just before I came up here," he said. "She agreed that it was impossible for her to go on this short notice. We even explored the family emergency clause in the contract, but we just can't find a way to do it. Emma isn't your family."

"Okay." I thought a second. "So, just how short *is* this notice?" I asked.

"You leave tomorrow evening at seven or so," said Lamar. "They tell me you gotta be there at least two hours before the plane takes off."

"From where, Cedar Rapids?"

Lamar shook his head. "O'Hare in Chicago."

"You can park at my mother's house in Evanston," said Reverend Thiese. "The airport shuttle will pick you up there, so you can save a bundle with parking."

"And it would cost almost twice as much airfare if you left from either Dubuque or Cedar Rapids," said Lamar.

"Here," said Kayla Eder. She handed me several printouts on letter sized paper. "These are your vouchers, for the shuttle and the airline tickets. Don't lose 'em. And a map to Ida Thiese's house in Skokie, and your hotel accommodations. Don't," she repeated, "lose 'em."

I glanced at the papers. They were complete with bar codes and everything, including my name. "Uh, thanks."

"You have to go to 53 West Jackson Blvd. in Chicago, to get your passport. There's a list here of what you need to give them when you arrive. The airline ticket information has already been forwarded to the passport people. Those things in the small envelope are two copies of your driver's license photo that you need for the passport. We got you on American Airlines, because you're so tall. They have better seat spacing in coach. Even though Lufthansa was cheaper. And they land at Heathrow airport, right in London. Otherwise you'd have to go to Gatwick and it costs more for your shuttle to the hotel."

"Okay." It was quite a bit to absorb this quickly. I wondered if I was getting too old for this. But excitement was starting to build, too.

"We booked you into a hotel in Kensington," said Olivia. "It's near the offices of a firm we do business with, and fairly close to New Scotland Yard. It's an easy tube ride to your daughter's apartment in Highgate."

"Uh, sure." Well, at least *she* knew it was New Scotland Yard.

"I go over there at least twice a year," she said. "You'll like it, and it's very easy to get around. And it's only 62 pounds a night."

"How much is that in dollars?" I asked. Now was as good a time as any to get the bad news about the exchange rate.

"Right now," said Allen Jones, "that would translate into roughly one hundred eleven dollars."

"So don't buy a hamburger that just has a seven and a dot followed by two zeros," said Kayla. "That'd be just about thirteen bucks."

Great. Our per diem, for meals, was fifteen dollars. For three meals.

"That's okay," said Lamar, reading my mind. "You can afford to drop a few pounds."

Chapter 5

Monday, November 10, 2003
Chiswick, London, UK
21:36 Greenwich Mean Time

The young man known as Hamza stood at the right-hand edge of the only window in the shabby flat, and peered through a crack in the curtain. The yellowish street light on the corner opposite revealed the same three cars that had been parked there for the last two hours. Otherwise, the street was deserted. He sighed, to relieve the tension. "Nothing yet," he said.

There were muffled sounds from the bedroom behind him. Concerned, he left his post and opened the bedroom door.

"Everything all right, then?"

"Brilliant," came the breathless voice of his associate, Anton.

Hamza looked in at their captive. Emma Schiller was breathing hard, from her exertions, but now that Anton had secured her ankles with the tape and was sitting on her shins, she was no longer able to kick the wall. Her taped wrists, coupled with the duct tape over her mouth, had not been enough. He, himself had decided not to tape her ankles . . . they were becoming raw from repeated applications of the silvery stuff. It had become necessary to remove the ankle tapes each time she was escorted to the restroom. Her wrists, however, could remain taped while she was eating. They had taped her mouth for the first time today when they knew they would be having guests. It had certainly been much quieter than the usual cloth gag. He sighed, again. It wasn't likely they could keep her quiet for very long, even like this. Perhaps especially like this. She had much more strength than he had expected, and was very much more resilient. He nodded. "Good. Don't hurt her." It was not their task to injure the woman, but to keep her isolated and fairly healthy.

Anton glanced at him with some irritation. "Right." He pushed his dark hair back out of his reddened face. "Tell her that."

Anton found dealing with the Emma very difficult. In the first place, they had decided to conceal their identities by wearing ski masks in her presence. As soon as it became apparent that they'd be spending twenty-four hours a day with her, the ski masks became much more trouble than they were worth. They'd tried putting a bag over her head, but that had its own set of problems, including the fact that she couldn't see. Every time they fed her, or took her to the restroom, they had to put on their masks and remove hers. It was much more annoying, just that simple thing, than he would ever have thought possible.

He and Hamza had both been instructed not to have any sexual contact with her whatsoever. Yet, with no female associate available, they had been required to see to it that the captive could bathe. They had tried to let her bathe by herself by shutting her in the bath with one hand taped to her ankle. Emma had nearly made it out the bathroom window, before they had heard the thumping noise she'd made trying to get her free leg through the small, high opening. Since then, one of them had been required to go into the small bathroom with her, leaving the door open so the other one could be certain there was no un-necessary touching. This had also become necessary as she used the toilet. It was embarrassing for them, and he suspected humiliating for her, although he wasn't nearly as embarrassed as Hamza.

Hamza, on the other hand, had been very surprised to discover their hostage was able to deliver an occasional roundhouse-like kick, as his bruised thighs could attest. He had never expected her to be this way, especially since Marwan had confided that he'd been sleeping with her before she was taken captive. Hamza had imagined someone rather more meek and pliable. Even as he thought about it, she bent her knees, and kicked out, barley missing Anton.

"Please don't kick," said Hamza. "Please." He was sincere. He was quite terrified that Anton would lose his temper, retaliate, and she would be injured. Then he knew that he and Anton would be held to account.

Hamza's true name was Jamal Essabar, although he had styled himself Hamza and was addressed as such by those within the activist movement headed by Marwan. He'd been born in London almost twenty years before, to Arab immigrant parents. His father worked as an accountant, and his mother was a social service worker. Politically as well as religiously, his parents were moderate, and although Hamza privately considered them to be afraid to acknowledge the injustices to their fellow Muslims, he respected them far too much to ever broach the subject. Hamza had been raised in London, and was currently a university student at King's College, majoring in computer science, with a minor in English. He had a fairly healthy opinion of himself, and was a good student. Irritatingly, he'd recently discovered that his school nick was Snivel. Nobody had called him that to his face, but he had ways of finding these things out.

Hamza and his associate, one Stefan Wentik, who preferred to be called Anton, had both been recruited by Imad in the last two months. Tonight, they were anxiously awaiting the arrival of their commander, so they could videotape the young woman captive one last time, and then be done with her. That, and get reimbursed. Getting paid was becoming very important, since he'd been required to fund this detestable little flat from his own funds. Still, it wasn't something that he'd mentioned directly to Marwan. He and Anton were expected to be dedicated, and payment was expected to be a secondary matter. He'd known Marwan for three years, and considered him the best teacher he'd had so far. He wasn't as aloof as most, and Hamza felt he could talk very freely with him. Hamza had chosen to take the names of one of the 9/11 hijackers as his code name, as soon as he had discovered that Marwan had done the same. Despite the high regard he had for his mentor, Hamza was determined to ask for funds tonight. He was nearly broke, and could not ask his father for additional funds.

"What do you think they want us to do with her?" he asked. "After tonight?"

"Take her far, far away," said Anton. "Antarctica would not be far enough."

Hamza nodded to himself. Not Antarctica, naturally, but somewhere suitably remote. He personally thought it would be Bangladesh. Rural Bangladesh. Backwash Bangladesh. He smiled at that. "Backwash Bangladesh," he said, pleased with himself.

Anton didn't respond.

Disappointed, he went back to the curtain, moved it slightly, and looked out once again. Nothing appeared to have changed in the last minute or so. His girlfriend, Pamela Arpino, would have appreciated "Backwash Bangladesh," as an address. She got very nearly all his jokes. Accustomed to seeing her every day prior to the hostage taking, he missed her a lot. He simply hadn't felt he could trust Anton to be alone with Emma for an extended period of time. Not that he'd told Pamela that. Well, not exactly.

The abrupt knock on the door startled him. "Yes?" he said, putting his hand on the chain lock, and peering out the peep hole. The lighting in the hallway was dim, but he recognized one of the men standing just outside. Marwan was in his late forties, tall, fit, and dressed in a black turtleneck with a dark grey jacket. The older man with him was almost as tall, but heavier, with grey hair, eyebrows and moustache. He was wearing a reddish or maroon turtleneck, a light grey sports coat, and carried a briefcase. He thought he also caught a glimpse of someone in the hall, but the two men were already coming through the door, and he had to step back to allow them through.

Hamza had no idea who the older man might be, and had no wish to attempt to establish his identity. Already, he had learned that the less one knew, the better for all.

"Welcome," he said.

"Hamza," said Marwan, "This is an associate of mine."

Mr. Kazan nodded. "I want to see her," he said to Hamza.

"Yes. Of course. We have her in there . . . ," he said, gesturing toward the bedroom. "Anton is with her."

Mr. Kazan glanced at Marwan. "Good," he said. "She should not be alone."

As Kazan passed him, Hamza caught Marwan's eye, and mouthed the word, Payment?"

"Don't be greedy, Hamza," he replied, in the soft, meticulous inflections of an educated Englishman. "Mr. Kazan must inspect the goods, appear in the last taping, and then we complete the transaction." He stepped toward the bedroom, pulling on a dark blue ski mask. "Not before," he said.

To Hamza, Marwan seemed more intense than usual, more excited. He saw that he almost forgot to put his ski mask on before he entered the bedroom. Since the captive knew him extremely well, that could have been a disaster. He followed him to the bedroom door, arriving just in time to see Anton remove the captive's hood, and to hear the old man say, "I am Mr. Kazan."

The bound, gagged captive attempted to glare at him, but kept blinking in the sudden light.

"I am to appear with you on your next tape. It's going to give me great pleasure to be seen with you."

Emma Schiller kept staring at the man, her eyes adjusting to the bright room light. She was terrified, but she was making every effort not to show it.

Mr. Kazan whispered to Marwan. "I wish her to appear very . . . emotional in this one."

"Yes," said Marwan/Northwood, understanding his role. He stepped forward, into the full view of the captive.

Emma saw Marwan/Northwood for the first time since she'd been taken captive. Although he'd spoken only a single word, it had been enough. She connected his voice with his build and clothes. She began making muffled noises, staring at him, and attempted to move toward him. Mr. Kazan reached out and pushed her back onto the bed.

With the young woman glaring at him, Mr. Kazan calmly reached out and patted her cheek. "Anger is not the emotion I wish to provoke," he said. "You . . ." and he indicated Hamza. "Put this on her." He handed him the shopping bag.

"Uh," said Hamza, taken aback. "I, we, let her do that for herself, we just . . ."

"You will do it," he snapped. He addressed the girl. "Stand."

There was no response.

"Stand," said Mr. Kazan. "You must do this, if you wish to see your loving family ever again."

Emma remained sitting.

Mr. Kazan put his hand in his pocket, removed a set of car keys, and took the single step that separated him from Emma Schiller. Even though she flinched backwards, he was able to thrust one of the keys under her right ear, and apply considerable pressure to the portion of her skull behind the ear. Emma made a strangled sound of pain and anger, but stood quickly.

"Now, dress her," said Mr. Kazan to Anton and Hamza. "Dress her in what I have provided," and he handed them the briefcase.

Hamza took it, and looked inside. "All that's here is a sweat-shirt. . . ."

Mr. Kazan never took his eyes off Emma. "I did not ask that you tell me the contents of the bag. You will simply dress her."

"Ah. . . ."

"Do as I say. And get the printing to face the front."

Hamza held the shirt up. It was white, with large black lettering reading "No More War, No More Lies." Spattered around the shirt were several splotches of red, apparently representing blood stains. He cleared his throat. "Is this the right shirt . . . ?"

"The questions will stop," said Mr. Kazan. "You simply do what you are told. You can do this? Good. So, put the shirt on her."

Dressed in the sweatshirt, Emma was seated in a folding chair, her arms bound behind her back. Mr. Kazan carefully adjusted Emma's head. "There . . . we want your head erect for this one. So the camera gets a very good look at you." He stepped back, and studied his work. "Yes. Yes, this will do."

She adjusted the camera and the lights herself. "Who runs the camera?"

"Me," said Hamza.

"Start when I tell you, and stop when I bow."

"Sure. . . ."

Mr. Kazan reached into his inside jacket pocket, and removed a navy blue ski mask made of a very thin layer of woven material. He pulled it on very carefully, making sure his hair was completely covered and that the openings for the eyes were properly aligned. He removed his jacket, and then stepped behind Emma, quickly pulled off the duct tape over her mouth, and said, "Begin."

"Goddamnit, that hurts!" said Emma. "What are you doing here?" she asked, clearly addressing Marwan/Northwood. "Help me, Robert! For God's sake. What are you here for? Get me out of this shit!"

Marwan said nothing, and Mr. Kazan delivered a short, sharp blow to the back of Emma's head. "Quiet."

Emma Schiller was many things, but even after this long in captivity, she was not about to be treated this way.

"Fuck off, you pathetic old. . . ." That was as far as she got before Mr. Kazan delivered a stunning blow to the side of her head.

"Do as you are instructed," he said, calmly. "Do not anger me. You have a purpose for the first time in your pathetic life. Act as if it were so."

"Stop hitting her," said Marwan/Northwood. "She's helpless."

With the ski mask, Mr. Kazan's gaze was even more intimidating. "This is my task. What is she to you but a means to an end?"

"I," he said, hesitated, and finished with ". . . I don't like to hurt people."

"You probably say that to everybody you fuck," said Emma. Her voice was weaker, but her will was intact.

Mr. Kazan grabbed a handful of the hair at the back of Emma's head, and slowly turned his wrist, pulling the hair and making her turn her head nearly onto it's side in an effort to avoid the pain.

"You're hurting me. . . ."

"Yes," said Mr. Kazan. "You will not speak filthy words."

"God damn it, Robert," yelled Emma. "You gotta help me!"

Mr. Kazan hit her again, hard, with her hair still twisted in his other hand. Emma screamed.

Hamza, taping as he was told, winced at the blow. He concentrated on keeping the action in frame, and hoping that Mr. Kazan wouldn't strike Emma again.

Anton had no such thoughts.

The taping took much longer than Hamza had anticipated. Emma, for one thing, just did not cooperate. She kept speaking out of turn, interrupting Mr. Kazan by making some noise, or suddenly straining against her chair.

Making the best of a bad situation, Mr. Kazan finally had them tape Emma's mouth over with duct tape once again, and had Anton laying on the floor at Emma's feet, just out of camera range, and hanging on to her ankles for all he was worth.

"You're certain you cannot do voice dubs?" asked Mr. Kazan.

Momentarily caught off guard by the unfamiliar term, Hamza said, "What?"

"A separate voice for me," said Mr. Kazan. "You cannot do this?"

"Not with this stuff," said Hamza. "This equipment. I can't digitize it, mess with it, and get it back to tape. You said you had to have tape. I could do it on a DVD disk, but I don't have the equipment. . . ."

Mr. Kazan exhaled in exasperation. "All right . . . all right. Again."

Finally, Marwan stepped in. "Emma," he said, pleadingly. "Just do this one last tape, dear. One last time. Then you'll be done, and you can go."

She glared at him.

He kept pleading, and very carefully brushed her hair into a more ordered disarray with his hand. "Please. You must do this. Just be quiet, while Mr. Kazan reads his statement. Then you can go."

Emma gave him a long look, and slowly nodded her head.

In five minutes they were finished. Mr. Kazan had given his statement one last time. Emma only moved enough to show she was alive, which was all they wanted her to do all along.

Mr. Kazan and Marwan/Northwood moved into the living area while Hamza and Anton put away the equipment, and laid Emma on the bed. Marwan/Northwood was pale and subdued. Mr. Kazan carefully removed his ski mask, and patted his forehead and neck with a handkerchief.

"Do you think you'll survive?" he asked Marwan, with a biting edge to his voice.

"Of course." He sat on the arm of one of the old stuffed chairs.

Even now, he was aware of the grime on the seat. "I'm just grateful that the business is over."

"For me, it is. For you, there remains one more task."

"And that would be . . . ?"

Mr. Kazan smiled. "Now you must dispose of her. "She will need to die."

"Die?" hissed Marwan/Northwood. "Bloody well die? Out of the question. My God, I'll not be killing anybody! This was never stated. I don't kill bloody anyone!"

"You can delegate what you will," said Mr. Kazan. "But she must die, but not before the 21st of this month. I need her kept for . . . contingencies. After the 21st. Not before."

Marwan/Northwood stood, and moved toward the door. "It was never even discussed. I won't have it. Unless I am no longer a part of this, I need the authority to make my own judgment as to when she is ready for release . . . and then release her as planned."

Mr. Kazan stopped him with, "It was very clearly discussed."

"It was never!"

"Not with you," he said, simply. "There are others who have an interest. The date stands. So. And she must die. You, yourself do not have to do this thing. They," and he indicated the two younger men still in the bedroom with Emma, "will do this for you. If you tell them it is so."

"I don't think that's so," he said.

"It is so. Remember the conditions. Not before the 21st. That is critical. It will ruin the plan if she is killed too soon."

"That was not in my plan." Marwan/Northwood was adamant. "I truly cannot do this. I'm not a killer. That's murder. How could I ever convince the court that she was a willing participant, if she's bloody well dead? The press? That I had the cooperation of the corpse? Don't be a bloody fool. If I am to continue with this mess, it must be on my terms, she must be released. . . . ."

"You shall find a way to do what I say," said Mr. Kazan. "The consequences for you, if you fail, are known to you now."

Marwan was stunned. The implications were suddenly and extremely clear. "Are you threatening me?"

"I do not threaten," said Mr. Kazan. "It isn't as though you have to *tell* her. If you have a problem with your conscience, play her along until then."

"I will not," said Marwan/Northwood, drawing himself up, "lie to her."

"You no longer object to killing as much as you object to having to lie to her?" Mr. Kazan smiled. "See how easy it becomes? Killing her is now the lesser of two evils."

Marwan stared at Mr. Kazan, his mind churning. Desperately, he said, "But, but, I'm the chairman of this group."

Mr. Kazan snorted. "Then, Mister Chairman," he said, sarcastically, "discharge your duty. Imad and I say that she must not be terminated prior to the 21st. That is our decision, not yours. She knows it is you who had her brought here, she has quite probably seen your two," and at this he nearly spat, "cell members. She must cooperate fully, and then she must die. Really, Marwan. Or Robert. Surely you must have known this would be the result. Or are you such an idealist?"

"Then," said Marwan/Northwood, in the last gesture of defiance he would be able to manage for quite some time, "you can bloody well have someone else do your dirty work!"

"Don't be such a coward," said Mr. Kazan, coldly. "You are in charge. Be flexible. Be creative. You will have her cooperation, to the very end. And then you will do what is necessary. Or," he said with a whisper and a tight smile, "perhaps you will all die."

When Hamza entered the living room – kitchen, Mr. Kazan was drying his hands near the kitchen sink. He peered at her reflection in the little mirrored calendar on the wall, and ran a comb through his hair. "Give me the finished tape," he said, holding out his hand.

Marwan/Northwood nodded, and Hamza handed it over.

"Don't disappoint us," he said, more to Marwan than Hamza. He opened the door, and glanced into the hall. "I will be in contact."

Then he was gone.

"There's a fuckin' scary one," said Hamza to Marwan.

"Indeed." Marwan/Northwood felt slightly ill, almost queasy, and his mind was racing. He'd been appalled at the long period that Mr. Kazan had given for Emma's retention, and he was frantically looking for an opportunity to "save" her. He needed to attend to first things first, to start the clock ticking, and to get himself out of here and back to his flat, where he could breathe and think. "There is one more thing to be decided."

"Where to release her?"

Marwan/Northwood took a deep breath. "Unfortunately, the plan has changed somewhat. What we need to decide is what you'll do with her for ten or eleven more days." He pulled out his wallet, and removed some bills. "Here . . . five hundred pounds. That's for now. You must keep her until the 21st." He held up his hand. "It's not for you to know. But she *must not* leave before the 21st." That was the easiest part of his statement, seeing as he, too had no idea why the 21st was important. "Do not attempt to contact me." He held up his hand, to forestall any comment from Hamza, and to make provision for whatever he might be able to accomplish with his persuasive powers between now and then. "I will talk with you before the 21st."

Hamza's next question was chilling. "Did I overhear Mr. Kazan say that she will die?"

Marwan/Northwood had always been able to think his way out of virtually every difficulty he'd ever encountered, and he was certain that he would be able to do so in this case. He just didn't know quite how. His mind had been exploring alternatives, and lies, all the time he was talking with Mr. Kazan. He needed time. He needed leverage. And the only leverage he could think of was possession and control of Emma Schiller.

"It was mentioned. But I, I am in charge, here. I intend to take her somewhere myself, to talk with her for a day or two, and then I shall convince Mr. Kazan to release her. I will relieve you of her shortly. And at that point, you'll find an additional five thousand pounds waiting for you."

"Hold on," said Hamza. "This bit wasn't part of the agreement." He wasn't bargaining for more money. Five thousand pounds was more than enough. He was trying to avoid an even more prolonged time with Emma, avoid any possibility of Emma suffering permanent harm, and desperately trying to think.

"There is no agreement. There is an oath of obedience. Or have you forgotten?"

There was a silence. Then Hamza said, "We didn't agree to anything so . . . so terrible. And we don't run a bloody rooming house, either." He turned toward Anton. "Do we?"

Anton spoke for the first time since Marwan/Northwood had entered the flat. "We do anything for the right price. I heard Mr. Kazan all right, and I know what the alternative is going to be."

Marwan looked at him, brow furrowed. "You speak English?"

"Well, that's obvious, now, ain't it?" said Anton.

"Imad," said Marwan to Hamza, "told me he was Bulgarian. You told Imad Anton here was a Bulgarian!"

"Oh, he is, he is," said Hamza.

"Are you?"

"You might say so, yes. I'm third generation," said Anton. "Grandfather granted asylum here in the UK in '47. You know. Right after the war."

Marwan looked from one to the other. "You moron," he said to
Hamza. "A Bulgarian is not someone whose ancestors fled bloody
fucking Thrace. My God." Disgusted, he glanced toward the bedroom.
"Do your job. Keep her until you hear from me. You wouldn't want
me to have to tell my friends to retain someone else, would you? Perhaps someone whose family hasn't ever emigrated. . . ."

The full implication of that wasn't lost on Hamza. 'Someone else'
would have much closer ties to someone like al-Qaeda or some other
group; and whoever it was would be 'cleaning' he and Anton up, as
well. "Right. Well, then. We won't disappoint you," he said.

"Oh, you have once, haven't you? Just see to it that you don't
again." He opened the door. "I don't want our relationship to deterio-
rate. That man is a force to be reckoned with, and I don't think you
want to aggravate him any more than he has been. I think," said Marwan, "that it's time for you to be very quietly compliant." He had another thought . . . that if he didn't yet have a place to take Emma that
Mr. Kazan wouldn't know about, there might be another way to have
her at a more, well, neutral location for a day or two, until he came up
with a safe place for him to take her, to persuade her that he was on
her side, and to think of a way to get out of this mess. . . .

"I've been thinking," he said.. "I suggest you all move out of here
as soon as you can. Tonight, if possible. Don't cancel the rent . . . use
some of the money to obtain another flat a long way from here. Take
care of business once you're there. I want no connection with this
place, understand?"

"You want us to fucking *move* her?" asked Hamza.

"That's exactly what I want. You figure out how to do it. No noise,
no fuss, no attention. Just do the thing. But don't contact me. I will
contact you before the 21st. On your cell phone. Absolutely no contact
until then. You're clear on that?"

"Right," said Anton. "The 21st. Absolutely."

"By that time, I shall convince Mr. Kazan of an alternate plan."
The door closed, and Marwan was gone.

In the silence that followed, Hamza inhaled deeply, held it, and let
it out in a long sigh. "Bloody hell," he said. "Now what do we do?"

"Obviously," said Anton, "we play musical rooms."

"Not me," said Hamza. "I didn't agree to kill her. Just grab her
and hand her over."

"Might as well, though, eh? The penalty's the thing, and if we
don't we could die. You know that. Besides, the money's better if
we finish the task."

"Sod the penalty," said Hamza. "Not the same thing."

Anton sighed. "Right. So, tell me, you know him?"

Hamza nodded. "He's Marwan. From the club, that's where I know him."

"Not his nick," said Anton. "Do you know his real name."

Hamza thought. "I don't know it," he lied. "She called him Robert. That could be it. You think someone like him would use his real name? I think I could find out. . . ."

"Oh, right. And the other one? Can you tell me who he is, then?"

"No. Never seen 'em before," said Hamza, truthfully, this time. "He said he was Mr. Kazan. You heard that bit. But I'm sure that isn't his real name, either."

"Well, that's just too fuckin' brilliant. *Because they know who we are.* They've actually been here, ain't they now? Your little rented flat, you wanker." He gave a disgusted gesture toward the bedroom. "Not to mention *her*. You've already got a life sentence just all bundled and tidy. If you don't finish the job and give them a chance to do whatever it is they want about her, you'll serve it. They can kiss us off any time. We're the ones who grabbed her, simpleton."

Hamza felt the walls of a grim reality closing in. "But . . ."

"Let me put it in language you can understand," said Anton, evenly. "It's we do what they want to *her*, or they do what they want to all three of us. Simple enough?"

"We never should have . . ."

"Shut up! Bloody waste of time, is what that is. We did it. That's all. Now we make the best of it."

Back at his flat on Ashburnham Road, Robert Northwood took stock. He was a man who needed to feel in control of his situation, and he was most uncomfortable at the moment. Somehow, between now and the 21st, he had to convince Emma Schiller that she wanted to go along with things. At least that he was her friend and was her savior, who had really had nothing to say about what had happened to her, and who had fought bravely and even heroically against the kidnapping plot. Difficult though that would be, he thought, it would surely be the easiest part.

"God," he murmured. He'd have to see her, of course. Possibly spend quite a bit of time with her. "Possibly fucking drug her," he said, aloud. "Might as well try brain surgery. . . . God!"

He'd read some mysteries, in his time, and had a vague memory of keeping the hostage in fear and doubt, in order to weaken their resolve. That part, he began to think, could be left to Hamza and Anton. Let her bake for a while. She'd be even happier to see him, and perhaps this time, she'd appreciate what he would say he was trying to do for her. Fearful enough, so if he then told her that he had thought of a way to save her life. . . .

"Possibly," he said.

But she had to stew in her own juice for a while. Indeed. But how long? And then, how? How to bring it off. Would Mr. Kazan actually kill her? He had no doubt of that. Would Kazan kill him? He would. Willingly.

"Never trust a bloody Arab," he said, to himself. Any awareness of his being largely responsible for his own predicament was fading, being driven into the back of his mind by fear, anger, and desperation. The fact that he'd inserted himself into a situation and a movement where he had absolutely no business venturing never had, and never would occur to him. He had entirely too much faith in himself to waste time even considering such things.

He decided that what he needed was time to focus his thoughts, and to prepare himself for the onslaught of Emma's reason and defenses. But, when? Today was Monday, the 10th. Tomorrow, and Thursday the 13th, he had his two weekly classes. He could not miss those, as he correctly felt that an absence, even with a very good excuse, would draw un-necessary attention. There was no way to take a mini-retreat until Friday, the 14th, as his next class after that wasn't until the next Tuesday the 18th.

Four days would certainly do. A day to go north, at least two days at his brother-in-laws little cabin, just south of Bothel near the Lake District, and a day home. He could even leave after three pm on Thursday, for that matter. Nearly five whole days. The shack would be available because his brother-in-law, who he considered an insignificant factotum for an insurance company, was conducting his annual inspection of one of the North Sea oil rigs.

He thought of it as the time necessary to think, and regain control of the situation; to reassert himself as the man who should be in charge. The fact that it was much more a case of his fleeing the reality of the situation might have crossed his mind. If it did, it was brushed aside. A mind as self involved as his could hardly be expected to spare the time to contemplate realities, when so much energy was required to bolster his perception of control.

He placed a call to his sister, and asked if she could let him use the cabin. It certainly wouldn't do to barge in on someone else. It was as he expected, very much available and stocked with canned goods. To forestall her questions, he merely said that he had to read a thesis for a friend, and didn't want to be bothered at home.

The real problem, naturally, would be this damned Kazan. But if he had Emma safely at his sister's cabin, he would be in a position to bargain. His last resort would be the police. He could always call the police. But the image of himself being countered by the testimony of Imad, Anton, Hamza, and Mr. Kazan was very uncomfortable. He'd rather have called the police now, but he had just told two men to kill Emma in a few days. How could he deny that? He'd have to get Emma to himself, convince her, and rely on the fact that her testimony about himself as the new Galahad would get him off.

That was it. And if it was leaked to the press just before . . . and there was the possibility of a book, too. He had a flash image of his photo on the back cover. He smiled for the first time that day. Publish or perish, indeed.

Satisfied, Robert Northwood went to bed and slept quite well.

Chapter 6

Monday, November 10, 2003
16:40 Central Standard Time

I sat down in a spare wooden chair in the Dispatch Center, and carefully placed my full coffee cup on the printer stand. Sally Wells, my favorite dispatcher, had her back to me, typing furiously on the teletype keyboard. "I'll be with you in just a sec . . ." she said, without turning around. "You really get to go to London?"

"Yeah."

"No shit," she said, pressing the send key and turning around to face me. "How come you're so lucky?"

"It's a long story," I said. "Believe me. Luck isn't the right term. It's kind of like your promotion." Sally had just made Chief Dispatcher, and was quietly tearing her hair out over scheduling and sick leave problems. "Be careful what you wish for."

"You got that right," she said. "So, when do you leave?"

"Tomorrow morning. So I'm gonna need a bunch of contact phone numbers, and any possible background data you can get for me on Emma Schiller."

"I don't think there's much . . . you have a DOB?"

I thought for a moment. "No. But she's pretty close to Jane's age. I'd think about 1972 or so . . . maybe 71 or 73."

"Oh, that's a hell of a help," she said. "I'll see what I can get. . . ."

"Go back as far as you can," I said. "I don't care if it's some juvenile simple misdemeanor. If anybody gives you any crap about juvenile records, refer 'em to Lamar."

She smiled. "My pleasure. You want traffic, too?"

"Yeah," I said. "I think we're not going to have much else, really. If that. But I want to take everything I can with me to London." It sounded very strange to say that.

"Okay." She grinned. "You really get to work with Scotland Yard and all that?"

"Yeah. And it's been New Scotland Yard for a hundred years, now."

"Lighten up. They'll like you better. Anyway, traffic citations . . . ?"

"Yeah. And that includes anything you know, or heard, about her or any member of her family." She looked startled. "And I already know about her uncle Virgil Breckenridge. He got ten years for embezzling mega bucks in St. Louis, a long time ago. As far as I know, that's the only member of her family who has a criminal record."

"Her cousin . . . oh, hell, what's her name . . . Addie Donnigan," said Sally. "You and Mike busted her along with about five or six others for meth about a year ago."

"No shit? I didn't know old Addie was her cousin. Well," I said, "you just never know. Must be on her mother's side . . ."

"Yep." Sally leaned forward, confidentially. "Do you think she's dead?"

"Beats me," I said. "I hope not."

"Come on, Houseman," she said. "What do you really think?"

I drew a deep breath, and then let it out slowly. "Anything's possible," I said. "The only thing I know for sure is that right now, nine and going on ten days after she's disappeared, is about the worst time to be sending me over there. Either get there right after she's missing, or months later afterward when all the false leads have kind of settled out. Not now . . . it's either too early or too late."

"Don't be so negative."

"Me? Negative?" I took a sip of coffee. "Don't be silly. Just a healthy pessimism. That's all."

"Sure," said Sally. "I think she's dead," she said, brightly. "You got anything on a motive?"

"I have no idea." I looked at her. "You really think she's dead?"

"Oh, hell yes," she said, "I bet five bucks on it. What else could she be?"

"Well, a hostage, maybe. . . ."

"No notes, no calls, as far as anybody knows. You don't just put hostages in the bank, Houseman."

"That's true. Who'd you bet with?"

"Norma. She's so naive, you know. But five bucks is five bucks."

"So, anyway, just in case you're wrong, tell me what you know about her."

"Well," she said. ". . . well, I don't want to tell you anything that isn't provable or anything, but . . . well, she wasn't any angel, you know."

"Like what?"

"Well, like she used to sleep around quite a bit."

"Really?" It was a rare day when Sally gave me news I'd already heard.

"Lots and lots of boys, I hear," she said.

"No kidding? Where'd you hear that?"

"You know my aunt Megan down in Manchester?"

"Yeah, kinda." I'd met her once, when she'd brought Sally's Thanksgiving dinner up to her at the dispatch center a few years back. Relatives did that sort of thing on most holidays.

"Well, you know, her daughter was at Iowa when Emma was."

"Didn't know that." Truthfully, I didn't know she even had a daughter.

"Well, she was. Anyway, when the news from England broke, she called me and she said that this Emma Schiller from Maitland had been 'pretty busy,' in college."

"What's her daughter's name?"

"Stanton."

"Stanton? That's her last name?"

"No, silly," said Sally. "It's her given name. Stanton Becker. You aren't going to talk to her or anything?"

"Just get me some data on her, too. I'll file it under Possible Background Source. Who knows? Being sexually, uh, active? That doesn't even stand out these days. So it might not be much of a motive, but anything could help. Jealousy, maybe." I took a sip of coffee. "You ever hear anything about her doing married men?"

"No! Good Lord, I just said she was busy, not some sort of slut, for God's sake."

I laughed. "Gottcha. So, then, you hear anything else?"

"Not really. I think about half the folks here in Maitland think she's already dead, though. From what they say."

"Well, that does make a bunch of us."

"But, you know . . . if she might be dead. . . ."

"Ah. Right. They won't say anything bad about her."

"Well, not for a few weeks after the funeral, anyway. But what about Jane? Aren't you worried about Jane? Being her roommate and all?"

That had occurred to both Sue and me, of course. Immediately. It had prompted a call to Jane, who had discounted our concerns by saying that there was absolutely no indication that it was anything but a chance meeting at or near the pub that had caused Emma to disappear. Jane was also adamant that, since she'd spent so much money to take those courses, she was going to be damned if she'd throw all that down the sink and come back to the US on some half baked theory that she could be in danger. In fact, her exact quote had been, 'Geeze, dad, she could just be having the time of her life, for all we know. . . .'

I nodded to Sally. "Oh, kinda concerned, I guess," I said. "But there doesn't seem to be any indication that it's other than random. Even the Metropolitan Police haven't suggested anything other than that."

"Well, if you say so," said Sally, with doubt in her voice. "But I'll bet you'll be glad to get over there."

"Oh, yeah. For sure. But me being there or not, Jane's pretty damned bright," I said. "She'll get worried if she needs to." This was entirely too reminiscent of a conversation Sue and I had just had. I said as much.

"Well, you know. We all worry too much, probably."

"I sure as hell hope so," I said, with complete sincerity. I stood up, and picked up my cup. "The thing that bothers me a little about the random theory is, well, it just means there isn't any evidence to suggest anything. So that would, you know, automatically make it look like it was random. The first piece of hard evidence could throw all the random bullshit into a cocked hat." I grinned. "That's the way this stuff works. Anyway, I'll stop up before I leave tomorrow, and pick up what you get. And as soon as I know what it is, I'll send you my phone number over there."

"Awesome," she said. "A number in London. Who all do you want to have that?"

"You can give it to anybody who can afford to call it," I said.

"Oooh."

"Yeah. Oh, and I need you to send a teletype to the Metropolitan Police in London, to let 'em know I'm heading over, and that I'd like to talk to them about Emma's disappearance."

"That's been done," she said. "Lamar's request about an hour ago."

"Oh. Okay, good. Anyway, then can you get me a number to call them. Somebody there, not just a generic. Whoever's working the case would be nice."

"I don't know how long this will take," said Sally. "There's a time difference. . . ."

"Six hours," I said. "They're six hours ahead of us. If it's 4 PM here, it's 10 PM there."

She blinked while she digested that. "Got it."

"You might want to write that down," I said.

"I think," she said, sarcastically, "*I'm* young enough I can remember that."

"Relax. Not for you, but for the rest of the office. I don't want to get a 'How's it going' phone call at three in the morning, London time."

By four o'clock, I was just about ready to head home and start packing. I stuck my head in Lamar's office. "Anything else?"

"I hope you ain't pissed off," he said. "About goin' over there."

"Oh, no. I'm more surprised than anything else. But don't get your hopes up. I'm just about certain I won't be able to accomplish shit."

"Maybe not," he said, "but it's worth a shot."

"That attitude surprises me about as much as anything," I told him. I'd worked with or for Lamar for more than twenty years, and it wasn't like him to do this. "Why you doin' this?"

"Shut the door," he said. "And don't repeat anything I'm gonna tell you."

"Okay . . ."

Even with the door shut, he lowered his voice. "First, I'm serious about it bein' worth a try. But . . . Rocky's gonna run again," he said. "And it's looking like it's really a close one this time."

By 'Rocky,' he meant Harold Stone. Rocky had been a candidate for Sheriff twice before, and had gotten a surprising number of votes three years ago. He was one of those completely inexperienced candidates, who had never worn a badge in his life, and was given to telling people that, if elected, he'd order his Deputies to ignore proper procedure and 'do what's right.'

"You're kidding?"

"No. So if you got any doubts about how much good you're doin' over there, just ask yourself if you'd like to work for Rocky."

"You don't think he can win, do you?"

"Folks didn't think I'd win, first time, either. Remember?"

I did. It had been very close, but Lamar had beaten Steve Burgess, the incumbent. "Yeah, but Burgess was a complete idiot." I looked him square in the eye. "I'm qualified to retire. If that s o b wins, I'll quit."

He chuckled. "If he wins, I won't be here, either." He got serious again. "But the people deserve better than Rocky."

"You got that right."

"So, Carl, have a nice trip. It ain't costing our budget a penny more, so Rocky can't bitch about that. It's been approved by the Board, so I got him there, too. And, if things go right, you might be able to help over there. If not, we tried." He smiled. "And if he bitches about it, most of the important people around here'll take his head off."

"And you didn't go yourself. . . ."

"You got it. My responsibility is right here."

"You're one smart son of a bitch," I said, with a big grin.

"I keep tellen ya," he said.

"I'll send you a postcard."

"Make it one of that double decker bridge they got," said Lamar. "I like that thing. One with it up to let ships through, if you can."

"Okay." I opened the door, and said, "I'll keep you posted."

He motioned me back in. "Not yet." When the door was safely closed again, he said, "You probably agree with me . . . that she's pretty likely dead."

"Yes."

"But there's always a chance," he said, almost making it a question.

"Sure. Just not much of one. I'm not basing that on any good evidence, you know that. Since there doesn't seem to be any. But I think the odds of finding her alive are really slim, and getting worse every minute."

"If they find the body," he said, "call me first."

"Absolutely. But, shit, Lamar, if she's dead, it could be years, if ever, before they find her."

"Well, you got two weeks. If you can't give me a happy story, just find out enough to give me something to base something on. You know?"

"Something 'professional' that'll keep Rocky off your ass?"

"That'd be nice. But this isn't just about Rocky. Let's find out what happened to this kid. I remember that fuckin' car wreck that got her dad. Hell, you were there, too."

"Sure," I said. I didn't add that I was there first. If he'd forgotten, it wouldn't make any difference.

"And I want to make absolutely certain that it ain't related to anything goin' on around here. For real."

"I'll do my best."

"And, Carl?"

"Yeah?"

"I'm serious about the terrorists and the meth. Especially the meth."

"Yeah. Well, we've sure as hell had 'em both. I'll check." That gave me a moment's pause. "Think I should take copies of that terrorist case over to show the London cops?"

"Couldn't hurt. Just edit out the stuff the Feds want kept quiet. You know. Go ahead and tell about that, if you want, but not in writing."

"Then I'm gonna have to get into the safe," I said. We had a double locked safe, for intelligence and other secure data. We each had a combination for one lock.

"We gotta make the copies ourselves, too," he said, standing. "Norma isn't cleared for this kind of shit." Norma had just been promoted from dispatch, and was our second secretary.

"Won't Judy be in tomorrow?" Judy was cleared, and I was anxious to get home.

"Yeah. We'll let her do it, and mail it to London, and that way you don't have to lug it all over the airport."

That was a good idea. There was some highly confidential stuff in that, and with all the searches and things, I'd end up lugging it in my carry-on. It was probably going to run five pounds or better, and I didn't want to have to be carrying it with me on the plane, either. Things get lost and stolen in airports.

I brought Lamar up to speed on everything I'd found out about Emma.

When I was finished, he just shook his head. "You can learn lots of stuff on this job that you really don't want to know."

"Yeah."

"Just think what it would be like if it was your daughter or mine. Hearing some of that stuff. Stuff that some people always take in the wrong way."

"I hope that day never comes," I said. "Not for either of us." It had come for him in a way. A murder victim had been one of his nieces, and the details about her personal life had bothered him. They'd bothered everybody, in fact. Not that she was a rotten person, or anything. She just tended to do strange things.

I saw the phone in the middle office light up just as we finished. The ring was disabled every evening by Norma, when she went home at 4:30. That was so it didn't bother Lamar.

A second later, the intercom in his office buzzed. We both faintly heard Sally say, "Lamar, its Carson Hilgenberg for you."

"Crap," said Lamar, handing me my copy of the file. Carson Hilgenberg was our new county attorney. He'd gotten appointed to replace a vacancy, when nobody else wanted the job. He was pretty young, and something of an idiot, but he normally meant well. His only saving grace was his secretary, who kept him on time, and properly equipped to handle his cases. And properly dressed, for all I knew.

"I'll talk to you tomorrow, before you go," said Lamar. "I wonder what he wants this time. . . ."

I took my file back into my office, got out my attaché case from the cranny under my desk where it had been gathering dust for a couple of years, and put the file in the lid pocket. There was a Snickers bar in the corner of the case that had to have been there for at least a year, probably all of two or three. I shut the case quickly. You never know when you might need a Snickers.

I was already past Lamar's office, on the way to the door, when he stuck his head out.

"Hey, wait up."

"Sure."

"I got some bad news."

Since he'd just talked to the county attorney, I figured that now that I was getting excited about going, I'd be kept home from London because there was a court case Carson Hilgenberg had forgotten to tell me about.

"I got court?"

"No, worse."

"Well, come on Lamar," I said. "Spit it out."

"Carson Hilgenberg's goin' to London, too."

"Yuck, yuck," I said. "Very funny."

"I ain't kiddin'," he said. "Carson Hilgenberg's going, too. He said he'd try to get away when we talked yesterday. We consulted with him about sending you. . . ."

"You're shittin' me?"

"Nope. I didn't think he could get out of the county . . . Christ, he's the only prosecutor we got. But he had vacation. So he's goin' over with you. And, well, it gets worse."

"I can't think how."

"Ah, well, ah . . . you two are sharing a room." He looked sad. "I'm really sorry, Carl. It just . . . happened."

As it turned out, Carson Hilgenberg, attorney at law, was running in the next election, too. That's one thing he'd talked with Lamar about . . . he wanted tips on how to run a successful campaign. I guess he thought what worked for a Sheriff would work for a prosecutor. Lamar, in good spirits, had told him that he'd be sending a deputy to England, to work the missing person's case. Lamar made the mistake of saying that it seemed to him to be pretty good political sense to do so. After Lamar had actually had to explain who she the missing girl was, Carson said he not only considered it a very sound political move, he thought that a prosecutor should go along.

"He said he'd be there to give the Deputy Sheriff legal guidance. I tried to talk him out of it, Carl. I really did," said Lamar. "But he said he only had five cases on the docket for the next three weeks, and he was going to get them continued. And that we could call the State's Attorney if we needed anything done really fast while he was gone."

"No. No way, man. I can't stand that little shit."

"He's using vacation time," said Lamar.

"No way. He's only been County Attorney for a year or so. County employees only get one week a year for the first five years." I thought I'd found a way.

"He's gonna be working," said Lamar. "Just like you are. But he's taking his week of vacation just to impress the voters. Besides, he's counted as a part-time official, since the County only pays half his salary. He can be gone quite a while before he violates the provisions of his office." He looked stricken. "You're gonna have to keep him out of this somehow," he said. "We can't have him get involved, you know? Not for real."

"Don't lay that one on me," I said. "I didn't ask for him, and I ain't gonna ride herd on him."

"Think of Emma," said Lamar.

"That's not fair," I said. "This isn't an expedition, for God's sake! You gotta talk to the Board of Supervisors, Lamar. There has to be something you can do about this."

He shrugged. "Carson's an elected official. That's all she wrote," he said, with a grim note of finality. "I know you can handle him, Carl."

Chapter 7

Monday, November 10, 2003
17:35 Central Standard Time

The first thing I tried to do when we got home was call our daughter Jane in London. It was 5:35, which made it 11:35 PM in London. I just caught her before she got to bed.

She answered with a tired "Hello."

"Hi, it's your dad."

"Hey. Nothing new yet, just to get that out of the way. She's still gone. How's Margaret?"

"Margaret's just fine," I said. We were referring to Jane's beagle, Margaret, who she'd left with us while she was in the UK. "Sorry to hear that Emma's still gone, but . . ." and I told her I'd be in London about 9:30 AM on the 11th.

"What? Here? No way!"

"Yeah. The Department's sending me. To assist."

"What about Mom?" Then, as she caught her breath, "Assist who?"

"I'm afraid not. The school won't send her . . ." I said, making a small joke. "No, she's okay with it. To assist New Scotland Yard, who else?"

"I hate to tell you this, but I don't think they really need it, Dad." She laughed, and it was the first time I'd heard her do that since Emma disappeared. "So, what airport? How are you getting in town? Where are you staying?"

I gave her the details. She said she'd meet me at the hotel about 3:30 PM or so, when classes got out.

"We can do supper or something," she said. "Wait till I tell Vicky. She's really been worried."

"And there's more. Carson Hilgenberg, the new County Attorney? He's coming with me."

She actually laughed again. Two for two, except I didn't think this one was particularly funny. "You're kidding?" I'd discussed Carson with her more than once.

"No."

"Well, you're going to have a long trip, Dad."

About 6:15, Sue suddenly said, "I'll bet you didn't get Traveler's Checks."

"Oh, shit." The banks closed their windows at 4:30.

One phone call to Allen Jones, president of Northland Savings Bank and one of the interested parties in Lamar's office this morning, and I was on my way to the bank. He came down in person, and issued the Traveler's Checks himself.

"You want this in hundreds or fifties?" he asked, opening a small box that contained the checks.

I had decided to withdraw five hundred dollars from our checking account, but Allen had persuaded me to go for a thousand. That left, by the way, less than four hundred dollars in our account, so I decided to transfer a thousand from our savings, which just about zeroed that account out.

"You got your birth certificate?"

"Shit. No, I don't. It's in our safety deposit box."

One phone call, and Sue was on her way with the key. She walked. It was only a block. We opened the box, got my birth certificate, and Allen very obligingly copied it for me.

While doing all this, Allen kept asking pointed questions that he'd been uncomfortable about raising in Lamar's office.

"What do you think the chances of her being alive really are, Carl?"

"Hard to say," I answered.

"No, come on. Just between us."

I took a deep breath. "Very slim," I said. "She's too close to her mother to take off like this and not let her know."

"Oh, I hope you're wrong," said Sue.

"Me, too."

"I agree about her not doing this to her mother," he said. "If she is dead, how long do you think it'll take to find her?"

"That's pure chance," I said, "if the Brits are being straight about not having any leads." I signed some more. "One of the biggest factors is the method of disposal. Some are more easily discovered than others."

He took the signed Traveler's checks, stacked them neatly, put them in two paper wallets, and completed his form. Then he handed them back to me. As he did, he said, "If you need more, just let me know, Carl. We can get a no interest emergency loan and get it to you within a couple of hours."

"Thanks."

"No questions will be asked," he said. "Except for one thing."

"Okay . . ."

"If you have to pay an informant, tell me. Don't tell me what for, just tell me. If you have to do that, we won't consider it a loan, and it'll come directly out of my personal account."

"Jesus, Allen, you don't have to do that."

"It'll be my contribution. I know there's no way that sort of money ever comes back. Just one thing. . . ."

"Sure."

He grinned. "Don't pay for any more information than you absolutely need."

If I'd had any lingering doubts about the community feelings on my mission to find Emma, that settled them for good and all.

Sue and I got to bed early, because we both had to be up and running at 07:00. That was normal for her, but I seldom rolled out of bed until about 10:00, as I began my shift at noon.

Neither of us could sleep.

"Did you remember to pack your other shoes?" she asked, wide awake.

"Yep," I answered, as alert as she was.

"And your sport coat?"

I hate sport coats, mostly because I hate ties. "There's not room." She'd convinced me to buy a sport coat a year ago, and I'd worn it once.

"There's plenty of room, I'm sure. I'll pack it for you."

"I'm not gonna need a sport coat."

"You will. Trust me. And I don't want you to feel out of place over there. They dress much better than . . . well than you do."

Sue had been very disappointed, but realistic about not being able to go with me. The fact that I was going to be cursed by Carson Hilgenberg's presence had give her a good laugh, though, and may have taken some of the sting out of it.

"And your brown belt, too? You need it with the beige slacks."

I chuckled in the dark. "Yes, that, too. You better get to sleep."

"I should let *you* get to sleep," she said. "This is unusual for you. Now, tell me again, how do you get a passport so fast?"

"They tell me you can do it in Chicago in a work day. So, that's why I get to arise at 07:00."

"Is Lamar driving you in?"

"What?"

"I said. . . ."

"Well, holy shit," I said, "I can't take my squad car and leave it in Chicago two weeks . . . and I sure as hell can't take ours. . . ." I turned on my bed lamp, and reached for the phone. "You're sure ahead of me on this one."

"Naturally."

I dialed the office, and recognized the voice that answered. "Hey, Betty, it's Houseman . . ."

"You should be asleep."

"Tell me. Anyway . . . ," and I explained the problem with the cars. "I know you call Lamar at 06:00. When you do, ask him if he wants to give me a ride."

"Just a sec . . ." she said, and I could hear her rustling through some papers. . . . "Just making sure," she said. "Okay, here we are . . . the previous dispatcher got a call about forty-five minutes ago . . . you will be riding with Carson Hilgenberg to Chicago."

"Oh. Well, swell." I guess I didn't sound too enthusiastic, because she laughed, and so did Sue beside me.

"But, I'll tell Lamar you called," said Betty.

"Thanks."

She told me that Carson was picking me up at 08:00.

"Delightful."

After I hung up, Sue said, "You sounded pretty funny. What's up?"

I told her about my ride. She thought it was very funny.

A few minutes later, when I was finally beginning to drift off, she said, "Now don't take up too much of Jane's study time, will you?"

"Huh? Oh, no. No, 'course not."

"Make sure she's safe, Carl."

"Well, sure." I was awake again. "Like I said, there are absolutely no indications that whatever has happened to Emma, that it's associated with Jane." Directly. I added that to myself. There was a fair chance that it might be someone they both may have known.

"Just promise you'll send her home if you start to worry."

I reached out and put my arm around her. "I started to worry the day we heard Emma was gone," I said. "How about I send her home when I think I'm worried in a rational way. Not that I can send her

home anyway. She's over 21. But I'll sure as hell make a strong sugges-
tion. That okay?"

"All right."

It must have been a good ten minutes later, as I was just dropping
off, when she said, "She's dead, isn't she?"

I was just a bit too far gone down the road to sleep to have the
safety mechanism kick in. "Yeah," I said.

"What!"

It was a long night.

She didn't forget the sport coat. She got it in. I wasn't sure I could
get it re-packed on the way home, but she got the thing in my suitcase.

Carson Hilgenberg honked his horn at my back door at about
08:20. Twenty minutes late. Sue had already left for school, after admonishing me once again that Jane was to be safe, in my estimation, or
I was to persuade Jane to leave London. Right. Like I was going to be
able do that, if she didn't want to go.

I lugged my two bags plus carry-on out to Carson's black Ford
Expedition.

"Hey, big guy," was his greeting. "Just toss 'em in the back, and hop
in. The Windy City Express is about to leave!"

Carson was about twenty-six or twenty-seven. That made him
about thirty years my junior. He'd been appointed county attorney
when the office was vacated, and nobody else wanted the job. He'd
managed to get through law school by the skin of his teeth, and had
failed to pass the Iowa Bar Exam the first time he took it, before finally making it two years ago. Sue had said, once, that I used the term
'idiot' way too often. She'd asked me to name two people who I thought
really deserved the label. I said "Carson Hilgenberg, and Carson Hilgenberg."

I have to give him some credit, though. He was an idiot in the
broadest, nicest sense. In fact, that made him the worst kind of idiot.
He was well meaning, friendly, and not at all unpleasant. He was fairly
well educated. And he really wasn't dumb, either. He was just the sort
who had always gotten by, and who would forget most of what he'd
learned about torts, but never forget those zany antics of rush week.
And he'd tell you about them. All of which meant that it wasn't possible to really hate him, and eliminated all sorts of satisfying and vengeful retorts. It did mean that I usually found him pretty irritating.

"Hello, Carson," I said, hoisting my bags into his SUV.

"I think this is going to be a worthwhile trip, don't you?"

"I sure hope so," I said. I slid onto the passenger seat, and fumbled with the belt. "We'll have to see."

He started forward just before I got my door completely closed. He's like that.

Carson talked incessantly all the way to Chicago, mostly telling tales from his fraternity days. I was enthralled. During one of his infrequent pauses, I allowed as to how I was concerned that my passport wouldn't be ready in time.

"Hell, Carl, it's a piece of cake. Don't worry. I've got a fraternity brother who just got one that way . . . no problems."

"Glad to hear it," I said, still concerned.

"Oh, yeah. He grabbed it the last time we went to Italy. . . ."

That got him going on the various times he'd been to Europe on what he termed the Hostelling, Drinking, and Screwing the Undergrads tours.

"You went with undergrads?" I was surprised.

"Oh, sure. I was sort of a proctor cum tour guide. Prime assignment. I got to go as an assistant to the instructor."

"They let you out alone with undergrads?"

"I called it my sex education tour. Only I wasn't the one who was learning."

"Right." I took a deep breath. "So, where all did you go?"

He seemed to have gravitated toward Italy and France, although he'd been to England and Wales.

"You got a favorite country over there, Carl?"

"Well," I said, "it's a little hard to say. Never been there."

"You're kidding?"

"Well, Sue and I sort of thought we'd go somewhere after we retire," I said.

"Let me tell you, you'll love Assisi. Really."

I knew it was in Italy. I listened to his glowing description of it all the way to 53 West Jackson. I don't know that it was related to his European travels, but I was glad Carson seemed to know Chicago so well. I never could have found the place. He'd been right. It was a piece of cake. It actually took less than an hour, all told.

Consequently, we were way early getting to O'Hare, the plane leaving at 7:30 PM, and us being there at 3:30 and all. We checked our luggage, and then headed toward our departure area. I thought Carson was going to get us arrested when he saw me empty my pockets at the security checkpoint and said, in a normal tone of voice, "Oh, you're not wearing a gun?" I think we were very fortunate I had just placed my badge in the tray.

"No," I said, ostensibly to him, but loudly enough for all the security people near me to hear very clearly. "The Department recommends we don't take our service weapons with us on flights." Jesus.

That conversation, unfortunately, distracted me. As I passed through the metal detector archway, the alarms went off. I knew right away what it was, but I got pulled aside anyway, frisked with a wand, and then motioned over to an adjacent area with a small chair, and asked to remove my shoes.

"It's the case for my reading glasses," I said. "It's steel. I forgot to take it out of my shirt pocket."

The security man just said, "Well, let's just make sure."

That's what it was, all right. Carson tried to help by saying, from his vantage point of having passed through successfully, "I'll bet it was your badge."

The security guy smiled. "You a cop?"

"Yeah." I nodded my head toward Carson. "He's not. He's an attorney."

"No? Really? I couldn't tell."

That made me feel a bit better.

We walked about half a mile to gate K12, past what seemed to be an endless variety of shops, restaurants, and bars.

"This place," I said to Carson, as we walked briskly down the concourse, "is like a shopping mall with airplanes."

He liked that.

After finding gate K12, which turned out to be about as far from our entry point as it could possibly be, we sat in the departure lounge and ate some uniquely expensive cheap sandwiches, drank pretty expensive bad black coffee, and finally got around to talking about the case when Carson stated, "You know, Carl, I bet she's dead."

"Who, Emma?" Of course Emma, I thought. Don't be rude.

"Emma. I don't know about you," he said, confidentially, "but I'll bet she's already been planted out on some moor or something. Could take years to find her. I read somewhere," he said, lowering his voice, "that there was this family over there on the moor, and they actually ate their victims! Can you believe that?"

I sipped my coffee. "So, then, why are you going over there? If you think she's a gonner."

"Hey, Big Guy, a chance like this comes along once in a lifetime. I mean, we get to do some routine checking, and have a lot of time left over for sightseeing. All in the name of public service."

The way he said sightseeing told me quite a bit. "Well, maybe," I said. "But this is a working trip. We have lots to do. I think we could be pretty busy, if things go right." Actually, I suspected that he was right. I just hoped he wasn't. And I didn't appreciate his attitude.

"I don't know about you," he said, evidently not having a clue as to the impression he was making on me, "but I intend to spend an hour or so at Scotland Yard, listen to their report, and then see what turns up while we're there. They can call us back if they find anything."

"New Scotland Yard," I said.

"What?"

I explained.

"Oh."

"Always nice to use the right term," I said.

"Yeah. Thanks. Hey, you think they've got a Hooters in London?"

"Oh, I wouldn't think so. . . ."

"I dunno," he said, brightly. "I'll have to check when we get in. They got these Philly Cheese Steak sandwiches . . . you ever have one?"

" 'Fraid not."

"How 'bout their Cuban sandwich?"

I shook my head.

"You tryin to tell me you've never *been* to Hooters?"

"I'm 'fraid so," I said.

"How about a Cinnabon?" he asked.

I shook my head. "Uh, no."

"Well, you're in luck. There's one right behind us!"

I went sort of reluctantly as we lugged our carry-on stuff with us, but each ended up with a huge cinnamon roll that was absolutely delicious. We camped in the dining enclave for a while, and Carson cranked up his laptop and checked his email.

"Wireless," he said. "I don't know what I'd do without it."

Mine, which stayed on the floor with my gym bag, needed wires.

He may not have known what to do without it, but judging from the short time he had it opened, there weren't any messages. He folded it up, and carefully wiped the crumbs from the case. "They don't buss the tables here very often. It's because they share 'em with other concessions. Jurisdictional problem." He took a drink of coffee, and carefully wiped his mouth with a paper napkin.

"I hope we find out one way or the other when we get there," he said.

"About Emma?"

"Yeah."

"Me, too."

"You know, I understand she had two roommates," he said, around his cinnamon roll. "Maybe I can score with 'em?"

"Only one, if you know what's good for you," I said. He gave me a questioning look. "One of 'em's my daughter."

He was unflappable. "So, like, I should try for the other one, right?" He grinned.

"If you want to see thirty-five."

"You know," he said, after a minute, "I remember Emma when she was in high school. She was a cheerleader; she was a senior, I think, when I was in seventh or eighth grade."

"That'd be about right."

"Boy, I had the hots for her."

I looked at him. "Must have done you a bunch of good."

"Oh, you know, like a junior high kid has the hots. Nothing serious." He flashed a big grin. "But I used to follow her around the halls, right after lunch. . . ."

"Carson Hilgenberg, junior stalker," I said.

"That's about it. Boy, it'd be a shame if she was dead. She had a truly gorgeous ass." He seemed to realize he'd made a mistake as soon as he said it. "I mean, you know, she was a great gal and everything. I just meant . . ." The sentence just sort of trailed off.

"Yep."

"Sorry."

"You don't have to apologize to me," I said. "You just might be a little more circumspect for a while. Especially in London."

The crowd in our lounge area changed about every forty-five minutes, and as it got closer to our flight time, I found myself looking over the passengers in the area and picking out potential hijackers or bombers. If you ever start looking for suspicious people, you'll find 'em everywhere. I mean, you're going to be wrong at least ninety-nine percent of the time, but you see 'em anyway. That gave me an idea.

"Look at that guy," I said, indicating a particularly unkempt individual with only a small bag. "Doesn't he look like a hijacker? I mean, really?"

"What?"

"Just look at him."

"Damn," said Carson. "You're right. Should we, like, tell somebody?"

"Oh, no. I mean, look at that gal to his right, back a row. The one with the big curly hair and the pocket pants. Lots of suicide bombers are young women these days, you know. And with that outfit on, who knows what she might hide in those pockets. Or that hair, for that matter."

"You don't think . . ." he asked, rhetorically. "No, no, she'd have to pass through the same security checks we did."

"Yeah, she's probably not. Well, unless a co-conspirator slipped her something from behind a food counter. They probably don't check airport employees nearly as close as passengers." This was fun. "You know, I'd be more likely to suspect that man there . . . the one with the beard and the backpack. See him?" I asked. "Almost looks like he's kinda hiding behind that pillar, doesn't it?"

"Shit. . . ."

"I'm gonna take a little nap," I said. "Just keep a mental list of the suspicious looking ones. If you've got something hot, tell me when I wake up."

"Sure."

"Give me about half an hour, would you?" With that, I scrunched down in the seat, and left Carson to fidget. I didn't sleep, but I enjoyed the silence.

Our plane was a 777. Big. Way big. We trucked our carry-ons way back to economy class seats 24 D & E. They turned out to be seats 2 and 3 in a group of five abreast. They were also right against a bulkhead. That meant that our seats were not only a little hard to get to, but once we got settled in, we found that they didn't recline more than an inch or two.

"This flight is supposed to last how long?"

"Seven hours," said Carson. "Plus or minus."

"Wonderful."

I was in the middle. Carson, to my left, was absolutely delighted to find an attractive young English girl between him and the aisle. He started a conversation immediately, beginning with his being a 'chief prosecuting attorney' in his County Attorneys' office. Chief as in only. Nonetheless, she seemed politely impressed. That was all it took. Although I felt a bit sorry for her, she provided a great distraction for Carson.

Seven hours and thirty minutes later, we landed at Heathrow airport, London. According to my internal clock, it was about 2:30 AM, and the day was just about over. According to Greenwich Mean Time, it was 8:30 AM, and the day was just beginning. A day we'd gained. It was now the 12th. According to my legs, it was time to go to the hospital.

Chapter 8

Wednesday, November 12, 2003
10:26 Greenwich Mean Time

Everything had gone much more smoothly than I expected, and only two hours or so after landing, we had checked into our hotel and were unpacking. All the concern about my obtaining a passport seemed a little silly by now, as I had only been asked two questions upon entry to the United Kingdom.

First, the man behind the little podium had asked me if the purpose of my trip was business or pleasure.

"Business," I said.

"What is the nature of your business?"

"I'm a law enforcement officer, over here to work a case with New Scotland Yard." And, with that, I presented him with my badge and ID. Zip. End of questions.

I'd had to wait for Carson, who had gone into some convoluted song and dance about being on official but confidential business. He did have a knack.

"Which bed you want?" I asked Carson.

He pointed to the one furthest from the window. "That one, if it's okay with you?"

"You bet," I said, and fell back on the mattress. "See you in four hours." And I was, I'm embarrassed to say, out like a light.

I awoke at 13:22 local time. Half past one in the afternoon. Great. I'd never be able to sleep tonight. Not only that, I was hungry, my back was sore, the heavy curtains were pulled, and Carson was no-where to be found.

I took a shower, dressed, and felt just a whole lot better. I opened the curtains, and got my first good look at Kensington Park. It was pretty. There was a largish brick building in the middle distance, and I made a note to ask somebody what it was.

We were on the fifth floor of the Thistle Kensington, overlooking High Street. There was a bunch of kids, looking to be about fourth graders, queuing at a crossing sign on an island in the middle of the road. They were all dressed alike, green shorts, skirts and jackets, and accompanied by two women who were wearing reflective vests. They all waited patiently and then crossed with the light, disappearing be-hind some trees just inside the park fence. It was the first time I'd ever seen real English school kids. Cool.

I opened the window. It seemed to be about 50 degrees, and the sky was partly cloudy. Not what I'd been led to expect, which was cold and rain all the time. Off to my right was a gold spire sticking up out of the trees. That required another note. When I got home, I wanted to tell everybody what it was that I'd seen. I got the impression that I was going to need a really good tourist map.

I was just sort of standing there, taking in the fact that I was actu-ally in London, when there was a small commotion at the door, and Carson walked in, arms full of sacks.

"Hey, you're up!"

"You bet. Where you been?"

"Shopping. I went down to this little store about two blocks that way, and got us some wine, and some pop, and some crackers and cheese."

I revised my opinion of him upward a bit.

"Lemme tell ya," he said, "we aren't in Iowa anymore. You can't believe the women here. I swear to God, I saw a dozen who were almost six feet tall, blonde, and absolutely gorgeous. In less than an hour!"

"Good for you."

"Honest, Big Guy, I didn't realize how much I missed city life."

"You call New Scotland yard yet?" I asked. I surely hoped not, but thought I'd better make sure before I called in.

"No, I thought I'd wait for you to do that. Wanna wait until to-morrow?"

"Oh, no. No, no. We get started now," I said.

The first real surprise was that the telephone number I'd gotten from Sally was just a general switchboard number at New Scotland

Yard. I asked for the Missing Persons unit, and eventually got an officer named Garret, who said that his unit in general was working the case. He then asked who I was, and what my interest was in the case.

That took a few minutes. His basic response was polite and correct, but there was a very strong tone of '*What in the hell* . . . ?' about most of his side of the conversation. That was all right, because I was pretty hard put to tell him just exactly why, myself.

Eventually, I was told that an officer Trowbridge would meet with us the next morning. I was given the number of the Missing Persons unit, I gave him mine at the hotel, and that was that.

"Get everybody all straightened out?" asked Carson.

"This ain't gonna be easy," I said. "I think he was just a little . . . oh, maybe you could say dumbfounded. I would be, too." I chuckled.

"Why?"

"Well, look. I mean . . . I'm sure he couldn't find Iowa on a very good map. But he knows it's one hell of a distance from here, and for a case where there is absolutely no evidence of foul play. . . ."

"Well, she *is* gone."

I reached for the crackers. "Yeah, but as far as I know there isn't anything that's turned up one way or the other. And I would suppose they have a fair number of missing persons cases in a city this size."

"Most of whom turn up?" he said, as much of a question as not.

"I'd think."

"I wonder," said Carson, "how long the average one is gone before they find they're all right?"

"That's a good question. But I'll bet it's not anywhere near this long."

"I don't suppose there's a prosecutor assigned this one, yet."

It's hard not to make a crack at times like that. "Well, probably not." After all, there wasn't a crime. Hard to assign a prosecutor if there isn't a crime. But I didn't say that.

"Well, not without a crime, I guess," he said.

I was beginning to think he wasn't such an airhead, but that his mind just was geared a little differently.

"Right." I figured I'd limit it to that.

"So, we go together tomorrow, right? To the police station?"

Now, New Scotland Yard was bound to be a bit more than a police station, but I let that go, too. He was a prosecutor, not a cop. "You bettcha. I think it's best if we're together. They'll have an easier time," I said, with a grin, "believing two of us."

It wasn't five minutes later that the phone rang. I thought it was going to be Jane. No such luck. It was an Inspector Whitcomb, telling me that he and a sergeant would be in the lobby of our hotel in ten minutes, and could we, perhaps, meet in the lounge.

"Sure. No problem."

"Very fine, then. See you in ten," and he hung up. I told Carson. That sounded good to him.

"Yeah," I said, "it does to me, too. I think."

"What? You aren't happy with this?"

"I'm not sure," I said. "Let's see how it goes."

The lounge area was very cozy, with comfortable leather chairs grouped in threes and fours around tables. Coffee or tea was provided with a complete service. Sue would really like this, I thought. It was really luxurious, heightened somehow because Carson and I were the only two patrons in the place.

We'd been seated for about a minute when two men dressed in sport jackets entered, and came directly toward us. They were middle height, fit, and had an air of complete assurance. One was about forty, one maybe thirty and a year or so. Cops. Without a doubt.

"Mr. Houseman?" asked the younger of the two.

I stood. There was about a nine inch height difference between us. And about a hundred pounds, to boot. I stuck out my hand. "That's me," I said, looking down at him. "And this is Carson Hilgenberg."

"Inspector Whitcomb," he said, presenting his credential wallet for me to see. "And this is Sergeant Trowbridge." There were handshakes exchanged. He turned to the waiter who was fussing around the next table. "Two teas, please." He smiled. "Let's sit," he said, "why don't we?"

We did.

"Sergeant Trowbridge tells me that you're a sheriff?" There was an air of amusement about that question.

"Yes. Well, no, not precisely." I noticed his eyebrows rise. "A Deputy Sheriff, from Nation County, Iowa," I said, and handed him my badge case. "Carson, here, is the chief prosecutor for our County."

"Ah, a barrister," said Whitcomb. He looked at my badge, and handed it back. "Very nice, and it's really a star. I've always connected rural US Sheriffs with cowboys and shootouts with cow punchers. Not really that way, is it?"

"No. Well, hardly ever, anyway. The best thing is that we don't ride horses."

He smiled. "So, now, it's my understanding that you're here regarding a missing persons case, is that correct?"

"Yes," I said. "A young woman named Emma Schiller. She's from our county."

Sergeant Trowbridge said her name at the same time I did.

"A name familiar to all," said Whitcomb, with a brief smile. "Well, then, right to the point. What has us wondering, really, is why you would be sent over here for a case where there's no evidence of a crime being committed."

"We attempted to explain that in a teletype we sent via Interpol," I said.

"Yes. Yes, that arrived this morning, I believe. . . ." and he glanced at Sergeant Trowbridge. "Is that correct?"

"Right," said Trowbridge. "I asked for any contact information after Deputy Houseman called today. Central communications gave it me."

"Interpol is notoriously slow," said Whitcomb. "When was it sent?"

"A while ago," I said. "I'm not sure exactly, but a good week. . . ."

"You see. Nonetheless, it offers assistance, but fails to mention your imminent arrival."

"That should arrive next week," I said, in an attempt at humor. "But as to the reason for our visit . . ." I explained the events that had led us to London.

"Local politics, then?"

"Only partially," I said. "It sort of greased the skids. But my Sheriff is genuinely concerned about Emma's disappearance, and so are we all."

"Most understandable," said Whitcomb. "Ah, Sergeant Trowbridge tells me you have the same last name as one of the missing girl's roommates? Would you be related, then?"

"Jane Houseman's my daughter," I said.

"Ah. And that would be another interest, then?"

"We all knew Emma," said Carson, speaking for the first time since the conversation had started in earnest.

"Yes," said Whitcomb. "And it's brilliant of you to have come to help us. Truly. But to be perfectly honest, we feel we should caution you not to go about questioning people. At least, if they indicate they would rather not talk to you, you should abandon that pursuit instantly. That would be harassment if you weren't to desist immediately. Since you lack jurisdiction. And, if there would turn out to be crime involved, you could muddy the waters, as they say, and quite possibly interfere."

"I'm very aware of that," I said. "Believe me. I also know that, if you think you might have a lead, somebody asking questions over the same territory could cause any possible source to dry up."

"Too right," said Sergeant Trowbridge, and earned a cautionary glance from Inspector Whitcomb for his trouble.

I made a mental note that Trowbridge had developed a possible lead.

"Just to put all our minds at ease," said Whitcomb, "you don't happen to have brought some sort of firearm over with you?"

"No," I said. "No, I wouldn't do that. I'd be completely illegal, doing that."

"Yes, indeed you would," he said. "Firearms are illegal in the UK. So, well, brilliant. Trowbridge here has brought you a copy of his report. You can look that over, and give him a call if you have any questions."

"Thanks," I said, taking the envelope handed to me by Sergeant Trowbridge. "So, do you have any leads?" I wanted to see a reaction.

Trowbridge looked as if he was about to nod in affirmation, when Whitcomb said, "Not really. But I assure you, we're still on the job."

"Okay," I said. "Well, just so you are aware, we do intend to talk with the folks in the pub where she was last seen. And with some fellow students, possibly." I grinned. "And her roommates, of course. Daughters aren't allowed to refuse to talk. But, part of our, ah, mandate I guess, is that we make absolutely certain that there can be no connection to any events occurring on our side of the Atlantic."

I had a reason for bringing that up. It was bound to make them curious, and if they did have anything they weren't sharing, it might put them in a mood to do a bit of a deal. Not right away, but if they kept coming up dry, they might remember the Iowa connection.

"What sort of connection were you thinking of?" asked Whitcomb.

"Oh, our county has a large reputation in the US of being one of the major sources of methamphetamine, for example. And you never know if somebody might have pissed somebody else off and they decided to get even."

"Internationally?" Inspector Whitcomb sounded amused.

"Oh, yeah" I said. "Could easily be. We have individual manufacturers who clear several hundred thousand dollars a year. They trade for dollars, they trade for ecstasy, they trade for heroin. They trade for sex, too, but I suspect that's gotta be pretty local to do 'em any good." Only Carson and Trowbridge laughed. "Anyway, it's really hard to say. The only foreign involvement we've actually proved in the last three or four years is a connection to Denmark."

"I am truly amazed," said Whitcomb, and he sounded sincere.

"So were we," I said, and this time we all laughed.

"Do you think Emma Schiller was involved in the narcotics trade, then?" asked Trowbridge.

"Not as far as I've been able to tell, and we have pretty good records," I said. "I'm not able to say she wasn't a user, because I really don't know. I can check that aspect with my daughter, if you'd like. She might know."

"I've asked that question," said Trowbridge, "and got the usual reluctance to say much. You must know how that is."

"Sure," I said. I certainly did. Nobody ever wants to snitch off a friend, and nobody ever wants to speak ill of the dead. It's kind of a universal thing. I was sure that Jane and Vicky weren't likely to be exceptions. "As time passes and there's no development, they'll open up more. Let me see what I can do."

"You must have lots of missing persons every year," said Carson. "Hundreds."

"Thousands," said Whitcomb. "And ninety-nine percent are found or otherwise proven to be all right."

"Well, that's encouraging," said Carson. "Isn't it, Carl?"

"You bet," I said, looking at Whitcomb. To us pessimists, that meant that if there were ten thousand cases a year, a hundred were missing permanently. "What's the usual duration of a missing persons case?"

Whitcomb shrugged. "I really can't say, right off."

"Less than a week, though, wouldn't you think?"

"Trowbridge here can check that for you, and let you know," he said.

From the look on Trowbridge's face, I figured he could probably rattle the figures off the top of his head. Not now, though, with his superior firmly in the lead.

"And, so," said Inspector Whitcomb, "we must be going. We'll be certain to notify you immediately if there's any change in the case." He stood, as did Trowbridge. "No need to see us out," he said, with a smile. "You can reach us at the same number, if there's a need."

After they'd gone, Carson and I stayed to finish our coffee. It was really pretty good stuff, and gave the lie to the reports I'd had that the Brits could only brew tea.

"Well, they were really nice," said Carson. "I feel much better about this whole thing, now. Don't you?"

"Not really," I said.

"You don't?"

"Oh, they were nice enough, but I get the impression that we're going to be kept at arms length by New Scotland Yard. That's why they changed the meeting from there to just meeting us here. From the timing of the two calls, I'll bet that Inspector Whitcomb thought all of us meeting at New Scotland Yard would lend an official air of acceptance to us. They don't want to consider us as colleagues or co-investigators, and if it comes to that, absolutely not part of a joint investigation team. They want to consider us as potential witnesses, no special privileges, no access to anything other than this report here, and press releases. So we meet in the lounge instead."

"Don't be paranoid, geeze, Carl."

"Yeah. But it's just exactly what I'd do if I was Inspector Whitcomb." I shrugged. "Well, like we've been saying, there is not a bit of evidence for a case except a simple missing person. Which isn't even a crime. Just a problem."

"Sure. But doesn't it seem to us that . . ."

I held up my hand. "Right, and there's the crux of the matter, I think. *It seems to us.* We have a hell of a lot less evidence than they do, and I honestly don't think they have all that much." I thought for a second. "But I definitely got the impression from watching Trowbridge that he has a lead, or at least the beginnings of one."

"Really? You think they know something they aren't sharing with us?"

"Bet your ass."

"Okay. Oh, well. You think they have a hot tub in this place? Maybe a sauna?"

Wednesday, November 12, 2003
15:01 Greenwich Mean Time

Back in our room, we looked over Sergeant Trowbridge's report. It was pretty thorough, considering. He listed the basic facts, gave locations, such as they were, and did the times and dates. What made it frustrating was that all last names other than those of Jane, Vicky and Emma had been blacked out. That was not going to be a help, but it wasn't the end of the world, either. At least we had first names to go on. I strongly suspected that, if we'd given Trowbridge enough warning, he'd have taken out the last names, as well, and simply numbered the witnesses.

"Hey," said Carson, when I handed him the first page, "they blacked out all the names."

"Yeah. But only the last names. Well, you know. It's an ongoing investigation that could easily turn out to be criminal. They're just being safe . . . just read it. It's a pretty good report."

The last place Emma was seen alive was in a public house called

The Gatehouse in Highgate. According to a Constable Gullford, who was the first reporting officer, five male subjects had arrived at the pub between five fifteen and six fifteen. They all knew each other, and had jobs that varied from school teacher to civil engineer. As far as we were being permitted to know, they were named Hugh, Todd, Martin, Walter and Peter.

"Ah, we're gonna need some last names, here," I said, "regardless."

"Huh?"

At least he was reading. "I said, we're going to have to get these last names."

"You really think we need to?"

"We do if we're gonna interview 'em," I said.

"Oh. Sure. This could take a lot longer than I thought, Big Guy."

I sighed. "Me, too." But for different reasons.

According to Constable Gullford, the next witness to arrive was our Vicky Bergin, at approximately six twenty or so. She had come from doing homework in their shared apartment, with a prior arrangement to meet with Emma and Jane around six thirty, for their Friday supper. Emma and Jane arrived together, at almost exactly six thirty. Emma was coming from her last class which ended about an hour before and Jane from a routine appointment with her academic advisor, one Robert. It was really hard without last names. Anyway, Emma and Jane had traveled to Highgate from downtown London together, having hooked up at Great Portland tube station, taken the Underground to Highgate, and had walked from the Highgate tube station to the Gatehouse pub, which was about a quarter mile. They had, according to Trowbridge, seen nothing out of the ordinary.

According to the accounts provided Constable Gullford by both Jane and Vicky, the Friday night arrangement was sort of a week's end treat they gave themselves, and was usually their only night out as a group. Both remembered eating fish, and said that all three had a couple of pints of beer apiece. Neither Jane nor Vicky said they thought they had consumed an excessive amount, and believed that Emma had not, at least in their presence.

By eight pm or so, Jane and Vicky left, Vicky because she had to do some laundry, and Jane because she wanted to get a start on a paper. They left together, and both had stated that Emma had begun a conversation with one of the men at a table near them. They had all met before, and Emma had taken sort of a shine to the one called Martin. Martin who? Just Martin somebody: boy that was irritating. Anyway, he was the teacher.

I handed the next page to Carson. "Not much yet," I said.

Page three was a summary of the interviews conducted by Trowbridge with the five male subjects the day after they were first interviewed by Constable Gullford. . . . They all recollected events basically the same as Jane and Vicky did, and all remembered Emma sitting down at their table after "the other two Yank girls had left." She apparently had at least one more pint, and spent most of the time talking with Martin. What Emma apparently had not known was that subject Martin had just gotten engaged on Wednesday. He apparently hadn't come right out and told her, either.

There was great reluctance on the part of Hugh, Todd, Walter and Peter to speculate on any prior relationship between Martin and Emma, but an "in-depth" interview Trowbridge did with Martin later, (appended, I looked ahead and it was there) had revealed that he and Emma had slept together on two previous occasions.

I stopped reading, and looked out the window. Well. If nothing else, it meant that we were probably going to have to edit the already edited report before we showed anything to Emma's mother.

Back to page three, I discovered that Emma had apparently made some fairly clear suggestions to Martin, on the evening she disappeared, that they spend some more intimate time at Martin's flat later on. Martin, apparently trying to be "diplomatic" according to Trowbridge, finally revealed his change of status to Emma just as he and his friends were preparing to leave the pub.

"There was an exchange between subject Martin and subject Emma that was somewhat acrimonious," was the exact quote in Trowbridge's report. "At one point, according to the statement of subject Mary, pub employee, subject Emma referred to subject Martin as a 'sly son of a bitch,' and further as a 'weasel,' and then expanded on the point that he, subject Martin, had failed to notify her, subject Emma, that he had any sort of a relationship with any other female at all. Subject Emma further appeared to have been quite concerned about subject Martin being less than forthcoming with his fiancé."

The five male subjects left the pub, and at that time Emma was still in the establishment, and had moved back to the table she and Vicky and Jane had originally shared. The five all remembered the time as "between half eight and nine."

"Hmm," I said, to myself. I handed the page to Carson, and continued onto the fourth sheet. A motive for subject Martin? Slim, but if he thought his fiancé was going to be told by Emma. . . .

* * *

Trowbridge proved to be just at thorough as I had hoped. He'd interviewed several employees of the Gatehouse, in fact all of them who were working that evening, and had found that only one, subject Mary somebody, described by Trowbridge succinctly as "female, 23, Caucasian, a two year employee of the Gatehouse, and a bar maid in that establishment at the time in question," had any memory of any of the events. Apparently subject Mary had indicated that she thought that subject Emma might have had a bit too much to drink, that she had conducted herself in an "argumentative fashion" and had "sulked" alone at her table for about fifteen minutes after the five male subjects had departed, before gathering up her jacket, paying her tab, and leaving alone. That was approximately nine o'clock, give or take half an hour. According to subject Mary, subject Emma had not left a tip.

As far as Trowbridge was able to tell, subject Mary was the last known person to see subject Emma within the confines of the Gatehouse, and was the last known person to see her at all.

The next page was a list of the Principal Witnesses, with dates of birth, addresses, telephone numbers, and places of employment. Unfortunately, all the data except the first names had been blacked out.

The three that I did know, the young women from Nation County, were spaced on the list in alphabetical order by last name, with other witness names intervening. Just a guess, but I thought it likely that if some of the persons on the list were in alphabetical order, so were the rest.

"Well, they're in alphabetical order," I said. "For all the good that does us."

"What?" asked Carson.

I handed him the sheet. "The girls are in alphabetical order," I said, "by last name. No reason to think the others aren't as well."

He glanced at the list. "Oh, yeah." He went back to reading page three.

The last page of the report proper was a summary, which stated that: "There is no evidence available to this officer at this time to indicate that there has been any foul play in this matter. This officer, along with Sergeants Givens and Constable Gullford have interviewed all identifiable witnesses in this matter, and have canvassed the route between the Gatehouse and the residence of Subject Emma, and have been unable to locate any persons who recollect seeing her on the night in question. Members of the public throughout the Village of Highgate have been notified via press releases and posters strategically distributed."

I thought that was pretty good police work, myself. His summary continued: "The particulars of this incident have been vetted by homicide and sex crimes units, and there are no indications that known offenders were, or are, in the vicinity of the area where the subject Emma was last seen, or was known to frequent. There is no indication of the involvement of any known offenders, although with the conspicuous lack of evidence there can be no comparisons of possible *modus operandi*. It is the recommendation of this officer that this investigation be held open until such time as the missing person has been located."

The last paragraph was completely blacked out. Judging from the size of the blackened area, it was about eight lines long. Shit.

There were two appendices, the one I'd already referred to, and another that was completely blacked out except for Trowbridge's signature. Well, it was more than I'd expected. And it gave us some pretty good places to start, really. Hard to top that. I handed the summary to Carson. "It's short but sweet," I said. "As far as I can tell, they've done a perfectly good job, especially considering what they have to go on."

When he finished the Summary page, he agreed. "You really think there's anything we can do?" he asked.

"I dunno, like I said. We just start checking around ourselves. We might turn up something. The deleted parts tell us that Trowbridge's gotta have some sort of information he's keeping quiet. But I have no idea what it might be."

"So you think, maybe, we can turn up the same thing?"

"Nope. Not a chance. He's got resources and we really don't. Not if he's lookin' at something he got from a snitch, anyway. He's got those. He's got records. He's got access to prior cases, too. Not to mention about a billion cops."

"Can't we develop one? A resource? Like a snitch?"

"Carson," I said, "imagine this . . . somebody from London comes to Maitland, looking for some information that might be crime related. Who you think they're gonna get for an informant, anyway?"

"Beats me," he said, cheerfully. "That's your territory."

"You bettcha. And I'll go on record right now that the best he's gonna be able to do is somebody like . . . Georgia Benson, for example." Georgia was a perfectly nice person, a waitress, and about the biggest gossip in Maitland. She was renowned for being wrong about ninety-nine per cent of the time.

"Ewww . . . you think so?"

"You see the problem. We find ourselves with a snitch over here, and I'll bet it's about that quality. Especially since we don't have anything budgeted to pay for information with." I was keeping Allen the Banker's offer to myself.

"So, what do you think? We sightsee for a couple of days and go home?"

"Oh, no," I said. "We're just getting started, here. We go talk to people. There's always a chance. Always. You never give up. And regardless, we'll sure be able to give Trowbridge a different perspective."

I looked at my watch. "Just about time for the girls to show up," I said.

"Do we let them read the report?"

I thought about that one for a second. "Sure. Why not? They ought to be able to give us . . ."

"Insights?" asked Carson, with a big smile.

"Good a word as any," I said.

"I wonder if we should take them to dinner, or anything?"

"That's a damned fine idea," I said. "Let's go to this pub . . . the Gatekeeper. We might as well talk business."

"Isn't that the Gatehouse?"

"Didn't I say that?"

"No, you said Gatekeeper."

We were beginning to sound married.

Chapter 9

Wednesday, November 12, 2003
16:14 Greenwich Mean Time

Jane and Vicky called from the lobby at about 16:00 on the button. I was ready to go on down when the phone rang, but Carson had to spruce up. Or, as he put it, "I always like to make a good impression on the ladies."

A good ten minutes later, with Carson all combed and cologned, we met "the ladies" in the lobby. I gave Jane a big hug. I was really glad to see her.

"Hey, dad," she said, "boy are we glad to see you . . . Is this Carson Hilgenberg? My God, *it is*!"

She shook his hand, and both girls smiled at him. "You were what?" asked Vicky, "Five or six years behind us in school?"

"Six, I think . . ."

"Well, look at you," said Jane. "An attorney now and everything."

"Yeah," said Carson, "who'd a guessed."

"I was your baby sitter a couple of times," said Vicky. "Wow."

"Me, too," said Jane. "When I was in eighth grade . . . you would have been about 4th or 3rd grade then, wouldn't you?"

"I guess," said Carson.

"Do you still like Spagetti O's?" asked Vicky.

"Not for a long time."

"They still call you Lowly?" asked Jane.

"No."

"Lowly?" I asked. "Why'd they call you Lowly?"

"Remember those children's books by Richard Scary?" asked Jane. "The ones you used to read to me?"

"Yeah?"

"Remember the character called Lowly Worm?"

I laughed. "No kidding?" I figured Carson was about as uncomfortable as humanly possible, so I said, "We were thinking, why don't we take you out to supper? Maybe up at the pub at Highgate?"

"The Gatehouse?" asked Jane.

"Sure. We have to go there soon anyway . . ."

She glanced at Vicky. "That okay with you . . . or would you prefer The Angel?"

"Oh, the Gatehouse is fine. That's all right."

I must have looked puzzled, because Jane said, "We haven't been back since Emma disappeared."

"Oh, then hell, we can just as easily go to the Angel."

"No, no," said Vicky. "It's okay. Fine. Really."

"You sure?" asked Jane.

"Yes, absolutely."

"Okay, then," I said. "How do we get there? Cab?"

It was explained to me that the Underground was the only way to go in London. It was less expensive, and almost as fast as a cab.

"We just need to get you and Carson your tube passes," said Jane, "and then it's just a few minutes from here. The nearest station is Kensington on High Street. Come on."

It might have been the nearest, but it was a good ten minute walk. I wasn't used to that.

As we headed in what I thought might be a westerly direction, I pointed to the big rectangular brick building in the park. "What's that? We can see it from our room."

"That's Kensington Palace," said Jane. "You know, where Princess Diana lived before she died."

"Oh, sure . . ." It looked nice, but it wasn't exactly my idea of a palace. I guess I'd seen too many Disney movies.

Traffic was interesting, to say the least. The first thing I had to do was learn to look in the right direction as we crossed the street. In the US, cars on your side of the street approach from the left. In London, they sneak up on you from the right. I suspected the streets in popular tourist areas were paved with dead Americans.

We passed a cluster of small shops, and then found ourselves in an area of clothing and department stores. "Your mother would love this," I said. "Don't tell her unless we have to!"

We had to cross the street at Church Street, to get to the American

Express office and get a bunch of traveler's checks changed into pounds. At approximately a dollar seventy to the pound, I made a mental note to be very careful in spending.

We crossed the street again, and on the south side of the street, identified by a large red circle bisected by a blue bar, was the tube station. The printing on this one said, in white letters, "Kensington High Street."

I was expecting a train station, or a bus station, or something dedicated like that. But as we turned at the sign and entered a large open area, we were in something of a small shopping mall instead. More clothing stores and food outlets. Interesting.

"See that place," said Jane, pointing to a small open shop to our left.

"That's Benjy's. Good cheap eating if you're on the move. Wrapped sandwiches, salads and candy bars. They're all over town, really."

"Okay." I glanced in as we passed. Bottled water, too. Excellent.

We made it past Benjy's and found ourselves in the station proper.

Getting our passes wasn't all that simple. I approached the window, with Jane hovering close by.

"I'd like to purchase a pass," I said. That's when it got complex.

First, we were advised to get them for a week at a time, because it was not only cheaper, it was much faster than buying one every day. I was good with that. Then we had to designate the furthest zone from the center of London we'd be traveling to. That beat the hell out of me, so Jane chimed in with "Zone Five!" So that's what I did. Then, the ticket clerk asked me a question I didn't get at first.

"Photo?"

"Pardon?"

"Photo," he said. "I need a photo for identification."

I thought he wanted a photo ID from me, so I showed him my driver's license.

He shook his head. "No, I need it for your ticket."

Well, that's exactly why I thought I was showing it to him. "I don't understand . . ."

This was the first time I got what was to be a familiar look of, "be patient, he's an American."

"No, sir, I need you to give me a photo. For me to put in your pass. If you don't have one with you, you can use the booth over there," and he gestured behind me.

I turned, and saw a standard photo booth near the entrance. Ah.

While Carson approached the ticket booth, I went to the photo kiosk and spent a couple of pounds on a strip of photos. When I got out, Carson was standing there waiting.

"I haven't used one of these since college," he said. "I suppose I gotta leave my clothes on this time . . ."

After that, it was a longer wait in the ticket line as more people had arrived. The ticket clerk smiled, cut off one of the photos from the strip, and viola! I had my first tube pass.

"You must carry this with you at all times," he said, "and be prepared to present it upon request." There were so many people behind me by now, that I just didn't take the time to ask why.

Then it was just a matter of slipping the ticket into the slot, and walking through the turnstile.

Jane came through immediately behind me, and we waited for Carson and Vicky.

"Here's a tube map," said Jane. "Don't lose it. It's bigger than the one that you've got there, and you should be able to read it without your glasses."

"Okay. . . ."

"Now, just watch what I do, and mind the gap."

"The what?"

She laughed. "There's a gap sometimes between the tube car and the station platform. Don't step in it. You could break your leg."

"Ah."

I've always liked trains, and the London Underground was a real treat. It was kind of crowded, but that was part of the fun.

"There's one of the big tube maps on the wall over there. . . . Let me show you how to get around. It's really easy."

"Okay." I thought it was going to be.

"We want the tube to Highgate, Dad," said Jane. "That's the Northern line. The black one. Right now, we're on the Circle line . . . that's yellow."

"Yeah, right," I said, grinning.

"Look at the map," she said. "We're here. We want the Circle line to South Kensington. We get off there and transfer to the Piccadilly line to Leicester Square. That's the dark blue one here . . . We get off there, and get on the Northern line going to High Barnett. We get off before High Barnett at Highgate."

"Sure. Like I'm following that. . . ."

"You'll get used to it," she said. "It really is easy. . . ."

I scrutinized my little map. It had occurred to me that we were gong to have to get back to our tube station at High Street, Kensington by ourselves.

Carson was being given the same briefing by Vicky. I hoped he was paying attention, but thought he was more interested in standing close to her. In contrast to Jane, who took after her mother, Sue, and was about five two; Vicky was five feet ten, and about 130 lbs., with big brown eyes and dark brown hair. From what Carson had been saying to me about tall women, she was pretty much his type. Well, not his type, maybe, but the type he was drawn to. I'd never been happier that Jane was five feet two.

The trip to Highgate was pretty much a blur, although I was paying as close attention as I could to the process. I did have time to be impressed by just how far underground the Underground really was in places, though. And how old the bricked tube walls were. I tired to imagine laying those by hand and gave up.

We got off at Highgate after about a twenty minute ride, as promised. We emerged from the station into a glazed area that was surrounded by trees. We followed the exit, and found ourselves on a street corner in what for the world looked like a small village.

"This is part of London?" I asked.

"You bet," said Jane. "We're pretty far from the center, though."

"Must be," I said.

"Close enough to get a few bombs during the Blitz, they tell me."

There was a red building adjacent to us. "This our pub?"

"Oh, no," said Jane. "Ours is that way," and she pointed up a long hill toward some buildings.

"Hey," said Vicky, "it's getting late . . . why don't we go to the Gatehouse first, before they get crowded, and then to our place."

"The Gatehouse," said Jane, "is only about two blocks from our place, on the other side of the hill."

"I'm all for eating first," said Carson.

So we did.

It was about a half mile to the Gatehouse, mostly up hill. The sidewalks were narrow, the streets the same, and it almost felt like home.

"This is a pretty time of year," said Jane.

"Sure is," I said. "Not to mix business with pleasure, but is this the route you always take? The three of you?"

"Usually, yes."

"The night Emma disappeared, for instance. Would this have been the way you two walked to the pub?"

"Yes."

There was very little traffic, either vehicular or foot. "It always this quiet?"

"Mostly."

I was beginning to feel the climb, as we were walking pretty briskly and I was talking. "Doing this every day would keep you in shape. On the night Emma disappeared, did you notice anything out of the ordinary?"

"No. Not a thing. We just walked up this way, and we were talking, and I was carrying my jacket because it was pretty nice out, and Emma didn't even have one. We didn't stop, and nobody was behind us."

That last statement would have sounded unusual if I hadn't been checking our rear frequently to make sure some faster walker didn't need to get by us.

"Nobody just standing around?"

"Nobody I noticed," said Jane.

"Hey, Vicky?" I said. She and Carson, who were ahead of us, stopped. "On the night Emma went missing, what route did you take to get to the pub?"

"From our flat," she said. "It's on the border of the little park. Pond Square. Just down from the Gatehouse. Kind of from the opposite direction we're taking now. The other side of the village."

"Did you notice anybody or anything unusual? That night."

"No. The detective called Trowbridge asked the same question. It was fresher then, but I still couldn't think of anything unusual at all."

I tapped my pocket. "I've got his report here. We'll go over it when we get to the pub. . . ."

The Gatehouse turned out to be a three story building, white mostly, which had those neat exterior frames in the Tudor style. I don't know exactly what I was expecting, except maybe a dark, probably smoky, kind of bar with a dart board. It was far from that. The interior was very bright, with blond wood, and several older couples and foursomes sitting around at nice tables, some drinking, but most having supper. There were also some younger people in the place, more to the rear.

The whole pub was kind of muted, but there were conversations going on all over the place. A nice, peaceful place to relax at the end of the day.

We got a table near a window that looked out on the street, toward a corner where there was a flower stand. It seemed to be doing a brisk business, and the woman vendor appeared to know everyone who passed. I made a note of that.

The waitress came, welcomed Jane and Vicky back, identified herself to us as Mary, gave us menus and asked us what we wanted to drink. We ordered a beer, and scanned the menu.

"Dad," said Jane, "I know it's bad for you, but you might want to check out the bangers and mash."

"What?"

"Just like it says. It's the sort of thing you'd make for yourself, if we'd let you get away with it. Sausage, mashed potatoes, peas, and all cooked up in a thin pie crust with lots of gravy."

Sold.

While we waited, I produced Trowbridge's report. "You want to look that over, and see if there's anything you can tell me that isn't in there?"

Jane and Vicky read it together. "All the last names are inked out," said Vicky. "That's pretty shitty."

"Well, they don't want us interfering," I said.

It turned out that the girls were going to be a big help in that department. Between them, they provided the last names for Hugh, Todd, Martin, Walter and Peter.

"That'd be Hugh Watson, and Peter's last name is Sloane," said Jane.

"And Todd and Martin are both named Granger, but I think they're cousins and not brothers," said Vicky. "Martin's last name is Farmer."

That was quick.

"How about the others?" I asked.

"Well," said Jane, "Our advisor's Robert Northwood. I can get you his office number, and his teaching schedule. And although I don't know her last name, 'subject Mary' is our waitress tonight."

"Okay," I said, making the appropriate note in the report. "Robert Northwood. . . ."

"That should be Professor Robert Northwood," said Vicky. "It's his course we're all three taking. In fact, it's the only one the three of us are in together. Jane is one of the lucky ones. She got the professor himself for an advisor. My advisor is George Bennett, and he's just a post-doc and a little dorky to boot."

"I really was lucky," said Jane. She told us how she'd gotten Prof. Northwood because Dr. Lymington, her original advisor, had been injured in a boating accident shortly after the semester began, and that Professor Northwood had taken on some of the advising tasks to help out. "He's just fantastic," she said.

"Pretty good looking, too," said Vicky, wryly.

Jane actually colored a little at that. "I love him for his brain," she said.

"Hey, nothing wrong with getting some if it helps your grades," said Carson.

He flinched a bit, and I was pretty sure somebody had kicked him under the table. It wasn't me, and I think if it had been Jane he would have left in an ambulance. Good for Vicky.

When our waitress Mary returned, I made sure she had all our orders before I said, "Excuse me. I'm Jane's here father. Do you mind if we talk with you for a minute when you're free?"

"I'm pretty busy right now," she said. "But my shift ends in about an hour." She smiled. "And, yes, I think I can spare you a few minutes."

"That's fine. No pressure, but I'm interested in Emma Schiller, you know, the girl who's missing. I'm going to be talking with her mother when I get back to the States, and I'd like to be able to tell her as much as I can."

"Oh, right, certainly, oh her poor mum, what a worry and all." She seemed genuinely concerned.

When she left, Jane said, with a pretty heavy note of sarcasm in her voice, "That was pretty slick, not letting on you were a cop."

"I'm not, strictly speaking. I don't think I could get any further out of my jurisdiction if I went to Mars. I'm just a tourist who happens to be a cop in another country." I grinned. "Does it really bother you?"

"No. Not really. But I want to be there when you tell you what you do for a living."

The manager came over when we were about half finished with our meal, and sat down. He thrust out his hand. "Ned Bunting. I'm running the establishment while the owner's on vacation. Mary tells me you're interested in the missing girl?"

"I sure am," I said.

"All the way from America . . . and friend of the family, then?"

I gestured toward Jane. "I'm her father, in fact."

"I don't know we can be of much help," he said.

"I'd appreciate it if you'd try," I said. "Maybe I can help focus things a bit. I'm a cop back in the US, so I'm familiar with how to try to sort this type of thing out."

"So she's dead, then?" he half asked, half stated. "Is that why you've come?"

I thought he assumed that pretty fast. Well, what the hell, most of us probably thought she was dead by now. "I hope not," I said, and gave him my very best and truthful explanation as to why Carson and I had come over to London. It took a minute.

"Politics?"

"Pretty much what actually got us here," I said. "But the root of the matter is that the whole town of Maitland is pretty worried about her. Especially her mother and the rest of her family."

"How big is this Maitland," he asked. "I can't say I've ever heard of it."

"About fifteen hundred," I said.

"A hamlet then?"

"Pretty close," said Carson. "More like a big room."

"Are you a police officer, too?" he asked Carson.

"No, I'm an att . . . ah, barrister," he said. "He's the Sheriff."

"And you're a Sheriff? With fast draws, and cowboys and all that?" He was kidding, of course.

"Some days, the cowboys seem like they're winning," I said. "But I've never been on a horse in my whole life, and the holsters we wear have safety things . . . you couldn't fast draw if you wanted to."

"You do wear guns, then?"

"Oh, yeah. We're even required to wear 'em off duty. And just for the record," I said, probably from habit because Lamar is known to have spies *everywhere*, "I'm a Deputy Sheriff. The Sheriff is elected. We're hired."

"I see. One of those 'don't call me sir, I'm a sergeant, not an officer. I work for a living,' bits from the army."

"Exactly." He was giving my hip a very curious look, and it took me a second. "Oh! No, I don't have one on now. Didn't even bring one. That'd be illegal over here."

"Just curious, there, mate," he said. "If things slow down a bit, I'll see if I can let Mary have a sit at your table for a few minutes."

Before Mary got to our table, Jane said, "So you let him tell her . . ."

"Sure. Just happened that way, though." I smiled. "Pure luck. But it's better because she trusts him and he's talked to us. Just let me do most of the talking, okay? At this first interview, anyway."

"Right," said Jane, giving me a look that would have done her mother justice.

Mary came over and sat down, but kept looking toward the door and around the pub, keeping tabs on the customers, apparently only too anxious to jump up and go back to work.

We talked for about five minutes. She hadn't noticed anyone leave with Emma, she was absolutely certain of that. She told me the same thing she'd told Trowbridge, including the remarks made by Emma concerning Martin's character.

"You didn't notice anyone leave within a couple of minutes after Emma went out, did you?"

Mary thought for a second. "No, I don't think so . . ."

"Or make a phone call, maybe?" I asked.

"No . . . but one could take a mobile into the loo," she said. "Then I'd not notice at all."

"Sure." I looked back at Trowbridge's report, and asked the time honored question cops always use to wind up an interview. "Can you think of anything I haven't asked? Anything at all?"

She couldn't. Well, she said she couldn't. I didn't know her anywhere well enough to say if she was telling the truth or not. I just took a shot.

"Have you overheard anything? You know, things people say about others behind their back. I'd think you might be in a position to overhear things." All I was doing was giving her a chance to vent her own opinion without having it attributed to her.

"Well," she said. "I might have. Yes. I can't remember who, but just the other night somebody was saying that he thought she was a little too involved with the native population."

"Really?" I shot Jane a glance, because her face was starting to flush and I was afraid she was going to say something to defend Emma. "You mean like Martin?"

"That could have been," she said. "You know about Martin, then?"

"Just that they were seeing each other, sort of." It's always a good idea to hide a detail or two.

"Oh, right, were they," she said. "I don't mean to speak ill of . . ." The pause was significant. ". . . of the absent," she finished, lamely. Just somebody else who thought Emma was dead. "But she did tend to be . . . I must say, she was quite a bit of the busy one, you know." The last came out with a rush.

"Anybody other than Martin?" I gave Jane another glance. She was angry, but I could tell she wasn't about to break the line of questioning.

"Oh . . . well, I've *heard*, mind you, that she was interested in others. Even at her school," she said.

"Really?" That did surprise me a little.

"Oh, yes. She was here with a professor somebody, oh, weeks ago, it was. And it didn't look as if they were discussing courses." She glanced around, and nodded at me. "Mind you, he did ask me. I don't go spreading gossip."

"I'm sure you don't. Did you get his name?"

"No."

I was afraid she was going to clam up after her disclaimer. "What did he look like? I really do need to know, so I can talk to him, too. Maybe he saw somebody hanging about before, somebody he isn't connecting with this disappearance."

"It's hard to remember."

Now, I don't know the British at all. So I didn't know if she was hinting at a little cash transaction, or if she was just being reluctant. I gave her the benefit of the doubt. "I'd really appreciate it if you could think back . . ." Nobody would forget what he looked like if she'd brought it up in the first place. I figured people all over were at least similar in that respect.

She came through. "Oh, tall, dark. Maybe forty, or a bit. A slender man. Tanned, which makes me think he was posh. Well dressed . . . not a proper suit of clothes, but expensive slacks and a polo shirt. Lovely white teeth."

And it didn't cost me a cent. Or a pence.

I looked directly at Jane and Vicky. "You two thinking of anybody?"

"No." The way Jane said that, I was real sure she just didn't want to say so in front of Mary.

"Well, Mary," I said, "thank you. You've been very helpful, and I'm sure you're anxious to get back to work."

"You're quite welcome," she said, primly. "And one other thing." She stood, and straightened her apron. "He came in one of those silver grey cars . . . Aston Martin, perhaps. Very becoming."

"No shit?" Carson decided to contribute. "A Vanquish?"

"Quite similar," said Mary.

"Holy shit! Carl, those things cost about a quarter of a million!"

"Oh, no," said Mary. "More like 130,000." Obviously a girl after Carson's heart.

Carson thought for a second. "You're talking pounds sterling. I'm talking dollars."

"Oh," she said. "Then you'd be quite close, wouldn't you?"

A teacher? A professor? I looked at the girls. Jane had an eyebrow way, way up. That was a sure sign of something being out of sorts. Then I looked a bit harder at Mary, and caught a hint. I gave her my broadest, friendliest smile.

"Or, maybe not an Aston Martin, right? Maybe a Honda?"

Mary smiled back. "Quite likely. I don't know that much about cars, at all."

"You knew the price range of an Aston Martin," said Carson.

"I browse the net," she said. "And I do know about the exchange rate."

I laughed. "Excellent. Very nice, indeed. But it was silver grey, right?"

"Yes."

"Anything else you'd like to share?" I was having fun, and I guess it showed.

"A word to the wise, of sorts," she said. "The press are much more concerned with her sex life than they are with her having gone missing. They say some very rude things. I don't know about the US papers, but ours here can sometimes be very rude indeed."

"Thanks. I appreciate it." She and I shook hands. "If you think of anything else. . . ." I always ask that. So does every other cop I know. It's almost as routine as talking about the weather.

"I'll let you know," she said.

Just like talking about the weather.

Chapter 10

Washington, DC
Excerpt from the Intelligence Briefing entitled: "Task, Collect,
Process and Use"
April 19, 2002

*T*he problem with the lag time between the terrorists deciding to do
something and actually getting it done can cause much confusion
among western agencies. If, for example, a terrorist response is being
anticipated to a particular event, there may be a bombing in an unanticipated location that seems to be that reaction. In fact, it is very
likely that the bombing could be a response to some completely different event that occurred years ago. We call this a disconnect between adversaries, and it's caused by those adversaries operating in
two completely different worlds. We're computer aided and any ex-
changes of data or voice communications that are not real time are
considered obsolete. We sometimes, if you will, think too fast for our
own good.*

Wednesday, November 12, 2003
20:03 Greenwich Mean Time

Carson and I accompanied Jane and Vicky to their flat, and stayed for
a cup of coffee. For a house-sitting job, it was a pretty nice place. Each
of the girls had their own room, and the kitchen was very nice.

"I got the impression back at the pub," I said, "that you two knew who Mary was referring to when she talked about the cool dude with the car."

"Okay," said Jane. "Look, I didn't get it from Emma firsthand, but Vicky did."

"It was probably Professor Latham. Edward." She looked a little embarrassed. "It wasn't like she was getting bad grades or anything. Really. She just thought he was pretty hot. She saw him a few times. I don't know how far things got."

"Best guess?" I asked.

"Oh, hell, she probably slept with him," she said. "She would. I mean, it's the way she thinks. Short relationships . . ."

"I can live with that," I said. "No problem."

"Wouldn't that be really sorta dumb, though?" asked Carson. "I mean, like she'd have to *break up* with her professor *before* the course was over. Shit, I think that'd have to have a really bad effect on the old GPA."

"To be honest about it," said Jane, "I don't think Professor Latham was exactly looking for a lifelong partner, either."

I cleared my throat. "But he does drive a silver or silver grey car, right? Super expensive or not?"

"Yeah, Dad, and it's a Honda."

"More in keeping with his means?"

"Yeah, I think so. I don't know what he makes, but it should be fairly good money. . . ." She looked at Vicky. "You have any idea how much professors make over here?"

"No. Enough, though."

I asked to see Emma's room, and Jane took me to it. I looked around in it without touching anything. I mean, we didn't know for certain she was dead, and I didn't feel I had the right to snoop. What I was looking for, mainly, was stuff like photos, mementos, things like that. Something, or anything, that might give me a direction. The only photograph was on her desk. It showed her, her mother, Janine, her late father, Harrison, and her baby sister Monica in better times. I hardly knew Monica, who'd been sort of an afterthought, and was about sixteen now. I didn't think that there would be much confiding done between sisters who were fifteen or sixteen years apart, and Jane had confirmed that.

Jane told me that Emma might have had a diary, but she'd never seen it.

"I know she had one in high school, and college."

I really wanted to know if she *had* kept a diary. It was tempting to look for it, but I was stopped by the fact, once again, that Emma was not known to be dead or injured, or in any way threatened. She could conceivably walk in at any time.

Well, I thought that for a few minutes. Then Vicky yelled from the living room.

"Get in here, everybody! Quick, ohmygod!"

We got there in time to see Emma's face on the tube. She was between two masked figures, apparently both male. She was bound at the wrists, her hair was pretty well messed up, and she had a swelling on her lip. Otherwise, as they say, she looked fine. Her head moved from side to side, as if she was addressing the two standing alongside her. Then she looked straight at the camera. She was moving her lips, but there was no audio.

The voice-over from Sky News said, "There is no audio to go with this tape, but the printed note we received stated that the missing American girl Emma Schiller was in good health, and that there would be more tapes to come, outlining demands."

The camera that had been focused fairly close on Emma backed off a little, and I could see part of a banner in the background. There was something written there, and it looked like some sort of Arabic script.

We all just stood there, as they re-ran the tape. Jane said, "Oh shit," once or twice, but that was it. We just watched.

The beginning of the tape had a newspaper spread out in front of the camera. It was the *London Times*, but the quality was so bad I couldn't make out the date.

"The headline," said the commentator, "is from the *Times* front page for twenty-ninth October, so it is a strong indication that the now understood to be kidnapped woman was alive and in this condition on that date."

Okay. So?

"That would be the day after she went missing, so the theory that some have had regarding her being off on a lark is fairly refuted. We will continue to await further developments, and have been told that there would be a comment from New Scotland Yard soon. While we wait, let us chat with. . . ."

Pundit time. Fill didn't interest me at that moment.

"Okay," I said. "This is good. We know what's happened to her now."

"Shh! Dad . . . ," said Jane.

I used the three minutes of blather from the tube to collect my thoughts, and to get ready to answer their questions as soon as they went to commercial.

All too soon, there was a shot of some young girl walking briskly down a street, with "Unsquare Dance" by the Dave Brubeck Quartet playing in the background. Vicky hit the mute.

"She looks so scared . . ." "Did you see her lips?" "She looked okay to me . . ." were all spoken pretty much simultaneously.

"She's alive," I said. "That's the good news."

"But, Dad, Jesus, look who's got her, why did they pick her. . . . ?"

"Well, we don't know for sure just who they are. . . ." You gotta try.

"Their terrorists, Dad! What else could they be?"

"Yeah. But it gives us all a chance to find her," I said, quickly. "Scotland Yard is very good at this sort of thing. So long as she's alive, there's a chance." Assuming that she was. That tape was pretty old.

"But, Dad, damn it all, they never get these hostages back!" Jane was very near tears.

"Sometimes they do . . . There haven't even been demands yet, as far as we know. . . ."

For what may have been the first time in my life, the commercials were over too soon, and we were back live. Not for news of Emma, but for news that might be about her. President Bush was due in the UK in a few days, and there was immediate speculation that Emma might be being held hostage in order to coerce him to do something while in the UK.

"Do you have any speculation on that, Robert," asked the commentator.

Whoever "Robert" was, I thought he was a little obnoxious. "One could hope for a demand to withdraw from Iraq altogether," he said. "Not that the current American administration would pay the slightest bit of attention. But it would explain the acquisition of an American woman."

"Acquisition?" It just came out. I couldn't help it. "Christ, it sounds like they just filled out a request for a volunteer."

"Dad. . . ."

On the TV, a woman named "Edith," chimed in. "Robert, I've been watching the tapes in the booth, and the technicians say they think it's a copy of a copy . . . What do you make of that?"

"It's so difficult to say, Edith. But I've taken advantage of the opportunity of the break to think about this. She's a student. The tape is of poor quality, certainly not professional. Perhaps, the photographer, too, is a student? Could we be dealing with some staged effort, here? Perhaps a cooperative effort to convince President George Bush of the error of his ways? I suppose we could only hope," and he smiled.

Even in the worst days of US television, I'd never seen something politicized quite so fast. I was certain we'd get nothing but blather for quite a while, now.

"Mute it," I said. "We need facts, and they don't have any."

Vicky did, but she was reluctant.

"We know it isn't a fucking prank," I said. "Pardon my language."

"No problem," said Vicky.

"We gotta call home," I said. "It's probably already on CNN, or it will be shortly. What time is it in Iowa?"

"About 2:30 PM," said Jane. "We need to call Janine. I don't want her to hear about her daughter from the media. . . ."

"Use your cell phone," I said. "In case Scotland Yard wants to call us about anything."

She did. She and Vicky called Janine Schiller's number four times, getting a busy signal each time.

The land line phone rang. Vicky answered, and started to break down immediately. It was her mother. They only talked for a few seconds, and then Vicky was able to get out that she'd call on her cell phone, to free up the line.

She'd just hung up when it rang again. It was Sue, calling to talk with Jane. Jane started to cry, too, but got her composure back very quickly. "Let me call on my cell, Mom, we have to keep this line open."

I sure hoped like hell that New Scotland Yard would call.

Carson, in the meantime, handed me his cell phone. "You want to call your office?"

I used our unlisted number. I got Sally, who sounded extremely stressed.

"Holy shit, you can't believe it," she said. "We've got both dispatchers and both secretaries on the phone, and the other lines are still ringing. The media is going nuts."

"I need to talk with Lamar."

"Okay, you must have seen the tapes, then?"

"Yeah. You get tape with sound over there?" ·

"No . . . Lamar . . . Lamar, it's Carl . . . Line twelve . . . Stay on the line after you're done," said Sally, before Lamar picked up. "I got some stuff . . ."

"Carl?"

"Yeah, boss. Zoo over there?"

"NO! What the hell ya think?"

"We don't have anything you don't, I guess," I said. "We did some interviews today, but we didn't know about this tape thing until a few minutes ago."

"You guys call Janine yet?"

"We can't get through," I said.

"I'll get somebody up there, tell her to either stop talking to the media, or to put her phone back on the hook, and then call you. Where you at?"

"The girl's apartment. She's got the number."

"Whatta ya think? Terrorists? She still alive?"

"Not now," I said.

"Can't talk now?"

"Yes, that's right. Very likely." I didn't want to add anything negative to the conversations going on all around me.

"Yeah. Chances of getting her back alive ain't so good."

"You got that right," I said, with feeling.

"Okay, do what you can. Scotland Yard cooperating?"

"Doin' just what I'd do in their place," I said, truthfully.

He paused, digesting that. "Well, don't let that stop ya," he said.

"No, I won't."

"What? Okay, hey, Sally's got something for you. Be good."

Sally was back on the line. "We got a call from the F.B.I. about thirty seconds before you called," she said. "They wanted some info, and said that you were the one to talk to, and then I told 'em that you were in London. They were real fuckin' surprised," she said, with some joy. "I gave 'em your address, and they want to have one of their people over there contact you."

"Okay. Which address did you give 'em?"

"Your hotel."

"Cool."

"What's going on, can you say?"

"Sally, if I knew *anything*, I'd be only too happy to tell you."

It wasn't five minutes after I talked with Lamar that we received a phone call from Janine Schiller. Jane answered the call. She and Vicky kept passing the phone from one to the other, as they would begin to lose it and manage to pass it to the other before starting to cry.

Then it was my turn to talk.

Janine seemed pretty composed, all things considered. We just discussed what the two of us knew, mostly from watching TV. I'd known Janine and her late husband, and we'd always been on good terms.

"Carl, I'm just so glad you're over there right now. It means so much to us." I could imagine the scene at her house, with sisters, brothers and cousins coming in.

"I'll do what I can, Janine," I said. "We've had a good meeting with Scotland Yard earlier, and they're working hard on this one."

"Help them, though," she said. "Promise you won't let them drop the ball."

"They won't do that, Janine, I'm sure." I couldn't imagine the British doing anything other than work this case with all they had available.

"Just promise us that you'll be there, too," she said.

"Sure. You bet," I answered. What can you say at a time like that? It sure wasn't the proper moment to go into jurisdictional things, or to tell her that I'd just be a spectator in the whole thing.

"And the County Attorney? I understand he's there, too?"

"Carson Hilgenberg," I said. "Yes, he is."

"That must be a great help," she said.

"It is."

"Would I be able to speak with him?"

"You bet, Janine, he's right here," I said, handing the phone to Carson. "It's Mrs. Schiller."

Carson took the phone, greeted Janine, and then started nodding. "Yes, ma'am, Mrs. Schiller," he said. "Yes, yes, we will."

It took me a second to remember that Janine would have been one of his high school teachers.

"You know it, Mrs. Schiller," he said. "We won't let you down." He looked at me in a desperate sort of way. "I think Carl has some more to say, Mrs. Schiller." With that, he handed me the phone.

"Janine," I said, winging it. "Look, we'll keep you posted. We can send regular emails, and get any reports that are available right to you."

"Carl, could you talk to Martha for a minute?"

Martha Dressler was Janine's sister. "Uh, sure. You bet." It's not easy when you know these people.

"Carl? Carl, this is Martha. How are things going over there?"

I told her pretty much what I'd told Janine.

"Carl, some of us were thinking we could really help if we came over, too. What do you think?"

Oh, boy. Even a small percentage of that clan would be five or six people. My first reaction was to scream and drop the phone, to tell you the truth. My training prevailed.

"Well, Martha, I don't know. We're the only ones the cops will talk to in any depth, and that's because they could demand we be fired if there are any leaks. They'd probably just turn you over to their PR people, and . . . ." The little wheels were turning, though. Having a couple of family members sitting on the doorstep of New Scotland Yard could have its advantages. The local press would have photo ops constantly. That would keep the case in the public eye. That could increase the chances of a tip, or of an informant coming forward.

"Yes?"

". . . well, ya know . . ." and I told her what I was thinking. "It'd have to be somebody pretty self possessed, and kinda tough," I said. "And they'd have to have very little contact with us, because we don't want the coverage on us. I don't know, Martha. What do *you* think?"

She didn't even hesitate. "Three of us, I think," she said. "We can be there in a couple of days."

"Okay."

"It'll be me, Harriet and Wendy." Harriet was another sister, and Wendy was a sister-in-law. "Wendy because she's the only woman I know who cries pretty." Martha had a mind like a steel trap, and when she was pissed, she was formidable.

"Sounds good to me," I said.

She complimented me on my quick thinking, and then kind of took it back when she said, "I don't remember you being this fast on your mental feet in high school, Carl." She'd been a year behind me.

"I seethed within," I said.

"It must have been pretty deep," she replied. "But we'll see you in a couple of days."

"Okay."

"Do you think this will have a good outcome, Carl? The hostage business?"

"I don't know," I said. "We can just hope and do what we can."

"Sure," she said. "I think you're right."

When all the phone calls were done, a sad silence settled down on the flat. Nobody really wanted to say anything, and we'd probably all said just about everything we had to say, anyway.

It was, well, not exactly awkward. Just uncomfortable. Finally, Jane asked if we wanted any coffee or tea. We did.

While Jane was in the kitchen, the phone rang again. It was Sergeant Trowbridge. I took the call.

"You've seen the tape, then?" he asked.

"Just what they showed on TV," I said.

"Ah. Well there was a bit more. Not lots, and just more of the same."

"Okay."

"We think the absence of audio is due to their not being able to get her to cooperate . . . verbally, you know. We believe they tried to have her read a prepared script, and she wasn't cooperating."

"Sure." I wondered how they knew that. "How can you tell?"

"We have a lip reader viewing the tapes now. That's his opinion at this point, at least."

"Oh, sure."

"They weren't either bright enough, or at all well informed about these things. We'd have thought they'd dope her first. Just enough to make her pliable. This is very likely a first effort on their part."

"That sounds reasonable. It looked clumsy as hell."

"Yes." Then his voice became even more serious. "That can be rather, well, hazardous, you know. For her."

"Agreed."

"Are you able to talk quite freely?"

"Not quite."

"Ah, then. Well, there was a note, as well. They call themselves the London Reform Movement for the Freedom of Khaled al Fawwaz and Ibrahim Eidarous and Lions of the Front for Jihad in Britain."

I'm used to speaking while I adjust. "Okay. . . . Long title . . . never heard of that one." You hear about having your worst fears confirmed, but it happens so seldom.

"Strangely, neither have we," he said, with just a touch of sarcasm. "We're still checking with other sources, but we can't make any connections with anyone at this point. It might be useful to keep in mind that it could be a hoax of sorts, or a dodge to keep us looking the wrong way."

"Are they saying what they want?"

"No," said Trowbridge. "They just tell us they'll be in further contact. No specific date. I thought we might drop round tomorrow, and discuss things."

"Here or at the hotel?"

"There would be fine, I'd think."

"Any idea what time?" I was trying to prolong the conversation, trying to adjust to the jihad business.

"We'll call ahead," he said. "I've got to go, now. Tomorrow, then?"

"Sure."

"We'd appreciate it if you didn't mention the name of the group to anyone, just yet. We'll want to release that at the appropriate time."

"Fine." Great. I'm really good at keeping secrets, but it doesn't mean it's easy.

"What did they say?" asked Jane, as soon as I put the phone down.

"Not much more than we already knew," I said. "There's just a little more tape, it's longer than the bite they show on TV. But nothing significant."

"Ransom?" asked Carson.

"No, at least not yet. They got a note with the tape, apparently. The kidnappers say they'll be in touch again."

"Oh, God," said Jane. "Oh, Emma . . . how long do you think this will go on?"

I shrugged. "There's no way to tell."

That little piece of encouragement seemed to be sufficient for the moment, so I didn't add that there was also no guarantee that it would turn out well. I think we were all adequately aware of that, anyway.

Carson and I hung around quite a while, but the girls didn't think it necessary for us to sleep over. They had to be up early for class, and they were now beginning to put a positive spin on the evening's events. Emma was, after all, alive. That was the most important thing.

We left the flat, and made arrangements to get together again after classes tomorrow.

Carson was unusually subdued. "I just got the weirdest feeling with that tape that Emma's not gonna make it."

"I kinda got the same feeling," I said.

"Did Trowbridge say anything you held back because of the girls?" he asked.

"He said they struck him as amateurs. The kidnappers. That that makes it kind of dicey for Emma's survival."

We walked about a minute in silence. I noticed that we only met two other people, and both were alone. I also noticed the streetlights on Southwood Lane. "I don't think I've ever seen such yellow streetlights," I said.

"I was noticing that, too," said Carson. "I was hoping it wasn't something I drank."

"Yeah. It makes everything look different."

We walked down the hill, back to the tube station. The entrance was a good block from the exit, and down a long flight of exterior steps. I felt like I was descending into the woods. It was kind of remote, although it was lit pretty well. "You don't suppose she went back into London that night, do you?" asked Carson.

"Why would she?"

"I dunno. Maybe she just went somewhere to meet somebody

else . . ." He shrugged. "Just talking to hear myself talk, I guess. It's easy to travel in a herd, here."

"I wonder . . . did anybody ever say if she had a cell phone or not? I can't imagine that the troops at NSY would neglect that . . . but it wasn't in the report." I didn't have a cell phone with me because mine wouldn't work in the UK, so I'd left it home. But Jane and Vicky had one, and I thought it was fairly likely that Emma would have one, too. I made a mental note to call Jane when we got back to the hotel.

Moments later, we discovered that the tubes in London apparently stop running at midnight. There was absolutely nobody around. We went to a small pub by the tube exit, persuaded the clean up crew to let us in, and called a cab. It was one of those big black jobs, the kind you see in all the movies.

Once we got in, I got another bit of education. I hadn't realized just how much we stood out, and how quickly we could be identified at US citizens. All I did was tell the driver the address of our hotel.

"You're Yanks?"

"Yeah. Just got here."

"Have you heard about that American girl, the one that was taken hostage?"

"Yeah."

"Bloody awful thing, that. Awful. Grabbing people off the street, threatening 'em and all that."

"It sure is," said Carson.

"I hear she was staying here in Highgate," he said. "Would you happen to know her?"

"We sure would," said Carson, before I could stop him. I glared at him anyway, but I don't think that he caught it.

"Well, you have my sympathy, there. My cousin was killed in an IRA bombing, a few years back. Awful thing for the wife and kids. He was a clerk walking home from work, when the bomb went off in a store. Instant it was."

"Sorry to hear that," I said.

"What's this world coming to, I always say." He glanced back toward us, over his left shoulder. To someone like me, who had always driven left-hand drive cars, it was unsettling. "Here's hoping she comes out of it well and good," he said.

"You got that right," I said.

"Bloody shame the pols get involved now, though. What with terrorism and all. They won't be able to let it alone."

That opened a whole new avenue of worry.

It was about 10:10 when we got back to the room. The message waiting light on the phone was flashing. I picked it up while Carson went to the john.

"There is . . . one new message for room . . . 515," said the bland, computer generated voice. There was a pause, and then Sergeant Trowbridge's voice came on the line. "Deputy Houseman . . . this is Sergeant Trowbridge at New Scotland Yard. It's 7:00 PM. There's been ah, a development in the Emma Schiller case. Pleas call me at . . ." And he gave his number.

I scrambled to find a pen and paper, found them in a drawer, and then had to replay the message to get the number.

"What's up?" asked Carson, coming back into the room.

"Something in Emma's case," I said. "Just a sec. . . ."

I wrote down the number, hung up, and said, "That was Trowbridge. He left a number . . ."

Another detective answered the phone, and told me that Trowbridge was out of the office. I explained who I was, and named the case I was interested in.

"Oh, you're the Sheriff from the States?"

"A Deputy . . . yes."

"Oh, right. Ah, I think Trowbridge's up in Stevenage about now. Let me give you his cell number . . . I know he wants to talk to you. Just a bit . . . ," and he gave me the new number.

I called it. After six or seven rings, he answered.

"This is Deputy Houseman. You have something on Emma's case?"

"I'm afraid we might. We've recovered a body. It's a bit difficult to identify at the moment . . . would you be able to assist us with identification?"

"Probably," I said. A body? But we'd just seen her on TV, for God's sake. "What's the condition?"

"I'd rather not go into it on the phone. We're at the Stevenage police station. Could you come up? We could have someone meet you at the train station. . . . We should be back at the hospital by the time you arrive."

He had to give me directions as just how to go about that.

I hung up the phone. "They've found a body that they think might be Emma," I said. "We have to go to a place called Stevenage right now." I grabbed a jacket and put the pen and notepad in my pocket.

"We're supposed to go to King's Cross station, and take what he calls a 'proper train' to a place called Stevenage. He said to take the express, and we should be there in an hour or so."

"Hell, we just saw her on TV! It can't be her," said Carson. He pulled his jacket out of the closet. "Can it?"

"I don't know," I said, heading out the door. "But I don't think they'd call us unless they were pretty fuckin' sure."

Chapter 11

We finally got to Stevenage at about midnight. We'd run into a little problem at Kings Cross station, and obtaining the right tickets, and . . . well, at least we'd gotten to Kings Cross in good time. Taxi's aren't cheap over here, either, but since the tube was closed, we'd had no choice.

The train ride seemed longer than it was. We speculated a little, but even that wasn't too lively, as we still had so very little information to go on.

We were met on the second level of the Stevenage train station by an officer who introduced himself as Constable Julian Richards, Hertfordshire police, who checked our identification at about the same time he shook our hands, and said he was very glad we were available. He ushered us to his patrol car, which I found uncomfortably small, and drove us immediately to Lister Hospital.

Richards ushered us down a ramp and into a remote area of the hospital where the deceased were kept until the proper funeral agents could take charge of them, and also where those necessary autopsies were performed. Trowbridge met us outside the door.

"Sorry to bother you, but we think we may have a match with your missing girl."

"No problem."

"Before we go in, let me fill you in a bit. She was, oh, discovered early this evening. By this officer, in fact," he said, indicating Richards.

I turned to Richards. "Cool, good for you," I said.

"Mostly luck," he said.

"You know what they say," I said, "about rather be lucky than smart."

"Yes. At any rate," said Trowbridge, "she was in this small freezer and we've had a devil of a time getting her out. All we could tell until she was removed was that it appeared to be a small person with reddish brown hair." He opened the door for us. "That description fit well with at least three missing persons in London, and two more throughout the UK. Now that she's out, and thawing, we can tell a bit more, you see."

My first impression was that it was much warmer in the autopsy area than I would have expected. Then I saw the body, and knew why. It was the damndest thing I'd ever seen. On the exam table was a human female, naked, beaded with moisture, and roughly in the shape of a cube. Her ankles were crossed, with the feet bent inwards. Her calves touched the backs of her thighs, which in turn were flat up against her chest. Her arms were pressed in tightly against her torso, with the forearms folded so they, too, lay back against the arms in a sort of hyperflexed position. Her head was folded tightly to her right, with her right ear pressed firmly into her right shoulder, and her face pressing into the recess formed by her arms and knees. Her long hair was matted to her right side, and pushed up between her feet. Her flesh was flattened on all the outside areas, like they were pressed against the other side of a glass surface instead of freestanding. Those areas were much whiter than the rest of her. Her external genitals were very much exposed, and everyone in the room assiduously avoided looking in that direction. I, myself, discreetly moved around to the other end of the body.

There seemed to be abrasions and ligature marks at her wrists and ankles. They were pretty rough looking, with well defined lines. The closer I looked, the more I thought I couldn't tell if they were from ligatures or simply from the severe folding that had taken place. I did notice that the skin of both knees was broken, and there seemed to be scabs on those injuries. Pre-mortem, so to speak.

"Shit," I said, softly. I approached the body more closely. Her face was mostly concealed by being pressed against her knees. "It sure as hell could be Emma," I said. "The hair's the right color, all right." I peered more closely. There seemed to be some pretty significant damage to her forehead and the right side of her face. It looked to me as if she'd been beaten up, probably with an instrument.

I turned back to Trowbridge. "How much longer till she can be unfolded?"

"The pathologist will start soon," he said. "He's waiting for a second pathologist. And, he wanted a cup of tea after he was able to remove her from that . . ." and he pointed to a small freezer that was standing in the corner, with it's top removed and leaning against it at an angle.

I was astounded. "She was in that?"

"She was."

"God, it doesn't look possible. . . ."

"The interior dimensions," said Trowbridge, looking at his notes, "are twenty-two by twenty-two by twenty-one inches."

"Emma's about five-one. . . . I never would have thought it possible," I said.

"We think there's some evidence that there was a bit of pressure applied to the lid, to force her into the space. You can see the cracks in the plastic liner of the lid, from her ankles, we think."

There was a sound behind me as Carson went back out into the hall.

"So, you have a suspect?" I figured that if the freezer had been found in a residence, they had their man. If it had been found in a commercial place, they would have at least the names of those with access to the freezer. Regardless, they had to be off to a good start.

"I'm not at liberty to say much right now," said Trowbridge. "If it is, in fact, Emma Schiller, I shall be able to tell you more."

"Okay. I hope," I said, "I can do a positive ID. I'd hate to have my daughter or Vicky see this. . . ."

"I agree completely," said Trowbridge. "Do you think your friend will be all right?"

"Carson? I dunno. . . ." And I continued to look at the corpse. "Are those goose bumps on the upper arms and thighs, do you think?"

"I think so," said Trowbridge. "Please step back now. We don't want any chance of contamination . . ."

"Sure. Any idea how long, postmortem, goose bumps will form?"

"You mean goose flesh? I'll ask," said Trowbridge. "Can't say that I know."

"Me, either," I said. "It could be interesting. She sure as hell had to be flexible when she went in there. And from the marks on the edges of the buttocks, it looks like she was in soon after death. Lividity. . . ."

"Indeed." He moved toward the door, determined to get me out. I followed.

"I've dealt with frozen bodies on a couple of occasions," I said, "but they've always been outside in the winter. We call those corpse sickles."

Trowbridge snorted, and I thought it might have been a laugh.

"Does it get really cold, then, where you're from?" asked Richards.

"Coldest it's ever been on a night I worked, was minus forty-seven, Fahrenheit, I think."

"Good Lord," said Trowbridge. "I thought only Canada reached those extremes."

"It was a blast of air they sent our way," I said. "Called an Alberta Clipper."

"Do you know what that would be, Centigrade scale?" asked Richards.

I looked at Trowbridge. "Not sure . . . about the same, though, I think. Don't they sort of converge about minus forty-five or so?"

"I think that's right," he said.

"But I've never seen one artificially frozen before," I said. "I think it'd take longer, in a freezer, because it's not as cold."

"The freezer had been unplugged for a bit," said Richards.

"Not good policy to jump to conclusions," said Trowbridge. Richards took the hint and shut up.

We continued the discussion as we emerged from the autopsy area and back into the hall. Carson was sitting on a bench, his head back against the wall, and breathing deeply. His eyes were closed.

"Carson, how you doin'?"

"I'm never going to be able to forget that . . ." he said, weakly.

"Oh, sure," I said. "Don't worry. It's gonna fade. Eventually."

We all sat or stood around, and I thought we were just waiting for the other doctor.

"One thing," I said to Trowbridge and Richards. "She sure didn't put herself in that freezer. You've got a case one way or another."

"Oh, indeed," said Trowbridge.

"Well," I said, "not to be asking questions out of turn, but if you've got the remains, got the freezer, there's an excellent chance that either you've got a suspect in custody, or at least you have a suspect."

"No more discussion until Inspector Whitcomb arrives," said Trowbridge. I couldn't help noticing the smile on Richards' face.

It did occur to me that Carson and I were the only 'civilians' in the area. Either the other missing persons had no relatives, or Trowbridge and company were pretty damned sure that this was Emma. I figured the odds were in favor of the latter.

It was after one am before the doctors and a couple of nurses came back to the autopsy area. Before they'd arrived, we'd peered inside twice, and both times the body seemed to be unfolding. It was just too weird. The last time I'd looked, whoever she was had sort of slowly assumed the appearance of a four-legged spider, with her limbs just beginning to touch the surface of the table. The unfolding forearms were nearly vertical, and the knees were at about a forty-five degree angle. The feet were staying flexed for some reason, so that her heels were touching the surface, but her toes were still pointed back toward her shins, with the soles facing inwards at a very unnatural angle.

"I'm Doctor Mallampalli," he said. "Rama Mallampalli. This is Doctor Barrington, and these are nurses Barnett and Wellesley."

He was clearly addressing Carson and me. We introduced ourselves.

"From the American heartland, I understand," he said, with a hearty handshake. "Well, we are honored. What brings you all this way? Our frozen guest in there?"

"If it's the one we're afraid it might be, yes, that's it."

"Well, let us go see just who she is," he said, and walked briskly into the autopsy room. "I think we can reduce the heating now," he said, and Nurse Barnett moved into a corner and adjusted the thermostat.

"Ah, yes, we're somewhat supine now," he said. "Come here, Deputy, and see her face. It's quite exposed. . . ."

I walked over, took one look, and was certain. "It's Emma," I said. "No doubt." I inhaled deeply. "Son of a bitch." You always find yourself hoping, right up to the last moment.

"You sound very sure," said Trowbridge.

"See that little scar, above her right eye . . ." I pointed. "I was present the night she got that."

"You are certain, then?" asked Dr. Mallampalli.

"Yes." I peered more closely. "Do you think that's a ligature mark on her neck, there, or do you think it's a fold line?"

"I shall have to make a determination on that point when I can see it more clearly," he said. He slipped some latex gloves on, reached out, and put pressure on the left knee of the thawing victim. There didn't seem to be much free movement in the joint.

"I would estimate another eight hours," said Dr. Mallampalli, "before we can commence the autopsy. I do not wish to damage any of the tissues." He turned and smiled at the rest of us. "Nor do I wish to freeze my hands once I am inside."

He looked directly at me. "You knew the victim, then?"

"Yes," I said. "My wife and I were friends of her parents, and she was a very good friend of our daughter. They're about the same age."

"My condolences," he said.

"Thank you."

"You will be attending the autopsy, then?"

"I'd think not," said Trowbridge. "Attendance will be limited to two officers who are officially on this case."

That was fine with me, and I said so. I hate autopsies of people I know. It really screws up your memories of them.

"And the results?" asked Dr. Mallampalli. "Just for the same officers?"

"I believe so," said Trowbridge. "If Deputy Houseman receives a copy, it should be from the investigative team."

I had no objection that, either. It was the same way we'd do it back home. I looked at my watch. It was nearly one in the morning. "I'm going to have to make a couple of notification calls . . . to the US," I added, quickly, forestalling an objection from Trowbridge. "And then I'm going to have to tell my daughter and her roommate."

"I'm afraid that's not going to be possible for a while," said a voice behind us.

I turned around. The speaker was a man in his late fifties, over six feet, thin, and dressed in slacks and a sweater. He showed Trowbridge his credentials. I didn't get a good look at them, and probably wouldn't have been able to tell the difference between a police badge and a public works icon unless I'd read the printing. But Trowbridge popped to like a rear rank private.

"Sergeant Trowbridge, sir. I'm the case officer present."

"Is there somewhere we can talk a bit?" asked the man.

"Yes sir," said Trowbridge.

"I'm Dr. Mallampalli, and this is Dr. Barrington." I thought Dr. Mallampalli had also reacted slightly when he saw the man's credentials. "I'm rather surprised to have you here."

The man ignored that. "You're a . . . Deputy Houseman, from the US?" he asked. It sounded rhetorical.

"Yes."

"Why don't you come with us, too." It wasn't a question, but more of a very polite order.

"Sure." I had a feeling that this was something I really didn't want to miss.

"I'm Carson Hilgenberg," said Carson. "Prosecuting attorney, Nation County, Iowa, USA"

"Indeed," said the man. "And you'll be waiting in the hall for us." He addressed Nurse Barnett. "You'll see that he's provided for? Coffee and the like. . . ."

She looked at Dr. Mallampalli. He nodded, vigorously.

"Yes," she said.

He then spoke to Constable Richards. "Would you be kind enough to stay with Mr. Hilgenberg, here? No telephone calls, now, either of you." His voice was gently admonishing, but somehow he brooked no arguments. "The autopsy room will be out of bounds, and there will be nothing regarding this unfortunate woman discussed until further notice."

Dr. Mallampalli said, "This way . . ." and we walked a short distance down the hall to a physician's conference room.

The tall man addressed me as soon as the door had swung shut. "The name's Adrian Blyth," he said. "MI5. I believe we have an agent Pollard of the FBI in common?" He stuck out his hand.

I shook it. "You're the one George talked to about Skripkin. . . ." I was thinking, MI5? No shit? I'd thought he was Special Branch. That had been important enough for me. But it wasn't the sort of thing you'd actually say. I was very impressed.

He smiled. "None other. I'm sorry we have to meet under such circumstances."

We sat around the small conference table. Dr. Mallampalli spoke first.

"This is quite extraordinary," he said. "Will the protocol regarding the distribution of our report change?"

"Oh, yes," said Blyth. "Dr. Haworth will be over shortly, to assist you. He may well have an assistant of his own in tow. Your report will be made to us, with a copy to Special Branch only. SO13. There will be no information given the press until we clear it."

"Ah." Dr. Mallampalli nodded. "Would you rather we typed or dictated it?"

"Regretfully, typing would seem in order here." He smiled.

"You trust my spelling more than I," said Dr. Mallampalli, with a grin. "It is good to see you again."

"Always a pleasure working with you," said Blyth. "All forensic samples and evidence shall be filed with Sergeant Trowbridge here, under a case number I shall provide."

"Not to worry," said Trowbridge.

Dr. Barrington spoke. "Is there anything in particular we should have the laboratory screen for?"

"Anything that would seem indicated," said Blyth. "She was a hostage . . . she may have been given something that would make her more pliable." He shrugged. "It's so hard to tell with the little we know.

Now if you men of medicine would excuse us, we've some very pedestrian business to conduct amongst ourselves."

When just the three of us were in the room, Blyth sat on the corner of the desk. "Sergeant," he said, "would you check in that refrigerator and see if there is anything for us to drink? Water, preferably."

As Trowbridge handed him a bottle of water, and I nodded that I'd like one, too, Blyth seemed to relax his guard. "First of all, you have my sincerest apologies. If I had been notified somewhat earlier," and he glanced at Trowbridge, "I would have spared you the identification process."

"That's okay," I said. "It's one of the reasons I'm here. Besides, I'd really prefer being the one to do it, rather than my daughter." What I think he meant was that he wouldn't have let me get involved in any way, but as long as I was here, he'd make the best of it.

"You also have my sympathies. I understand you knew her?"

"Pretty much. It's a small town, we all know each other."

"Indeed. This is a very interesting case," he said. "Let me begin by saying that MI5 is not a police agency. We don't make arrests or such things. We rely on Sgt. Trowbridge, here, for the real work." He smiled at Trowbridge, who just blinked back. "We are merely good citizens, who gather intelligence."

Right, I thought. Sure. But I just said, "Okay. Kind of like the NSA, then. The real one, not the movie version."

"Exactly. And like them, we also do not assassinate people."

"Bloody shame," said Trowbridge.

"Well, yes, on occasion," said Blyth, with another smile. "Nonetheless . . . we do get on somehow. Now . . . Deputy?"

"Carl is just fine. Really."

"Right. Well, Carl, as long as you're in up to your elbows, I'm going to ask you to cooperate with us for a bit."

"Sure."

"Unofficially. Has to be that way. Right, then, here we go. Nothing we say here goes elsewhere, you understand? Good." He sighed. "We've received a second tape. Or, more properly, the BBC has done. Again, it's from a group calling themselves the "London Reform Movement for the Freedom of Khaled al Fawwaz and Ibrahim Eidarous and Lions of the Front for Jihad in Britain." Again, the wan sort of smile. "With such a clumsy title, I believe we have some true amateurs here. This time, however, there is a clear demand, although still not with any audio enhancement. They are demanding the release of all political prisoners being detained under ATCSA in Belmarsh, or they say they'll kill her. I have to tell you that from their title, we expected no less."

"But now that she's dead? I mean, it's totally meaningless." He didn't answer immediately. "Isn't it?" I asked.

"Well, one would certainly think, wouldn't one. Not that we'd actually release prisoners, you understand, regardless of her state of being. But they also refer to a forthcoming tape and additional set of demands, and we'd just as soon not let anyone know that we know she's dead. Not just yet."

I don't know if he thought I'd ask a question or not, but I had absolutely no idea what was going on and I didn't want to look any dumber than I was. I think Trowbridge felt the same way. Finally, I said, "Okay. Just so I have some idea, can I assume that Belmarsh is some sort of jail or prison, and those letters you mentioned before it stand for what?"

"Ah. Yes. Pardon me. Belmarsh *is* a prison," he said. "A very secure detention facility. And ATCSA is an acronym for the Anti-Terrorism, Crime and Security Act, put in place in 2001, shortly after September 11th. It expanded arrest and detention powers."

"Oh." I twisted off the cap on my water bottle. "We're way out of my league, here."

"Indeed," said Blyth, "and I apologize. But I'm afraid I'd like to have you do something for us."

I must have looked very curious, because he smiled. "Not to worry. You'd be very nearly un-involved," he said. "I've told you this much because of the incident you and friend George of the FBI lived through two years ago. What we ask of you this time is your fullest cooperation."

"You've got it," I said. I meant it.

"You aren't to be allowed to tell *anyone* that Emma Schiller is dead."

I considered that for a second. "Oh, boy. Well, sure, okay, but . . ." A whole lot of stuff was going through my head. "This is gonna mean that I've gotta go back to my daughter's flat . . . and they're gonna be all concerned about her being held hostage, okay. And I've got to sit there and not tell them that she's dead?"

"Yes."

"Some of her relatives are coming over, to see what they can do to obtain her release," I said. "I can't tell them, either?"

"No. No, I'm afraid not. I know it's asking a lot."

"No shit," I said. I inhaled, held it, and then let it out with "Then there's my boss. I'm gonna have to lie to him, at least by omission." I chewed my lower lip for a few seconds. "He can't know?"

"No. Not yet."

"So, for how long? Any idea?"

"No. None."

"A guess?"

He shook his head. "No idea. Not forever, surely. But just how long depends on too many variables."

I waited a second, hoping to get a partial list of variables from him. None were forthcoming. This was going to be a tough one.

"Okay. I mean, sure. Of course. It's gotta be done, it's gotta be done."

"Good. Speaking of your boss a moment ago . . . just why is it you're here?" He sounded like somebody had told him, and he just hadn't been able to believe it.

I explained everything to him, as quickly as I could. I think he just pretended to understand.

"Ah. Well, then, I'm glad we understand our respective positions."

"Yeah." I turned my palms up. "Yours is easier to state. For mine . . . I'm absolutely not in any position to do much about the situation. But can I at least have your best guarantee that these bastards will get what's coming to them?"

"I think I can say that, yes. Special Branch will certainly see to that. I do apologize, about you're being dragged into it like this and all. But I wasn't told about the body recovery, or about the call to you to assist in identification, until it was too late to do anything about it." A little exasperation crept into his otherwise laid-back voice. He looked at Trowbridge again, as he said it, not so much to place blame, but to let him know that they'd be discussing something along those lines shortly.

"That's okay. I sure understand that." I took a big gulp of water. "Are you familiar with this particular group?"

Blyth pulled his PDA from his pocket. "The London Reform Movement for the Freedom of Khaled al Fawwaz and Ibrahim Eidarous and Lions of the Front for Jihad in Britain?" He closed it. "Not the faintest glimmer of recognition. It does sound as though someone had combined two or more groups. . . . But given the little we do know about them from their activities, I'd say more of an amateur enterprise."

"Would you be able to give me some more background on 'em, when you get it?"

I think he started to automatically refuse, and then caught himself. "Ah. You're looking for some connection to the group you and Agent Pollard encountered in the US, aren't you?"

"I'm almost afraid to. But, yeah, that's what I'm thinking."

"Do you have a link in mind? To Emma Schiller?"

"No," I said. "But I just want to be sure."

"Indeed. I *will* let you know that, as soon as I can. Do you have a list of those names?"

"I'll get it to you as soon as I can." I hoped it would be fairly quick. I'd have to contact Lamar and Sally, and make sure things were being done.

"Right. I *will* tell you what I can. I promise you that." He slowly twisted the cap on his water bottle counter-clockwise, then back in a clockwise direction. It was very quiet.

"Well, then," I said, "good enough. I know how this sort of thing goes. So, okay, I hate to assume things . . . but I'd guess that since you've got her recovered, and in a freezer, you have an address for a suspect. Am I right?"

"Unfortunately, no."

That surprised me. "You do have someone in custody?"

"No."

I was about to ask if someone had mailed them the god damned freezer, but thought better of it. He didn't seem to be lying to me, nor trying to mislead me. He just wasn't going to tell me everything he knew. I wasn't happy about it, but it was fair enough. Exactly what I'd probably do if I was in his shoes.

"Okay . . ." I said. My head was getting busier and busier. In the airplane, I'd thought quite a bit about what would have to be done if Emma were actually dead. "Since I'm going to have to keep quiet about this, what am I supposed to do with the funeral process? I mean, there has to be a coffin, when you're done with her. Arrangements to have the remains shipped back. . . ." I took a drink of water. "You're gonna have to give me a hand, here. I can't for the life of me see a way for me to do those things in secret."

I don't think Blyth had thought that far in advance, either, but he was unflappable. "Certainly," he said. "I'll have our people help you make the arrangements as we go. We have friends in high places." He smiled again. "I promise you we'll hold you to this for the shortest possible time. But when we give you the go ahead, all the arrangements will have been made."

"Thanks," I said. "Now, what about my friend Carson out there . . . he's just a local prosecutor, and he's kinda new at this. He knows she's dead, now. That could be a problem."

"Can we help with that?"

"Maybe. They got room at Belmarsh?"

Blyth snorted. "Short of that."

"Maybe if you could talk to him yourself, before I do? I'll keep an eye on him, but it'd be nice to have the foundation laid first."

Blyth nodded. "Of course." He blinked, and then said, "How did you get here, if I might ask?"

That took me a second, because I thought at first that he was asking about the whole process with Lamar, and I was sure I'd just told him about that. Then I got it.

"A cab, then the train." I had an excuse. I was really tired.

He looked over at Trowbridge. "I should have thought you'd arrange transportation for them, especially at this hour."

"I was already here," he said.

"Shall we do the right thing, then, and provide transport for them back to their hotel?" It really wasn't a question. We got Constable Richards, and a car, put at our 'convenience' to take us home.

Chapter 12

On the way back from Stevenage with Constable Richards, Carson and I had a little chat. I wasn't quite sure what Blyth had said to him, but he kept repeating the same phrase.

"Jesus. We could go to prison if we say anything."

"True," said Richards. "Official Secrets and such things . . . very serious business."

"Sure enough," I said. "So we just don't." I looked at Carson. "Right?"

"Oh, right. Bet your ass we don't. Jesus, Carl, we . . ."

"I know. Prison. Look, it's gonna be a lot easier than you might think. Really."

"That's true," said Richards.

"With those consequences? I hope to God," said Carson. "But a man can slip up, you know?"

"Yep. But, look, hey. It's easy at first, so you have a chance to get the hang of it. But then things are gonna be said, things are gonna be done. . . . And sometimes just not talking won't even come close to covering it. Sometimes you have to make misleading statements. I just try not to outright lie. But it gets harder as you go, the longer it gets. Believe me." I was trying to sound reassuring, but I thought I was blowing it.

"Sure. . . ."

"The tough part is looking shocked when they finally find out that she's dead. I mean, we'll need to be just as surprised as anybody, and just as devastated. Understand?"

"Yeah. Sure. We could go to prison," muttered Carson. "That man was from MI5. That's who James Bond works for. Shit!"

"Too right," said Richards. "But good old double oh seven works for MI6, actually. That's the foreign end of things. MI5's domestic, you know." He seemed to be getting a kick out of this. Well, in a way, so was I.

"Same difference," said Carson. "But it's an Official Secret. Tell nobody. And afterward, after we all know . . . ?" he asked. "What do we do . . . ? I mean it's over, then, and we can just *tell* 'em? Right?"

"About tonight? Nope. We never tell about tonight unless it's okayed by the Brit authorities."

"God, Carl, this isn't easy."

"Listen to me. After we all know? That's the toughest time. For the next thirty years. Because we can't *ever* let on that we knew. You got that?" I really felt I needed to prepare him for the reality of the whole thing. I was especially concerned about Jane. If she ever found that I'd known well before she did, she'd never forgive me.

"Never?"

"Not until I'm in my grave, how's that? After I'm dead, you can tell anyone you want. That way you can go to prison alone."

"You're serious?"

"Dead."

"You've done this before?" It was beginning to sink in.

"Not over here. But, yeah. A few times. Not quite like this. Usually just dope cases, where we bust somebody and roll him over. We can never let on he talked, you know? But, you know, it gets easier if you just don't think about it. Don't dwell on it. Just suck it up and keep quiet. Like attorney-client stuff, you know?"

He thought about that. "Yeah. But, sooner or later, they're gonna figure all this out. Somebody will. Jane and Vicky aren't stupid, not by a long shot."

"I know."

"What am I supposed to do, change the subject?"

Richards took that one. "Artfully," he said.

Carson didn't look too damned convinced. Hell, I wasn't sure he could pull this off either, but I had no choice at this point but to hope that he could.

"You've got it easy," I said. "If you just absolutely gotta talk about it, talk to me."

That seemed to lighten his load a little. It sure didn't lighten mine, though.

Just to change the subject, Constable Richards told us that he'd been with the Metropolitan Police for ten years, before transferring to Stevenage, where he'd been for four.

I gave him my pedigree, and we talked some cop stuff for a few minutes. War stories are the same everywhere, I guess.

As long as we seemed to have so much in common, I ran my theory by him about the identity of the suspect being limited to the owner of the residence, or the persons with access to a commercial property. I went a little further, and suggested that there might even be a suspect either in custody, or being actively sought.

"I mean, they at least have to have the address where they found the freezer."

"You'd think so, wouldn't you?" said Richards. "And you're absolutely right in your reasoning. Unfortunately, that's not the way it happened. In your position, you wouldn't even be able to guess, I think. I'm of a mind to tell you what really happened." He swiveled his head and looked at us. "Can you blokes keep another secret?"

"I know I can," I said. I gestured toward Carson. "Not too sure about him, though."

Richards laughed, and Carson protested. "Hell, they can only send me to prison once . . . I might as well know another one."

"I think you should know," said Richards, "that I was the one who found the body. It was subsequent to a traffic violation." He paused for effect. It worked. "She was in the freezer, right enough, but the freezer was in the back of a car."

That surprised me, I have to admit. I suppose that's why I said, "No shit?"

"Indeed," said Richards. "There was this car, a Jazz, one of the little hatchbacks? Nice, though. Well, it was acting dodgy . . . you know. Hanging about, making hesitant turns about the park area. Stopped in the traveled way, he did, and turned up the wrong way, and backed up. I start in behind him, and he gets nervous, you know the way they do. Suddenly all careful. I'm nearly ready to stop him, you know, but I'm hoping for one more glaring error to put down in the report, when he starts what he has to think is evasive maneuvers. Hard turns, picks up speed. Well," he said, with increasing enthusiasm, "I activate the lights and the siren, and stick to him like glue. It's only moments, and I'm talking to base, saying I've got myself a live one, and he stops like that!" He clapped his hands and then put one back on the wheel. "I slide on past, due to the wet and all, and I'm out of the unit in a blink, but I see two of 'em running off like a pair of bleedin' Olympians, going in two directions, not even shutting their vehicle down before they leave."

He chuckled. We all seem to enjoy this aspect of our work. "Right, then, I'm on my best speed, heading for the driver, and I notice as I pass the vehicle that it's beginning to move about again, and I stop so fast I slide, and I'm turning about to try to get in and stop the bloody thing before it gets into housing and hurts someone, and it hits a tree with a grand thump. Up goes the bonnet, and the hatchback springs, the air bags bang out, and there's steam and all, it was quite a sight!"

"Shit!" I like stories as much as the next guy.

"Shit, indeed. So there I am, the blokes both gone into the gloom, and the car what would have stopped regardless when it hit the tree, so I'm standing there, having accomplished nothing but witness a crash that occurs after the driver has fled!"

I loved it. "I wish I could have seen that," I said.

"Well, then, you know how it is. I call the station, and my sergeant is on the way, and he orders me to stay put, so I figure there's nothing for it but to have a poke about, you know, to see if I can discover evidence telling why the two occupants have fled. So, the first thing I see is this cube-like edifice standing up in the back, against the back of the seats." The glee faded completely from his voice, as he continued, "I thought I'd just have a look inside, calculating that what was in there could well be contraband, and that was why they fled, you know? So I opened the lid. . . ."

It got pretty quiet in the car.

"Well," he said, "you know what I saw. I thought my heart would stop, just then. Totally unexpected, it was. Totally."

It stayed quiet for a few seconds. "You know who the car belonged to?" I asked. It was obvious to me that the plate and registration would be the first, most automatic think they'd look at.

"Right," he said. "Stolen that very evening, from where it was parked. In Chiswick, on Elliott Road."

"Chizzick?" I asked. That's what it sounded like.

"Right. The owner's a man of doubtful intelligence, as he left it unlocked with the keys inside. Was coming right back out, you know. We can go by there if you like. It's not too far from your hotel."

"Cool," I said. No matter what, it helps to see someplace involved in a crime. It just gives you a sense of things. "Owner checks out, I'm sure?"

"Right. The Mets gave him a very clean bill of health." Richards looked over at me. "It wouldn't do for you to be following up on this, now."

"No, I won't. Promise. Hell, I wouldn't be able to find it again in a million years. Trust me." That was absolutely true.

*   *   *

It was very dark when we went up Elliott Road. Nothing remarkable at all, to tell the truth. Richards didn't know just exactly where it was on Elliott Road, but we got to see the general area. It was really quiet. So, at least, I could put a location to where the car had been stolen from. That sort of thing helps, believe it or not.

We got to the hotel after 4 AM. I wasn't even tired, mostly because it was about 7 PM Iowa time. Suppertime, in fact. The problem was, there was no room service, and absolutely nothing within walking distance seemed to be open.

"I'm not gonna be able to sleep," said Carson. "All I can think about is Emma, you know, the way she looked. God, she used to be so pretty."

I remembered the purplish face, and the blotchy lividity. "You've never seen a dead body before?"

"No."

"That can be rough, the first time. Nobody who's been killed like that ever looks normal. They can't. All the muscle tone's gone, you know? That's what gives faces character. Especially then if they've been put in unusual positions, or frozen, or whatever. They just don't look the same."

"Yeah . . . but that first view. You know, she wasn't covered up or anything."

"Yeah. Well, she wasn't really her anymore. I'm sure she didn't care."

"Oh, sure," he said. "And the other thing isn't helping, either."

"What's that?" I asked, knowing what was coming.

"You know, having to lie, or go to prison for telling the truth. Those bastards are serious."

I almost laughed. "You'll adjust," I said.

"We really could go to prison, you know."

"That could be a real kicker," I said. "I mean, attorneys never get sent to prison for lying, and then they send one there for telling the truth? Shit, Carson, you could be famous."

So there we were. Emma dead as hell. Murdered, by kidnappers who were making some demand about releasing prisoners. And us not being able to tell anybody who cared about her.

"You think this might have some connection to the terrorism thing you and the Feds got into that time in the barn?"

"No. I mean, I can't see how, and the odds on that being connected are a million to one." I took off my shoes. "It did surprise me, the political motivation. I do think it has a hell of a lot to do with her being an American, though."

"What makes you say that?"

"Nothing. Just what I think. And I'll tell you something else I think. . . ."

"Go for it," said Carson.

"I think the Brits suspect that it might have something to do with G.W. Bush coming here."

"You're shitting me?"

"Just think about it for a minute. You'll see what I mean."

He shook his head. "No evidence for that. Nope, Carl, there isn't any at all."

"Not yet." I grinned. "Like I said, it's just something I think. But wouldn't you, if you were Scotland Yard, or MI5? They *have* to think that. And so do the Secret Service. They can't take any chances, so they *have* to know. That's gotta be why they don't want anybody to know that they know Emma's dead. They want to see what the next demand will be. See if it says anything about the President."

"But, shit Carl," said Carson, getting excited, "the guys who ran off and left Emma in the freezer *know* they left her, for God's sake."

"Exactly. And if they're two idiots acting alone, it's over. No new demand, because it's not going to mean shit to them. They know they have no bargaining power any more. But if it's not just two idiots," I said, slowly, "there's a chance that the two flunkies who gave her up are going to split just as fast as they can. Let's say they work for some real, honest to God terrorist group. Somebody who told 'em to dump the body way away from where it had been killed. Would you want to piss those guys off and tell 'em you screwed up and gave the body to the cops?"

"Well, no. But . . . ?"

"Especially if nobody reads in the paper that there was a body found in Stevenage, right? Regardless of motivational shit, nobody who thinks the boss will off 'em if they fuck up is going to run right out to the boss and say, 'Hey, guess what?' Right?"

"Well, yeah. Sure." He didn't look quite convinced.

"And from what we've seen, whoever held her wasn't exactly a polished professional, now, were they?" I thought that was a very good point.

"True." He was getting into it, too.

"But what if somebody who was a pro told 'em to grab her? Somebody they're afraid of? Somebody who wanted to use her for some higher reason?"

"Like what?"

"Beats the shit out of me," I said. "But let's work on that."

Thursday, November 13, 2003
Chiswick, London
02:58 Greenwich Mean Time

Hamza and Anton, who were effectively the only two functional soldiers of the London Reform Movement for the Freedom of Khaled al Fawwaz and Ibrahim Eidarous and Lions of the Front for Jihad in Britain, were walking along Mayfield Avenue, tired, cold, but buoyed by a small success. They had been taking great care to elude their pursuers all the way from Stevenage, by taking sudden route changes, going to ground in the restroom of the train station, referring to each other by fictitious names in the cab from the station, giving the driver an address several blocks from their true destination, and other similarly inspired tactics. The fact that they had not been followed was unknown to them.

They were now nearly at the flat of one Hanadi Tamish, known to them as Ayat. They had met her only once, at a meeting of their cell in Marwan's favorite pub; and had been told that she would provide legal assistance if it was ever needed. The assistance that had been meant was more along the lines of legal advice for articles and posters. At the time, both Hamza and Anton had looked at the young woman very skeptically because she appeared too young to be a college graduate, let alone an attorney. Because of that, she'd made the amateurish mistake of giving them her card. Since neither of them knew the address of Marwan or anyone else in the cell except the one on Hanadi's card, she'd been their only choice. They certainly couldn't go to ground with someone who wasn't a cell member. Calling Marwan was absolutely out of the question.

That it never occurred to them that they would now be leading someone straight to another terrorist was an indication of both their amateur status and their state of mind. Neither man would have considered himself to be in a panicked state: that is the nature and the power of panic.

Things had begun to go terribly wrong with the captive Emma on November 11th, in Hamza's flat. They had only been trying to sever the ties with the seedy place. To do that, Emma would have to be transported away from the flat. It had been as simple as that. All quite reasonable, if one assumed Emma's cooperation in the move. That had been a mistake. Regardless of their liberal application of duct tape, she not only fought, she had effectively disabled Hamza during the battle with a strong, two-footed kick to the groin. Anton, who had wrapped his arms around her head to avoid being butted, found himself alone in the struggle with her. Although they'd had duct tape around her wrists and ankles, binding them securely, she had been able to whip her head and feet around, nearly squirming free of their grip, and the resulting kicks had finally scored a direct hit on Hamza, who had gone down hard, taking the struggling girl with him, and hitting the back of his head on the wooden floor. Although he hadn't lost consciousness, he had unsteadily left the room, and Anton had heard him retching moments later.

Now alone with Emma, Anton continued to try to subdue her. The duct tape over her mouth, which at least muted her yells and screams, also effectively restricted her from breathing through her mouth. Anton felt that she had tired sooner because of that, and was grateful.

When Hamza went down, Anton had become furious at their captive. In his efforts to subdue her without assistance, he resorted to slamming her head against the wall, the bedpost, and the small nightstand. In so doing he not only succeeded in stunning her, he broke her nose, causing it to bleed. Paying little attention to her condition, Anton had merely grabbed her by her waist, and slung her onto the bed. He had then turned his attention to Hamza. While he was occupied with assisting his retching partner to the toilet, Emma Schiller had aspirated blood, swallowed blood, choked, vomited, and subsequently suffocated.

Anton discovered her condition when he re-entered the room some ten minutes after leaving her.

He shook her shoulder. "Wake up, whore."

There was no response. Worse yet, the woman's head lolled about as he shook her, and her fingernails were turning blue. Anton felt as if he, too, had been kicked in the groin.

"Wake up . . ." he said, as he tore the duct tape from her mouth. A trickle of blood mixed with vomit drained out, between her bluish lips. He checked for a carotid pulse, as he looked at her wide open eyes. The pupils were, as the doctors would have said, fixed and dilated. There was no doubt in his mind. She was dead.

He'd been trained in CPR, and it occurred to him that she might be saved even yet. He looked again at the contents of her mouth, and decided he could more easily deal with her death.

His mind was racing. Dimly, he realized three things. First, Emma was dead, or as good as. Secondly, he had been the sole cause of her death. And last, it was a week too soon according to their instructions. Instructions from people who he was convinced had the will and the capability to kill him for his mistake.

He found himself back in the loo, staring down at Hamza on the floor by the toilet, his mind moving so fast that he was hardly aware of having walked there. "Bugger," said Anton.

Hamza, in considerable pain, looked up, and said nothing.

"Best get up," said Anton. "The bitch's dead."

"What?" came painfully and incredulously from Hamza.

"You did her, mate," said Anton. "She's bloody well deceased."

Hamza's features contorted, not with pain, but with fear. "No . . . I didn't. . . ."

"Well, she's dead," said Anton, feeling his composure beginning to return. "I know I didn't kill her. She must've hit her head when the two of you took the tumble."

"No," said Hamza, horrified. "I didn't . . . I couldn't. . . ." His head was still foggy with pain, now jolted by fear, and he was struggling to remember if he'd even hit her above the midsection. He only remembered hanging on to her by her waist, then her legs, and then the blinding pain when she'd twisted away and he'd been kicked, and both of them had hit the floor.

"Well, I couldn't hit her in the fuckin' head, now could I? I was holding onto it with both hands." Anton's thoughts were beginning to coalesce, as Hamza's confusion deepened. "Well, I know I couldn't have done it, I never struck her . . . you must have."

Hamza struggled to his feet. Nausea swept over him, but he refused to retch again. The pain was too great. "No," he managed to get out, as he hobbled into the bedroom. "No, I think . . . no. . . ." He looked at Emma. There was no doubt in his mind that she was, indeed, dead. She seemed somehow deflated, an object more than a person. How could he have killed her? Confronted with the fact of her death, and what was to him the obvious fact that Anton had, truly, been holding her by her head, he was left with it being his own action. He didn't remember doing anything like striking her head, but the pain had been so intense, he couldn't remember anything immediately after she'd kicked him.

"I didn't . . . I don't remember. I didn't hit her in the head. You let go, for her to hit the floor. What are we going to do?" he said, as much to himself as to Anton.

Anton now took complete charge of their joint thinking. "I bloody well let go, I didn't want her to get my stones as well. But you took her right down. Don't try to blame me, mate."

"I didn't mean to . . . imply that." He stared down at the dead body of Emma Schiller. "I don't know what to do," he said, weakly. "Marwan . . . Allah have mercy. She's dead."

"Worried are you? Well, me, too, but I'll stick by you. There are ways around that. We just have to show a fresh dead body on that date. But one that we killed then, right?"

Hamza stared at him, uncomprehending.

"We claim we killed her a few days from now . . . get it? We wait . . . then do her after the 21st, as far as anyone knows. We can control that. We can fucking well shoot her a few hours before that Mr. Kazan comes to make sure we did it."

"But, but she's dead. She's dead now. . . ."

"Well, bloody hell, let's just freeze her. Get her out a day or so before he comes, let her thaw, then just bloody well execute her, man, and she'll look fresh from the market."

Hamza just stared at him.

"And it gives us *time*, mate. Thinking time is what we need right now, agreed?"

Hamza nodded his head. That much he could agree with wholeheartedly. "But . . . but won't they be able to tell?"

"What do you think Kazan is going to do? Whip out a bloody knife and perform a sodding autopsy on the slag?"

"Uh. . . . No, I . . . no. Not if we do it right, and we just tell him what she did . . . because they were late. Not our fault. . . ." His mind was beginning to shut itself away from reality. "We must freeze her."

"It's brilliant, ain't it? Just put her on hold, so to speak."

"Wait . . ." said Hamza. "No, it won't work. It won't because Marwan will be coming back for her *before* then. He has a plan. To save her . . ." he said, and he started to cry.

Anton slammed him in the shoulder. "No bloody crying! Marwan said we move her today, right?"

Hamza nodded.

"So, we bloody well move her. He isn't going to contact us for a few days. We get her somewhere else, and we say we were unable to contact him and tell where she was. It's his bloody fault then. Marwan can piss off, far as I'm concerned. He's no bloody threat at all. It's that Mr. Kazan we got to impress, he's the one that'll kill us if things go wrong. Do you see?"

Hamza nodded. He did. Clearly.

"Be happy," said Anton. "All we got to do is give her a ride now. The hard part's done, for sure."

"What?"

"Well, look on the bright side, will you? At least we don't have to kill her, now do we?"

*   *   *

The only freezer available was the small top loading one in the kitchen. They tried to think of a way to get her out of the flat, to a place with a larger freezer, but there was no way they were about to carry her out the door in a recognizable fashion.

"We can't muck about here," said Anton. "If we wait, shell stiffen up, and we'd have to wait days until she gets loose again." He picked the little freezer up, inverted it, and dumped the contents on the floor. "Here we go . . ."

It had been a tight fit. They'd had to remove her clothing, because it tended to bind, and kept her from folding enough to get her in. After trying head first and feet first, they found that, by stuffing her in buttocks first, folding her arms tightly across her chest, and then pressing her knees to her chest as well, and by pushing on her feet . . .

"There," said Anton, when they had her shoved in as far as they could. "She fits."

About five inches of feet and the very top of her head protruded above the top opening lid.

"That's not good enough," said Hamza. "Look . . . she sticks out."

"Close the lid. We take turns sitting on it until she gets frozen. Then it'll stay in place as long as we want. It'll work."

And so it did. They traded off sitting on the lid about every half hour. During one of his turns, Anton began discussing her body.

"Her tits were smaller than I'd like. How about you?"

"Do not say that! We must respect her. She is *dead*."

"You killed her," said Anton. "You respect her. But she's just an American whore. Be truthful. Didn't you think they were too small?"

Hamza held his hands over his ears. "Stop saying that. Don't say that. Don't talk about her that way."

Anton grinned. "Didn't color her hair, though, did she?"

Hamza started toward the door.

"Don't run off and leave *me* here to hatch this bloody egg," said Anton. "She's yours, all yours. Don't forget that!"

Hamza turned slowly, defeated. "I assume all responsibility. But I owe her a debt, and she must not be mocked. I took her life . . . I must protect her honor."

Anton looked incredulous. "Honor? American women have no honor."

"Do this for me."

Anton thought for a moment. He was now certain that he'd convinced Hamza that he was the killer. Excellent, he thought. He had every intention of telling Mr. Kazan that Hamza had, indeed, killed the hostage. If Hamza believed that himself, ever so much better for Anton. Satisfied, he said, "Yes. I will. For you. I am sorry."

That had been the end of the first half of the disaster. The second half occurred the next evening, November 12th, when Emma was pretty solidly frozen, and they could take her out of the flat in the small freezer.

Both young men had decided that it would be extremely uncomfortable for them if Marwan, or worse, Mr. Kazan, paid them an unexpected visit and found out what had happened. Hamza had the bright idea that they could drive somewhere remote, find an accommodation, and rent a room until the 21st.

"As long as it has electricity, we can keep her there."

"What about whoever cleans the room," asked Anton.

"You can refuse that sort of thing. We can't stay here."

"Too true. Right, then, but we can't take her on your motor bike. We need a car."

"My mother has one," said Hamza. "Down in Portsmouth. I could go down and get it."

"I ain't staying here with this bitch-sickle," said Anton. "Not and have you forget to return."

"We can't both go. And my mother would never let you have her car," said Hamza.

"Sod your mum, then. I'll get us the wheels." Anton put on his jacket, and headed for the door. "Be ready to go as soon as I get back. It won't do to be waiting around. We'll need to move fast." With that, he was gone.

Hamza was beginning to appreciate the apparent loyalty of Anton, and his resourcefulness. He hated the attitude toward Emma, but there was just so much he could do about that.

What Hamza didn't understand was that Anton felt very strongly that Marwan liked Hamza much more than he liked Anton; and that Marwan would be more likely to suspect that Anton was lying about what had happened to Emma. Anton was staying with Hamza for the sole purpose of protecting his own interests. His loyalty was to himself.

In less than an hour, Anton returned to the apartment. They struggled with carrying the freezer down a flight of steps, and then out the back entrance to the alleyway. Carefully, they set the container down on the curb, and Anton pointed to a green Honda Jazz. "Care to take her for a spin?"

"Where did you get that?!"

"Borrowed it, in a manner of speaking. Let me pop the back, and we'll just set her in. . . ."

"You mean you stole it?"

"Nah," said Anton, being deliberately offhanded and nonchalant about it. This ensured that Hamza was convinced it was stolen, and increased Anton's value in Hamza's eyes. In point of fact, he'd walked to his married sister's flat, pounded on the door, and convinced her to let him borrow her car.

Once Emma was packed, they decided that, since Hamza had his mother in the south, they'd go northward. Just to throw off a possible search by Mr. Kazan.

"Where?" asked Hamza, who was relying more and more on Anton to make his decisions.

"The A1 gets us all the way up north, and won't go through some of the more crowded places like the M1 does. Newcastle upon Tyne is it then? I went there once, with a friend. Fine place to get lost."

"All right," said Hamza. "It's a very long way. . . ."

"Even better," said Anton, pulling into the street. "I don't drive much, you navigate."

"I haven't a map. . . ."

"Sod the map, I can get to the A1. Just keep me on track is all."

Northward they went. All the way to Stevenage, just fifty kilometers north. Anton was hungry, Hamza would be much more comfortable with some sort of map, and they needed petrol.

Stevenage isn't a particularly large town, but at night, it's not too difficult to become lost. They'd been debating how long Emma would keep since she wasn't plugged in. Hamza wanted to get something to keep moisture from leaking out, and giving them away if they were stopped. Anton thought that was foolish.

"She's frozen solid," he said. "Won't thaw for hours and hours. Not to worry."

"How long is it going to take us to get to Newcastle upon Tyne? Eight hours?" His voice was rising in pitch.

"More like six," said Anton.

"Just pull off the road, we can do a scout. The map says that there's a Greenway petrol station on Cutty's Lane, just off our road . . . turn off at the next intersection. . . ."

Just to shut him up, Anton turned onto Broadhall Way.

"Now where?"

Hamza had his head buried in the map. "Left . . . to the north . . .

Monkswood Way, and then keep on, and then it becomes King George's Way, and then it's very close, to our right. . . . ."

"What? This is Monkswood already. How does this turn into . . ."

"Keep on!"

"Where . . . ?"

"There, back there, on the right!"

"Bloody hell, you've caused me to miss the turn," said Anton, failing to find a turn off King George's in time, and turning onto a street called Fairlands.

"Just wait . . . that's a drive down there . . . turn about . . . you could have, just then . . . then this one . . . pull in there and turn about."

As they entered a park area, Hamza saw a police car on their left, pulled into a parking zone. Anton was just slowing, preparing to turn into the same place, when Hamza alerted him.

"No, no, not here! Cop car!"

Anton, who had nearly slowed to a stop, accelerated, and turned to his right. It was a dead end, and re-tracing their course, they found themselves headed straight back to the police car.

"Fuck this!" said Anton, and stopped, reversed, and tried to make it into a small paved area behind them.

"Not here, he can see us here!"

Anton then started forward, they went past the police car at a legal speed, and then turned quickly to the left as they re-entered the street.

"He's behind us. Oh, oh. Oh, no! He's following us," said Hamza. "Act normal!"

"We'll dump the car," said Anton. "You listening to me? We dump the car, and we get out and run in opposite directions, and meet up . . . over there," he said, pointing to a mall area.

As he pointed, he swerved. Blue lights came on behind them.

"Fuck me! He's on us. Hang on!" The car swerved abruptly onto a narrow park path, then over a bump, and back into the park lane. The police car took a more direct route, and was now closer to them than before. They could hear a siren.

"When I say run, get out!"

"We can't leave her here. Our prints are on the freezer!"

"You can bloody well stay and wipe them, then!" yelled Anton, slamming on the brakes, and stopping the car. "Run!"

They met in the mall parking lot.

Hamza gave Anton a hug, as soon as he was sure it was him.

"Don't! Stand back, don't draw attention, you idiot!"

Hamza did as he was told. Both were exhilarated by their escape, and the ramifications of the last few minutes hadn't sunk in.

"That's the train station over there," said Anton, pointing. "See?"

"Yes," said Hamza.

"We go over individually. You go down over that way, and I'll meet you there in about ten minutes."

"Why can't we go together?"

"They're looking for two men, stupid. We don't attract as much attention alone. We can melt into the crowd at the station. It's simple. We just get there alone."

When they saw each other again, they were the only two people on the upper level of the station. Otherwise, the red trimmed covered area was deserted. Even the concession area was closing down. They had to ask the clerk for directions to purchase tickets.

Once down to platform level, there was a young couple, also waiting for the train to London. They had to stand there for ten minutes, in full view of the whole world, had it cared to look. It didn't.

They got in to King's Cross Station well after midnight. They were forced to spend their last cash on a cab. It was either that, or walk nearly five kilometers to Hanadi's flat in Brewery Square, just across the Thames from the Tower.

When they arrived at the correct address, they buzzed the intercom at the entrance that bore her name card. It hadn't occurred to them that she might be married, or that she might live with roommates.

A sleepy female voice answered, after a few rings, "Yes?"

"Marwan has sent us," said Hamza. Which was, in a sense, true.

There was a long silence, long enough that Anton pushed the buzzer again.

"Who are you," asked the voice, more alert.

"Anton and Hamza, we have your card, remember?"

She did remember, because they were two of four people Marwan had introduced to her. "When I press the lock, come to the top of the stair, I'm the apartment on the left."

Hanadi, while putting on sweats and stepping into sandals, was assuming that Marwan was in some sort of difficulty with the police. Mentally, she was listing the things that he could have been arrested for. Ever since the BBC broadcast the first of the tapes of the hostage Emma Schiller, she had been dreading the midnight call. Marwan hadn't told her anything more than they were taking a "willing" hostage, and that they were going to stage a "mock execution." Terrified, because she knew full well that the penalty would be the same, or nearly so, if they actually did take a hostage and then claim to kill her. She had come very close to calling her father and seeking advice, but had resisted. She didn't want it to sound to him as if she weren't truly committed to her course of action. Many times, he had told her to choose her positions wisely, and then to adhere to them. Many times.

There was a soft knock on her door. She looked out the peep hole, recognized the two bedraggled young men, slipped the three deadlocks, and said, "Come in."

They were obviously upset, and excited, and had not the faintest idea of what to do. In a rush, they told her about being pursued by the police, and abandoning their car.

"Stevenage . . . that's north, isn't it?"

"About an hour's drive," said Anton.

"I'm not truly clear about what you need," she said. "I don't understand what you were doing in Stevenage late at night. Or at any time."

Hamza inhaled deeply, looked at Anton, and said, "We had her. In the back."

Hanadi's insides began to turn cold. "Who? Who did you have?"

"You know, the hostage. Emma Schiller."

Hanadi swallowed hard. "Would you like some coffee? I need to think." She moved toward the stove. "So the police have her?"

"Safe bet," said Anton.

"When you told Marwan," she said, assuming that he had truly sent them to her, "what suggestions did he have?" She was vaguely surprised that he had not called her before their arrival, but knew security must be carefully observed. Perhaps the time was not right.

"We, uh, didn't call anybody," said Hamza. "We just came here because you were the solicitor, you know."

Hanadi filled the kettle. "Marwan doesn't know?"

"No. Ah, we really don't think it would be good to call him yet."

"I disagree. He must be contacted," she said, scolding like a mother. "After all, this Emma person must be telling the police everything she knows."

"Not likely they'll learn much there," said Anton.

"I do not know her," said Hanadi, "but I know she is an American student. She will tell all she knows, believe me."

Her two fellow cell members exchanged glances. "No," said Hamza, sadly. "She won't tell them anything . . . because she is dead."

Hanadi felt faint. She reached out and held on to the counter as she said, "She is dead?"

They both nodded.

She was irrationally terrified that Marwan had shot her. "Who killed her?"

"He did," was Anton's instant response. He nodded toward Hamza.

That was even more of a surprise for her. She turned to face them squarely, leaning against the counter for support. "You were driving about with the body of a woman you had murdered in the back of your car? They can trace it, they'll know it was yours. . . ."

"No sweat," said Anton. "It wasn't our car. We stole it."

Hanadi, whose area of expertise was in contracts, had appeared in criminal court exactly one time, representing a client's son on a traffic charge. Here they had handed her a murder and a felony theft.

"Your fingerprints," she said, dazed. "They will find those . . ."

"I told you we should wipe the freezer," said Hamza.

"And I told you to bloody well hang about and do it yourself. Sod off!" said Anton.

"Freezer?"

They told her everything, then. Every detail, even the ones they'd only assumed. And, of course, on the part of Anton, the ultimate lie that Hamza had killed Emma. They included Mr. Kazan, the taping, and the most significant of all the details, at least to Hanadi. They told her that Marwan had ordered them to keep the girl hostage, at least until the 21st.

Hanadi was stunned. These things were never part of the original plan.

"You must mean that Mr. Kazan told you to keep her. . . ."

"No, no, it was Marwan. To my face," said Hamza.

By now, they were seated at her kitchen table, drinking coffee. "You cannot stay here," she said, as the situation began to truly sink in. "I can't be any use to you if I am in the jail with you. She is no longer alive, so she can no longer exonerate you by saying she was actually cooperating."

"Do you really think that Marwan could have pulled that off?" Anton glared at her. "At that last taping . . . I did not get the impression that he could pull that off."

She continued as if he had never spoken. "You cannot stay here at all. Where will you go?"

They had no idea.

Her legal training began taking over as she sat with them, and so she said, "We need to think. To have a plan. You must go somewhere they won't think to look."

"Hide. Oh, that's absolutely fuckin' brilliant," said Anton. "Did they teach you that in Law School?"

She glared at him. "By logically, I mean you have to *think every-thing through*, and do it quickly. A process that is obviously unfamiliar to you. If you want me to help, we must *think* together. Do you understand?"

Neither man said anything.

"Therefore," said Hanadi, "we need to establish criteria. Where they won't think to look. Where you can stay for some time. Where you have access to us, and we to you. That means we must stock it with supplies, and that we must establish a contact procedure." She stopped. "Do you comprehend any of what I've just said?"

"Yes," said Hamza, appreciatively. "I just don't have any place other than my real flat, or my mother's in Portsmouth." He looked at his partner. "You?"

Anton considered a second. "What about the place where we went with Marwan? When he took us to the old tube station . . . on Down Street?"

Hanadi expressed some surprise. "He took *you* there, too?" She had gone with him on a guided tour of the old station. He'd explained to her that these tours were quite rare, never admitting more than a half dozen people, and were very difficult to arrange. He'd said that he had some influence because he was writing a book about the Underground. She couldn't imagine anyone letting them in at all, not to mention allowing two members of a tour to slip away and remain below ground. She said as much to the two young men at her table.

"Tour?" said Anton. "Not likely. He's got his own way down. He goes to a building, then the sub-basement, was some sort of a shelter years back. And presto. Through the wall and into the tube."

She was astonished.

"He said that he'd been told about it when he was chatting up the owner," said Hamza. "The tube wall was only five feet from the sub-basement. Told the owner he was up to researching the tubes for a class at University. Nobody knows about it but him, I think. And the owner."

"And us," said Anton.

"Why not just stay in the basement?" asked Hanadi, reasonably.

"Because the bloody owners go down there sometimes, your honor. It ain't abandoned like the station. You have to *think everything through*," he said, with a smirk.

She blushed.

"It's a restaurant, upstairs at the street level," said Hamza. "They store vegetables and things in the basement. They have a key they leave for the delivery trucks. It's under a stone in the rear, a little dock."

"It's too close to Buckingham Palace," said Hanadi. "They'll be watching."

"Oh, bugger fuck," said Anton. "It's not close enough to matter. You can't even see bloody Buckingham Palace from there."

"And, since it's a restaurant," said Hamza, "we might be able to borrow some food, late at night. They'll never miss it."

"Steal it, you mean," said Anton. "Just say what you mean. For a bloody killer, you're so careful. . . ."

"Shut up!" said Hamza too loudly, almost immediately regaining control of himself. "Don't say that. It was an accident."

"A fine difference that'll make," said Anton. "Ask her."

Hanadi looked sad as she said, "That is true, I'm sorry to say. After kidnapping her, to kill her even accidentally is a murder." She looked to Anton. "For both of you, in fact."

That settled him down.

Mr. Kazan, whose true name was Ahmed Bhatti, was the proprietor of a small antiquities shop on Great Portland Street, just a few blocks south of Regent's Park in Marylebone. He rose at 06:45, just like every day for the last thirty years, and made his morning coffee. Today, he thought, would be the day to begin to move the plan to the next level. At approximately 7:10, shortly before leaving for his place of business, he placed a telephone call to Chief Inspector John Bassingham, New Scotland Yard Special Branch, at his residence. Chief Inspector Bassingham's wife, Molly, answered.

"The Bassinghams'," she said, brightly.

"May I speak with John?"

"Certainly," she said. She thought she recognized the voice as belonging to one of John's 'Baker Street Irregulars,' as she called them. She simply could not abide the other terms that were applied to police informants.

As he waited for John to come to the phone, Mr. Kazan reflected on the purpose of his mission. Imad had been the first to propose recruiting a non-Islamic Englishman into the group, to be used operationally. The particular operation would also be of an experimental variety, whereby the operation would merely serve as a diversion from the real operation. The plan had been opposed from the outset by the fact that it was wisely considered a mistake to trust a non-Islamic associate with a major operational role.

Imad had persisted. He said that it would give the British pause, that it would create the image of the movement being more universal, and not confined to the Islamic world. Anything, he maintained, that disconcerted the infidel was a bonus.

One of the attendant imams had rather condescendingly explained to Imad that those benefits would only accrue if the Englishman were exposed. Mr. Kazan would never forget the sly, satisfied smile on Imad's face.

"Yes?" said John, a few moments later.

"It is Ahmed. How are you this fine morning?"

"Absolutely brilliant," said the Chief Inspector. "Yourself?"

"As well as can be expected," said Mr. Kazan. "Time passes all too quickly."

"I don't suppose this would be regarding a bargain coin, would it?" That was the code phrase that Chief Inspector Bassingham always used to indicate that the line was clear, and that he was alone.

"Unfortunately," said Mr. Kazan, "all that is new is an Antoninous Pius Sestertius, just bronze, I'm afraid. I can let you steal it for ten pounds." The type of Roman coin varied from conversation to conversation, but the ten pound steal was the confirmation that he, too, was unattended.

It is worth noting at this juncture that Mr. Kazan had not been associated with any particular terrorist group until the late '80s. He was not a plant, nor was he the result of long-term planning by anyone but himself. He had gotten involved with certain terrorist related groups for financial gain, being paid well to launder funds. His primary connection with terrorism had been his cousin in Tripoli, who had been killed during the Israeli occupation of Beirut in 1982, while with the Palestine Liberation Organization. Although no member of the PLO himself, Mr. Kazan discovered he had a predisposition to be both anti-Israeli and anti-American.

"So. What have you got for me today?" asked Bassingham.

"The unfortunate American girl, the one who was taken hostage?"

"Yes?"

"Allah grant that she be well," said Mr. Kazan. "I have heard that a group of crazy ones have taken her. You know that, of course. But I was also told that the leader of this group is an Englishman."

"Really?"

"His name, I am told, is Robert Northwood. I believe he is a professor of English here in London."

"Really?" This time Chief Inspector Bassingham spoke just a bit more loudly.

"This is only what I am told. I, myself, of course have no knowledge of such things."

"Of course." Chief Inspector Bassingham thought quickly. "That *is* surprising," he said. "Any idea how he got himself involved in such a sordid business?"

"I hesitate to say this, because it is only a suspicion," said Mr. Kazan. He paused for effect. "I believe he is the actual leader of the group."

"Really?"

"This is based only on one small statement. I cannot be certain, and I mean no offense."

"Naturally not," said the Chief Inspector.

"That is all I know," said Mr. Kazan, apologetically. "Do you wish me to ask further in this matter?"

"As always," said the Chief Inspector.

"I will pass to you what I can discover," said Mr. Kazan.

"You've done well, once again."

"Than you," said Mr. Kazan, letting a bit of his true pride into his voice. "I hope that it will benefit you."

The Chief Inspector put down the phone. Ahmed had originally been an informant in an embezzlement case many years before, and they had maintained an occasional relationship since then. When Bassingham had been assigned to Special Branch, and in particular SO-13, which was the counter-terrorism unit, Ahmed had been of use on two occasions. This made him a reliable informant. That he was a confidential informant went without saying. As such, his true identity was recorded, he was assigned a number, and he was never referred to by anything other than that number in any communication.

The inspector picked the phone back up, dialing another Inspector.

"Freddy? John here. Six zed one nine just rang me up. Do a check on a Robert Northwood, would you? He's likely an English Professor, somewhere here in London. We'll meet in my office before nine."

Mr. Kazan, the most urgent business of the day already completed, left his flat and walked downstairs to his antiquities shop, confident that he was in control of the situation. He was not, of course, aware that Emma was dead. Neither was he aware that a particular abandoned tube station, adjacent to a restaurant well known to him, had been compromised by Imad's ego. Imad had told Mr. Kazan that it was he who had discovered the proximity of the tube station to the restaurant, and that it was he who had visited the tube station. Imad *had* told the truth when he said that he was the one who had the idea of using the restaurant as a storage facility, which would permit access to the abandoned tube station, and an exit to the surface completely separate from and un-related to the Camel restaurant; and that he himself had persuaded the Islamic owner to allow him access to the storage basement. It had not been a conceit on the part of Imad to claim the complete credit; he had done so primarily because he thought the locations so perfect that he feared that Mr. Kazan would prevent their use if he had known the origin had been Robert Northwood.

In the latter assumption, Imad had been entirely correct.

Once in his shop, Mr. Kazan waited for another of his "special customers," a certain Nadeem whom he had known for many years, and who was the orchestrator of the planned use of the stored explosives. Nadeem had coordinated the two plans; the first being the diversionary kidnapping of the American woman, which had appeared so foolish to Nadeem that he considered it ideal to draw attention from the British Security away from the primary attack. The participants, with the exception of Imad, were entirely dispensable, and Imad would be pulled from the group prior to the start of the operation.

Nadeem's masterpiece was the primary attack. That attack targeted the British Royal Family, and involved what Mr. Kazan considered the coup of the century. Nadeem had managed to insinuate three of his fighters into the kitchen staff at Buckingham Palace. It had taken two years to accomplish this feat, but the personnel were in place, the explosives were within reach, and all that remained was the execution of the attack itself.

As the financial representative of the men hiding in the Afghan mountains, Mr. Kazan's approval of the plan was required, and he had approved with great enthusiasm. Nadeem and Mr. Kazan were in some ways a fortunate mix; in other ways, they were not. Nadeem was an adaptable thinker, and his operational experience had left him able to improvise in the face of a changing situation. He was also possessed of a fierce emotional intensity, coupled with a religious fanaticism that was necessary to inspire suicide bombers. In this mode, he was susceptible to precipitate action which was not necessarily the best course. If he had been the subject of a briefing given at MI5 or the FBI, his primary motivation would have been considered religious.

Mr. Kazan was a set piece man. He would form an image in his mind of the way a plan was to unfold, and any deviation from that pre-conceived image would cause him some alarm. He was also of a practical, patient outlook that had been responsible for his success as a double agent. In an MI5 or FBI briefing that considered Nadeem's motivation religious, Mr. Kazan's primary motivation would have been considered political.

The proposed attack, or strike as Nadeem referred to it, had originally been planned for the Queen's birthday in 2004. In an attempt to take advantage of an unexpected opportunity, the plan had been quickly changed in mid-October to coincide with the US presidential visit in November. It was now set for the 21st of November, 2003. On that day, the majority of the Royal Family, or at least those who counted to Nadeem, would be in residence, having gathered for the occasions involving the presidential visit. On the 21st, President Bush was to leave London, and travel to Sedgefield, in the north of England, to meet with Prime Minster Blair. According to Nadeem, on that day the withdrawal of the US Secret Service from the area of Buckingham Palace and the transfer of many British Security Service personnel to the north, coupled with the inevitable fatigue and relaxation that would follow the general stand down of the enormous number of additional British security personnel assigned the presidential visit, would create the perfect opportunity to execute the plan.

Some of the explosives from the restaurant basement, safely disguised and concealed in their cheese boxes, had been in the Palace kitchen area for more than a month. Smeared with a thick layer of goat's cheese, they had easily passed the inspection that included a bomb dog.

Special pockets had been completed for the three intruders, sewn into their working clothes, which would enable each of them to carry upwards of ten kilograms of Semtex on their person.

More of the explosive was to be loaded into a small truck which made daily deliveries of fresh fruit to the mini-mart that occupied one half the old entrance to the Down Street station. The explosives were to be transferred from the sub-basement of the restaurant, up the emergency stair, and out the emergency exit that could only be opened from the inside.

Once loaded, the truck would proceed to the north wall of the garden of Buckingham Palace, and be detonated. Although this would very likely not endanger the Royal Family in any way, it assuredly *would* have the effect of over-stretching the security personnel assigned to the Palace itself.

In accordance with the standard drill, the Royals themselves would be taken to a secure area within the Palace. Concentrated in that fashion, they would be easy targets for the three bogus employees. The first was to self-detonate in the closest possible proximity to the first security obstacle he encountered. The second, who was to be ten seconds behind him, was to clear the way for the third, who was to rush into the presence of the Royals and blow himself, and them, to pieces. If the security was as thin as they hoped, there was a strong possibility that the second suicide bomber would be the one to reach the Royal Family; in that case, the third man was to wait to see if there were any survivors.

All three bombers were to detonate their explosives if detained. Regardless of any damage to the Royal Family, the fact of three explosions within the Palace was certain to make a point.

This was why Emma Schiller was to be kept alive until the 21st. Her diversion needed to be credible up until the last moment. That was why the final tape would demand a meeting with the US President. The very mention of his name would ensure a larger portion of British Security would be traveling to the north of England on or before the 21st, in order to increase protection. But to do this, it was critical that she be demonstrably alive on that day.

Chapter 13

I'd had a bad night's sleep. Carson had had an even tougher one, because at least once I had sort of come around to a familiar sound. I remembered sitting up in bed, the room infused with a flickering glow, and finding Carson sitting at the desk playing Spider Solitaire on his laptop. I let it go, and got back to sleep eventually.

I have no idea what woke me at 05:48, for God's sake. I just sat up, and there I was. It was one of those awakenings when you know that, tired or not, you aren't going to be able to go back to sleep.

I looked into the next bed, and saw that Carson was out like a light. I was as quiet as I could be in the bathroom, but the shower must have done the trick. When I came out, he was sitting in his skivvies, looking out the window with the TV on.

"Nice day," he said. "Just like yesterday. Not supposed to rain. About fifty-five degrees or so."

"Good. Shower's all yours."

"What are we gonna tell the girls?"

"About Stevenage? Not much," I said. "If we start a story, we'll just get into deep trouble. Just keep on acting like we want to find her, I guess."

"Yeah." He stood. "The water for the instant's still pretty hot."

He seemed really down. "Something getting to you?"

"Just about everything," he said. "You seem to be doing okay."

"I don't dwell on it," I said. "I mean, it isn't like the case is over, or anything. The killer is out there. Or killers. I think we should do what we can to get information from the girls, stuff they might not have thought was important. We can do that."

"Sure." He didn't sound convinced.

While he was in the shower, I took a few minutes to plug my lap-top in, and then begin to write my notes for yesterday. I wanted to make sure I had everything down I could get before talking to a bunch of people. I've found that the more you talk about recent develop-ments, the more you begin to edit and focus on certain facts. Then it's easy for what you begin to see as peripheral data to get shoved deep into the background. Do the notes first, and you can talk about them all you want without having the contents of a conversation bias your reporting.

When I finished with my notes, the first email I sent was to my favorite dispatcher, supersally@nationcounty.sheriff.gov. This is what I said:

SALLY, WE'RE GOING TO NEED LOTS OF DATA ON THE CASE WHERE WE WERE IN THE BARN WITH GEORGE AND HESTER. WE NEED THE FILE. THE TAPE SHOWING EMMA TELLS US THAT THERE ARE VERY LIKELY TERRORISTS INVOLVED. I DON'T THINK THEY'RE THE SAME BUNCH, BUT I WANT TO MAKE SURE. I ESPECIALLY NEED NAMES AND CODE NAMES FOR THE ONES WE KNOW. IF WE HAVE TO ASK A FAVOR OF GEORGE, SEND ME HIS PHONE NUMBER AND I'LL DO IT.

TELL LAMAR I'M SENDING HIM AN EMAIL. BE SURE HE CHECKS.

FOOD IS GOOD. WEATHER IS NOT RAINY.

CARL

The second one was to Sue, at housemans@maitland.k12.ia.us; and at cshouseman@aol.com, just to make sure she got it either at home or at work.

HI. ALL IS AS WELL AS CAN BE EXPECTED. THE BRITS ARE DOING A FINE JOB. ASSUME YOU HAVE SEEN THE TAPE. I THINK THERE WILL BE ANOTHER ONE. I WOULD STRONGLY SUGGEST THAT YOU NOT WATCH, AS VICTIMS TEND TO GET WORSE LOOKING AS TIME PASSES.

JANE IS DOING WELL. SHE'S REALLY WORRIED,
THOUGH. I THINK SHE'LL BE FINE, BUT IT MIGHT
TAKE A WHILE. VICKY SEEMS OKAY TOO.
I DON'T HAVE MUCH HOPE FOR A REALLY GOOD
OUTCOME HERE. I HATE TO SAY THAT.
CAN'T WAIT TO COME HOME. MISS YOU.

LOVE
CARL

The third went to bossman@nationcounty.sheriff.ia.gov. That would
be Lamar. Our network kept anyone from reading his email but him,
with a password. So, if he remembered to check and if he remembered
his password, he'd get my message. If not, Sally would tell him to check
after she got mine. Anyway, I wrote to Lamar:

LAMAR,
NEW SCOTLAND YARD IS DOING A GOOD JOB
OVER HERE. SEE IF YOU CAN CONTACT GEORGE
POLLARD AT FBI, AND SEE IF DCI CAN PUT ME IN
CONTACT WITH HESTER GORSE. GET WHAT INFOR-
MATION YOU CAN FROM THEM REGARDING THAT
LITTLE THING WE HAD IN THE BARN.
THINGS HERE DON'T LOOK ALL THAT GOOD FOR
EMMA, SO TRY TO PREPARE FOLKS BACK THERE FOR
THE WORST. THERE IS A CHANCE THERE WILL BE
ANOTHER TAPE RELEASED. I ASKED SALLY TO GET
THAT TERRORISM CASE FILE OVER HERE ASAP. I
KNOW IT COSTS, BUT IT'S REALLY, REALLY IMPOR-
TANT TO DO A FED EX NEXT DAY THING. REGULAR
AIRMAIL WILL TAKE TOO LONG, AND THIS IS UR-
GENT. REALLY URGENT.
GONNA NEED A VACATION WHEN THIS IS DONE.

CARL.

I needed the names from that file, the aliases, and physical descrip-
tions. I was about as certain as I could be that this wasn't connected
with anything we'd had, but you always have to check.

So much for correspondence. It was, according to my calculations,
about one in the afternoon in Iowa. Either that or one in the morning,

but I was just too tired to play with the math. I logged all three emails in my calendar, and sat back and looked out the window, just like Carson had done. The instant coffee, in those little foil tubes, is pretty good. I found that if you put both the caffeinated and the decaffeinated portions together, you got a fairly strong tasting cup of coffee. I was just finishing my cup when Carson emerged.

"You call the girls yet?"

"No. I'll give it at least another half hour."

I heard a familiar clopping sound as I turned back to the window. There was a large group of horsemen coming down High Street in a long column of twos. They turned, and headed into the park area. The riders had military uniforms on, sort of a drab green, and some of them had yellow reflective vests on. It finally dawned on me that it was Horse Guards. It had to be. Taking their horses for exercise. I thought that was pretty cool, and thought to grab my camera just after they were out of sight.

It was about 6:45 when I called Jane and Vicky. They were just up, and getting ready to come in our way for class. I told them Carson and I would do our thing with the London police, and that we'd try to keep busy. We were to meet them at about 4:30 up in Highgate for supper.

Carson and I went downstairs and ate breakfast in the hotel. Just as I was leaning back, pleasantly full, sipping a good cup of coffee, and wondering if I'd be able to go back upstairs and catch an hour's sleep or so, this woman came in to the dining room, looked around, and homed in on us like she was radar guided.

"Pardon me, but you're Americans, aren't you?" Her voice told me she sure wasn't. Very English.

She was in the American tourist uniform of blue jeans and tennis shoes just like we were, so I'm not exactly sure how she knew it was us. Later, I got the impression we'd been fingered by the concierge, but I never did find out.

"Yes, we are," I said.

"My name is Sarah Mitchell. Would you be here regarding the missing American girl?"

Nothing like getting right to the point, I thought, so I said, "Yeah. And you need to know that for . . . what reason?"

"I'm a correspondent for the *National Sun Express*," she said. She seemed to think we were familiar with that paper, and I didn't discourage her.

"Okay . . . and . . ."

"I'd like to interview you."

"We don't have a thing to say," I said.

"Why don't we just talk a moment," she said, sitting at the table. "I may have some information you should have."

I was curious. I was also my normal urbane self. "Uh . . . well, you want like . . . some coffee or something?" I was pretty budget conscious, too. I didn't want to offer breakfast.

She took the coffee offer. While she got out her PDA, I looked her over pretty closely. I guessed she was in her mid-thirties, or thereabouts. Pretty. Very close cropped brown hair. Long neck, long fingers. Nice sweater, medium brown. Although we were seated, I'd guessed her height at about five ten or so, when she walked over to the table.

"I understand you're a police officer in the US?"

I wondered who she'd been talking to. I had enough experience with the press in the US to know that denying that would only cause problems. Besides, she'd already said that she 'understood.'

"Yep."

"Bring your shootin' iron?"

I looked pointedly at her chest. "Are those real?"

I thought she might leave then, but instead she smiled brightly. "Point taken. Neither of us will dignify those questions with an answer, then."

"Okay. But, for the record, no I didn't. And we call them service weapons, when we refer to them. Not 'shootin' irons.' Do you have some sort of identification, or credential?"

I glanced at Carson, and he was still looking at her chest. He glanced at me, and shook his head very slightly.

She reached in her back pocket, and produced what looked like a credential, along with a business card. She gave me the card.

"How about yourself?"

I pulled out my badge case, and opened it. "All I got. . . ."

"Oh, that's a pretty one," she said, leaning a little toward Carson. "And are you an American cop, too, then?"

"I'm an attorney," he said.

"My," she said. "I don't suppose an attorney has a fancy star, does he? Well, then. Could I have your full names?"

"You said you had information you thought we should know," I said. "Let's go there first."

She sat back a little. "You knew that . . . Emma . . . was seeing a young man up in Highgate?"

"Yes." She looked a little disappointed at that.

"You work quickly," she said. "Then you also knew she was seeing one of her professors?"

"Sort of." In fact, I had not known that. Interesting.

"Do you know that he's an activist in a pro-Islamist cause?"

That ensured my cooperation. "No idea," I said.

"Well," she said, satisfied, "he is that. Does petitions and
marches and things to get some terrorist blokes released from Belmarsh. Interesting, no? He has at least the same focus as the group
that nabbed Emma. I can give you more, but I'll need an interview
in exchange."

"Why don't you go to the police with this?"

"They and I have . . . oh, let's just call it an adversarial relationship." She smiled. "Besides, I'm sure that the boys and girls in Special
Branch are way ahead of me."

I thought I could understand why. As she had been talking to me,
there had been a man at a table across the dining room, trying his best
to be subtle about working a small camera he kept pointed in our direction.

I nodded toward him. "He with you?"

She turned, as if there had been more than one. "Him? Yes," she
said, turning back. "That's Bobby. We've been doing stories together
off and on for years."

"Back home," I said, "the press usually asks before they take . . .
candid shots."

"That's quaint," she said. "You're from the heartland, aren't you?"

"Yep."

"I'm sure it's a very nice place, but it's likely not what you'd call
cosmopolitan, is it? The press here are somewhat different."

"Got it. Anyway, thanks for the information. Got any more good
stuff?"

"Not until after I get an interview." She smiled.

Although I was certain her demeanor was just part of her job, I
smiled back. She was an unexpected bright spot on a very bleak day.

"What do you want to know?"

She leaned forward. "Let's start off with why you're here. . . ."

This time, wisely, I left out the politics with Lamar. I just said that
he was concerned, and wanted to have someone over here to be of any
assistance to the Metropolitan Police. She bought that right away, and
I decided to leave the political part of the explanation out from then
on. It sure made it a lot easier.

"Now," she said, "intrepid investigative reporter that I am, I noticed that your last name is the same as one of Emma Schiller's roommates. What's that connection?"

"Jane Houseman's his daughter." Carson picks the damnedest times to contribute.

"Really? How remarkable. I mean, I'm sure it's a coincidence, after all?" She had kind of a twinkle in her eye when she said that.

"It just happened that way," I said. "It's a rural county, small population. We bump into relatives all the time." That sounded a little lame, even to me. Even though it was true.

She transitioned smoothly to Carson. "And you? Do you think your partner here needs legal council? Or that, maybe, one of the girls might?"

"No," he said. "I'm just concerned for the same reason that Carl's boss is." That was true, but without knowing the local politics of the thing, it sounded pretty lame, too.

We gave her a fairly good interview. We made absolutely no mention about Emma's death, or even the fact that we'd been talking to any authorities except the courtesy call from New Scotland Yard. I made sure to mention that we were very impressed with their efforts. We also went into the number of people in Nation County that were greatly concerned about Emma, and made it very clear that we had not known anything about her being held hostage until after we arrived in the UK.

The whole business ate up a good hour. About halfway through, I motioned to her photographer, and he joined us at our table. He seemed sincere, but not terribly interested in the case itself. We paid for his tea.

At the end of the interview, I said, "What's the name of this professor?"

"Pardon?"

"The one you said Emma was dating. The one whose name you said you'd give us after the interview."

"Oh. That one. Yes, it's Robert."

"Robert who?"

She smiled. "Best I can do. It's what I have."

I was sure she was lying. She wanted to keep the last name from us so she could use that as bait for the next interview. Too bad for her. I thought I already knew it.

After they thanked us and left, we found ourselves with much of the day ahead of us with nothing to do. There was no point in going back up to Highgate until we collected the girls after classes. We decided to see at least one sight. We started walking west, on High Street. Carson needed an adaptor for English current for his shaver. On the way, we stopped and bought our very own cell phone. The first person I called was Trowbridge, and gave him the new number.

Kensington Palace was right across the street. We walked through the park, which was, by remarkable coincidence known as Kensington Park, and found ourselves standing in front of the south gate. It was kind of bleak, with the leaves leaving the trees. The stark black wrought ironwork, with gilded tops, was nice. There were three small notes attached to the gate, each with a flower. Not the flood of flowers I remembered seeing on TV when Princess Diana died, but the gesture was still poignant. Especially since we'd found out that Emma was dead just last night.

After a few moments, Carson said, "Maybe we could do something more cheerful?"

"Yeah. Let's walk over this way. There's that big gold thing over there. Let's see what that is."

We passed a white statue of Queen Victoria at the intersection of two paths. We read the inscription, just to make sure.

"Wasn't she the one who was married to Prince Albert?"

Carson and I had gone to the same high school. "You read that in Lit class? About her as a young girl?"

"Yeah, I think I did. He was . . . from Saxe-Coburg-Gotha, I remember having to remember that for the final."

"The shit you think you'll never use," I said.

The big gold thing turned out to be the Albert Memorial. It had been raised after Albert's death, and was Queen Victoria's tribute to him. It was very impressive, and we spent about fifteen minutes reading the names of the scientists and trying to guess who the smaller figures were. We went down the steps of the memorial, re-crossed High Street, and found ourselves in front of an enormous, round brick building. The Royal Albert Hall.

"I wish somebody would memorialize me like this," said Carson. "She really must have thought highly of him."

We were both quiet, apparently having the same thought.

"We gotta do something for Emma, when this is done," I said.

"Absolutely."

"Something really nice." I looked back across the street to the gleaming memorial. "Really, really nice."

Washington, DC
Intelligence Briefing entitled: "Task, Collect, Process and Use"

The current group of terrorists are very much influenced by fundamentalist religious beliefs. Previous organizations such as the Red Brigade and Bader-Meinhoff, which were politically motivated and, although violent on what we would now consider a small scale, were more concerned with a message; the current group are motivated by religion and have as their central objective a large number of victims. Rather than campaigning for something that could be considered rightfully theirs, for example; these newer groups are more vengeful in nature, and will kill those who oppose them whether it gains them an advantage or not. It sometimes appears that their ultimate objective is to kill all who oppose them. This would have what they would consider the agreeable result that politics would be unnecessary.

The truly committed can justify any action as being the will of a supreme being, and therefore are able to suspend any social constraint they otherwise would feel toward another human. This serves to reduce their susceptibility to typical interrogation techniques.

This phenomenon has produced one other effect that is remarkable. Persuading those committed by religious purpose to abandon their cause is extremely difficult, if not impossible.

Chapter 14

Thursday, November 13, 2003
12:29 Greenwich Mean Time

I'd placed a call to Sergeant Trowbridge about 10:45 or so, and told the switchboard operator that I'd be back in my room between twelve and one. To save money, we'd gone to Benjy's near the tube station, and stocked up on submarine sandwiches, chips, and bottled water. The only hard part was trying to look like we weren't carrying our lunch through the lobby.

We'd just finished, when the phone rang. It was Sergeant Trowbridge, returning my call.

I asked what was new, and got a response that surprised me.

"We'd be most appreciative if we could talk with you later this afternoon. Around three?"

"Sure." I knew better than to even ask what about over the phone. Then he asked, politely, if there was anything new with us. I told him about the interview.

"Ahh . . . I'm not so certain that was wise. With whom did you speak?"

"Just a sec," I said, and fished out her card. "The *National Sun Express*, it says . . . the reporter was a gal named Sarah Mitchell."

There was a short silence at the other end. Then, "That's not a good one to share things with. Not at all. I do hope you didn't tell her anything."

"She already knew who we were. She knew quite a bit about the case. We didn't mention anything we weren't supposed to."

"I do hope that's true."

"Don't worry. She did have some information for us, though. About a professor, and who he was dating. And his connections with a certain group." I was trying to be circumspect due to an unsecured line, and hoped he might have at least some idea what I was talking about. Apparently he did.

There was another of those pregnant pauses. "I think we'll be sending a car for you straightaway," he said. "Do not, and I cannot emphasize this enough, do not talk with anyone. Not even to ask the time. A car will be there in less than five minutes. Go directly to the lift, and stand in the lobby. There will be a uniformed officer there for you."

"Ah, okay, sure."

I hung up, and said to Carson, "If you gotta use the head, do it now. We have to be in the lobby in four or five minutes."

"I'm good. What's up?"

"He wanted to see us about three or so. Then, well you heard. He wasn't all that happy about the interview, but when I mentioned the bit about the professor, he just about crapped. I think we might be in for an interesting afternoon."

I don't think it took more than three or four minutes to get to the lobby. There was a constable waiting for us.

"You'd be the two gentlemen from the States?"

I made another mental note to find out just why that seemed to be so obvious. "That's us."

"Right this way, gentlemen," he said, and ushered past the concierge's station, out the door, and down the steps to the marked police van that was sitting at the curb, looking about as conspicuous as only a marked patrol vehicle can.

It was a fun ride.

We were driven to a place called the Paddington Green police station. It was really close to the Edgeware Road tube station. That would make it convenient for us later. It was a more modern building than I was expecting, by a long shot. Mostly concrete and glass, it was probably a hundred years newer than our Nation County Jail.

We were ushered in, assisted with security and ID, and escorted through secure doors to an elevator. We were met on the second floor by Sergeant Trowbridge, who escorted us with very few words down a hall to an office identified with a 221 in small numerals. I could tell just from the thickness of the door and the acoustic tiles on the ceiling that it was a secure room.

The door shut, he relaxed just a little.

"I've been called twice after I made the first call to tell certain persons what you told me that Ms. Mitchell told you some things. You've stirred up quite a bit of interest."

"Sorry," I said, and meant it.

"Not to worry. Blyth, whom you met last night, is on his way over. Along with, I suspect, his special team. Have a seat."

We sat.

"We've begun security surveillance of your daughter and her friend Vicky, this morning."

"What?" That took me by surprise. "Is there a threat?"

"No, no. It's not that we think they're in imminent danger," he said. "But just a precautionary sort of business. There's someone assigned to each of them. We'll arrange a formal meeting, and an explanation of the procedures involved, later today."

That told me that they wanted to watch them for a while without them being aware of it. Cop work is like that . . . you never want to take a chance, I guess. As a cop, I could appreciate the tactic. As Jane's father, I was both grateful and irritated. That's not a comfortable combination.

It was a very long ten minutes of small talk before there was a knock at the door and Blyth entered. He was accompanied by three younger people: an athletic looking woman of about twenty-five, short blonde hair, who was close to six feet tall, and had bright blue eyes; an equally tall, thin man with short dark hair and glasses, of about the same age; and a shorter reddish haired man who was probably all of thirty.

"Hello," said Blyth. "I'd like you to meet Alice, Mark and Geoffrey. They're all incredibly energetic, and fortunately for me, they're a large part of my unit." His face cracked with a wide grin. "I refer to them as Vera, Chuck and Dave."

I laughed, but Carson didn't. Wrong generation?

"Hello," said Alice, extending her hand. "Pay him no mind."

Carson and I were both standing by that time, and we shook her hand. "It's nice to meet you," she said. That was a good start. Mark and Geoffrey were equally polite, and Mark seemed to have a keen interest in the two of us.

"Never met a US Sheriff before," he said, sounding very pleased. "Brilliant."

"Show him your badge," said Trowbridge.

I did so.

"My," said Mark. "Are all Sheriff's badges that fancy, then?"

"At least in Iowa," I said. "I'm just a Deputy." That got a quizzical look. "We do the actual work. The Sheriff himself just kind of runs the place."

"The same the world over," he said.

"A little respect, please," said Blyth. "I shouldn't want to have to tell Mum." He made motions for everybody to sit. "So," he said, "I'm given to understand that you've made the acquaintance of our very own Sarah Mitchell?"

"At breakfast," I said. "We ate at the hotel."

"Ah, nothing's sacred these days," said Blyth. "Well, then. Let me begin with this; you're aware of the tabloid press? Sensationalist journalism, and all that?"

"Oh, yeah." I knew where this was headed now. I shook my head, and said, "I think I know what's coming. Sorry about that. We got trapped."

"I suppose that couldn't be helped. You've just had an interview with one of the most, well, sensational of them all, at least of the current lot." Blyth cleared his throat. "So, then. Just what did you tell her?"

"Not a word," said Carson, out of the blue. "Carl did all the talking. I didn't tell her anything."

He was still just scared about prison I guess, but he was beginning to sound like a little brother. Just a little exasperated at him, I said, "First of all, *I* said nothing whatsoever about last night. She knew who we were. She asked for some routine stuff. I told her why we were here in London. Left the politics out, you'll be glad to know." He smiled. "About as low-key as I could make it, I think. She knew that my last name and Jane's were the same, and I couldn't think of a good reason to try to hide the fact that she's my daughter. Just cause trouble in the long run, I think. Other than that, not much at all. I did," I added, to make myself sound a little brighter, "manage to get her to tell me a couple of things first."

"Good," said Blyth. "Did she appear at all reluctant to exchange this information with you?"

"Hardly. I had nothing to pressure her with. She just started with asking if I knew that Emma was, well, active with dating. I said I knew that. I could tell her stories, in fact. But, I didn't say that," I added quickly. "Then she asked if I knew she was dating one of her professors. Emma, not the reporter. I said I knew that, too, but I really didn't. I figured she didn't need to know that. So she went another step, because she wasn't going to get an interview if she only told me stuff I already knew."

Alice nodded. Approvingly, I thought.

"And that's when she said?" continued Blyth.

"She said his name was Robert. Then she asked me if I knew that this professor was an activist, and in a group whose purpose was the same as that stated by the hostage takers on that tape."

"The one that was aired, then?" he asked.

"Yeah . . . anyway. . . ." I stopped for a moment. "Well, hell, wait a minute. No. It sure as shit couldn't be, could it? I mean, there was nothing in that tape . . . no voice. No audio. Well, son of a bitch. It was an attached written note, wasn't it?" I looked at Sergeant Trowbridge. He nodded. "Okay, sure. A note, but that wasn't published. . . ."

"No, it wasn't," said Blyth. "That's explainable; as I'm sure she has very good contacts throughout the journalistic community." He seemed just a little distracted. "What I'd like to know, though, is just where she got this information regarding this professor fellow."

"I can't help you there," I said.

His eyes positively twinkled. "Don't be too sure, Deputy Houseman. Why do you suppose she told you all that she did?"

I considered what I knew. "Oh . . . I'd say there's a good chance, based on you guys' reaction, that she got a hold of something pretty good. I'd also say, since she told me so early on in the bargaining, that she doesn't really realize exactly what she's got. Not quite. And the reason she only told me his first name might be that she wanted my cooperation in her story. Personally . . . I think she'd got the last name, and wants to dangle that out there, because she doesn't think we'll be able to get it on our own. She's right, as far as that goes. Well, either that, or she just wants to stir stuff up. Maybe?"

"Very good," said Blyth. "Her disreputable broadside is due in the stands in time for the evening rush. Another miracle of the computer age. Let's wait to see what she says."

"Then again," I said, "maybe she's got a hard-on for this professor. . . ."

"Well, yeah," said Carson.

"Regardless," said Blyth, "we may have to ask you to stay in her good graces for a while. There's every possibility that she knows more, even if she doesn't realize that she does. You may have to talk with her again."

"How difficult could that be, now?" I asked, more of myself than anybody else.

"Best wait until we've seen her article," he said. "How goes it with your daughter and . . . Vicky, isn't it?"

"Not bad. So far, we've only talked on the phone today." But as long as we were on the subject; "You mind if I ask her and Vicky about this professor? Whether Emma ever went out with him?"

"By all means. If you'd not mind having one of us there."

"Sure, we're gonna meet up at the Highgate tube station about 4:15 or 4:30." That seemed good enough to me. We talked for another fifteen or twenty minutes, and he said that there had been one or two 'minor developments,' that, if they panned out, he'd share with us. We were not to initiate contact with the professor, or anybody we thought might have taken part in Emma's abduction. We were to stay away from the University, as much as possible, and were to make no attempt to interview students or faculty.

"Of course, if someone initiates contact with your lot," said Blyth, "you'll let us know immediately."

"Oh, absolutely."

Alice said, "I just want you to know that I think I can appreciate what you're going through. Having to be less than truthful with your daughter. It's a horrid situation."

"It's gonna get worse," I said. "But thanks."

"If there's any way we can help," she said, "please call." She handed me her card. "A cover story, perhaps? Or a distraction . . . ?"

She was dead serious. I appreciated that more than I could ever tell her.

I took the opportunity of giving her our new cell phone number. Or, at least, trying. I couldn't remember it, and the paper I'd written it down on was at the hotel.

"Just call up your number on the display," said Carson.

After a few seconds my fumbling delay was getting pretty painful, so I just gave it to him. He pressed a combination of keys, and read the number off almost instantly.

"That's what the children are for," said Blyth.

Carson brought up the funeral arrangements, and we were once again assured that matters would be expedited, as soon as the remains were no longer being held in secret.

After that, Carson and I found ourselves, once again, at loose ends. That was difficult, because I knew that all the "other guys" were busy digging, interviewing, and maybe even doing some surveillance. I just couldn't get comfortable with doing nothing.

Anyway, we didn't want to go back up to Highgate, at least without the girls, because we wouldn't even know where to begin with talking to people up there.

We decided to go to the Victoria and Albert Museum, to kill time. The Museum, or the V&A as it was called, was absolutely fascinating. So much so, it was nearly 3:15 when we finally got away.

"Don't you feel guilty about this?"

"What?"

"Oh, you know. Doing tourist stuff. Shouldn't we be doing more cop stuff?"

"It's not guilt," I said. "I just ain't happy not being in on the good shit. We'll get more cop stuff in before we're done. But, damn it, I tried to tell everybody that it would be like this. *This is not our case.* We haven't got anything official to do. And we only get to cooperate when we're asked."

"Yeah, but. . . ."

"Yeah. Well, hell. Lighten up, Carson. We'll get busy yet today. Trust me." It looked to me like Emma's death had really gotten to him. Too.

We got to Highgate, and waited at the tube station for Jane and Vicky. I noticed a guy kind of hanging around, then wandering off, then coming back again. He ended up just outside the main exit onto the sidewalk. He looked like an accountant or something. He sure didn't seem threatening, but neither would a professor have yesterday. I kept sort of an eye on him, but didn't say anything to Carson. We'd been there about five minutes, when Alice showed up.

"Would you mind if I talked with your daughter and Vicky about that professor, too?"

"No, not at all." I'd expected somebody from MI5 to be around a little later, but this would do. "Glad to have you." I considered how stupid I was about to sound, but went ahead. "You see that guy outside? Just to the left of the door?"

"Indeed."

"Where?" asked Carson.

"Just a sec," I said. "I can't point just now. He should be the only one out there." I had my back to the window at the time.

"Okay," said Carson. "What about him?"

"That's just what I was going to ask," I said. "He's been there since we got here, and I think he might have been on the tube with us, but I'm not sure."

"No," said Alice. "He's been waiting in the station for the better part of the afternoon."

"You know him," I said. A statement, not a question.

"Oh, indeed," she said. "But it would be best not to notice him. He's a sensitive one."

"What are you *talking* about?" asked Carson.

"We're discussing our Phillip," said Alice, with a smile. "He's been

one of the people assigned to you since the hostage business was revealed. I believe he expected you to continue outside. You'll find there's
one with Jane and Vicky now, too. Been with them all day, in fact."

"Security?" asked Carson.

"One would hope," smiled Alice. "Wouldn't one?"

As Jane and Vicky emerged from the station a couple of minutes
later, I became aware of two things almost simultaneously. First, there
was a man who was following them. Or, rather, accompanying them
at a discreet distance. As soon as he saw the three of us, he just kept
going out the door. A better job than 'our' Phillip.

The other thing I could tell was that Jane was absolutely furious. I
think Alice caught it, too, and sort of hung back a little bit. Jane had a
rolled up newspaper in her hand, and was saying, "Have you seen
this? Have you seen this shit? What the hell is going on?"

Rolled up and all, it was pretty hard to tell what she was talking
about.

"Seen what?"

They were on to us by that time, and Jane pulled the roll open.
"This *shit*!"

She handed it to me, and she'd had it rolled so tightly, it was difficult to keep it open. It was a copy of the *National Sun Express*. The
banner headline read "COOL IT GIRLS, DADDY'S HERE!" and had a
photo of Carson, Sarah Mitchell and me at breakfast. The caption
read, "He Didn't Wear His Gun At Table." A subhead line read "NEW
DEVELOPMENT IN THE CASE OF AMERICA'S SWEET TART."

I scanned the article pretty quickly. Basically, all it had for real
content was just what we'd told the reporter. She'd added all the sensational stuff via headlines, captions, and subheadings. It didn't look
as if she'd actually misquoted me at all.

"What the hell is going on, Dad?"

It took a few minutes, but we got it explained. I'd seen Jane mad
before, but I couldn't ever remember seeing her so outraged. At least
this time Carson didn't point at me and say I'd done all of the talking.

Alice had sort of edged closer, and all of a sudden, Jane pointed at
her and said, "Who's she? Another reporter?"

"No," I said. "She's a cop." Well, she was, sort of. I introduced
them to Alice, who just said she wanted to talk with them about some
stuff. That took a little of the heat off, at least. Jane was mad, but not
mad enough to argue extensively in front of a stranger.

We all talked and walked, stopping every so often to allow a more
detailed explanation.

"I should have warned you about this rag," said Jane, finally, not so much totally calm, but more like tired of being angry. "This isn't the first nasty bit this, this ... *sleaze* has done. This whole crappy 'Sweet Tart' bit really pisses me off. It's the *third* time she's used that in a headline. I swear to God, if I ever . . ."

"Well, now we all know," said Carson. "we won't let that happen again." Nice try.

"She did an interview with us," said Vicky, speaking for the first time. "We told her about the guy Emma was seeing, the one from the pub. That was the first time this Sweet Tart business came up. She was sure Emma ran off with him."

"Even though he was still here?" I was surprised.

"Hell, she never checked, Dad. She just wrote it."

"Oh, perfect," said Alice. "True to form, at least."

"She does this all the time?" asked Jane.

"Very nearly."

"Oh. Then it's not just us?"

"Not at all," said Alice. "Between her and her editor, I'd say they try to do something like this with every story they cover."

Jane sighed, and looked toward me. "I guess you had to say you were somebody's dad?"

"She already had my name," I said, "so I couldn't very well claim Vicky. And I didn't think I could pull off brother or uncle. . . ."

A small smile appeared on Jane's face for a second. "Well, definitely not brother."

We were standing near the intersection of Southwood Lane and Castle Yard, just about the first really level part of the quarter mile to the girls' flat. There was nobody else around, so Alice took the opportunity to jump in with both feet.

"Do either of you know a Professor Northwood?"

"Sure," said Vicky. "Why?"

"Was Emma dating him, do you know?"

There was a momentary silence. I was afraid that Alice had pissed off Jane all over again, but Jane just said, "She did a couple of times."

"Would that have been for dinner," asked Alice, "or an evening out, or just coffee . . . ?"

"This is important, right?"

"Yes," said Alice. "Perhaps very."

"Okay." Jane took in a deep breath, let it out, and said, "She went out with him a bunch. Maybe ten, fifteen times. That we know about. It started with coffee, and went from there. She slept with him, I'm sure, because she told me she did."

"Mmmm," said Alice. "Do you know where they went, usually? Unusually?" She smiled.

"Well, unusually," said Vicky, "the four of us went to an old Underground station."

"How unique," said Alice.

"Yeah," said Vicky. "Weird. Not your average date. We had to pack a lunch, and we just climbed up and down this circular staircase."

Alice's brow furrowed. "Which station?"

"Wasn't it . . . Downey?" Vicky was asking Jane.

"Close,' she said. "I can't quite pull it up . . . just a sec." If there was ever any proof needed that she was my daughter that would have done it.

"Do you remember where it is?"

"Over by Buckingham Palace," said Jane.

"But behind it, sort of. You know, along Piccadilly."

"Hyde Park?" asked Alice. "Green Park? Those are the tube stations along Piccadilly . . ."

"Oh," said Vicky. "It's not a *functional* station. I'm sorry."

"Down Street," said Jane. "That's it. It's an abandoned tube station on Down Street."

Alice nodded. "Brilliant. Yes, that would be it. Why there? Any clue?"

"He's writing a book about the tube system," said Jane.

"It's a hobby of his," said Vicky. "He got us in on a tour."

"Really?" asked Alice. "How interesting. Was it fun?"

"It was kind of neat," said Jane. "Old, and we had to go down a spiral stair that was more than a hundred steps. Musty. But full of historical stuff. Hey, Dad . . . you'd like that. It was part of some military facility back during the Second World War . . . there are still some old military signs and stuff."

For a moment, there, she sounded just like Jane from the pre-kidnapping time. Interested, enthusiastic, happy. Just for a moment.

"Is there some reason you want to know this stuff?" she asked Alice.

Alice looked around. So did I. The only two stationary people I could see were Phillip and the other security man, about a hundred feet back down the hill, and on the other side of the street.

"Do you know anything about Professor Northwood's political opinions?"

"No," said Jane. Vicky just shook her head. "Why?"

I had to give Alice credit, she didn't hedge, or try to be cute. She just played it straight up. "He's a member of a group who have the same goals as the people who kidnapped Emma."

I think that would have been a conversation stopper anywhere. On Southwood Lane, Highgate, London, England, it sure as hell was.

"Where should we eat?" asked Carson, glancing at the Gatehouse.

"Oh, not there," said Jane. "Not tonight. Not with that article today. What about Zizzi?"

"Who's Zizzi?"

"Not who, Dad. It's a place, just kind of behind the Gatehouse. Italian. Good food."

I was for it.

Chapter 15

Thursday, November 13, 2003
The Basement of "The Camel"
17:48 Greenwich Mean Time

It was time for supper for Hamza and Anton, too. They were in the sub-basement of a restaurant across the alley behind the old Down Street station. They'd gotten there in the very early morning hours, with Anton pulling on the back door as Hamza used the half inch spring steel bar that was used to prop the door open to slip the interior hook. Marwan had showed them the method, and said that he used it when they needed to take things to the secret place. He never divulged just who had showed him how to do this, but it was obviously an employee of the Camel.

They'd gone immediately through a small opening behind a counter, and into the abandoned tube station. They'd hidden their duffle, and scrambled back into the restaurant basement, looking for food.

Not knowing who their ally on the inside might be, the two fugitives were most reluctant to be seen. They were dining on things they were able to find in the sub-level storage area: onions, dried fish, dried apricots, and dried prunes. There were four large, wooden boxes of what they thought was goat cheese, but since the label was in Arabic, they weren't sure. It was at least cheese, and Hamza was grateful for that. Unfortunately, they were each drinking from their last bottles of water.

"At least it's clean," said Hamza. He was looking at the pattern on the old tiled floor, done in light and dark green, and cream. "Dry, too."

"It's a palace," said Anton. "Just like Windsor, except for the five foot ceilings. I hate this fish."

Thinking the ceilings were a good foot taller than that, but wanting to avoid an argument, Hamza said, "Well, it's supposed to be prepared with spices and oils. . . ."

"Shut fucking up," said Anton. "Just shut up and eat. And think of someplace else we can go."

"Want some cheese?" asked Hamza, a minute later.

"It can't be worse than this fish," said Anton.

Hamza got up, pried open the wooden box, opened the greyish wrapping paper, and very carefully used his pocket knife to slice off a small, even piece of the cheese. Satisfied that it hardly looked disturbed, he did it three more times, two slices each. Then, very carefully, he rewrapped the paper, and quietly tapped the box lid back in place.

Hamza got up with the intention of replacing the wooden box on the shelf, when the sound of a door opening in the level immediately above, and the sound of feet on the stairs, caused him to grab the box and head for concealment. Anton, more self-possessed, quickly and quietly went up the steps to the closed door, and put his ear to it. Then he very carefully switched off the light, and used his flashlight to light his way back down. "Where are you?" he hissed.

Hamza blinked his light from behind an old wooden table that was covered with onions. Anton joined him.

"Should we go back into the station?" was the whispered question.

"Too noisy," said Anton. "Shhh. Wait a bit. There are two of them."

With their lights extinguished, it was pitch black in their little room. At least the abandoned tube station had some lights. Now that it was completely dark, though, they could see a light through a fine crack in the door at the top of the stair. A few moments later it went out.

"Right," said Anton. "Back to the station. We'd best come back here when they've closed and gone home."

"What about this?" asked Hamza, holding up the cheese box.

"Bring it." Anton thought it would be safest to just bring the thing, rather than take a chance returning it to its place. "They'll never miss it."

Their entrance to the long abandoned tube station was underneath an old, worn counter with a marble top. Once the counter doors were opened, they revealed a narrow, horizontal slit in the basement wall, which had been originally covered with a grate. That obstacle long gone, they were able to slide through on their bellies, traversing some eight feet of very narrow, rectangular tunnel with stone walls. The opening was no more than two feet high and four feet wide for its entire length. Just small enough and long enough for Hamza's claustrophobia to begin to gain hold of him.

"Hurry," he gasped, pushing the cheese crate in front of him. He'd just had the irrational thought that Anton might somehow die in the short tunnel, and trap him. He told himself not to be foolish, just as an image of the stones around him slowly crumbling and collapsing caused him to nearly cry out.

Their exit was into the old tube station WC proper, near the urinals. Their passageway had been part of the old ventilation system that led from the toilet facilities to the roof of the original restaurant building.

Hamza was breathing rapidly by the time Anton eased himself through, and got to his feet.

"You've got your share of anxieties, don't you?" asked Anton.

Hamza was too happy just being out of the shaft to care. "They're my . . . hobby," he said.

Anton took the cheese box from him. The two made their way through the toilet area, and through a swinging door onto a platform area in the station proper. This area was lit, although dimly, by a work light. They had been advised earlier to continue toward the far end, where the old track bed disappeared into the darkness.

They cautiously jumped down onto the filled in bed where the tracks should have been, and used their own lights to find their way to a steel door. Opened, it led down four steps into an old generator room, where they had stored their things. The old, grey electric motors, boxes and cable runs were still intact. Dusty, but intact.

There was a lightbulb in the corner, and Anton reached up and screwed it all the way back in. They had decided that not using the switch by the door was a good idea. This way, they were able to control the lighting in the large space, and anyone coming in the door would not be able to simply turn on the lights. There were three other lightbulbs they had unscrewed, as well.

"How did Marwan find this bleedin' place?" asked Anton.

"He took a tour," said Hamza. "He's writing a book on the Underground, he says."

"No, dolt," said Anton. "Not this station. The entrance under the restaurant."

"Oh, that," said Hamza. "He was eating there, and had a book with him he was reading, about the old Underground."

"I thought you said he was writing it," said Anton, carefully opening the cheese box.

"His won't be the *only* one. Just the best. He's doing research."

"Oh, he told you that, did he?" He unwrapped the thick paper, and selected a piece of cheese.

"It's a reasonable assumption," said Hamza, shaking off the last of his claustrophobia and pulling two bottles of water out of their carton.

"Fuck!"

"What?"

Anton was spitting the cheese out of his mouth. "Fucking awful!" He wiped his mouth with the back of his hand. "I'll never be hungry enough to eat that shit!"

Hamza reached over, and tore off a small corner of the cheese brick. "It can't be that bad . . . must be feta." He put the morsel in his mouth. His eyes widened, and he spat it onto the floor. "That's not cheese!"

Anton was making a snorting, gasping, gurgling sound that passed for a giggle. "See!"

"Really," said Hamza. "Really, that isn't cheese. . . . . But it smells like cheese. . . ."

"Sod the smell, it tastes like shit. Well whatever it is, you can put on *your* crackers at bedtime," said Anton. "I'm just glad she gave us some tinned meat." He took a large onion from his pocket. "I'll cut this up . . . cleanse our sad fucking palates."

Hamza glanced around their hiding place. "How long do . . . ?" He was drowned out by a rush of air, a roar, and the sound of a tube train passing a few yards down the tunnel on one of the active tracks of the Piccadilly line. It was a huge, rushing, thundering sound that prevented any communication for at least a minute.

After a few moments, Anton said "What?"

"How long? Do you think she was right when she said a week?"

"To stay down in this hole? I should say a fortnight, at least."

Hamza looked dismayed. "Truly?"

"I'm off in a couple of days, mate," said Anton. "Unless Marwan himself comes down and tells us different."

"I hope it's him and not Mr. Kazan," said Hamza, as the rush of air began again, and the conversation was halted for the time being. Alone with his thoughts, Hamza was again combating a tinge of claustrophobia. He kept telling himself that there was another way out, the old spiral stair to the surface. It was at about the midpoint of the station, about two hundred feet away. But, he thought to himself, it was still clearly marked. The "Way Out" sign was done in the cream with maroon trimmed station tiles.

As the noise subsided a little, Hamza said, "How far down do you think we are?"

"Probably not more than fifty feet," said Anton. "Why? Getting all nervous again, are we?"

"No," Hamza said, lamely. "Just thinking about . . . oh, fire?"

The rushing sound started up again. It was a peak hour for the Piccadilly line. He comforted himself with the knowledge that it would become less frequent, and stop at midnight. At least their sleep wouldn't be interrupted. Hamza had never felt lonelier in his life. What was even more disagreeable, he hadn't thought it was possible to miss Pamela so much. Could he possibly get her down here?

Highgate
18:30 hours

Zizzi, it turned out, was just behind the Gatehouse. That was convenient. Alice was on her cell phone as soon as we got inside the place, and while she was distracted, Jane asked, "Who is she, really? A watchdog, or do Vicky and I need security?"

"She wants some information," I said. "Security is already being taken care of."

"What? Taken care of? How?"

"When we leave," I said, "remind me to point out the two cops who've been with you all day."

"What? Nobody said anything to us . . . I'm not sure I like being watched, Dad."

"They aren't watching *you*," I said. I know Jane pretty well. "They're watching for nasty people who might be watching you."

She gave me that one, mainly, I think, because she was just a little more frightened than offended. But it was probably pretty close.

"Did *she* arrange for it?" asked Jane, indicating Alice who was still on her cell phone a few feet away.

"I don't know. Maybe. I'd say that it was her, or her boss."

"Jeez, Dad, she's not any older than Carson," whispered Jane.

"True," I said. "But I think she really knows her stuff."

We got our menus, and I took the chance to glance around the place. Nice, very clean, very modern, with a quiet atmosphere. It was the sort of place I could really enjoy. And it had a skylight. That just about made my day.

We all ordered Calzone, of various sorts. I figured that, at home, it'd require me to walk an extra two miles or so to burn off the calories. Since here in London I was already walking five times as much as I usually did, my calculations said I was ahead of the game, so I could pretty much eat what I wanted. That's my kind of math.

"What's it worth if I don't tell Mom?"

"Any DVD you want for Christmas. But it's gotta hold for all the rest of the time I'm here."

Jane thought a second. "Okay . . . how about *Lord of the Rings 2.*"

"Done."

"The director's cut, Dad. The extra scenes, and the background stuff and the interviews. Widescreen."

What the hell. I figured I'd get to borrow it, anyway.

The Calzone was fantastic. As we ordered coffee, Alice said, "I hope you don't mind, but I've asked someone to join us for dessert."

Given that that meant we were going to have dessert, I was overjoyed. "Fine with me."

"A word as to why," she said, "before she arrives. It's Sarah Mitchell, I'm afraid."

"What?" Jane's blood pressure was starting to go up again.

"Just allow me," said Alice. "I've not told her who I am. As far as she knows I'm your solicitor, who has advised you to talk with her. What I told her was that I'm representing your interests, but I'm convinced she drew the proper wrong conclusion." She was very intense. "I'm not able to go into all the details, but I want to know everything she knows about this Professor Northwood, and just how she found all that out."

There was silence.

"Good. Now, just be yourselves," she said, and very quietly reached over and took Jane's table knife. "Just to be on the safe side," she said, sweetly. "That's the good girl." She handed them back right away, but it broke the tension.

"Why do you have to know this?" asked Vicky.

"If you'd read the article from my point of view," said Alice, "you'd see that she has come upon information . . ." She was interrupted by the appearance of Sarah Mitchell in the entryway. Alice stood. "Over here," she said, waiving. "Over here." Although she'd done nothing I could see, her demeanor had changed from extremely self-assured to just slightly over-demonstrative driven by uncertainty. In other words, a young attorney who was just a little wet behind the ears. I was very impressed.

It was pretty obvious that Sarah Mitchell wasn't. The first thing she said after saying a greeting to all of us that somehow managed to exclude Alice, was: "I hope this is important. I do have another interview yet tonight."

"I'm sure we won't keep you long," said Alice.

"I'm afraid my editor got to the headlines of that article," said Sarah Mitchell, indicating the rolled up edition that Jane had on the table beside her. "He does that."

"Sure," said Jane. The way she said it, I nearly reached over and took her silverware myself, although I suspected she'd be able to make do with her bare hands if it came to that.

"I just need to know a few things, so I may advise these people properly," interjected Alice.

"You don't get that from me, ducks," said Mitchell. She looked at Alice closely. "Are you certain you've been admitted to practice yet? You seem somewhat younger that I'd have thought."

"Why, thank you so much," said Alice. "Now, then, so long as we're all here, I think you should know that they wish to cooperate fully with you, in getting to the bottom of this matter."

That surprised Mitchell. She wasn't alone.

Alice continued in that vein, explaining that we were having some difficulty with the authorities sharing data with us, and that we had information that we, as a consequence, were not sharing with them.

The hook, so to speak, was in.

"Well, you'll have to give me some idea . . ." said Sarah Mitchell. "I'd need something rather special. . . ."

Something special enough to let her break somebody else's confidence. I got that, so I thought I'd serve up a good one. "Okay. There was a terrorism incident back in Nation County, oh, about a year ago. All we want to know is whether or not these are the same people, or affiliated with them or . . . well you know." I shrugged.

"Really? What kind of incident? I need something of interest over here."

Jane got back into it at that point. "Dad was just about killed, and another officer was shot," said Jane. "A chemical thing at a meat plant, wasn't it?"

"Yes," I said.

"We can't divulge everything," said Carson. "But I can have the proper form faxed over, and if you'll sign, we can show you the stuff that isn't covered by National Security."

My respect for Carson went up again. He sounded like a US Attorney.

"Chemicals?"

I leaned forward. "Ricin," I said.

Her eyes widened. "Truly? That's fascinating, but it hardly gets us over here to my readership."

"It will, trust me. All I need," I said, "is some names associated with this Northwood dude. I have some access, and I can run 'em by the names I already have." I gave her a knowing look. "The Feds had to let us have the names of all the dead. And those that got killed in Nation County, especially. We already had the connections with particular groups identified. We can do some group stuff, too."

"You sure about that?" asked Carson. He was looking directly at me.

"Yep. FARC especially, but the al-Qaeda connection was made right in front of us, so . . . yeah." If you talk among yourselves in the presence of an interested party, you add a huge layer of 'authenticity' to a deception.

"Truly? With a connection to over here?" Sarah Mitchell was leaning well foreword, elbows on the table.

I looked back at her, and included her that way. "Oh, yes. But, you know, this organization you say he hangs around with? This . . ." I reached back, took out my notebook, and read the name aloud. "This . . . London Reform Movement for the Freedom of Khaled al Fawwaz and Ibrahim Eidarous and Lions of the Front for Jihad in Britain . . ."

"Yes?"

"That's just way too clumsy to be real. You can't even do a decent acronym . . . listen . . . LRMFKFIELFJB. A name on everyone's lips. You got any idea who they really are?"

"Not a clue," said Sarah Mitchell.

"That's valuable," I said. "And in exchange for that you want something from us?"

"What he means," said Alice, "is that . . ."

"I know what he wants. He *is* a cop. I did connect them. It was easy."

"Really?" asked Jane.

"All I did," interrupted Sarah Mitchell, "was go to his website. I'd already been to the website of London Reform Movement for the Freedom of Khaled al Fawwaz and Ibrahim Eidarous and Lions of the Front for Jihad in Britain." She ran through the name smoothly, having committed it to memory. Unlike me. She leaned back. "I sent an email to the website, and he fucking answered it from his university computer address. He's the bloody chairman."

"No shit?" came from Jane. She beat me by a tenth of a second.

"Oh, indeed," said Sarah Mitchell. "You'd think the coppers could find out something that simple, right?"

I glanced at Alice, and she winked. Apparently they had.

"I'd sure think so," I said.

"Well, don't count on it. I haven't identified this Imad fellow just yet," said Sarah Mitchell. "He's second in command or something. Imad is probably a code name, just like your Robert Northwood goes by the code name of Marwan. You might want to run that one by your files."

I wrote that one down. "Good . . ."

"There's a female member," said Sarah Mitchell. "Secretary. She rejoices in the code name of Ayat, but I believe her true name could be Hanadi."

Alice's eyes widened just a bit. Whether she hadn't known, or hadn't thought that Sarah Mitchell was able to get that far, I didn't know.

"Now, before I give you any more," said our intrepid reporter, "why don't you give me something worthwhile from those files you have. Like a name?"

"Skripkin," I said. "Yevgenny Skripkin. Lived in Lambeth. Was a member of The People's Freedom and Reform Movement."

Her brow furrowed. "I remember that. . . . I do, I remember that!"

Alice looked positively aghast. I decided not to do any more names tonight.

"He's one," I said. "Enough for tonight?"

"This *is* a London connection. A bona-fide London connection. You cosmopolitan devil, you," said Sarah Mitchell. A look of considerable satisfaction came over her face. "Absolutely no one will have this. . . ."

"That's true," I said. Skripkin, really, was an idiot who hung around with a variety of people, and who had absolutely no intrinsic value himself. Well, as far as I knew, anyway.

"What do you say you work on the connection that Professor Northwood has with the tube system?" she said. "My sources tell me that he does."

As far as I knew, her source on that one was probably his website. When you hand out BS at the rate we were doing, you get to recognize it pretty fast, too.

"That's not much of a connection," said Jane, suddenly. "He even offers to take little tours on Saturdays. If he likes you. Claims he's writing this book about it. The tubes. A history, he says. The three of us went with him to an old tube station once . . . just a second. . . ." And she took out her copy of London A to Zed. She leafed through it for a second. "It's near Piccadilly."

"It was probably their first date, you know?" said Vicky.

Jane looked up. "Yeah. I think it was. Emma wanted a little company. He really didn't expect us, I think." She smiled to herself, not looking up. "But Emma was the one he asked. She asked us to come along." She looked at her guide again. "It's right near Buckingham Palace . . ."

"A tour to Hyde Park Corner Tube Station?" Sarah Mitchell looked skeptical.

"No, no. Near there. It's abandoned. There are lots of them . . ." said Jane, without looking up from the guide. "Down Street. It's Down Street."

"Never heard of it," said Sarah Mitchell.

"Well, it's there," said Jane. "Old, red building. Little shop in half of it." She pointed at the place, and showed the map to the reporter. "Right here. . . ."

"Well, let me check with my editor, then. I should see him tomorrow. When do you think you might have those files? I need to see at least part of them, to verify that they're real."

"I sure hope tomorrow or the next day," I said. "Depends on how they're sent."

"Let me know as soon as you have them. We'll talk more, then."

As soon as she'd left, Alice let out a long sigh. "Well, that was a cock up on my part. I'd *expected* to be the one who did most of the talking."

"We did all right, though, didn't we?" I thought we had.

"Oh, you were all brilliant," said Alice. "Please, *please* don't promise any more names."

"Skripkin's a nobody," I said.

"I assume you're right," she said. "But let's vet the names before we share them, could we?"

"Sure." I wasn't worried. In fact, it had been sort of enjoyable to play with Sarah Mitchell's head that way, not to mention Alice's, and I found my mood elevated higher than it had been since we'd arrived in London.

"And, Jane," said Alice, "with anyone else but us, could you not remember the name of the old tube station? Vague is the key, now."

"Sure."

"But I think it went rather well," she said. "I believe she'd been misdirected."

"Oh, boy," said Jane. "You know, I'm really encouraged. Really. I think we really have a chance of finding Emma. I really do."

My mood fell abruptly. I'd almost forgotten that Emma was dead.

* * *

We all went back to the girls' flat after supper. The girls invited Alice, who declined. I think both Jane and Vicky were ready to like her.

We discussed some non-Emma things, like movies and books and television programs for a while. Nobody else remembered *The Prisoner*, and only Jane had ever seen an episode of *The Avengers*, so I listened a lot.

Eventually, the conversation got back around to Emma and the hostage business.

"Does anybody have an idea where she might be being held?" asked Jane.

I couldn't very say 'the morgue,' so I just shrugged. "It's impossible to tell from the tape," I said. "But I think it's a fair assumption that it was done in the UK. Logistically, you know? It would just be the simplest thing to do. I don't think there's any way that they could reliably smuggle somebody out of the country. Not fast, anyway."

"I don't know," said Vicky. "I saw this thing on TV once, a rich guy smuggled this girl on his plane . . . said she was sick."

"TV," I said. "They do that."

"Besides," said Jane, "why take her out of the country?"

"Why not?" said Carson.

We narrowed it down, eventually, to what I'd said at first. Simplest way.

"So," said Jane, "since that's at least a possibility, and since Professor Northwood hangs around abandoned tube stations . . . why don't we check there? They could be holding her there, couldn't they?"

I shook my head. "If I remember that tape, it looked an awful lot like she was in a room . . ."

"A set," said Jane. "Any theater major could do it."

What could I say to that? "Okay . . ." would have to do.

"Terrorists tend to do things in the least complicated way they can," said Carson. "Like your dad says. Cheaper, easier, and less chance of a mistake. They don't like unnecessary complexity."

"I suppose you're right," said Jane. I knew her well enough to know she wasn't anywhere near done with that train of thought.

"We don't have class tomorrow afternoon," said Vicky. "I don't know about you," she said, addressing Jane, "but I could cut my morning class, no problem. I feel the same way you do. There could be a connection. We really should check it out."

"You two," I said to Vicky, "are entirely too much alike."

"Well, Dad? You guys want to go, too?" Just the way it was said, I knew Jane was going.

"Why don't we just call the cops and ask them to do it?" I was being as reasonable as I could, I thought. All it earned me was dirty looks from Vicky and Jane.

"Look, okay, let me call 'em tomorrow, and just see what they say? And if they show no interest at all, then I'll ask if we can go there. Okay?"

They really needed to do *something*. I knew that. I personally didn't think it would do a bit of good to go rummaging around in some musty old tube station. I also thought that, if it could be arranged, it would be good for the girls to do that. Accompanied, of course. But any way you cut it, I knew they weren't going to find Emma and her kidnappers down there. They'd be about as safe as they could get.

Chapter 16

Hanadi was faced with a dilemma. She was extremely reluctant to call Marwan, since she had been told he'd actually ordered the death of the hostage. She feared for Hamza and Anton, for one thing. If Marwan had changed so much, what else had happened? For another, she certainly did not want to have the police discover she had been the one to call him to tell him that Emma was dead. That would be tantamount to signing her life away into prison, and for absolutely no purpose. Calling the police would have been the very best action she could take, without a doubt. Unfortunately for her, that also meant that she would have to inform on Marwan, Imad, and the rest. She was not about to do that. If she were to discover that she had been deliberately lied to by Marwan and Imad, then, perhaps, she would do so. But not now.

Hanadi would not have deemed herself particularly religious, since she did not believe that her religion was the central focus of her life. She had been raised in a religious family, however, and morality was at least as important to her as the law. She needed to know the extent of her obligation to Marwan and the committee. She needed a guide.

She placed a telephone call to a fellow Muslim whose morality she respected. He had studied the religious texts very intensely, and she thought him to be as informed as anyone she knew. He was not an imam. She knew that. She also knew that he was an admirer of the Infantada and Jihadist movements.

His advice to her was that a killing, regardless of age or sex or circumstance, was permitted by their religion if it "was justified in the eyes of the Mojahed."

The Mojahed. The warriors of God. "Even a woman?"

"If it was necessary in the mind of the warrior. Why are you asking this?"

"I was . . . just curious. A member of my firm and I had a discussion. It was nothing, but I wanted to know your thoughts."

"I see. So, you have them. Is there anything else, Hanadi?"

"No," she said. "Your health is good?"

"As is yours, I hope."

She then called a Muslim counselor whom she had known since her undergraduate days. She asked him the same series of questions.

"To capture and then kill a woman? It would be a horrible stain on the entire Muslim community. It could not be tolerated."

"What if it were accidental?"

"The taking of a hostage accidental?" He laughed ruefully. "Hardly."

"No, but the death. An accidental death. Would that ameliorate the situation?"

"Ah, Hanadi. Your study of the law has changed you. That is a barrister's argument. Morally, it would be a disaster, accidental or no. Do you understand me?"

"Yes. And thank you for answering my question."

"Hanadi?" He said her name just as she was about to end the conversation.

"Yes?"

"Please tell me you are not involved in anything foolish."

The question surprised her, and she hesitated for a moment before she said, "Me? Of course not. You know me. The logical one. No. It's just the news on the telly, and I started to wonder if it might be thought justified, you know?"

"Absolutely not, and you're not the first to ask that question."

"No, I suppose not."

After those calls, she could think of nowhere else to turn. Reluctantly, she decided that the two in the abandoned station could survive for another day. She would make an appointment with the most respected member of her firm, Sir Henry Culbertson, and ask his advice on a theoretical problem. He was a kind man, and she was confident that she would receive the best advice.

Regardless, she remained appalled at the turn of events that had resulted in the death of Emma Schiller. The plan, so clearly elucidated by Marwan/Northwood had merely been to kidnap the American, make a demand, and release her shortly thereafter, regardless of the response. She could still hear him say, "If it produces the release of some prisoners in Belmarsh, so very good for us. If it doesn't, and we release her unharmed and none the worse for wear, then good on us anyhow. We have shown compassion. And we can always claim it was a publicity stunt, and that Emma knew about it all along, willingly cooperated. Our word against hers. The scandal sheets will absolutely devour that one. Publicity is the life blood of any movement." He had seemed very pleased with himself at the time.

She could not, for the life of her, understand what had happened to change that plan into a murder, accidental or not.

Thursday, November 13, 2003
07:22

We'd gotten to bed early, by about midnight or so. For once, there were no interruptions. Unfortunately, I was unable to go to sleep. You know how it gets, sometimes, when you're just too damn tired to drop off? I took a couple of melatonin tablets, a couple of Tylenol, and after a while, I woke up. 7:22, according to the clock. I felt pretty good, considering. While Carson snored at the ceiling, I brewed up some hot water and instant coffee, and turned on the TV. I kept the sound off so Carson wouldn't be bothered, and watched CNN's headlines at the half hour. President Bush was coming over, on the 18th. People were unhappy about Iraq. I switched to Sky News. England was gearing up for the World Rugby Championships. They sounded very hopeful, although they'd never actually won the Championship before. It sort of reminded me of Cubs fans.

I poured a second cup of coffee, opened my laptop, and checked my email.

The first one was from Sue.

WE ALL SAW THE TAPES, AS YOU KNOW. WE DON'T THINK SHE LOOKS TOO BAD. OUR HOPES ARE UP. DO YOU KNOW ANYTHING ABOUT THOSE DEMANDS? ALL WE GET IS SOMETHING ABOUT RELEASING PRISONERS.

ALL IS FINE HERE. NOTHING NEW AT WORK. REALLY, REALLY MISS YOU BOTH. GIVE JANE A HUG FROME ME.

LOVE, SUE

That was nice to get. It did, though, make it just that much harder to keep from telling her that Emma was already dead. I could just picture the hopes that seeing her on those tapes had generated. Damn.

The second was from Sally.

I KNOW YOU'RE NOT HAVING A GOOD TIME, BUT HOPE YOU CAN HAVE SOME FUN SOONER OR LATER.

THE REPORT WENT FED EX NEXT DAY AIR. LAMAR NEARLY HAD A HEMMORHAGE. YOU HAVE ANY IDEA HOW MUCH THAT COSTS?

CONTACTED HESTER AND SHE WILL BE IN TOUCH VIA EMAIL. CAN'T FIND GEORGE ANYWHERE, AND HIS FIELD OFFICE IS NO HELP AT ALL. WE THINK HE MIGHT BE ON SPECIAL ASSIGNMENT OR SOMESUCH.

YOU NEED A DISPATCHER? I'M ALL PACKED.

SALLY

Cool. The file was on its way. The third was from Lamar.

ORDERED SALLY TO SEND PACKAGE. NO PROBLEM. KEEP AT IT. EVERYBODY ALL EXCITED ABOUT THE TAPE. I AGREE WITH YOU.

It wasn't signed, but it really didn't have to be. I was sort of amazed that he'd actually sent one himself.

The fourth was from Hester Gorse, Special Agent, Iowa Division of Criminal Investigation.

HEY, CARL!

I DON'T ENVY YOU THIS ASSIGNMENT AT ALL. I SAW EMMA ON A TAPE LAST NIGHT. SHE LOOKS GOOD, BUT IT'S NOT A GOOD IDEA TO GET ANY-BODY'S HOPE UP AT THIS POINT. THE DEMAND SOUNDS A LOT LIKE THEY COULDN'T THINK WHAT TO ASK FOR. YOU KNOW WHAT I MEAN?

I CHECKED WITH SALLY, AND SHE SEEMS TO HAVE THE COMPLETE FILE. I HAD SOME NOTES, AND WILL GET THEM OVER TO YOU.

GEORGE IS ON SOME SORT OF NATIONAL

SECURITY THING, STILL, YET, OR AGAIN. I'M TRYING
TO CONTACT HIM, TOO, BUT SO FAR NO LUCK.
SPEAKING OF, STAY LUCKY.

HESTER

The luck thing was because of the old saying, "I'd rather be lucky than smart." I'd always agreed with that.

So. Well, at least the file was on the way. I looked out the window at the people walking their dogs in Kensington Park. It was a beautiful, sunshiny day, the people wore light jackets or sweaters, and the dogs wore busy as only dogs can be. Almost none of them were leashed inside the park, and they were flying all over the place. It was relaxing, just to watch the park and the traffic in the street below. I could have spent my day doing just that.

The phone rang, waking Carson, and jolting me back to the real world.

It was Sergeant Trowbridge.

"I was emailed a copy of the autopsy report early this morning. Do you want to come over, or could I forward it to you?"

I gave him my email address.

"Excellent. The only alteration is the victim's name and sex. I've left it off, just in case things go awry. Will that do?"

"Sure."

"If you have any thoughts, feel free to email a reply. But," he added, quickly, "if there's something urgent, use the phone. I only get to my email twice a day."

"Got it. By the way, my reports on the terrorist incident in Iowa are being Fed-Exed, next day air. Should get it today or tomorrow."

"Excellent. Perhaps you should run that over to Blyth, first? They do that sort of thing. . . ."

"Sure."

He sounded pretty busy, beginning another conversation as he hung up. I thought it was nice of him to call.

I brought my email program back up, and there it was.

VICTIM: AGE: 33   SEX:
PLACE OF DEATH: UNKNOWN
DATE OF DEATH: UNKNOWN
PATHOLOGIST: MALLAMPALLI
DATE OF AUTOPSY: 16/10/03

FINAL ANATOMICAL DIAGNOSES:

SKULL FRACTURE, LEFT TEMPORAL BONE,
    RECENT 2 CM FRACTURE MAXILLIA AND
    1 CM FRACTURE, CONCURRENT, OF NASAL
    BONE
FRACTURE OF NASAL CARTILAGE
BRUISES AND ABRASIONS, FACE AND NECK,
    RECENT
LIGATURE MARKS, BOTH WRISTS, RECENT
LIGATURE MARKS, BOTH ANKLES, RECENT
ABRASIONS, BOTH KNEES, RECENT
ABRASION, RIGHT ELBOW, RECENT
BRUISES, UPPER RIGHT ARM AND SHOULDER,
    RECENT

POSTMORTEM FREEZING

AUTOPSY INDICATES: ASPIRATION OF BLOOD
    AND VOMITUS. AIRWAY COMPLETELY
    OBSTRUCTED BY BLOOD, VOMITUS, AND
    MUCUS.

TOXICOLOGY FOLLOWS. INITIAL CONCLUSION
    THAT TOXIC SUBSTANCES NOT DIRECT
    CONTRIBUTORS TO DEATH.

CAUSE OF DEATH: ASPHYXIATION

That was it. They hadn't sent the main sheets, which was all right with me. All they do in those is routine things like weigh your liver, and stuff. What I had was more than enough to tell me what had happened. She'd drowned, in effect. Since the blood and stuff was aspirated, and the airway was completely blocked, it took her a little while to do it. That was an ugly way to go. I hoped that she'd been knocked unconscious before the process started.

"What's that?" asked Carson, referring to my computer screen.

"Autopsy report," I said. "Have some coffee, before you read it."

"What happened to her?"

I told him. "I sure hope they get whoever's responsible," I said.

"I'd like to get 'em first," said Carson.

Now, as a cop, you learn not to say things like that. You just go out and do the job of arresting and charging, and let it go at that. It's usually satisfying enough. But, here, there was absolutely no chance I'd be able to do that, even if I could. I wasn't even a private citizen. I was just a tourist.

"It'd be nice," I said. "Not a chance, though. Not unless you want to thump people at random. Taking the chance that you just arbitrarily got the right one."

"Yeah."

"I think you'd have to smack around about fourteen million people, just to be sure," I said.

"I get it," said Carson. "Really."

"Assuming that it's somebody who lives in the London area . . ."

"So, what do you want to do today?" He poured some hot water into a cup, and added the tube full of instant.

"I'm not sure. Maybe go to that tube station? I dunno."

"That'd be a waste of time." He took a sip. "Wouldn't it?"

"Probably. But if the professor's been there, and is interested in the place . . . Hell, Carson, I don't know. But it might help Jane and Vicky."

He looked at his watch. "Don't they do the Changing of the Guard at eleven? We could go see that, and then to that station. They said it was close."

"I wonder if they take a tour today? I'm sure they won't let us in without a guide."

"The liability laws are a little different over here," said Carson, staring out the window. "Here, they just tell you to be careful. You screw up; you're on your own."

"No shit? That's refreshing." I thought a moment. "So, then, how do their attorneys eat?"

I stopped at the desk on the way to breakfast, to see if we could get into the Down Street station. The concierge gave me a really strange look when I asked him to check. We went in the dining room, ate breakfast, and he had his answer for us on our way out.

"They *do* have tours, sir," he said. "But only twice a year and you've missed them both."

We called the girls in Highgate as soon as we got back to the room. They were very disappointed.

"You have pretty good contacts, Dad. Could you see if there could be something special done? Like have somebody go with us, who can get in any time?"

"Very unlikely," I said. "They'd require some sort of guide, and . . ."

"Try, would you?" It was the same tone she'd used when she'd tried to wheedle the keys to the family car out of me ten years ago. She got the same answer.

"Well . . . Okay. But all I can do is ask."

"That's great! Oh, and the security dudes came by. I guess we should have told them that we were cutting classes today."

"Oh, yeah. I'll bet."

"They said that one of them can 'go on days off' now, if Vicky and I promise to stay together."

It made perfect sense to me.

"You know what?" she asked. "I'll bet that if we go to that abandoned station, our security guy has to come, too. You think?"

"Probably."

"Then all we need is a guide, or a key," she said, brightly.

I called Blyth's office. One of his staff took the call, and said that he'd get back to me regarding the station as soon as he had some free time. I started to give my new cell phone number to the person at the other end, and he repeated it to me before I was finished.

"Is that it?"

"Yep."

"Brilliant. We have everything then. He'll call."

I considered it a plus that the number was so readily available.

Blyth called just as we were sitting down to lunch with Jane and Vicky at a place called Prezzo, just off High Street.

"I've done some checking," said Blyth, "and we can get you in for a look round tomorrow morning."

"No kidding?"

"We've secured a guide," he said, "but there's a bit of a problem with security. Your girls' escort is going to have to be given a day away, due to your president's visit. It seems that just about everyone will be working from Tuesday next through Friday."

"Everyone?"

"We are supposed to field about 14,000 personnel for security."

"Jesus."

"Oh that he were included," he said. "Nonetheless, the Underground require you have official accompaniment. I had a chat with my friend O'Toole who operates the tube, and he was very gracious and wishes to express his concern for Emma. He said that he was more than willing to do anything to help get her back." He paused. He'd had to lie, too. "So. I have a volunteer on my staff who will tag along on her day off. It shall be Alice, naturally. She seems to have taken quite a liking to your girls. She'll meet with you at the Down Street entrance at 09:00 sharp. Shouldn't take more than an hour or two."

"She doesn't have to do that . . ."

"True. But she does want to do it. She'll be good company, and I'm sure you'll find her quite resourceful."

I smiled to myself, remembering the 'barrister' bit. "I've seen that. She certainly is."

Jane and Vicky were quite happy that their security tail had been taken off. I'm sure they didn't think they really needed it, and I could only agree with that. The odds were very great against either of them being targeted at this point. Although, to be truthful, I thought they were safe because Emma was dead, and that another hostage or two wouldn't fit with whatever their plans were. I wasn't sure why Jane and Vicky were so certain, and I didn't ask.

We spent the rest of the day at the girls' flat in Highgate, looking up tube information on the net, and periodically checking with our hotel to see if the FedEx package had arrived. I took the tube back down to our hotel to pick up my laptop. I was inordinately proud of myself for making it that far without getting lost. I have to admit the color coding of the tube lines helps a lot.

When I got back to Highgate, I found that the others had been shopping while I was gone. We were now the proud possessors of flashlights, or torches as I was informed they were called over here; much bottled water; two 'tins' of Walker's shortbread cookies; and a travelers first aid kit.

"Good Lord," I said. "You guys expecting to be gone a long time?"

"We just got things we might need," said Jane.

"A first aid kit?"

"Sure, Dad. If we do find Emma, it might be a good thing to have. Not to think negative, you know? But just in case." She was so serious, I almost told her. Almost.

Rather than lie, or say something I knew would mislead, I said, "How good are those shortbread cookies?"

"They're delicious," she said. "But they're for tomorrow."

She gets more like her mother every day.

"Did you remember to bring your camera? There might be evidence we need to record."

As a matter of fact, I had, but just to record the occasion for Sue. I came close to spilling the beans again.

"Got it," I said.

"Do you have a tape recorder?"

"Uh . . . no. I didn't bring one." I hadn't been packing to do a crime scene investigation.

"Geeze, Dad." She held out a small recorder. "I use it for lectures. There's a fresh tape inside."

Chapter 17

Friday, November 14, 2003
Thistle Hotel
High Street, Kensington

Carson and I went downstairs for breakfast about nine or so. Afterward, on our way out, the concierge at the near desk flagged me down. I had a package.

It was FedEx, and it was my files on both the Skripkin case and on that terrorist incident we'd had back in 2002. It must have weighed ten pounds. The attached slip told me that it had cost $128.00 to ship it. That doesn't sound like all that much, but our average postage budget for a month at the Nation County Sheriff's Department was about $30.00.

We hustled it right back up to the room, and I emptied out my carry-on bag and inserted the files. Carson thought the cost was funny.

"I can just see Lamar hand delivering letters all over the county because you spent three months postage!"

"No," I said. "It's part of the annual budget. He'll wait till I get back, and have me do the hand delivery." I was only half kidding.

I called Blyth's office, and told the woman who answered that my files had come, and that he could contact me via my cell phone. I also told her that I'd have the files with me, so we could drop them off any time today.

"You're not gonna lug that around all day, are you? Seriously?"

"Safest place," I said.

"What, with all the pickpockets in London?"

"We run into Fagan, you distract him, okay? While I run off?"

"No, really, Carl. Is that safe?"

"I feel better about it this way." We went back downstairs, and hiked west on High Street to the American Express currency exchange.

Jane and Vicky were in class, so we had the morning and the first half of the afternoon to ourselves. We decided to head over to the Imperial War Museum because we couldn't think of anything constructive to do without blowing our pledge to secrecy.

We found our way to the Lambeth North station on the Bakerloo line, after taking an unexpected excursion to a place called Willisden Junction, in the opposite direction from our destination. It pays not only to read the damned signs, but to study the Underground map posted in the cars, as well.

I like riding the tube, though, so I didn't consider it time wasted. My phone rang just as we got headed back in the right direction.

"Yeah?"

It was Blyth. "I understand your files have come?"

"Yes!"

"Good. From the volume of your voice, I'd say you were somewhere in the tube."

"We're headed," I said, more quietly, "to the Imperial War Museum. Just wanted to see it."

"Excellent choice. How soon will you be there?"

"Ah . . . we're just pulling out of Willisden Junction, so . . . what? Thirty minutes?"

There was a pause. "What on earth are you doing in Willisden Junction?"

"We got on the wrong train," I said, and got amused stares from three or four of the nearest passengers.

"You certainly did. Why don't I meet you at the museum in an hour? Give you time to see a bit of the place."

"Sure, fine!" I said, yelling again as we accelerated.

"Under the big guns," he said.

"Which ones?"

"Can't miss. . . ." And I lost the connection. I hoped I could find the right big guns, and told Carson as much.

I needn't have worried. There were these two enormous 15 inch guns at the entrance. The placard told me that they were 54 feet long, weighed in at 100 tons each, and since they were mounted at an angle, thoroughly dominated the landscape.

"Think these are the guns?" asked my sarcastic little partner.

*   *   *

We wandered into the museum for about twenty minutes, and then came back out just in time to see Blyth and Trowbridge coming up the walk under the guns.

"Why don't we go on in," said Blyth. "We can sit in one of their offices, I'm sure, and look the files over. Perhaps find some coffee or tea."

He greeted a man who looked like he was in charge as "Freddy," introduced us as a "pair of my American friends," and Freddy very obligingly ushered us upstairs, and into an office. It was his, I think.

We had coffee as we went through the files. When Blyth got to Mustafa Abdullah Odeh, he looked up.

"I know of him," he said, pointing to the name. "He had a connection here, as well. I didn't know he was involved."

"Yeah," I said. "The FBI didn't want his name out. I don't know how they accomplished that, but they did."

"You just quietly take him into custody," said Trowbridge.

"Well, yeah. But I shot him."

"What?" He looked truly startled.

"I didn't kill him," I said. "Just shot him in the leg. But he got treated, at least at first, in a local hospital."

"Why did you shoot him?"

"It says here," said Blyth, "that he was pointing a shotgun at you at the time."

"Yeah. And I was pointing my gun at his buddy, who was sort of on the floor with an AK-47 he couldn't quite get to. I pretty much shot Odeh because the other one couldn't' really get to his gun . . . it was sort of fast, you know?"

"It must have been exciting," said Trowbridge, with just enough sarcasm to get his point across without offending.

"No. It just sort of happened. No satisfaction, really. No sense of doing some sort of righteous deed. It just had to be done."

"I'm sure," said Blyth.

"What happened to the other man?" asked Trowbridge.

"He didn't make it."

"You killed him, then?"

"No." I grinned. "To be absolutely honest about it, I ran out of the building as fast as I could after Odeh went down. FBI sniper took the other guy out when he came outside with the AK and started shooting."

"Oh." This time Trowbridge sounded a little disappointed. I did notice that Blyth was grinning, too.

"I would have shot him," I said, still with a grin, "except I was hiding behind a tree by a hog lot, and I don't think I could have hit him from there. It was hard enough just seeing him."

"Tales of the Wild West," said Blyth. "You should write a book."

"Not on your life," I said.

Chapter 18

Saturday, November 15, 2003
Down Street, London
09:04 Greenwich Mean Time

We sighted Alice standing out in front of the old station when we were nearly a block away. We waved, and she did, too.

The entrance to the abandoned tube station turned out to be painted red brick, with the actual entrance door on the right, and a place called the "Mayfair Mini-Mart" occupying the left half of the building.

An older gentleman in a blue sweater came out of the mart, and walked right up to us.

"My name is John Hicks," he said. "I do some of the guided tours of the tube stations. Glad to be of help."

Hands were shaken all around.

"Your barrister here," he said, referring to Alice, "tells me that you're looking for possible clues?"

"That's right," I said. Good old resourceful Alice. "Our missing friend, Emma, has been here on a tour before."

"So have we," said Vicky, indicating Jane. "It's a fascinating place."

"Oh, indeed," he said, busily unlocking the entrance. "Quite a history. I'll just tell you about it as we go. That way you don't have to ask questions, and if there's anything like a clue, just tell me to stop," he said, cheerfully. "Just to start us off, this is one of the stations designed by the famous Leslie Green. Very recognizable." He returned his attention to the door, and seemed to be having a little difficulty with the lock.

Alice, who was wearing black slacks and a black windbreaker, motioned to the backpacks that Jane and Vicky were wearing.

"You'll be staying, then?"

Jane laughed. "No. But we just brought some stuff we might need."

"Well, then, let's have a scout," said Alice. "Assuming we can gain entrance."

There was a rush of air as the door opened.

"Overpressure from trains," said Hicks. "It will also be very noisy. The main Piccadilly track runs right past, of course . . . ," and the rest was lost as he entered the building.

There was also, I noticed as we descended a concrete stairway to the next floor, a strong smell of the general tube traffic. Oil, grease, hot metal, a little ozone, and kind of an indefinable mustiness permeated the place.

"Now do be cautious," he said, as we reached the top of a spiral staircase. "Stay to the outside, if you would, please. The widest portion of the steps. It would be all too easy to slip."

That sounded like good advice, especially from the man at the bottom of the file, who would be wiped out if somebody at the top tripped and caused everyone to come cascading down on top of him.

The walls were done in maroon and a cream colored tile. Well, maybe cream colored. They could have begun life as white, I thought. This station was old.

In contrast, the caged aluminum stair looked almost new. Like all spirals, it narrowed considerably toward the center. The outside made particularly good sense for those of us with the largest feet. I did sneak a look over the inside edge, near the top, as we went down. The shaft was fairly well lit, and seemed to go down a good 75 feet.

"The stair is kept in good repair," came wafting up from below me, as there was a pause in the noise of passing trains. "This would serve as an emergency exit for passengers between Hyde Park Corner and Green Park. For that same reason, the lighting is maintained."

That made sense. It also explained the white arrows on green background signs pointing up, and the legend, FIRE EXIT.

"How you doing, Dad?" Jane knows I have a problem with heights.

"Fine. Do we have to use these to come back up?"

"Yep. This one, matter of fact."

"Then ask me that on the trip back," I said. As I get older, my knees start to give me trouble after a while on steps. I'd already lost count, but there had to be between 75 and 85 steps on this stair. "Is there another level down?"

"There's but one platform level," said Mr. Hicks. "Just served the Piccadilly line, you know." There was an audible rush of air, sort of a deep, wheezing moaning that got progressively louder, announcing the approach of another train. "It was built in nineteen oh. . . ." His voice was drowned out again by the rumbling and whoosh, as the train went by down below us. Several seconds later, as the noise subsided, and the air rushed back past us to fill the under-pressure in the tube, he was still talking. ". . . Churchill in the early days of the War. Before the Cabinet War Rooms were done. He hated the place."

I took my digital camera out, and snapped a shot down the stair.

"They originally used lifts," he said. "Those were disabled years ago. Too dangerous, you see. We do sometimes have unwanted guests. Mostly homeless people, but sometimes young people. Mostly hooligans. They paint things on the walls. Well, I suppose they need something to entertain themselves."

Mr. Hicks apparently talked all the time, and not always to us.

"The maintenance crews winkle 'em out," he said, in a voice lowered enough to make me strain to hear. "Bless 'em."

Another train came by. I kind of hated to miss Hicks' monologue.

I was surprised to find there were doors along the descending shaft, better than halfway down. One was just a doorway, to an empty room. The others, Hicks opened for us. They were, well, vintage bathrooms. Steel looking fixtures, very grimy.

"You can see how much dust there is here," he said. "With the doors closed there the moving air from the trains doesn't dust things off like it does elsewhere." He turned to us. "Some say that Churchill used this bath, in the early days. Can't prove it, but it's what's said."

I noticed Jane peering into the two toilets. She saw me looking at her, and moved back toward me. "Just looking for signs of recent use," she whispered.

I decided that I'd better get more into the act.

"So, it should be difficult to tell if there have been trespassers? I mean, not much chance of foot tracks in dust or anything?"

"Only here," said Hicks. "Were you thinking that someone could use this for passage?"

"We're not certain just what we expect to find," I said.

"Some of us think they might have kept her here for a time," said Jane.

Mr. Hicks thought about that one for a moment. "I'd not consider that likely, Miss. But I suppose that we need to look at 'possible,' don't we? I mean, since the Yard doesn't seem to be able to find her anywhere else. But the maintenance crews store things here, and come through from time to time. And there's the monthly inspection by the safety lot. To make sure the way is clear for the exit. But they certainly don't go everywhere. . . ."

He was interrupted by another train's passage. They went by here at full tilt, and were a whole lot louder than they were in a functioning tube station.

After the noise subsided, he said, "There *are* nooks and crannies . . . do you wish to concentrate on those?"

"Yes!" said Jane.

Well, that settled it. I think we could have learned a little more on the way, but Mr. Hicks was on the scent, so to speak.

We went down another concrete stair, and onto the old platform area. We hardly paused, but Mr. Hicks did say, between passing trains in the adjacent tunnels, "The track area has been paved over, as you can see. It was for secretarial personnel during the war."

The platform looked to be about a hundred yards long, and there was another flight of concrete steps toward the middle. That seemed to be where we were headed.

"This is the bridge," said Mr. Hicks, "that crosses the east bound Piccadilly line. That's the line this station was originally on. . . ."

I was looking for footprints, along with Jane and Vicky. Nothing looked particularly fresh, thought the dust wasn't very thick. You could see the traces of prints, particularly the types with soles I referred to as Waffle Stompers. They were just faded, though, as though the dust had had several weeks to re-settle since they were made. The floor tiles were cream and purple, and the purple segments were very good for checking the prints.

"You see anything, Dad?" Jane's voice sounded anxious. She apparently didn't see anything fresh.

"Not really . . . but, boy, this place is sure big enough." I said that to give her ample credit that there was plenty of room to build a theatrical set that would represent a small room.

"Yeah," she said, sort of distractedly, "like I said. . . ."

We were just coming down the steps, after crossing the bridge, and were nearly on the second platform that would have accommodated trains running east, when Jane and I both saw the fresh prints.

Tennis shoes, both sets of them.

"Jesus Christ, Dad," she said, in a normal tone of voice. "Look. . . ."

"Yeah." Now what? Either they were workers, or maybe some homeless denizens of this place. But they sure weren't Emma's tracks, and by deduction, certainly not those of her abductors.

We all stopped, and got an extra minute or so to think as another train went whooshing and roaring by. By the draft, and the sound, there was an opening on this side of the tunnel that connected to an active track.

"Are they closer, now?" I asked Mr. Hicks, as the sound subsided.

"Indeed. The emergency entrance to this area is right over there . . ." and he pointed to an alcove on our right.

As it got progressively quieter, Alice said, "Do you recognize those tracks, sir?"

"No, but then I probably wouldn't," said Hicks. "The workmen usually wear boots . . . are those boot tracks?"

"No," I said, quickly. "Those are tennis shoes."

"Trainers," said Alice.

"How odd," he said, and began to walk right over them.

"Sir," I said, touching his arm. "We need to be careful . . . they might be evidence of something." I had to play the role.

Carson was giving me a look as if to say, "Evidence of *what*?" But he stopped just before stepping on them himself.

I asked Jane if she had a pad and pencil. She did, and I made a rough sketch of the prints. "Anybody got a ruler?" Vicky did. A very small tape she said she carried to use when shopping for antiques for her mother. Cool. I noted the dimensions, and then placed my pencil down beside the tracks, and took a couple of photographs.

"Just don't sharpen this pencil," I said.

"Why?" She took it from me, and put it in her pack.

"I just used it for scale. Sharpen it, it looks smaller, and the size of the shoe print increases. . . ." I chuckled. "I speak from experience."

Yet another train roared through the active tunnel, as we moved toward another alcove on our left.

"These are the old WC's," said Mr. Hicks. "No lights in here to speak of, so be very careful where you step. . . ."

As he said that, and another train roared right behind the last one, I thought I saw an abrupt change in the color of the wall just inside the WC entrance. I blinked, and it didn't change again. By that time, Mr. Hicks, Carson and Jane were already around the corner, with Alice close behind. I went next, followed by Vicky.

I turned on my flashlight, and was just turning the corner into the restroom itself when I distinctly heard Mr. Hicks say, "Who are you?"

At the same time, Jane yelled, "Dad. . . . !" and Carson hollered "Look out!"

Somebody was suddenly running out of the WC entrance, and heading right at me. I shifted my weight to block him, and he swerved, and without really thinking about it, I thrust my flashlight with my right hand, and speared him in the forehead as he was passing me. A shot like that is almost impossible to block, even if you can react in time. All you can really see is the small end of the flashlight, and that for just an instant before it smacks you in the head. It sure as hell got him. The blow almost sprained my wrist, but he hit the floor on his back with a very satisfying thud. I found myself looking down at a broad face with glassy, crossed eyes, and a half-moon shaped cut almost dead center in his forehead that was just beginning to ooze blood and get bluish at the edges. There was a large folding knife on the tile beside him, and I kicked it away, and started to lean down when Jane screamed, "Dad!" from deeper into the unlit room. I left the guy, whoever he was, laying where I'd knocked him, and went thundering into that dim, echoing place. Any other sounds were overwhelmed by another train, but I saw a short, thin man take a swing at Carson, who jumped back out of the way. The man had a knife, too.

Alice delivered a sweeping kick to the back of the guy's legs, taking him instantly to the floor. Almost before he hit on his back, she twisted his wrist really hard, really fast. The knife came away, and skidded across the floor. She used his arm as a lever, and twisted him over on his stomach, wrapped his wrist up toward the middle of his back, and held it there with her knee. It happened so fast that Carson was still backing up when she was completely in control of the assailant. I was very impressed.

Jane was sitting on the floor, Mr. Hicks standing over her, her back against the wall, and in the fresh silence, she simply said, "He stabbed me. I can't believe this."

"Where?" I was kneeling beside her.

"Here," she said, pointing at the area of her left collarbone.

I pulled her sweatshirt aside. He certainly had. There was a very deep cut, about four inches long, between her collar bone and the back of her shoulder. It was so deep it was spreading, and looked about half as wide as it was long. My first thought was the brachial artery was cut, but the blood was running out freely, not spurting.

"Where's the first aid kit?"

That's when we heard Vicky yelling outside the restroom. I didn't quite understand what she was saying, but Alice was off like a shot, leaving Carson sitting on the suspect.

"Vicky's got it," said Jane, dully. Shock.

"No problem . . ." I said, as I tried to tear her sweatshirt. I couldn't get the thing started due to the thick seams. I pulled off my sweatshirt, then my tee shirt, and folded it up as fast as I could. It made a poor compress, but it would do for the moment.

"There. Now that's going to be all right. How do you feel?"

"Dizzy."

"Normal. No problem." I pulled my sweatshirt back on. "You *should* feel dizzy with that. That's good." You say the damnedest things at times like that.

"And kind of cold." She looked me right in the eye. "Am I going to die?"

"No." I said that with all the confidence I could muster. It didn't look like an immediately fatal wound, but I wasn't sure about the bleeding. Between shock and blood loss, it might be possible to lose her.

She let out her breath. "Good," she said, weakly. "I don't want to do that."

I got out my phone. "What's the 911 number in England?"

That got a little smile. "999."

I couldn't get a signal.

"That won't work down here," said Mr. Hicks, who looked and sounded a little shocky himself. "Only in the active stations. . . . Antennas, you know."

"Okay . . . you all right?"

"Yes, how's she doing?"

"Okay so far. We need medical help. The sooner the better."

"Yes. There's an emergency connection in the other tunnel. . . ." And off he went at a pretty good trot.

"It's so dark," said Jane.

"I'll see if we can get you out to a lighter area soon . . . don't want to move you now." As I said that, I covered her right eye and flicked my flashlight beam into the left one. Its pupil constricted instantly. Good. I pressed two fingers of my left hand against her neck, and got a strong carotid pulse. Even better.

"Can you feel your fingers?"

"Yes . . ."

"Move 'em for me, okay?"

She did. "Like that?"

"Yep. Any tingly sensations or anything?" I kept talking, hopefully getting her attention and delaying or reducing the emotional shock, at least.

"No . . . no, not really."

No nerve damage, either. So far. "Okay, you're doing great. Now just keep that arm in your lap, like. Don't move it. Let the clot form."

Vicky came flying into the restroom. "Jane, oh my God! Oh my God, is she all right?" She sounded very near to crying.

"So far," I said. "She got stabbed by the one on the floor over there. The one under Carson. You've got the first aid pack?"

"Oh, my god, oh, yes, I'm so sorry . . ." she rattled off as she shrugged off her backpack and produced the kit. There was some pretty good stuff in there. Two large compresses, for example.

"Why?" asked Vicky, and she tore open one of the compresses and handed it to me.

"What?" I asked, as I took the compress.

"Why did he do this?"

"I don't know," I said. I shined my flashlight back onto the wound, and applied the first compress.

"Was it him?" asked Jane, a little foggy.

"What, kiddo? Try not to move your arm . . ."

"Was it him . . . over there?"

They *had* both had knives. "I think so . . . I don't know."

I looked over at Carson. He was paying close attention to the man on the floor.

"But, why?" asked Vicky again.

That was a very good question. It looked to me that we'd interrupted a couple of vandals, or homeless people, or something. They'd panicked. And I was going to kick myself for years for letting Jane come down into this place, knowing damned well that she wasn't going to find Emma.

"We must have interrupted something," said Carson, still on top of the suspect.

I thought he might be right, and suspected it was a dope deal.

"Can I have some water?" That was Jane. I opened my bottle, and she took it in her right hand. I let her bring it up herself, because I wanted to see how she was doing.

She took three pretty good gulps, no noticeable trembling, and then held it down. "Thanks." No immediate nausea, either.

"Keep it. You're going to dehydrate a little, so keep drinking water. It's good for you." I pointed my flashlight at the bottle, just in case there was some trace of blood in it. I didn't think the knife had gone into her lung, but you never know about these things. It was clear.

"Where did Alice go?" I asked Vicky.

"The guy you knocked down . . . he got up, and started to run away. I yelled, and started to chase him."

"You should have just let him go," I said. Just a cop thing.

"Alice almost got him. He wiggled into this little hole. . . ."

"He's gone?"

"Unfortunately," said Alice, as she came into the room. "How's Jane . . . ?"

"We need help," I said. "I think she'll be all right." Just a little lie. "But I don't want her to try to go up those steps."

"Have you called 999?"

"Couldn't get out," I said, looking back toward Jane. "How you coming?"

"Okay . . ." but it was a weak okay.

"Mr. Hicks went to an emergency phone."

"Good," said Alice. "May I take a look at that?"

She moved the blood soaked compress off Jane's shoulder, and peered at the bloody wound. "I don't think it got the artery," she said.

"Yeah."

As Alice and I put the second compress on the wound, I noticed there was plenty of blood pooling in the wound to show bubbles if she had an injured lung. There were none.

"No bubbles, kid," I said. "Better and better."

"What?" asked Jane.

"No bubbles in the cut. Your lung is just fine, too. Lookin' good."

"Thanks. . . ."

When the second compress was firmly in place, Alice went over to our captive.

"Who might you be?" she asked.

There was no answer. He did struggle a bit, but he was on his belly, and Carson was pretty strong. He wasn't going anywhere unless Carson let him. Secured, Alice patted him down thoroughly. She made a neat little pile of personnel effects near him, including a wallet, a cell phone, some papers, and assorted keys.

She looked in his wallet, and I assumed she'd found an ID card of some sort. "So what brings you here?" she asked. There was no answer.

"Ask about Emma," said Jane. She said it softly, but I could have sworn the guy heard her.

"Let's worry about you right now," I said.

After that, all we had to do was keep Jane hydrated, warm, and wait for assistance.

Four bobbies arrived first. They were really good. Two stacked the assailant up, handcuffed him, and kept him securely in a corner. One came instantly to check Jane, and the other started taking names. Alice identified herself, her true self, and began telling them what had happened. As soon as she got to the part where a second man had fled the scene, one of the bobbies who was on the suspect took off with her to try to track him down.

When the firemen and the ambulance people got there, I don't think I've ever been so relieved in my life. It seemed like it had taken them hours, but I was told later that it had been twelve minutes after Mr. Hicks placed his call that they'd gotten down to us.

They conferred while they examined Jane, and decided while the prisoner would walk up all the stairs to a waiting police car outside the old station, it would be best to flag down a train and take Jane to the next station, where she could be transported up by escalator. I didn't know they could do that, but they did. With Jane on her stretcher, the rest of us walked to the emergency access door between Down Street and the live Piccadilly line, and waited. Sure as hell, two trains later, one slowed, stopped, and we found ourselves on our way to the Green Park station. There weren't too many passengers in our car, but they were all pretty dammed curious. Even for Englishmen. When we got to Green Park, up we went to the surface, where we were met by an ambulance and two police cars, and hustled across the Thames to St. Thomas' Hospital Trauma Unit.

I rode in the ambulance with Jane. She was getting really groggy, now that real help had arrived and she felt totally secure. When we went flying by Parliament, siren yelping, she looked out the window and said, "Wow." Then she sort of went away for a few minutes.

I glanced at the Paramedic who was working Jane. "She looks pretty good to me, now," I said. "What do you think?"

"You're her father?"

"Yes. I'm also a cop."

"Very good. There's no exit. I can't say for sure, but it looks like the downward path of the instrument was deflected by her clavicle. We need to do X-ray. Wouldn't want any possible fragments of the bone to be moving about. Looks like we missed the major vessels, which is good. Might have impacted the scapula. . . . She ought to be just fine . . ."

Jane was checked again by a nurse, as soon as she got through the door. That's when I found out that what I called the ER, was in fact the A&E, or Accident and Emergency unit. They referred to it as 'Re-sus.' They said that it was short for resuscitation, but it sounded a lot like recess as in playground the first time I heard it.

I registered for her, as she was still going in and out of awareness, as the nurse said. They took her into an exam and treatment area, the fourth in a series of five large bays on the left just as we got inside the double doors, and with her surrounded by people in blue scrubs, the curtain closed. The rest of us waited outside. That's when I really started to get angry at myself. I couldn't very well say anything to

Carson, as Vicky was right there with us. But I kept telling myself that, if I had only told her that Emma was dead, we never would have gone down there in the first place. If I had been more serious, I would have gone in first, of course. But I damned well *knew* that Emma wasn't going to be there. So I'd relaxed. And she'd walked right into a couple of . . . what?

"What do you think they were? Homeless people? The one I got the best look at sure didn't look homeless. Gang members? Dopers?"

"I don't know," said Carson. "They sure didn't belong there, that's for sure."

"The one you knocked down," said Vicky. "Outside? He looked sort of dingy, you know, but not poor. Just hadn't cleaned up for a few days."

"Where the hell did he go?" I hadn't given that much thought.

"He ran to this little rectangular hole, about waist high. In a lobby-like area. Alice just about had him, she blew past me like I was just taking a walk. . . ." She looked helpless. "He just slipped right through, just before she got to him."

"You should have seen her take out the guy with the knife," I said.

Vicky looked at Carson. "I thought that you . . . oh, so Alice did that?"

"Well, uh, we sort of were there together. She's, you know, fast. Faster than me, this time."

Lame, Carson. I got out my cell phone, and checked the signal strength. Very good.

"Gonna call your wife?" asked Carson.

"As soon as I know something for sure," I said. "She doesn't know anything right now, so she isn't worried."

"What do you think?"

"I think she's going to be all right," I said. "God, I sure hope so. She's pretty tough, you know?"

"She sure is," said Vicky. "She'll be just fine."

She didn't sound any more certain than I did. I mean, I know about this sort of thing, but I've seen just enough to know that somebody can go sour on you at the snap of a finger, and it's always unanticipated. Something that's been overlooked, or missed, or just not thought about. So I sat there and worried for about fifteen minutes.

A nurse came out, and told us that Jane was looking, "Very good," and was being prepped for surgery, and would we like to "wait upstairs? That's where we'll bring her when the surgery is over."

She didn't say how long. They never do, but you always hope they might, just this once.

Almost two hours after we got settled in the upstairs waiting area, a doctor came out of a door, walked over to us, and said, "You must be with Jane?"

I told him who I was.

"She's doing absolutely fine," he said. "I'd expect to have her up and about by Monday. The proper angle does make a difference. The blade cut about half way through the clavicle. Lucky it didn't break. If it had gone in underneath rather than above, things would be very different. As it is, the knife just nicked the brachial vein, and she may have some nerve bruising, but otherwise we merely had to stitch her up. The X-rays showed no debris that we'd missed. She's lost a bit of blood, and we've given her two units."

"Excellent!"

"You should be able to see her in a few minutes. . . . I understand you're a policeman over in the States?"

"Yes."

"Then I suppose I needn't tell you, but it took a powerful blow to cut the bone like that. If the knife had been dull, it would likely have broken it instead of cutting that way."

"Or at a more canted angle . . . yeah, I know. Or a steeper one."

"She's very lucky. "

"I couldn't agree more," I said. "Thank you, doctor. For everything."

I decided to wait until I actually saw her, before I called Sue. Mothers want firsthand information.

A couple of minutes later, I was ushered into her room. She was still out, but there were no tubes in or anything, except for a very small drainage tube leading from her injured shoulder, and an IV drip that said it was a saline solution. She was pale, but breathing well. About all I could have asked for.

I called Sue at home. It was nearly three pm London time, so it was about nine in the morning in Maitland, Iowa.

Sue answered on the third ring.

"Hi!"

"Why, hello! I wasn't expecting to hear from you this early." Then intuition started to kick in. Just that fast. "Is everything all right?"

"Not too bad," I said. "Unfortunately, Jane's in the hospital."

"What? What? Where?"

"St. Thomas' here in London."

"Is she sick? Was she in an accident?"

"No, she's not sick. She got hurt while we were taking a tour of an abandoned tube station this morning," I said.

"How on earth . . . How bad is it? What happened?"

I was doing a rotten job, and I knew it. But this beating around the bush was also getting nowhere. "Listen, we stumbled on what I think were a couple of homeless people. One of them had a knife, and Jane got cut."

"Oh, my God!"

"She's just fine, I'm looking at her now, and she's just fine."

"Let me talk to her."

"Ah. Well, she's not quite up to that, not just yet. She's still coming around. . . ."

"Coming around?"

"She had to have surgery, on her shoulder."

There was a momentary silence. "How serious was this cut?"

"It was more of a stab, really. But she's been through the surgery, and she's just fine. All stitched up. I can hardly see the wound," I said. That was true. It was bandaged pretty well.

"When will they release her?"

"Monday, they say."

"Monday?! Monday . . . I'm coming over there. I think I can get there by then."

My backside was saved by Jane's eyes blinking open, and her whispering "Can . . . water?"

"Sure," and I reached over to her tray and got her a cup with a curved straw. She took a sip.

"Who are you talking to?" came over the phone. Jane recognized Sue's voice, and said, reasonably loudly, all things considered, "Hi, Mom."

"You wanna talk to her?" I asked into the phone.

Of course she did. It was a short conversation, but while they talked, I decided that I wasn't even going to make a token resistance to Sue coming over. This was really a family emergency, as her school rules defined it. And if they could get me a passport the same day, they could sure as hell do the same for her. We could pay off the credit card cost for a couple of years.

When I got the phone back, the first thing I said was, "Let me know as soon as you get a flight. Try to get into Heathrow, it's really close. I'll find a way to meet you."

"Right . . ." I could tell she'd been crying.

"She's really fine," I said. "Just still a little dopey. But I know she could use you for a few days, just to make sure she takes it easy and stuff."

After I broke the connection, Jane said, "Mom comin' over?"

"You bet."

She gave a very faint smile. "Can she bring Margaret?"

Margaret is Jane's dog.

Chapter 19

Saturday, November 15, 2003
16:00 Greenwich Mean TIme

Carson, Vicky and I were just standing around in the waiting area while a couple of nurses did stuff with Jane, when two women showed up. They weren't together, but they got off the elevator about a minute apart.

The first was Sarah Mitchell, sans photographer, at least as far as I could tell, although I began glancing around the area immediately.

"How is she?" was the first thing she said.

"She'll be just fine."

"Do you have any idea who the assailant was?"

"Look," I said, and I sounded tired even to myself, "I really don't have the time right now. Really."

"I know, but. . . ."

At that moment, the second woman stepped out of the elevator. It was Alice.

I waived, and stepped right over to her, intercepting her a good fifteen feet from the redoubtable Sarah Mitchell.

"Mrs. Peel, I presume?" Alice actually blushed. "You did a fantastic job back there," I said.

"How is she?" asked Alice.

"Gonna be just fine," I said, as I heard voices behind me. Carson was talking to Sarah Mitchell. I got some satisfaction that, at least this time, he wouldn't be able to blame all the leaks on me. Unfortunately, the voices were getting closer.

"We should talk," said Alice, under her breath. She raised her voice as Carson, Vicky and Sarah Mitchell approached. "Would you excuse us? I have some advice for Mr. Houseman. . . ." I'd almost forgotten she was my 'solicitor.'

As we walked away, I looked sternly toward Carson. He didn't even seem to be aware we were leaving. Vicky smiled, and nodded. She'll keep an eye on him, I thought. I hoped.

Alice and I strolled down the corridor, past the nurse's station, and turned into a short dead end kind of place that had a window. Nobody else was there.

"Our very own alcove," said Alice. "Excellent. Now, to begin with they weren't homeless," she said. "They were bedraggled, but they definitely were not homeless."

I knew who she was talking about. "I agree," I said. Sometimes you just have to say something.

"Special Branch assure me that the one we have is not a gang member. Just why he was there, we don't yet know. He had complete identification on him. You saw that. He's simply not talking, as yet. He hasn't been charged as yet, but he shall be confronted with a charge of attempted murder."

Good. "What's his name? If you can tell me."

"Jamal Essabar."

"Middle Eastern?"

"Yes. But that doesn't mean much . . . and certainly not what you might think." She said that with a smile.

"Yeah. So, what does he do?"

"We're checking. I came over as soon as I could. We may even know by now."

"I'm curious, that's all."

"Of course. That's very understandable. Did you see that cheese box on the floor, near the far wall? It was behind where I had him on the floor."

Now that she mentioned it, I thought I had. "About so long . . . ?"

"Yes. That's the one."

"Yeah. Wood. So that's what it was. Sure."

"It was labeled as cheese in Arabic," she said. "The small hole where the first subject got away? It leads into a sub-basement of a near-eastern restaurant. They apparently stole the cheese from that location, as I'm told there are several identical boxes in the basement. I looked in the box to see how much they'd eaten . . . to tell how long they might have been hiding down there.

"Excellent." I meant that. Good piece of work.

"There were just a few millimeters off one end," she said.

"Okay . . ."

"There's something about it's origin that we're checking."

"What?" I was thinking about several things, and the unexpected observation threw me for a second.

"The cheese. There's something about the cheese that's got some attention from our experts. I can't say what, as yet. But I have an idea what it is they're so concerned about. I was just old that as I was leaving."

"You have experts in cheese?"

"Not precisely." She smiled again. "Also, there were blankets and some other food items. There's also a small bag of trash that contains two empty cans of soup that match one of the un-opened cans they had in their little cache. My guess is they'd been bivouacked there for a day or two, at best."

"But we have no idea why they were there?"

"Not as yet."

"Anything on the identity of the second one?"

"No." She lowered her voice even further. "We do have two men we believe to be them, on surveillance video. They're walking, after leaving a car in the vicinity of the restaurant, last night."

"You had the place under surveillance?" I was astonished. Impressed, but astonished.

"Oh, no. There are cameras in place all about London. The Mets run them, and they hold video for a time. We just asked for a look up on the cameras that might cover their access routes. The installation at the intersection of Down and Brick Streets got them."

"I didn't know that."

She gave me a questioning look.

"About the cameras. How cool."

"Quite useful," she said.

"I'll bet. Over in the US, I think the ACLU would go nuts if we really tried that."

"We had a few murmurs," she said. "Now, they're ignored until they make themselves useful in criminal cases. Then they're appreciated."

Her information seemed to be at an end. "I just can't believe we'd run into those guys. Damn it. I would have been more alert, I guess, if I hadn't known what I knew."

"You mean about Emma."

"Yeah. Honest to God. That fricking little secret just keeps making things worse and worse."

"Yes," she said. "And in unanticipated ways." She took out her

PDA, and checked it. "Oh, yes. The most important question . . . would you be able to identify the second man again, if you were to see him?"

"You bet. Not a doubt in my mind."

Her brow wrinkled. "You're certain? It was gloomy, and you only had seconds. . . ."

"He's got a crescent shaped cut in his forehead from my flashlight," I said. "Just a little off center. It was only oozing when I saw it, but he should have a hell of a bruise and a lump, by now, too. Other than that, he's stocky. Thick, squarish head. Dark hair. Sort of a beard . . . not all that bushy. Brown eyes. Dark brown jacket." I chuckled to myself. "Dazed or glassy look, if you find him soon enough."

We headed back down the corridor. "You know," I said, "I'm always telling Jane that there's no such thing as a coincidence. I mean, not in life in general. Coincidences do happen. Just not in a case you're working on."

"Indeed."

"Those two shouldn't have been there." We walked a little further. "So, I have to conclude it isn't part of the case, don't I?"

"Logically."

"Yeah. Did you know that Sue . . . excuse me, my wife, is coming over to be with Jane?"

"No. What a wonderful idea."

"It sure is. Really. But it's also somebody else I've got to lie to, now. Any idea when they're going to "discover" Emma for public consumption? This is getting old in a hurry."

"I think when we receive the next tape. . . . Perhaps after that. It *is* becoming more difficult for you, isn't it?"

"Yeah."

Her cell phone rang, and as she answered it, I rejoined the group outside Jane's room. Carson was just finishing up with some of the lurid details of Jane being stabbed, and of him being one of those who disarmed the villain. I let him go on. It had nothing to do with Emma's case, and his over-cooperation right now would make him even more believable when he got back into denying the Emma details. Was I rationalizing? Probably. But I was just so damned tired.

Just as he wound things up, Alice rejoined the group. She had a frown on her face, and I hoped that she hadn't been zapped for hanging around with us.

There was just a pause in the conversation, and then Sarah Mitchell said, "I have a proposal for you, if any of you have the time."

"What would that be?" I didn't want any headlines with Jane, especially with the Sarah Mitchell treatment.

"I think I can . . ." and she lowered her voice so far that we all leaned in, ". . . now this has to be just between us right here. Nobody contacts the authorities, understood?"

Nobody said anything.

"Right, then," she continued. Her voice got even lower. "I believe I can put you in contact with Professor Northwood."

Alice's eyes widened, but she didn't say a word.

"Really?" I sounded as skeptical as I could. "He's a hard man to find."

"I have a source," said Sarah Mitchell. "But in exchange, I need you to do something for me."

"I knew that was coming," I said, lightly. "I don't know what we could have that you'd want."

"Given the tone of the last article," said Alice, officiously, "I really do feel that, if you decide to talk to this woman, I should be present. There's an enormous potential for libel."

To my surprise, Sarah Mitchell just sighed, and said, "Fine. Fine, I don't object to that. But no one says anything outside this group. That's an absolute condition."

"I'm afraid I must tell my senior partner," said Alice, not missing a trick. She gave a brilliant smile. "I suspect they're like editors?"

"But not one other person," said our intrepid reporter. "Not one."

"I swear I shall tell no one else," said Alice. "Absolutely."

"Well, then, what I'd like from you is permission to go with you back to the Down Street station. At least a couple of you. I understand," she said, looking at me, "that you might not be available. I'd like you there, but I do understand."

That was big of her. "Thanks."

"I do have a heart," she said, brusquely. "So, then, what shall it be?

"Photos, I suppose," said Alice.

"Of course. A reenactment."

"Then I must insist, that while I accompany those who are going, my photograph must not be taken."

"Shy, are we?" asked Sarah Mitchell, looking up at her.

"Professional conduct," said Alice, primly. "We serve our clients best if we aren't the focus of any articles." That was certainly true.

"Trust me," said Sarah Mitchell, "you won't be the focus. But I agree. No photos of you." She turned to Carson. "You'll be coming?"

He looked at me, and I nodded. With Alice there, he couldn't get into too much trouble. After all, Alice could probably whip him with one arm tied behind her. Not that he'd necessarily mind that.

"Sure," said Carson. "You want to go back, Vicky?"

She surprised me by saying that she'd go. I did think that her desire to find and rescue Emma was the predominant reason, and I felt bad about that. But I also suspected she wanted to be along to keep an eye on Carson for personal reasons.

"So, in exchange," I said. "We get . . . what?"

"Let me contact my source," said Sarah Mitchell.

"We get the location first, before anybody goes," I said. "And we talk with him first, too. Not that I don't trust you. It'll just work better that way."

"Done, unless it takes two or three days to firm him up. I can't be dealing with old news, and your president is here Tuesday. Your lot will hardly be the most interesting Americans here then. Oh, and there's another little condition, if you don't mind?"

"What?" asked Alice.

"This is my exclusive, the story in the station. And it's my exclusive with the professor, as well."

"The professor? How can you go exclusive on that?" I asked.

"Because I'll come with you to chat him up," she said, brightly. As if to clinch it, she looked at Alice and said, "And I suggest your solicitor be along for that one, too. In case tempers become an issue."

After she left, Alice said, "And just when I thought this case had turned into a true gallimaufry. . . ."

"A what?"

"Gallimaufry. A disorganized mess." She smiled. "What I think you over there would refer to as a bit of a cluster fuck."

"You got that right," I said. "We over there would."

"You'd best get back in to be with Jane," said Alice. "I need to make some calls. . . ."

Chapter 20

Saturday, November 15, 2003
16:45 Greenwich Mean Time

Blyth checked a printed list on his desktop, dialed his phone, and said, "John, please. It's Adrian."

Chief Inspector John Bassingham came on the line almost instantly. "Blyth? Just about to call you."

"Me, first, John. Have you heard from Goodenough?"

"Not since this morning."

"Ah. Just rang me up. They've found a fair bit of Semtex in the Underground."

"Bloody hell!"

"My words, exactly, John."

"Where?"

"An abandoned station, Down Street. Piccadilly line between Hyde Park and Green Park, actually."

"How much is a fair bit?" asked Bassingham.

"In the actual station, some five kilos, I believe."

There was some relief in the Chief Inspector's voice. "Ah, well, it could be much worse, now, couldn't it?"

"Yes, but here's the interesting part, John. They've found a bit more in a sub-basement of a restaurant near the station. One can pass directly from the restaurant, it seems, and into the station."

"Don't make me ask you how much was in the restaurant, Adrian," said Bassingham. "I hate it when you enjoy these."

Blyth chuckled. "Done. Forty-one kilos, to be exact, John."

"Bloody hell! Surely not?"

"Well, about fifteen kilos of Semtex, actually. And twenty-six kilos of Torpex/RDX. The difference, Goodenough assures me, is minimal."

"Twenty-six kilos of RDX?"

"Indeed."

"That could very well mean two sources," said Bassingham. "And two very different targets, as well." Torpex/RDX was known for its underwater use, while Semtex was normally associated with explosions in dryer environments.

"Or not," said Blyth.

"There's got to be a target in mind . . . who controls it?"

"That's the question, John, isn't it?" Blyth leaned back in his chair. "Absolutely no word from signals. No informants have gotten to us as yet. No information coming our way about this one, at all. No source. The Semtex was definitely manufactured after Lockerbie, by the way."

"Metalic traces?"

"Right." Semtex was manufactured in the Czech Republic, and they had added metal traces to make it detectable by airport X-ray equipment after the Pan AM flight 103 that crashed at Lockerbie, Scotland in December of 1988. Semtex had been the explosive used in that incident. "They tell me it also has that odor." The odor, too, had been added to what had originally been a nearly odorless plastic explosive.

"How'd you lot get involved?" asked Bassingham.

"Strangely, as seems all too likely these days. The American girl. Schiller, in the hostage tapes?"

"Yes?"

"One of her roommates, actually. She and some friends, including the one girl's father, went looking for the Schiller girl in the abandoned station," said Blyth.

"And they stumbled on explosives? Unlikely, Adrian, don't you think?"

"Would have thought so, yes, but our girl Alice was along. They disturbed two men lurking in the old station, and one of them stabbed the American girl. In the confusion, one suspect succeeded in fleeing. Crawled through an access, I'm told, and eventually led us to the restaurant."

"How contained is it?" asked Bassingham. "The information?"

"Only we folk, so far as the explosives are concerned. The Met handled the stabbing. The Fire Brigade was first at the scene. They bundled the victim off via tube, in fact. Stopped one of the trains . . . Down Street is an emergency fire exit. Ought to have been some surprised passengers on that one. And a bloke named Hicks, who takes the occasional tour group through Down Street. They're chatting up the one they arrested even as we speak. I've not word on that, yet. He's at Paddington Green, if you want to send someone over."

"Islamic?"

"I believe so, yes."

"Damn," said Bassingham. "I was hoping . . . ah, well. Lord, I hope it has nothing to do with our friends around Finsbury Park."

"Nothing at all, so far," said Blyth. There was a mosque at Finsbury Park that had been raided at least twice, having been used by some radical Muslims to plan, and store, for terrorists acts. It was an extremely sensitive issue, and not having it involved in any way with this mess would be a very positive thing.

"Who's doing the interview?"

"Just the Met, so far, John. Alice has hung about, but mainly because she was a witness. I'd like to be rather circumspect regarding this. I really want that last tape from these people, whoever they are."

"As do I. Let me send a pair over. Do the Mets know about the explosives?"

"They discovered them, John."

"So the world will soon know about the station and the stabbing and the explosives . . . and the connection between the injured girl . . . she did survive, I assume?"

"Indeed," said Blyth, "and it's good of you to inquire, John." He was relieved that Bassingham had not asked how the little party had obtained access to the station.

Bassingham made a growling sound over the phone. "It's not been the best of days, John. As I was saying . . . the connection with the hostage business will be made, of course."

"Yes. But just as a coincidence, thus far."

"Why on earth were they looking in that abandoned tube station? Are you holding back on me, John?"

"Not at all. They're aware of the connection between that professor . . . ," and Blyth referred quickly to one of the files on his desk. ". . . Northwood, and his anti-Belmarsh movement . . . ah, yes, this London Reform Movement for the Freedom of Khaled al Fawwaz and Ibrahim Eidarous and Lions of the Front for Jihad in Britain. . . ." He shook his head to himself. "Longish name. Very amateurish, to be connected with all that explosive."

"So unwieldy and juvenile as to sound spurious," said Bassingham, "isn't it, Adrian?"

"Indeed. But for the Semtex." Blyth made a note as he talked. "But back to the point, this Northwood has, I'm told, a passion for old tube stations. He'd had all three girls there as a group some time back, on a tour. They simply thought that they might be holding Emma Schiller there."

There was a long pause on Bassingham's end. "Who revealed the connection with the professor?"

"The media, of course. You should talk to more of them than just the *Times* staff, John."

"Who in the media?"

"You've heard of Sarah Mitchell? Of the *National Sun Express*?"

"The quintessential sensationalist."

"The very one, John. You do read more than the *Times*."

"What have you started for damage control?"

"We never let you down, John. Our Alice has managed to pass herself off as the solicitor for the Americans. They've talked to this Sarah Mitchell this evening, at the hospital, and she thinks she knows where this Professor Northwood can be located."

"Truly?"

"And Alice has managed to get herself invited to go with them to talk with him."

"How did this reporter find out about Northwood?"

Blyth felt some satisfaction that he had gotten this far ahead of his friend, although he would have rather killed himself than to let on. "She revealed the Northwood connection to the Americans at breakfast today. Not more than an hour before we received the information from you over at Special Branch."

"Remarkable," said Bassingham, dryly.

"Indeed, John. Indeed. This very same Sarah Mitchell came up with Northwood all on her own, it seems. And accurately, as well. Cited his political involvements."

"Regardless," said Bassingham, "with Mr. Bush coming over on the 18th, the explosives are very worrisome. I suppose we need to tell the Americans?"

"Yes. We do. I know one with the advance party, we've done things together before." Blyth looked at his watch. "He should have arrived this afternoon. We're on for a bit of supper. We should meet him together. Could you make ten at eight?"

"Likely," said Bassingham. "Oh that I had your budget. Regarding this injured girl . . . what hospital is she at? We'd best lay on a detail."

"Over at Tommy's. A nice touch, John. Her father will appreciate that."

"Oh. Well, the terror connection does free up a resource, now. Yes, I suppose he will. He's that Sheriff?"

"Just a Deputy, as he'll tell you. Yes. He knows about Emma Schiller being dead, you know?"

"Yes. We had a chat about that cock up at the morning briefing. He's kept it to himself, has he?"

"Alice assures me that he has done so."

"You're aware, Adrian, that we have a budget hearing shortly. I do seriously intend to grab some additional funds, and spirit Alice away from you."

"I don't feel threatened, John," said Blyth. "Best to Molly."

After the call was terminated, Blyth looked at his note. It consisted of just four words.

"Nab the Professor first."

MI5's job was security, and its current prime focus was gathering intelligence regarding counter-terrorism. Blyth's particular section cooperated with the counter-terrorism police units; in this particular case, the subdivision of the Special Branch of the Metropolitan Police known as SO13. SO13's job was to bring terrorists to justice. Blyth's section of MI5 was to provide Special Branch with the intelligence that was needed to do so, for while SO13's mandate was to arrest with a view to prosecute, MI5's mandate was to "frustrate" terrorist operations within the UK. Frustration, in all its forms, had many fewer legal complexities than the traditional police functions. From Blyth's standpoint, his job was accomplished if the identified and targeted terrorist operations were prevented from acting. After that, prosecution was all well and good, but it was a secondary effort. Because of that, he had found over the years that he had to be very careful to time the release of information to the police, lest they rush off and arrest someone before it was absolutely necessary. Premature arrests had a nasty way of drying up sources.

With that firmly in mind, he dialed Alice's cell phone. She answered on the second ring, with her usual "Hullo?"

"How are things with our American cousins?"

"Going quite well, I think," said Alice.

"Excellent. The cheese was two types of bad stuff, I'm afraid. Quite a bit in the other location, and I was told less than an hour ago that there is a chance there was a bit more before we got there. Can you be in the office . . . oh, let's say half an hour?"

"Done."

"Very good. There's a young lady I'd like you to meet."

He terminated the call. Alice was one of his most successful interrogators, at least in the softer forms. People had a way of confiding in her, especially female suspects and informants.

Saturday, November 15, 2003
19:50
St. Thomas's Hospital

I sat in Jane's room, watching her sleep. She still looked pretty pale, but healthier than she had before.

They'd given her some meds right after supper, and she'd started to fade into a deep sleep. Before she did, she informed me that she was really sorry we hadn't been able to find Emma, and wanted to be sure there had been no news about her that we hadn't shared.

"You don't have to protect me, Dad. If bad news comes in, you can tell me."

"I know I can. Now go to sleep . . ."

There's something about your kid being hurt, you know? I mean, no matter how old they are, they really are still your child, and you just feel awful. I started going over the blame trail in my mind. Would any of this have happened if I hadn't come over here? Well, I mean, I knew Emma would have been taken. And killed. That was a certainty, whether I was in London or not. But the rest of it? If I hadn't come over, Jane never would have been connected to Blyth, and never to Alice. The whole trip to the tube station couldn't have been arranged if it weren't for Blyth. That, therefore, was attributable to my being there.

I sighed, and took a sip of cold coffee. The Northwood connection would have existed whether or not I showed up. I was comfortable with that. But the whole damned thing with the press had been exacerbated by my presence. Strike two.

With me there, Jane could have been in a position to know immediately that Emma was dead. There would have been nobody but her and Vicky to identify the remains. But I was here, and I'd been tapped to ID the remains. MI5 asked me to keep it secret, and I did. So, now, there was a positive negative in the equation, so to speak. By being there, I'd come into information that could have kept her out of the old tube station because it was no longer necessary to look for Emma at all. But I hadn't told her. That just kept coming back. I hadn't told her because she didn't have a right to know. She had a need, all right. Even more, now. But all my training, and all my experience, told me that she had to have both before I could tell her. Not being in the right job, she never would have that right.

Shit.

* * *

I guess being so tired all the time didn't help, but my beating myself up was getting to be sort of an avocation. I knew that if I didn't stop it, I'd find myself telling her. That would be a disaster, on several fronts, not the least of which was the British security breach. I had heard of the National Secrets Act, but knew nothing useful about it. I just sort of assumed that, if I weren't covered by that, there was some other law that would get me tossed into the slammer, at least for a while. No thanks. Then I'd be even less use to Jane, the case, and all that.

Except I really hadn't been much use to date, except to get Jane stabbed. Well, that and maybe having something to do with an officer being posted just outside her door. Hopefully, I'd had *something* to do with that.

Saturday, November 15, 2003
Hampstead Heath
21:16

Alice and Blyth arrived at the unexceptional looking building in the park, exchanged greetings with the young man at the tourist information desk, and went directly to the third floor. In room 302, they met with a technician who was to record the interview, and who provided them with the current view of room 306, where the young woman was seated talking with Geoffrey, the "Dave" of Blyth's trio of young assistants.

The young woman, wearing blue jeans, a hooded sweatshirt, and trainers, looked to be about twenty, and was the girlfriend of Jamal Essabar, aka Hamza. Her name was Pamela Arpino, she was nineteen, and she was very frightened. She had been informed that she was talking to a representative of Her Majesty's Government, but had not been told the name of the agency.

"But, why can't you tell me why I've been brought here?" The state of the art digital sound system easily reproduced the slight quaver to her voice.

Geoffrey replied in a cool, distant tone, exactly as he'd been instructed. "As I told you, someone shall arrive soon, who will be able to explain that more fully than I."

Her eyes darted about the room. "I don't even know if I *should* talk with you. . . ."

"You are free to go, you know," he said. "But I can't emphasize strongly enough that it is in your very best interests to stay until you've gotten to the bottom of this."

Alice smiled to herself. Geoffrey was quite good at transferring the semblance of initiative. "She's been here . . . ?"

"Fifty one minutes," said the technician, glancing at the elapsed time readout on the screen.

Alice glanced at her notes. "We don't have lots and lots of good information, do we?"

"I have great faith in you," aid Blyth, and meant it. This was to be one of those difficult interrogations where the subject had committed no known offense, and in this particular instance, very likely no offense whatsoever. That significantly reduced the leverage for the interrogator.

Alice pursed her lips and furrowed her brow as she looked at the three sheets of paper in the file. One of them consisted of three photos of the captive taken that afternoon. The only thing of any real significance on the other two sheets was that the knife she had taken from Jamal Essabar in the old tube station had absolutely no traces of blood on it. That told her that he had not been the one who had stabbed Jane Houseman. The blade did, however, bear trace elements of Semtex. Most of the rest of the data consisted of things she should try to discover. "We must start somewhere . . . I think I'll go across the hall now."

"I'll be here in the gallery," said Blyth. "If there's anything you need, just pick up the phone."

The room was rigged with a regular telephone, which Alice would use to communicate with the control room if she wanted anything. By doing so, she would give the impression that it was the only link to the outside, and very likely would erase any thought of the room being bugged that might have occurred to Pamela.

Alice knocked softly on the door of 306, and she heard Geoffrey say, "Just a moment." The door opened, and he ushered her in with, "Just the person we've been waiting for. This is Pamela . . . Pamela, this is . . ."

"Alice," said Alice, thrusting out her hand and appearing to cut Geoffrey off. In fact, he'd given her their cue to use whatever identity she felt necessary. In this instance, she felt that her true first name would serve her best. "Very good to meet you."

Geoffrey glanced at his watch. "If you'll not be needing me?"

"Fine," said Alice. "We'll do very well on our own."

As Geoffrey made his way back across the hall to 302, Alice said, "Have you been told just why you're here, Pamela?"

"No." Her voice was clear, but with a slight quaver.

Alice produced her credentials. "I'm with MI5, the Security Service." As Pamela's eyes widened, Alice continued with, "We'd very much like you to tell us about a young man you know named Jamal Essabar."

Pamela had been very concerned about Jamal's behavior of late, and his sudden inaccessibility since late October, not seeing her at all and only talking to her occasionally on the phone, had convinced her that something bad had happened to him.

"Is he all right?" was all she could think to say.

"Do you think something's happened to him?" Alice's voice was full of genuine sounding concern.

As a matter of fact, Pamela did, and was not so sure that what had "happened" might not have been MI5 itself. Like many British subjects, she believed that MI5 an omnipotent, darkly secretive agency, which could do anything from dodgy tricks to murder in the name of the Crown. She was wrong for the most part, of course, but the effect of the misconception was plain to see. As a consequence, she was as wary and cautious as she could be. "It's what we always think when the police knock at the door, isn't it?"

Alice nodded. "I do that," she said. She pushed the photo sheet toward Pamela. "These were taken this afternoon. That's when I met him, and he's quite healthy."

Pamela seized the photos. He looked, to her, to be very tired, and his always neat hair was disheveled. "What have you done to him?"

"I found myself in a situation where I had to knock him about," said Alice, with more truth than she would have wished. "He had a knife, and he was threatening. I didn't injure him permanently."

Pamela nodded. Alice appeared to her to be quite able to knock Jamal down. "I can't imagine him with a knife," she said, slowly. She was choosing her words very carefully. "Are you sure it was him?"

"I took it from him," said Alice. "But that's a matter for the Mets to deal with. It does place you in a position to help him."

"It does?"

"I'm trying to understand what has happened with him. An explanation might help him. But I need to know as much as you'll tell me. How did you two meet?"

"At school. Kings College. Here, in London. We're both in computer science."

"What year?"

"Second."

"You're doing databases, then?" Alice smiled.

"And systems. Yes."

"In Java?"

"Yes."

"Well, be patient," said Alice. "You'll be getting to an individual project soon. Much more fun." She looked down at her meager papers. "When did you meet?"

"Last year. We started in two of the same class sections. We sat together."

Alice continued in that vein for several more questions, establishing general background information. She decided to end that section with a generic question. "So, then, when did you see him last?"

Pamela's face took on a worried cast. "Well, really, on October 28th. I think it was. It was a Tuesday."

"In class?" Alice was nearly holding her breath. October 28th was the day that Emma Schiller had been taken captive.

"No. He hadn't been in class for two or three days. He said he had something important to do. I gathered it was his politics. No, we met about four or so."

"Where?"

Pamela looked Alice straight in the eye, with defiance. "My apartment."

"Nothing untoward about that," said Alice.

Pamela relaxed a bit. "Sorry. He's quite religious. He tries to avoid things like that. Being alone with me in an inappropriate place. His parents wouldn't approve."

"Of course." She made a small note. "And their names are?"

Pamela shrugged. "I wouldn't know. I'm not sure he has any, really. No, that's not true. But I'm sure he's never mentioned me. I've never met them, and he only refers to them as father and mother. He's not sure of their reaction to me."

"Why?"

"I'm not Muslim. I can tell he doesn't want that to make a difference, but he's afraid. You know?"

"I think so," said Alice. "So, you haven't seen him for a while. You did say "really." Sort of for all intents and purposes . . . ?" Pamela nodded. "So, you did see him after that?"

"He said that he'd be gone for a few days. He thought he might be able to see me, but he wasn't sure. But a week went by."

"And did he see you?"

"Just for a few minutes. We met in that park in Chiswick. The one close to the roadway. Near that old loo that they mostly use for storage

I think. I just saw him for a few minutes. Really. And he called me, after that, too." It had become important to Pamela to convince Alice that Jamal was serious about her and their relationship.

"I believe that. I'm sure he missed you. From where?" Alice looked up to see a blank look on Pamela's face. She smiled at her, reassuringly. "Sorry, I tend to get a bit confusing. Did he call you from his home? School?"

"From a flat."

"A flat?"

"That's what he said. A flat."

"But not his flat?"

"No."

"Ah," said Alice. "You don't know whose it was?"

"He said it was his."

Alice gave a little laugh. "I'm sorry. I must have misunderstood. I thought you said it wasn't his. Right, then. So, moving right ahead. . . . ."

"It wasn't."

"Wasn't what?"

"His . . . oh, bugger. He said he had to rent another flat. Just for a while."

"Why on earth . . ." said Alice.

Pamela's lip quivered just a little. "I think . . . no, I thought. . . ." She looked Alice in the eye. "You're older . . . what do you think?"

Alice cleared her throat. "Ah. Yes. Well, then, let's get to the bottom of it. What did he tell you?"

"He wouldn't tell me. Do you think it might. . . ."

"Another woman?"

"No. I don't know. Do you?"

Alice shifted into a big sister role. "Between us," she said, confidentially, "there's every chance you'll never know. Men are like that." It was nearly always a good move to widen the wedge.

Pamela sighed.

"Did he say where the flat was?" asked Alice. "Or give you a number?"

"In Chiswick." Pamela reached into her backpack, and then paused. "Can I see him? If I tell you?"

"I can't promise that, not at this time," said Alice.

Pamela removed her hand from her backpack, and sat it back down on the floor next to her. "I don't remember the address," she said.

None of that, thought Alice. She changed tack instantly. "Why would he be in possession of explosives?"

"What?"

"Explosives. Plastic explosives, to be more precise. Why would he have them?" Alice had intended to startle Pamela. It worked.

"Oh, God. It's that Belmarsh business, isn't it? What have they got him to do?"

"What Belmarsh business?"

"Oh, that damned free the political prisoners group he's involved with. They're nobody, really they're not."

"What group?" Alice felt the warm glow of the lucky interrogator beginning to well up in her solar plexus.

"Oh ... it's here," said Pamela, unzipping a side pocket of her backpack, and rummaging for a moment. "Here ... the London Movement for the Freedom of Khaled al Fawwaz and Ibrahim Eidarous." She looked up. "This is it," she said, handing the folded green flyer over to Alice.

Across the hall in Room 302, Blyth smiled, and said, "That's our girl."

"How did he find himself involved with a group like this?" asked Alice.

"That professor Robert bloody fucking Northwood," spat Pamela. "That's how."

Over in 302, Geoffrey shook his head. "Luck sack," he said.

"Indeed," said Blyth.

"That would be ... ?" asked Alice, and spelled Northwood for Pamela.

"Yes."

"Professor, is he? Computer science?"

"No, English," said Pamela. Alice looked at her quizzically. "He has an English minor. Jamal has. He had a class of his."

"And how does this relate to this?" Alice held up the green flyer.

"Old Bobby Northwood," said Pamela, disdainfully, "wants to be a bloody Arab."

"Oh, shut up!"

"No, for true! He really does, the old letch."

"No!" Alice leaned back in her chair. "An Arab? Whatever for?"

"He thinks it's romantic, probably," said Pamela. "I'll just bet there's a girl. He's always trying to chum up to younger women, you know? Thinks he's all posh, very attractive. God's gift."

"He thinks that?"

"Nobody else does. Some boff him for a grade now and then. They say. He's just too old. Yuck."

"How old is he?"

"A hundred," said Pamela. "Oh, no. But all of forty."

"That old," said Alice. "Ancient, isn't he?"

In 302, Blyth muttered something about "overplaying her hand."

"You're not so bad," said Pamela. "Really. Look, you've got this already, probably. Here. I won't help him if I hold back." With that, she reached into her pack, and produced a small notebook. She opened it, went to a particular page, and handed it over to Alice.

"What's this?"

"Oh, it's his 'special' flat in Chiswick. He never did tell me. But I followed him back there. This is the address. I don't know which flat."

"Ah. Did he know this?"

"No. I felt bad, you know? Because I didn't trust him."

Alice reached for the phone. "Do you mind? I want some checking done on this."

"No, go ahead . . ." said Pamela, and leaned back. "Please, let me see him, won't you?"

"Can't guarantee," said Alice, as the phone rang through. "Alice, here. I have an address in Chiswick we should check out. . . ." She gave the address to Geoffrey, and then glanced back up at Pamela. "Hungry?"

Pamela, looking rather surprised, nodded.

"Be a dear," said Alice on the phone, "and run out and . . . one moment. Pamela, want to have at some curry?" Receiving an assenting nod, she said to Geoffrey, ". . . could you order us some take-away? I don't have the number committed to memory or anything, but there's this lovely little restaurant. . . ."

Chapter 21

Saturday, October 15, 2003
Chiswick, London, UK
23:58 Greenwich Mean Time

Chief Inspector John Bassingham, Special Branch SO-13 looked around the little flat. He stood well out of the way of the technicians processing the scene. With him was Adrian Blyth of MI5. They had arrived at the flat some ten minutes apart, Bassingham having called Blyth as soon as the warrant had been obtained.

"So, Alice is still talking with her?"

Blyth nodded. "As I left, they'd just finished up an enormous amount of take-away. I expect Alice will know all there is to know by two this morning."

Bassingham nodded. "Look there, Adrian. They must have done the taping back there. . . ."

The first Forensic Services Counter-Terrorism Team investigator on the scene had closed the flat to non-specialist personnel as soon as she observed the blood stains on the mattress, the dishing of the plaster wall where a roundish object had obviously impacted, and the severed pieces of duct tape in the kitchen. That was less than a minute after she'd entered the flat. She had been advised of the particulars of the Emma Schiller kidnapping case within minutes after the first tape had been received, and had been in the loop ever since. She was making notes to herself, including mention of the laptop, the camera tripod, and the black bag she believed to contain a floodlight and tripod. As she finished up, she approached Chief Inspector Bassingham.

"This could easily be the place," she said. "The tripod . . . and I'll be surprised if that long bag doesn't contain some sort of lighting rig."

"Indeed."

"John," said Blyth, "I'd appreciate it if you'd allow our people to check that portable computer first."

"Ah . . ." said the woman investigator, "we're quite able. . . ."

Blyth nodded. "You are. Undoubtedly. But I have some reason to believe that there is a certain category of information being dealt with here that may exceed your clearance."

"Indeed?" She was a little put off, because the MI5 crowd often used that excuse, and she always had a lingering doubt that they were being absolutely straight with her.

Bassingham said, "You can sign it over to them, as the experts, you know. You'll be able to have everything you need. Isn't that true, Adrian?"

"Of course, John."

The investigating officer, who knew very well who Chief Inspector Bassingham was, could only agree. But she made a mental note to very specifically detail these events, just in case.

"Shall do," she said.

"They expected to return, didn't they, John," said Blyth.

"I'd think they did originally," he replied. "Then they were too afraid to do so."

The investigator wisely edged away at that point.

"I'd be amazed," said Blyth, "if the one who gave Alice the slip would come here. But I do think he might well fly to our professor. I'm assured by the younger members of my team that they can have that portable over there scoured in an hour or two. The one we've got seems rather bright. It would be a very nice thing if he kept records."

"It would. Good that you've got your people lined up for it, then. You lot are luckier than we are. If I touch it, it will contain card games and little else."

"You will give us someone to stay with it, won't you? We'd best stay close together on this one."

"No sign of our cheese?" asked Blyth.

"None."

One of the searchers approached them. "I've some telephone numbers here . . . would you like me to copy them down for you?" The actual note would not be available for some time, due to the processing of the document examiners section.

"Oh, indeed," said Blyth. "John here will appreciate that one."

When they were more or less alone again, Bassingham turned thoughtful. "They're making it too easy to find our hiding professor, aren't they?"

"It does appear that way," said Blyth, "doesn't it? We've got the request in to the Secretary for an intercept on Sarah Mitchell. You know how loathe the Secretary is to do that sort of thing. The press and all, I mean."

"Indeed."

"Still, I think we've made a good case. I'd hope to be having people hanging from her eaves by noon."

Bassingham snorted. "Really? And a fine set of eaves she has, too."

"Now, John. I do worry about the foreign involvement here, though."

"Really? Afghani? Iranian?"

"No, American. Whoever has leaked this professor's address . . . it went to Ms. Mitchell, on purpose. Likely based on her treatment of the case, but also on her being the only one to get the American visitors to talk."

"Are they trying for another hostage, do you suppose?"

Blyth shook his head. "Difficult to say. I shouldn't think they would, unless they know we've found the dead one. It worries me, though, John."

"It's all in the knowing, Adrian. Now that's the dicey part isn't it?"

Hanadi's Flat
Near Tower Bridge, South Bank
London, UK
01:26

Anton had spent the better part of the day, since his narrow escape from Alice, hiding in the men's room at the McDonald's restaurant near Marble Arch Underground. When the traffic would bear it, he would slip from his stall and grab more paper towels, both damp and dry, for his forehead. When he would do so, he would look in the mirror. The place where the big man had struck him in the forehead was a deep purple, with a curving cut that had produced a flap of skin, which tended to fall away from his head like a small door opening. He kept pressure on it, a scab would form soon that would at least hold it in place. He alternated between too hot and too cold, and the throbbing of the wound was distracting.

When customers came in, he had found that by pursing his lips, making loud farting sounds, and alternating those with groans, nobody even lingered, let alone tried to enter his stall. He knew he was only safe for a while until the noon rush, but he simply could not think of another way to wait undisturbed.

He remembered the stunned look on the face of the woman he had stabbed. He hoped that he'd killed her.

"What the bloody hell were they doing there?" he asked himself. And the big man with the weapon . . . if he ever saw him again, he'd by Allah kill him, too. The fact that he'd been flattened, and then chased by a woman, and barely escaped was fading quickly. Revenge was the thing.

That, and hunger.

He was concentrating so hard that, when the employee came in to mop the floor, Anton missed the call of "Anyone here?" The sound of the wheeled bucket penetrated, just about the time the employee attempted to open the door to Anton's stall.

"Give us a minute!" he yelled.

"Oh, sorry! I'll wait outside," came a young voice.

After a moment, Anton anxiously peeked out. Whoever it had been was gone, but the bucket and mop were still standing near the sinks. Inspired, he rubbed his forehead hard enough to cause some bleeding to recommence, stepped over and kicked the bucket as hard as he could and threw himself against the entry door, at the same time yelling "Bloody hell!"

It worked even better than he had expected. The assistant manager, after applying a bandage to the wound on his forehead and yelling at the hapless employee who had left the bucket, insisted that he have a free Quarter Pounder, fries, and a Coke.

He ate quickly, but happily, and left the restaurant with his head well enough bandaged to avoid immediate attention from passersby.

By walking leisurely all the way, to avoid attention, he was able to make the four and a half miles to Hanadi's apartment by two in the afternoon. She had been home, but was very distressed to see him. Distressed, in fact, was the very word she had used.

He had tried to explain to her what had occurred in the abandoned tube station, but since he was none too clear on that himself, it was a very difficult task. He soon grew tired of repeating the small amount of information he had, and became angry.

Hanadi mollified him by brewing coffee and cooking an early supper.

Hanadi's main concern was to get this man out of her apartment for the last time, ever. To that end, she called the only one she could completely trust. Imad. She did not tell Anton who it was she was calling, she merely got through to him, and said, "You must come here immediately. It is vital. It is absolutely vital."

As she ended the connection, Anton emerged from the bathroom and said, "Who were you calling?"

Hanadi, skilled in maintaining the upper hand, merely said, "Imad."

"It must have been long distance. He's gone back to Syria." Anton had received this information from Professor Northwood, who had appeared distressed by the notion that Imad was to be fighting American and British troops.

"No. He has not." Hanadi had not been part of the deception regarding Imad's supposed recall.

"I'm sure," said Anton, "that he doesn't confide to you."

"Would you like some aspirin?"

"No." He would not admit to her that his head hurt.

"Ice?"

"I can take pain. Stop treating me like a woman."

At that moment, she could have sworn he was her father.

It had been a very long day for Hanadi, as well. She had met with the senior member of her firm, Sir Henry Culbertson just before noon. She had attempted to explain her situation as a hypothetical, referring to herself as a close friend of hers who needed advice. Sir Henry had not been fooled for a moment, of course, but had very graciously allowed her to continue. When she had finished, he had seemed absorbed in thought for several long seconds, and then had said: "This friend of yours has been very, very foolish. There appear to be no avenues open to her that lead anywhere but to disgrace and disbarment. She is a knowing participant in a foul crime, one that began in a deliberate fashion with kidnapping, and led to murder, regardless of how winding the path became. Regardless of how noble the motivation for the initial involvement. She deepened her guilt by aiding and abetting co-conspirators after the fact. A most egregious error. Her situation may be hopeless, I'm afraid. Her only chance, her only real option now, is to go to the police and tell them everything, and to cooperate with them in tracking down all the members of this . . . cabal." He waited for a response from her, but none was forthcoming.

"Hanadi, I can only tell you that this firm will recommend a good barrister for your 'friend.' But we shall have no involvement in the matter other than that. Anything more would be detrimental to our reputation."

This time she'd said, "I understand," in a very soft voice. Sir Henry had been her last hope, and she'd known the odds were greatly against her.

"Thank you, Sir Henry," she said, and turned to leave.

"Hanadi?"

She stopped at the door. He surprised her by stepping around his desk, and walking toward the door.

"Tell your friend that every minute she hesitates to go to the police, the more remote the chance of a reduction in her sentence. Every minute, Hanadi."

He opened the door for her. "And thank you for coming to me," he'd said, as she left.

The enormity of the recent events had stunned Hanadi. The abrupt change in her fortunes, coupled with the horror of realizing that she had, indeed, been an accomplice in the kidnapping and subsequent murder of a completely innocent woman had simply stopped her in her tracks. She had gone home, looked up the number for New Scotland Yard, written it on a pad near her phone, and had actually started dialing it twice. She had failed to complete the call both times, because she could not bring herself to betray . . . what? Her friends? Only Imad, of the persons she knew to be involved, was a friend. But, yes, that was a strong factor. Her sense of loyalty and commitment to freeing the prisoners in Belmarsh? Hardly that, now that it was so likely she was to join them. Her religion? To an extent, but just how much of one was difficult for her to determine. Her family? That, as well, she thought. Her profession, which she had worked so hard to achieve? Yes. Without a doubt. Thoughts of her profession brought her back to her family again. The only time her father had ever praised her was when she had graduated from law school. The entire framework of her life was being dismantled before her eyes, and she herself was the primary cause of the fragmentation. She had nowhere to turn. She had never felt so lost and lonely in her life.

She had considered Imad to be her last, best hope, but to tell him that she had even considered betraying the group would very likely result in her not only dying almost immediately, but dying in disgrace. Now, she would be lying to him, too.

She felt like wrapping herself up in a blanket, curling up on her bed, and crying herself to sleep. It was just that there was neither the time nor the opportunity for that.

A Small Hunting Cabin Near Bothel
The Lake District, NW England
02:30

Robert Northwood, in blissful ignorance of everything that had happened since he last saw Emma alive, well and irritable; took a last sip of brandy, and prepared to retire. He had reached several decisions regarding his approach to Emma, and had managed to convince himself that he was, in fact, about to regain control of himself, his fate, and the little group of kidnappers. He always managed to feel better after a little time alone, in which to reflect on his superiority.

He planned to call his Department on Monday, tell them he was feeling under the weather, and couldn't make classes on Tuesday. That meant that he didn't have to return to London until Wednesday, the 19th. He'd decided on the approach for Emma.

It had been his experience that, the more time he spent trying to convince a woman of anything, the less likely they were to agree with him. His plan, therefore, was to sweep into the flat where Emma was being held; pretend he was there secretly, and free her before anyone could stop them. He'd briefly considered staging some sort of fight with Hamza and Anton, but had discarded that. He thought he could trust Hamza not to get carried away, but had severe doubts about Anton. He'd just have to contact them Wednesday, tell them to stage an absence, and go rescue her at that point. He thought he'd take her to his flat, where he could offer her a shower and a good sleep before she and he went to the police. He could see no way that she could turn that down, after his rescuing her. Seduction, as he referred to it, would follow naturally. It had also been his experience that, even if they regretted it, after a young woman had slept with him once, she would very likely consent to repeat the adventure at least two or three times. He'd talked with his sister about that this very evening, although she had what he thought to be an opinion that was skewed by their relationship.

"The first times for adventure, Bobby dear," she said, "and the next few times she's simply attempting to convince herself that she hasn't been the fool."

Regardless whether his sister was right or not, that meant a good two or three days before Emma would make any serious attempt to break off the relationship. With the blandishments he had in mind, he felt certain that he could persuade Emma to go along with the scheme. He was at his best during times like those.

At about this time, back at Hanadi's flat, Anton was being beaten nearly senseless.

Chapter 22

Monday, November 17, 2003
Heathrow Airport, London
09:25 Greenwich Mean Time

I met Sue by the currency exchange, just at the exit from the American Airlines baggage recovery area. I saw her first, pushing a cart with her three bags, and looking very lost.

I was holding a large piece of white card stock I'd gotten from Vicky, and had carefully printed SUE on it in big black letters. She saw it, and waived.

I gave her a huge hug.

"By God, it's good to see you!"

"Why are you here? Where's Jane?"

"She gets out of the hospital later today, Vicky's with her. She's just fine!"

"Well, it's good to see you, too . . . did you rent a car?"

"Cab," I said. "Faster." It was the reference to speed that prevented any questions regarding cost. If you've been married as long as we have, you just do that automatically. As we hustled toward the cab, me pushing the luggage cart, I said, "Where do you want to stay? With me at the hotel, or with Jane at her place?" It was pretty well rhetorical.

"Why, with Jane. Besides, isn't the County Attorney staying with you?"

"Yep."

"Then where would he stay? Surely not with Jane and Vicky!?"

"We would have worked something out," I said.

"We'll just go right to Highgate, then," I said, as a driver approached.

* * *

On the way, Sue sort of alternated with worry and wonder. I think she would have been totally overwhelmed with being in London, if it hadn't been for her concern for Jane.

"How did this happen?" That was one of her first questions, and the underlying theme of the next ten or so. I tried to explain, but it was pretty difficult. Act of God didn't quite cover it, nor did coincidence, or bad luck, or anything else that came to mind. At the root of it all, at least for us, was the fact that I had not only allowed Jane to go into what turned out to be an unsafe location, I had actually been there at the time.

I couldn't very well explain that my guard was down because I knew that Emma was dead, and therefore hadn't any concern at all that we'd find her or her kidnappers. That, at least, was the explanation I'd come up with for myself.

We were in the midst of my stumbling my way through the possible explanations when my cell phone rang. Saved by the bell cannot be overused.

"Houseman," I said.

It was Blyth. "I hate to interrupt your meeting your wife," he said. That kind of surprised me, because I didn't know that he knew that Jane was coming.

"That's okay. What's up?"

"We're going to have to talk with you for a bit, as soon as possible. Something, oh, questionable has come up. Shouldn't take more than a few minutes."

"Sure. Hang on a sec . . . how soon do you need to do this?"

"As soon as possible. It may be important, it may not. One of those irritating situations."

"Sure. Ah, my wife, Sue, and I are headed to Highgate, to drop her luggage at Jane's apartment. Then we plan to go to St. Thomas'. About an hour?"

"Very good. Alice is at St. Thomas' even as we speak," he said. "She's interviewing, ah, Vicky. And Mr. Hilgenberg, the prosecutor. And your daughter, if she's up to it."

"Oh?" I thought Jane would be up to it, all things considered, but I also thought it had better be very important for her to be bothered right now. "What's the problem?"

"Not a secure line," he said. "Alice will tell you when you get there. Just information we need, nothing sinister or dicey. Be assured."

*   *   *

We got to Jane's apartment, dropped off Sue's luggage, took a moment for her to use the facilities, and started walking to the tube station.

"This is a very pretty place," she said. "This is part of London?"

"Yep. Depending on who you ask."

"I think I'd paint that wall behind the sofa a softer color," she said. "What?"

"The wall behind the sofa. Just as you leave Jane's."

"What color is it now?" The things a trained eye can notice.

"Blue," she said.

We were headed down Southwood Lane, just before we began descending toward the main road. "Look over there . . . what's that?"

"Downtown," I said. "The London you read about."

My phone rang again. It was Carson.

"Houseman. . . ."

"It's me," he said. "I just got out of an interview with the important people." That would have been MI5, I thought.

"Yeah?"

"Did you know that the two little bastards in the tube station were involved with this professor and the kidnapping?"

"What?" I took a deep breath. "What?"

"You bettcha."

"They told you that?"

"Not in so many words, but they're asking if we told anybody we were going down there. Anybody who could have tipped somebody else off is the unsaid question. But that means that it was no accident, doesn't it?"

It sure sounded like it to me. "We ought to be there in forty-five minutes," I said.

"Good. They're talking with Vicky right now, and then they want to talk to Jane."

"She up to it?"

"Well, she's dressed, and walked down to the coffee shop with us a while ago. I think so. Yes, I think she is."

"Excellent. I'll tell Sue how she is."

I terminated the call, and did exactly that.

"She's walking?"

"Sure. It wasn't anything that would prevent that, once they got her stitched up. Carson says she's doing fine." I could see that, fine or not, Jane was in for some great mothering.

"When will she be released?"

I'd forgotten to ask. Just like me. "Carson didn't say," I said. That was true, and avoided nicely the fact that I hadn't asked, or so I thought.

"I didn't hear you ask," said Sue, as we started down Archway Road toward the tube entrance. "Isn't this lovely?"

"Yeah. Ah, when we get there, there will probably be a couple of British officers there, they're asking questions about the incident."

"Still?"

"Well, yeah. I think there might have been a development. You know, additional evidence, did we see notice anyone else lurking in the shadows, or something of that sort."

"Lurking in the shadows?"

"Oh, you know. Just details. I was just joking about the lurkers."

"Yes." We started down the exterior steps to the tube entrance. "Oh, this is just lovely." She looked up. "I didn't bring my umbrella. . . ."

"Don't worry. Clouds or not, it hasn't rained once since we've been here. I don't even carry mine anymore."

We got off at Westminster. That way we had to cross the bridge, and she'd get to see Parliament and Big Ben across the street from the station. I didn't tell her why we were going to be getting off there.

When we got to the surface, it was noon. Inadvertent but perfect timing, and she could hear Big Ben tolling the hour as we stepped out of the glass doors.

"Oh, my God!" She sounded pleased.

"Really cool, isn't it?"

"It's gorgeous." She glanced around. "But I certainly hope we don't have to walk far. . . ."

Wouldn't you know? It was raining. Not hard, but it was enough to make us hurry across the bridge, and miss lots of scenery. On our left as we hustled to the bridge, was the statue of Queen Boadicea and her chariot, and I said to Sue, "Remind me to tell you about Alice."

"Alice?" asked Sue, from under her jacket that was being used as a substitute umbrella.

"The closest thing to Mrs. Peel I've ever run across," I said. "She's sort of assigned to us, and she's great."

When we got to the hospital, we met Jane, Vicky, Carson and Alice, who were waiting for us in the lobby.

After much hugging and tearing up between Sue, Jane and Vicky, with Alice looking like she could join in at any time, they finally got around to telling me that Jane had checked out, and they were waiting for us to get there before they went back to Highgate.

When Sue was introduced to Alice, Jane said, "And this is the one who clobbered the guy who stabbed me. . . ."

Sue told her how grateful we all were, and Alice said, "Well, as it turns out, it doesn't appear that the one I got was the one who struck you. His knife didn't have any blood on it at all. We think that it was the one that Mr. Houseman struck, who was the real culprit."

"Really?" I have to admit, I felt pretty good about that.

"Indeed. That's one of the things we'll be talking about. But, some lunch first?"

Bless Alice. We took a cab. Due to the rain.

Highgate
15:26 Greenwich Mean Time

We all got back to Highgate at about 3:30, and while Jane protested, Sue got her to put on her sweats, grab a comforter, curl up on the couch, and drink a cup of cocoa while Sue started making macaroni and cheese. We turned on the TV, half expecting to see something about Jane being stabbed. Nothing, strangely enough. I think that might have been because two things were taking up most of the news space: the US Presidential visit and the attendant controversy over Iraq, and the fact that England had beaten France in the semifinals of the World Rugby Championships. England had never won the World Cup, and they'd just made it to the final game. They were scheduled to be playing the Australian team in Sydney, Australia, for the championship on Saturday. As far as I could tell, the rugby folks were slightly ahead of the political pundits.

"You know," I said, "I've never seen a rugby game."

"Match," said Alice.

"Okay, match. Never seen one."

"You shall have to remedy that," she said. "Watch Saturday night. It's quite exciting."

"I'll do that," I said.

"Well, while you wait," said Alice, "I do need to interview you."

"Did you mention our trip to the Down Street station to *anyone*, before we actually went?"

I thought back, and got the answer I would have expected. "Nope."

She sighed. "Neither did anyone else, it seems."

"This is bad?"

She glanced at the rest of the room, who were paying very little attention to the two of us. "Remember our conversation about coincidences? At the hospital?"

"Sure."

"As it turns out, this very likely was one."

"You lost me," I said.

"Both suspects not only know Professor Northwood," she said, softly, "they're members of the group who took Emma."

"How in hell . . . ?"

"The little fellow we've got said they were; a search of his flat in Chiswick revealed that it was the place we've been looking for. There was, ah, evidence present. Of the political things, as well."

"Well, Jesus Christ," I said. I said it softly, but the dropping of the name got everybody's attention.

"What?" asked Jane.

I looked at Alice, praying that she'd field that one.

"It begins to appear," she said, "that the two men in the Underground were, in fact, associated with Emma's disappearance."

Jane said, "Yes!" and immediately started to tear up again. So did Vicky.

"I'm not at liberty to provide the specifics," said Alice. "But they do seem to have been involved."

As everybody started talking at once, I leaned closer to Alice, and whispered, "You gonna tell 'em?"

She shook her head. "I'd best call the boss," she said. "He may have the time to stop by. . . ."

Outside, the rain had stopped. Now that we were all inside for a while.

Since Sue had gotten Jane so comfortable, we did take-out, or take-away, from Zizi about 6:30. Alice and I went to pick it up, or take it away. I just love the language differences.

Anyway, we were alone as we walked over.

"Explain to me again how this could have happened."

"The connection between the parties?"

"That'd be it," I said.

"I'm not completely sure, but it seems that our dear Professor Northwood took many, many people on his little tours of the Underground. I don't think it was for the specific purpose of using the place for terrorist purposes, though. Just a fascination with the whole idea of abandoned tube stations."

"There isn't such a thing as a true coincidence, is there?" I asked.

"Apparently not in this case," said Alice.

I sighed. "What else have you got on these people?"

"Oh, we've got his cell phone, his laptop, his video recordings that they didn't use . . . everything we could want."

"Fantastic," I said. "That's great." It came out as sincerely as I could make it.

"By the way, the creepy one you knocked over is named Anton, as far as we can determine. Do you think you could identify him? We're looking for him now. As well as others."

"No doubt," I said. "How many others?"

"As far as I've had time to discover, several. It does appear that there were at least two main players above Professor Northwood. One in the group, and one rather . . . separate, shall we say."

"How close are you?" I asked.

"Special Branch will have more information on that. I've not seen the material, just been told that we've got it. So it's a best guess."

"Good enough," I said. "I hope to God that Blyth will tell everybody that Emma's dead."

"Likely not just yet," she said. "To the best of my information, we have as yet not received the next tape."

"I thought you said you had. . . ."

"The attempts, I think. They did many takes, apparently. They don't appear to have been able to edit much at all."

We had stopped in the little park called Pond Square Garden, facing each other and thereby clearing each other's back of possible eavesdroppers. "There are explosives involved here," said Alice. "Quite a bit of them, in fact."

"No shit? At his apartment?"

"No. Elsewhere," she said. "Can't really say right now, you know."

"Yeah."

"But with your president arriving soon, we absolutely cannot afford to take chances."

That had, I'm sorry to say, completely left my mind. "Oh, yeah. Sure. I mean, hell, yes." It would be an underlying worry for the British Security Service right now. "But, you really think the business with Emma has something to do with Bush?"

"We don't know."

"I know I'm way out of my league, here, but . . . well, I just can't for the life of me see how that would be."

"I'm not so certain we can, either," she said. "But that wouldn't make it any the less embarrassing if something were to happen and we'd missed the connection." She smiled again. "You and I shall just worry about the things directly effecting Emma, and now Jane. Agreed?"

"Works for me," I said, and we resumed walking. "Do you think they're at risk?"

She shrugged. "I don't know."

Hanadi's Flat
Near Tower Bridge, South Bank
London, UK
19:26

Anton awoke to find himself propped up on Hanadi's couch. His first realization was that he was breathing through his mouth. He wrinkled his nose, and felt the blood clots in both nostrils. The taste in his mouth was bad, his throat was uncomfortably dry, and he was able to open only one eye.

After a few seconds, he attempted to straighten up, and pain shot through his right arm, his ribs on the right side, and the small of his back. He moaned, and the slight extra pressure made his lip feel like it was being torn off his face.

"Don't move about," said Hanadi. "Do you want some water?"

He tried to say yes, and ended up nodding.

"Dump it on his head," said Imad.

Hanadi glared at him, and put a small glass of water to Anton's lips.

After a small swallow, Anton gingerly turned his head so he could see more of the room with his only functional eye.

Imad, and two other men, were looking at him. They were just sitting there, almost as if it were a social occasion. Anton recognized the other two from his infrequent visits to the mosque in Finsbury Park. They were often standing just outside the place, and seemed to be serving no purpose other than to look at people who passed by or entered. He'd been told they were Algerians, but he had no way of proving that.

"Hello," he croaked.

"Fuck you," said Imad. "You idiot."

Anton had a vague recollection that, between blows, he had told Imad that Hamza had killed the girl. Then, later, that he had killed her himself, but that it had been an accident. He had a somewhat clearer recollection that he had said that it was justified by jihad. That had been just before the heavy blow had sent his mind to another place.

"It was," Anton managed to get out, ". . . accident."

"It is not that you killed the bitch," said Imad. "She was not material."

Anton looked at him, but could say nothing. He struggled to understand why Imad was so angry, if she meant nothing. He failed.

"You did not tell us," said Imad. "That was your failure. You tried to conceal the body by moving it. That was incredibly stupid. You failed at that. That was beyond forgiveness. You crept back here. That was foolish, and has endangered Hanadi. That is unforgivable." He looked down at the battered face of his minion.

Anton struggled to say, "We were afraid of what you would think." What he was actually able to get out was only, ". . . afraid . . ."

"Really?" asked Imad, sarcastically. "And you don't even know all you did, you fool. You idiot. You led the police to that Underground station. *That* is your ultimate crime."

Anton just couldn't understand what Imad was talking about. Their hiding place? Hanadi, too, hadn't any idea why that was such a terrible thing; but she wisely refrained from comment.

"I am told that you stole boxes of cheese from the restaurant, and took them to the Underground station with you. Is this true?"

Anton nodded, very slowly. It hurt.

"Did you eat any of it?"

In his muddled state, Anton could only think that all this was about stealing cheese. "Yes."

"Did it taste good to you?" asked Imad.

"No." Perhaps, thought Anton, if they knew that it did not taste good, they would not hit him again. "Bad taste," he said.

Imad glared at Anton. Thus far, his mistake was not at all apparent. "That cheese was very important to us. It was placed where it was because that was a location the police would never think of to find such things. You led them directly to it."

Anton looked blank.

"You not only did that, you took some of it with you to your place of concealment. You made a trail." Imad was not certain just how this had occurred, but it was quite apparent that it had. He was assuming that the police were the ones who Anton and Hamza had confronted in the abandoned tube station, because Hamza had been arrested and Anton had obviously been pursued back through the narrow passage into the restaurant. The resulting search by the police had taken the rest of the "cheese." His conclusion, based on available information, was that a police informant had somehow come into this information. At the moment, he was struggling with the obvious conclusion that the informant was either Robert Northwood or Hanadi herself. He did not want that to be true.

"There is another who must talk with you," he said, slowly. "Anticipate that." He looked down at the battered face of his soldier. "He is very angry. You see, because you did not tell us of your incredible error. . . ." He became so angry himself that he had to pause for a moment. Then he said, "The last tape has already been mailed."

Highgate
19:41 Greenwich Mean Time

Blyth telephoned during dinner, and wondered if he could come up and see us. There was no question about that. He and Trowbridge showed up a few minutes after we were finished.

If Sue thought Alice was charming, and she did, Blyth and to a lesser extent Trowbridge were the icing on the cake.

Blyth in particular was very gracious, and said if there was anything she needed during her stay, she should feel free to call him.

"Oh," said Sue, "I really can't think of a thing."

"Never underestimate the recuperative powers of the London theater," said Blyth. "Our shop can easily provide complimentary tickets to any of them. You wouldn't," he said, to Jane, "even have to applaud too hard."

"I'd just love that," said Jane.

"And I'm sure Sergeant Trowbridge would stand the dining arrangements," said Blyth.

Trowbridge kind of winced, but was equally gracious when he said, "It would be our pleasure."

After a few more minutes, Blyth asked to borrow me for a moment, and the two of us stepped outside.

"You haven't heard from the intrepid Sarah Mitchell as yet?" asked Blyth.

"Not a word."

"You shall. I expect she'll be setting up a meeting for the 20th, or thereabouts. Thursday."

"Okay." I didn't ask how he knew.

"I'm terribly sorry about having to prolong this, but there are very extenuating circumstances. Alice has told you about the explosives?"

"She said there were some. Yes, she did."

"There was a substantial amount, actually. Are you familiar with Semtex?"

"Only that I know what it is," I said. "Pretty much like C4, isn't it?"

"Close enough. There were two boxes labeled as cheese in the tube station where you had your encounter. They contained Semtex, to the tune of some five kilos in the two boxes."

I thought back to the few explosions I'd witnessed. Five pounds would have been much more than I'd ever seen used. I did remember a demonstration we'd had, where a two pound block of C4 had been set off. They'd placed it on top of a Tupperware bowl with a lid. The bowl had been full of water, and had been placed on top of an old Dodge van. We were standing back a hundred yards when they set it off. The explosive had driven the water from the bowl through the roof of the van, through a bench seat, through the floor, and had cut the drive shaft clean through. All that damage had been done by a column of water, after getting an initial push from the explosive. The blast at a hundred yards had felt like I'd been hit with a well swung pillow the size of my whole body. Not enough to knock me down or anything, but strong enough to halt me in my tracks. That had been a two pound block of plastic explosive. Five kilograms, the amount in the tube station, was roughly eleven pounds.

"That's a hell of a lot," I said.

"Indeed," said Blyth. "There was more in an adjacent sub-basement, about another forty-one kilos, I understand."

I did the math. That was about ninety pounds. "Shit."

"Precisely, yes. The whole lot was located too close to Buckingham Palace for our comfort," he said.

"I didn't know we *were* that close."

"From the old Down Street station to the Palace itself . . . a bit over half a kilometer, I'd say."

More math. I was worse with kilometers than kilograms. "How far would that be in . . . miles . . . or feet?" I asked.

"Oh, about two thousand feet, in fact. A bit less."

"Just over a quarter of a mile. . . . You can get there underground?"

"There is a sewer," he said. "Not to worry about that venue. It's not connected to any tube line, and there are surveillance cameras down there." He had sort of a distant smile on his face. "We do owe the IRA something for their attentions. That, and with your president coming over so soon, we've had foot patrols down there, too. No, we aren't too concerned about the sewer. But just chucking bits of it over the walls would be quite a threat. In a vehicle, driven with sufficient resolve, or worse, two vehicles . . . one to make a hole, the other to drive though . . . There are going to be sleepless nights."

"Yeah." I could barely imagine. "I've lost track. When does he get here?"

"Your president? Tomorrow," he said.

"Jesus."

"No, Bush." He got a kick out of that. "At any rate, we still need you for a bit. We want to continue with your arranged meeting with Northwood. We've met, and we think it may well work best that way."

"Sure. Just me, though, okay? And maybe Carson. Nobody else."

"Just those you decide to invite," he said.

"How's this going to work?"

"We have located him," said Blyth. "A cabin in the Lake District. He's under constant surveillance, and shall be all the way to your meeting. We've visited his flat, and interior surveillance is now up and running. He is, by the way, considered to be non-violent. But taking no chances, we looked about, and there are absolutely no weapons in the flat, except kitchen utensils. He's an escape risk, of course. But not a violent one."

"Good to know. I hope you're not relying on me to chase after him?"

"If you were to merely hang on to his belt. . . ." He chuckled. "Alice will be along, and I feel certain she can handle him."

"Me, too."

"I'm told you referred to her as Mrs. Peel?"

"Yeah," I said. "Only Alice is better." I looked him in the eye. "So, why do you need us, then?"

"Authenticity. We want him to be comfortable with you, and what better place than his own flat? You will lend presence, and Alice will be able to act as solicitor. Sarah Mitchell will be asking lots of questions, and that shall flatter what we have found to be his considerable ego. We want him to tell you things he wouldn't tell us, at least not readily."

"Well . . ."

"He won't be wheedling for a deal with you," said Blyth. "He'll be receiving guilt, plus the surprising information that Emma is dead."

"He doesn't know?"

"We believe he does not," said Blyth. "Remarkable as that seems. We shall release the information in a timely fashion. It should unsettle him."

"I'll be damned. How can he not know?"

Blyth told me. When he was done, I believed what he'd said. It had that ring of truth about it. My years of dealing with self-involved petty criminals told me that it could very well happen like that. Hell, even the one real terrorist case I'd worked showed me that. The dipstick had just left too soon. "That sounds like it could happen that way," I said.

"We think so," he replied.

"Do you think there's any continuing threat to Jane, or anyone else in our group over here?"

He thought for a moment. "I don't know."

"Will you have someone watching out for them? Especially when I'm gone?"

"Even as we speak," he said.

That made me feel better, but it looked like the sleepless nights were going to include me.

Chapter 23

Tuesday, November 18, 2003
Thames House, London
09:10 Greenwich Mean Time

A drian Blyth left his morning briefing, and took the elevator to his office. It was unusual for him to have attended the briefing, but this had been an important occasion. Last night, MI5 had communicated the information regarding the incident at the Down Street station to the FBI in Washington, DC. The explosives were the highest priority during that call, with the identification of at least two of the suspects as UK born Muslims being a high second. The link to the abduction of the American girl, Emma Schiller, had been a strong third. The elements of a possible assassination plot coupled with a hostage taking, and the involvement of a possible radical Muslim terrorist connection had hit the FBI like a bombshell. The last that Blyth had heard, the FBI was going to attempt to convince the President to either postpone, or to radically change the scheduling of his trip to the UK. Postponement, candidly discussed, was fairly well ruled out. The change of itinerary was a distinct possibility, however, and would cause a massive realignment of security forces. Frankly, Blyth believed that the suggested changes would be refused. To secure entirely new areas of visitation would be impossible, and simply mixing the order of the events would only serve to disrupt the already strained security forces. As usual, he was right.

His secretary took the call just as he passed through her office and was opening the door to his own.

"It's Chief Inspector Bassingham," she said, and she handed him a note as he passed.

He stepped across the threshold, and picked up the phone as he came round the end of his desk.

"John," he said as he sat, "good of you to call."

"You were right," said Bassingham. "The Yanks are going to go ahead with the original itinerary."

"I think that's for the best. We can shift some personnel, to increase the coverage." He glanced at the note in his hand. It told him to see the Director as soon as he was able.

"It's provoked a bit more of a reaction than that," said Bassingham. "I've just been speaking with a presidential aide named Rich. They have this minigun that they can mount in one of these huge American SUV's . . . You know, like we have in helicopters?"

"The door gun on a Chinook," said Blyth.

"The same. It seems this is 5.56 mm, and they want to have it with the presidential motorcade."

"You must be joking?"

"I fear not, Adrian. They want it to go with him everywhere."

Blyth had a quick mental image of the carnage that could be caused by an arrangement such as that one. The minigun fired 100 rounds per second. In a crowded space such as was common in the streets of London, especially one filled with onlookers, a couple of two second bursts could shred a crowd. If a vehicle were moving, the accuracy would be very questionable.

"Well they bloody well can't have it," said Blyth. "They could kill a hundred people in seconds."

"I agree," said Bassingham. "Unfortunately, I don't have that say."

"Neither do I," said Blyth, "but the Secretary certainly does. I shall see to it. Good Lord."

"As long as you're at it," said Bassingham, "there's a bit more. It seems they can have US helicopter gun ships here very shortly. Bring them in on a C-5 from Germany. They'll be asking for permission to fly them in our airspace, to cover the routes."

"Just who is this Agent Rich? Doctor bloody Strangelove in disguise?"

Bassingham gave a strained laugh. "I *am* suspicious. Honestly, I think he's a bit new to his position."

"Reassure him. We'll provide the security. They can assist with their usual methods. Agents, side arms, and continued liaison. Their Secret Service are very good at working with us. I know that President Bush in unpopular in some circles, but they should know that he's safe here. Not necessarily popular, but we'll keep him safe."

"You might like to take this up with Eliza."

Eliza referred to Elizabeth Lydia "Eliza" Manningham-Buller, the Director General of MI5. "I suspect she's already on this one," said Blyth. "I've a note to see her."

"Excellent," said Bassingham. "I've great faith in her."

Blyth did, too. The Director of MI5 had been a high level liaison with the US Intelligence Services in the '90s, and knew her way around the Washington system as well as anyone. She also had a solid working relationship with some extremely highly placed personnel. "She'll make things work," said Blyth. "We just can't slip up on our end."

"Right you are, Adrian. By the way, there's been another development that should stir things up a bit more."

"Please say that was a joke," said Blyth.

"Sorry, can't. The Beeb just received another tape from the kidnappers of Emma Schiller."

There was a momentary silence. "What does it say, John?"

"Haven't seen it myself. It should be here in a few moments. Care to send someone over?"

"Yes. And invite the Americans, too. We really had better."

Highgate
11:35 Greenwich Mean Time

Last night, it had been decided that regardless of the presence of security people outside, I would spend the night at the girls' flat. It was a night filled with tension, not because I was afraid of somebody machine gunning the place, but because Sue and I have this tendency to discuss the day's events before we fall asleep. We'd been true to form, with the addition of discussing events that had occurred since I'd been in London. I found myself in the trying situation of trying to fill Sue in on what we'd learned, without filling Sue in on what we'd learned. It was especially difficult as my being so damned relaxed in the Down Street station was because I *knew* Emma was dead. Sue didn't actually say it was my fault, but the implication was clearly there. Well, hell, she was right. I felt terrible about it, but did manage to fall back on the truthful and honest feeling I'd had when I heard that the two dudes in the station were actually part of the kidnapping of Emma.

"It was just too much of a coincidence," I said. "Honest to God. They just shouldn't have been there."

"But Jane was right, wasn't she?" said Sue. "She thought that underground place had something to do with Emma, didn't she?"

I made a sort of growly sound of chagrin. "Yeah. But they shouldn't have been there, damn it. There was *absolutely* no evidence there that Emma had ever been hidden in that place. None. They had no reason to go there." That was about as close as I could get to it, without saying something about their fleeing all the way from Stevenage to the tube station after they lost control of Emma's remains.

"Well, I don't know why you think *that*," said Sue.

What could I say? "You've got to be awful tired," I said. "Jet lag is tough."

"You're changing the subject."

When you're caught, always fall back on the security aspects of a case. "I had one reason, that I can't tell you, because the Brit's told me because I was an officer. It's a need to know, right to know thing, and it goes way back."

There was a long silence, and I was hoping she'd fallen asleep. No such luck. "Do you think I'd tell someone?" she asked, icily. "Someone over here? Someone I have tea with every afternoon, maybe?"

"I just can't," I said. "You know that."

This time, she turned over. I heard her say something, but I couldn't quite make it out.

"What?" I just had to ask.

"I said," said Sue, her voice raised just a bit, "bullshit."

I thought for a second about resuming our years long conversation about intelligence and criminal history data. But just for a second. "Yeah," I said. "G'night."

"Good night."

We'd spent a better morning at the girls' flat, with Sue and Vicky doing fussy things for Jane, and me meeting Carson at the tube station and back to Zizzi for more take-out. Away.

As we were crossing the little park on our way back to the flat, Carson said, "You know, if it's getting a little crowded up here, you could always let Vicky come down to the hotel . . ."

I looked at him. "You're not serious?"

"Maybe."

I hated to tell him this, but I had already decided late last night that I'd be much better off back at the hotel. "I'll be back at the hotel tonight. All my stuff is there."

"You could have asked me to ring it up today," he said. We stopped at the south side of the park, for a bus to pass. "I'd have been glad to."

"The County's paying for that room, my boy. No hanky panky."

"Ah." He sounded a little less than sincere.

"Whatta you mean, ah?"

"Nothing."

I stopped on the other side of the street. "Come here a sec."

"What?"

"Something happen in our room when I wasn't there?"

His face got red. "Oh. . . ."

"With who?" I stepped closer. "I can't tell you how serious I am."

"Well, she just needed somebody to talk to, you know? She was a little scared after all this stuff. And you were off doing your thing. And we had a couple of hours to kill."

"Who?" Please, God, I thought, don't let him say Jane. Whoever else, I'm fine with it. Just not Jane.

"Vicky. Who else?"

Thank you, Lord. "I was thinking, you know," I said, trying to come up with a name. "Maybe that newspaper woman."

He looked startled. "You gotta be kidding!"

"Well, no." But that settled it. Tonight I was back in the hotel. "But I swear to God, Carson," I said, doing a pretty good impression of being angry, "if word of that ever leaks out, I'll kill you myself."

He grinned. "I forgive you in advance," he said, "because it was so worth it."

Jane was feeling a little weak, so we played Scrabble until about 2:30, when Alice called and asked if she could drop by.

She got there a few minutes later, so I knew she'd called on her cell phone. Those things make you re-evaluate timing.

After a brief greeting to everybody, she asked if she could talk with me outside. Sue got sort of a scowl at that, but I don't think anyone else noticed.

We stood just outside the door.

"The BBC has got another Emma tape," said Alice.

"You're kidding?" I say that way too much. I've got to learn how to be inscrutable someday.

"They demand a meeting with your president, by the evening of the 20th, or they say they'll not only kill Emma, but that there will be other serious consequences."

I thought for a second. "They had to have recorded that before last Saturday. Assuming that the other consequences involve those explosives."

"I agree, but remember, we don't know that those were all the explosives they had available. It would make *some* sense to split them up. All one's eggs in the same basket. If, in fact, explosives are involved at all."

"Okay. What else could they do?"

"Another hostage, perhaps? Something with incendiaries? It's really very difficult to say."

"Because you still don't know for sure just who they are," I said. It was a statement, not a question. "As far as I can tell, you've got the lower echelon. From what's been said, it doesn't sound to me like this Professor Northwood is anybody's idea of a major player. Right?"

"Likely," she said.

"So there's still a bunch of uncertainty, isn't there?"

"Oh, yes, indeed." She shrugged. "It's increased the tension a bit. Your American security people as well."

"I can understand that."

"We did think of simply taking Northwood instanter, but the plan stays the same. Your security people agreed."

It being that I didn't *have* any security people, I assumed she meant those with the president. It kind of surprised me that they had agreed. I've only met maybe two Secret Service people over the years, at least that I actually got to talk with at any length, and they sure hadn't struck me as the sort who take any chances at all, if they could help it. I said as much.

"We need to know how widespread this is, for one thing. It's frustrating, I give you that," she said, "but we don't want to delay obtaining the information further by having our professor whisked off to Paddington Green and into the clutches of his attorney."

"Sure." I could understand that. "So . . . what? You want me to beat him up for you?"

She laughed out loud. "No. Not that it's a bad idea . . . just too complicated in the long run. Questions, but mostly listening. Let me maneuver him. I'll do most of the talking, in a believable way."

"My solicitor," I said. "That's why I pay you so well. Anyway, I can assume that he doesn't know of the screwup of his buddies? With Emma and the explosives?"

"We are quite sure he does not. He's not even aware of the impending meeting with you and Sarah Mitchell."

I raised an eyebrow. "Then how?"

"He's apparently taking a short sabbatical. Sarah Mitchell is communicating with his school, and has found the date of his return. We, in turn, have communicated with his sister, who has no idea what is afoot. She will cooperate."

I wondered how they'd gotten her to do that, but didn't ask. Later, I heard that there were a couple of Special Branch people with her in her house when Robert Northwood came back from the cabin. They were introduced as some of her husband's assoicates, and he never got any wiser. Resources. They must be great.

"Doesn't Sarah Mitchell know about the new tape?"

"If she doesn't, we suspect she certainly shall. BBC have agreed not to air the tape for a grace period. She might not be the most scrupulous person, but to scoop BBC would be disastrous for her. Whoever gives her that information will make that perfectly clear."

"Hmm. Okay. I mean, you guys know that stuff. Okay, then. It's still set for Thursday?"

"Yes. The day after tomorrow. She's confirmed that, and will likely contact you later today."

She seemed very sure of herself. I felt that I could pretty safely assume that they had Sarah Mitchell totally wired by this time, and very likely followed as well. That was good. It meant that there would be very few surprises on that front.

"Okay."

"We two, and Carson, if he wishes to accompany us, shall meet tomorrow to go over details and procedures. After noon, but before four."

"Sounds good. Can I ask you a question, promise you won't laugh?"

"Of course."

"Sarah Mitchell. Ah, she doesn't work for you guys, does she?" I asked. It had just crossed my mind.

"Certainly not, thank God," said Alice. It seemed to brighten her day.

Since Jane wasn't feeling too peppy, the rest of that Tuesday was spent playing Scrabble, eating popcorn, and just sort of hanging around Jane and Vicky's flat. We watched some of the anti-Bush protests. They were really more that than anti-American or anti-US. I wondered how long that would last.

We decided that it would be best for Jane to rest the whole day, so we did take-out or away for supper again. This time Carson and Vicky did the honors, going to the Gatehouse for our food. I had bangers and mash. Sue glanced at it disapprovingly, but didn't say a word.

I re-thought my position about heading back to the hotel with Carson, especially in the light of Alice's offhand remark about ". . . possibly another hostage." I figured my place was in Highgate. Carson was a little disappointed, because I told him Vicky's place was in Highgate, too.

He wanted to go on the Northwood interview, and I really didn't see anything wrong with that. We talked about it briefly between us. Sue overheard some of what we said, and it took an hour to reassure her that we'd be just fine. I finally ended up saying, "I came here to help out. That's just what I'm doing. They asked, and I agreed. It's perfectly reasonable."

"Are you sure it wasn't your idea?"

"Absolutely. I haven't any say in what goes on over here. None. I just cooperate with them when I'm asked."

For some reason, she seemed happier that I wasn't able to directly effect anything. I sure as hell wasn't, but as long as she was mollified, I was happy.

Then Sue said, "Are you sure you want to go, Carson?"

"I am," he said. "Absolutely."

"You aren't just saying that?"

I intervened. "Don't be such a teacher," I said. That was one of our mutual signals for 'stop interfering.' Hers to me was to not be such a cop.

Jane came to my rescue. "It wasn't Dad's idea to go to the tube station, Mom. It was mine. I asked to go. He just went along with it. Really. I don't think he thought I was right. If he had, I don't think he'd have agreed to let me be along."

Just how she knew what the underlying issue was, I'm not sure. I guess it's a daughter-mother thing. Anyway, we changed the subject.

After supper we watched *Air Force One* landing at Heathrow. The TV coverage was constant, with the time between the drive and the arrival of the motorcade at Buckingham Palace being taken up by a fascinating variety of pundits and commentators. We had a good time, and consumed another round of popcorn.

"They just don't seem too happy with us, do they?" said Carson.

"I think that's a fair statement," I said. "You know what? I didn't vote for Bush, and I don't care who knows it. But some of this is getting me just a little pissed off."

That seemed to be part of the general feeling. It got a bit more pronounced when it was announced that the president wouldn't be addressing Parliament, because several of the members refused to guarantee they wouldn't boo and make catcalls.

"That would never happen in an address to Congress," said Sue. "I thought the British were more dignified than that."

Carson spoke up. "I took a class in the British Parliamentary system. They do things like that. It's probably not as awful as we think."

"Well," said Jane, "they'll be on somebody else next week. Probably us again."

"Who?" asked Sue.

Jane produced the newspaper. The one with the "America's Sweet Tart" headline.

That kept Sue up most of the night. I mean, she was jet lagged already, and the adrenaline rush just about did her in. The fact that I was quoted, and the fact that Sarah Mitchell had done the interviews and she was the one that we were going to cooperate with. . . . Well, it was a sleepless night, all right. I thought Blyth didn't know how lucky he was just having to worry about little things like security.

Chapter 24

Wednesday, November 19, 2003
The Residence of Chief Inspector Bassingham, London
06:38 Greenwich Mean Time

Molly Bassingham, waking from a sound sleep, answered the telephone on the second ring.

"Yes, Bassingham's . . ."

"May I speak with the Chief Inspector, please? It's Sergeant Trowbridge, ma'am."

Sleepily, she handed the telephone to her awakening husband. "It's Sergeant Trowbridge," she said.

"Yes," said Bassingham, his voice heavy with sleep.

"We've a huge flap on," said Trowbridge. "I believe you'll want to come straight over."

Chief Inspector Bassingham heaved a large sigh, sat up on the edge of the bed, and said, "Tell me now. I'm up."

"Ah . . . well, it seems that some reporter fellow for the *Mirror*, one Ryan Parry, has, uh, managed to pass himself off as a footman at Buckingham Palace."

"What!"

"Ah, indeed he has. He, ah, provided his true name. Merely neglected to say he was a reporter. Used one of his mates from his pub as his character reference. Some bloody idiot didn't vet him properly. He's the same bloke who investigated the security at Wimbledon last summer."

"When?"

"Pardon, sir?"

"When did he sign on? How bloody long was he there?"

"Some two months, sir."

"Two bloody fucking months!" He found himself without words for a moment. "What sort of access?"

"We aren't exactly certain, but the paper claims he was standing right behind the president at his arrival. Helped lay out the room niceties for the president and his entire party, it seems."

"Bloody hell," said Bassingham, softly.

"He was scheduled to serve breakfast to Ms. Rice, the US National Security Advisor, and Mr. Powell, the Secretary of State, this morning," continued Trowbridge.

Bassingham simply groaned. "So, then. How did we catch him?"

"Well, sir, it seems we didn't," said Trowbridge.

"Who did? Oh, bloody hell. Not the Americans?"

"Oh, no sir. They certainly did no such thing. I'd venture to say they were as surprised as we were. He, well, sir, he appears to have simply walked off the job late last night. Before anyone was aware of who he was."

After a short silence, Chief Inspector Bassingham asked the awful question. "And how do we know all this?"

"It's in the morning paper, sir."

"Jesus Christ." Bassingham felt drained.

"He seems to have taken photographs," continued Trowbridge. "Says that he had a camera with him at all times, and that it was never noticed by any of the security people."

"Send a car," said Bassingham. "Ten minutes."

"It's out front now, sir."

Chief Inspector Bassingham put the phone down. Molly was looking at him. "Bad news, dear?"

He hardly knew how to begin.

Adrian Blyth's day began somewhat earlier than his friend John Bassingham's, with a jog in the park at 06:00 sharp. His first call came on his mobile phone, and was from a member of the team that had "cleared" Robert Northwood's apartment. Clearing, in this particular instance, had involved talking a look through his computer files, and downloading them onto a portable hard drive.

"We may have something of interest here," said Agent Rose.

"Very good," puffed Blyth. "You must rise at four. What have you got?"

"That little group this Northwood's a member of? There's a person named Ayat, apparently was the recording secretary or something of that sort. Kept minutes of their meetings." He chuckled. "Forwarded them to Northwood via email. Email is registered to one Hanadi Tamish. We're checking for her address now."

"Minutes? Well, that was a bit foolish, now, wasn't it."

"It was all of that," said Rose. "There seems to be just three members who say anything, and usually just those three who attend the meetings. There were others, on one occasion. One of them was the little chap we have in custody, in fact."

"Another smoking gun," said Blyth.

"Indeed, sir. The other chap is referred to as Anton, and we believe that's the same one who led Alice on the chase in the tube station."

"Excellent."

"The most interesting set, though, could be this one . . . our Mr. Northwood and a man called Imad, who is the third principal, had a rather involved discussion, duly recorded, back in June. Regarding tactics and targets in London that would disrupt things a bit."

"Really?" Blyth was nearing the end of his fourth and final lap. "Such as?"

"Well, a kidnapping was discussed a bit. Northwood specifically mentioned an American girl, but not by name. To 'divide the alliance,' as he put it."

"Indeed," said Blyth, breathing harder as he neared the end of the lap.

"Also discussed was blowing up at least a portion of the Thames Tidal Barrier."

Blyth slowed to a walk. "Again?" It seemed that blowing up the Thames Tidal Barrier was the favorite scheme of every lunatic group they encountered these days. "That's remarkably un-original. Grammar school, in fact."

"This one does suggest the use of a thousand pounds of Semtex."

"I see. Perhaps not grammar school, then. Assuming they actually having a fair quantity of Semtex does lend credence. Does it say how much they actually have got?"

"No. There's no other mention of Semtex, or of any other explosive, in any other minutes. In fact, the recording secretary has to ask how it should be spelt."

"Interesting. Who tells her?"

"This Imad fellow. Sounds knowledgeable."

"Specifically a thousand pounds, though?"

"Yes, sir. That's what it says."

"I'll read the minutes today, but tell me, what impression have you got from it?"

Rose hesitated. "I'd say that there's another bunch, separate from this lot. But closely related."

He sounded a little hesitant. "Something wrong?" asked Blyth.

"Ah, well, I wouldn't even think that, really, weren't it for them actually having explosives in their control, now. These three main participants, well they don't seem to have what it would take to actually *obtain* Semtex. To my mind."

Blyth found that very interesting. Rose had been about this business for a long time, and had very reliable instincts. "Get them to my desk by nine, would you?"

Blyth was just re-entering his home when his mobile phone rang for the second time. It was Chief Inspector John Bassingham, who had some news of his own.

After Bassingham had given him the sordid details concerning the bogus footman at Buckingham Palace, Blyth said, "Well, I should guess that's going to make it damnably difficult to tell the Americans that we can handle the security, isn't it, John?"

"Not to mention the Home Secretary, the PM, and the Queen," said Bassingham. "Just to name a few. Christ, what a cock-up."

"Indeed."

"I'd like to wring that Ryan Parry's neck for this."

"Oh. Yes, him. Isn't he the one," asked Blyth, "who did the bit at Wimbledon last summer?"

There was a black silence.

"Ah," said Blyth. "I thought so. Well, we mustn't shoot the messenger, John. There is obviously a hole in the security fence that needs fixing."

"Yes," sighed Bassingham. "But it's going to be a severe distraction at a very bad time."

"Who's for the headsman on this one?"

"Percy, I'm afraid. It's all his operation over there."

"A shame," said Blyth. "Although I suspect we shall all be wise to check our pension funds over this. By the way, I do have some good news," he said, and told him about his earlier call. The information retrieval in the Northwood case was a shared venture, and Bassingham would very likely have the same information presented to him at some point this morning. Blyth simply didn't want to take the chance that it would be lost in the flap over the Palace.

"A ray of sunshine. Thank you," said Bassingham. "And, we're nearly at my office. It looks to be one of those endless days."

"My thanks for the prior warning," said Blyth. "Didn't realize you were in your car. If there's any way we can help, do let us know."

"You might send me an application form," said Bassingham, and terminated the conversation.

Highgate
10:02 Greenwich Mean Time

"Hey, Dad! You . . ."

The rest was unintelligible. I was shaving, and was lucky I even heard Jane over the running water. "What? I can hear you, but . . ."

"Get in here!"

She was in the living room. As I came around the corner, I saw a Royal Carriage, on some sort of State detail, with liveried people, and beautiful horses. "Yeah?"

"See that? One of those guys is a newspaper man!"

"What?"

"The footman . . . see him, that one there!" She pointed to a head within a superimposed circle on the screen.

I must have looked remarkably blank, and with half my face covered with shaving cream, a little silly as well.

"He went undercover at the Palace. Buckingham Palace! He was there for months. Taking pictures. He was right up to Bush, and Rice, and Powell, and everybody, not to mention the Royal Family. And *nobody* caught on!"

"Holy shit," I said.

"Yeah! He walked out last night. Nobody had the faintest notion," laughed Jane. "He's done this stuff before. He gave a buddy from his local pub as his reference!"

I watched as more footage showed the same footman at a Palace window, making sort of a surreptitious signal to whoever was running the camera from outside the Palace grounds.

"Heads are gonna roll," I said.

"The Tower, at least," said Jane, thoroughly delighted.

"I hope it's none of our guys," I said, and turned to go back to finish my shave.

"What?"

Communication is a strong suit in our family. "I said . . ."

"Our guys?" asked Jane. "Like, who?"

"Blyth could be a candidate, I'd think. I don't know just how much he has to do with Palace security, but it could be him. Trowbridge, too, for that matter. Special Branch is probably involved somehow."

"Oh, I hope not. Alice?"

"I wouldn't think so." As we talked, I got interested again, and sat down on the couch.

"Forget something?" asked Sue, looking at my soapy face as she came in from the kitchenette.

"You really gotta see this, Mom. You're not gonna believe it. I wonder what Vicky's going to hear at school?"

"Wonder who this reporter works for?" I asked. "Oh, boy. Not anything to do with Sarah Mitchell, I hope."

"No, really not," said Jane. "This was the *Mirror*. An exclusive. They have to say that every time they broadcast this story."

"You know," I said, "it's kind a funny, isn't it? I mean, it's serious, too. But it *is* funny. . . ."

There was general agreement.

"I'm really glad, though," I said, "that whoever's responsible, I'm not in their shoes right now."

"Tyburn," said Jane. "That's where they used to do the public hangings. Tyburn hill. You suppose we should go hang out, just in case?"

The pun was intended.

Buckingham Palace
10:44 Greenwich Mean Time

Ralph Vincent was the US Secret Service Agent assigned to coordinate the security around the presidential entourage while in the UK. He was standing in the inner courtyard of Buckingham Palace, among several vehicles which had arrived bearing some dozen additional personnel for his detail. Inside, the president was meeting with British Conservative Party and Liberal Democrat leaders. Separately. Shortly, they would be off to Banqueting House, Whitehall Palace where he would deliver a speech. After that, he would meet privately with family members of British soldiers killed in action in Iraq.

Vincent was with his British counterpart, Percy Uxbridge, who had just returned from a brief personal talk with the Home Secretary.

"I'm really sorry," said Vincent. "It could happen to anybody."

"Nice of you to say so," said Uxbridge.

"Regardless, we're gonna need additional sweeps ahead of the man. I know you've done a great job, but you understand where I'm coming from on this."

"I do. We're pulling in additional specialized personnel for the remainder of the visit. We're re-vetting anyone hired in the last thirty-six months, by the way. As well as all the family members he's to meet this afternoon."

"Really? The last thirty-six months? That's a little severe."

"That has nothing to do with your president," said Uxbridge. "It's the entire list of personnel who may have any close proximity to the Royals, Parliament, and the various government agencies."

"That's gonna cost," said Vincent.

"It is. MI5 are on twelve-hour shifts as of this morning." Uxbridge straightened himself and said, "Senior staff on twenty-four hour availability. So, this group is going to conduct a sweep, is it?"

"Yeah. We really appreciate you letting us do this.

"It would be damned difficult to object at this point," said Uxbridge. He produced a brittle laugh. "I can be assured none of your agents is in the employ of the *Washington Post*?"

Vincent laughed. "Don't think so, Percy. If there is, we shoot him."

There was a bass hum, faint at first, growing louder very quickly. Moments later, a United States Marine Corps CH-53E came into view, its grey paint making it hard to discern against the cloudy sky. It went into a hover, and disappeared behind the inner section of Buckingham Palace.

"That's the one?" asked Uxbridge.

"Yep. That one will pick him up, if there's an incident. If he's not injured, they fly him straight up to Wethersfield, to the E-4B up there. Call sign Gordo. If he's injured, he doesn't go to Gordo, he goes straight to the nearest hospital. If his health permits, he goes straight from there to *Air Force One* at Heathrow." He pressed his hand to his ear, to monitor some radio traffic. "*Air Force One* has medical facilities. Gordo doesn't."

"Right. The helicopter flies car and all?"

"You bet. If the limo is operational, it drives right up the ramp and into the chopper. If the limo is down, we pick him up in an alternate vehicle. We have LZ's picked out all along the route. The RAF was very helpful."

"Well, we should go back inside," said Uxbridge. "I can't begin to tell you how I hate this. Everything, all our scheduling, has been thrown into a cocked hat. We'll have to reassign personnel ad hoc, which is going to play bloody hell with many of our other operations."

Great Portland Street
11:00 Greenwich Mean Time

In his antiquities shop, Mr. Kazan sat, a copy of the *Mirror* in his hand, having just finished the article about the sham footman at the

Palace. He was staring into space, his mind racing. He had a potential catastrophe on his hands, and was frantically considering his options. First and foremost, he needed to use his assets wisely and decisively. The number of terrorists available in London who possessed the two seemingly opposed characteristics of patience and a willingness to blow themselves up was very small, indeed. Those who could gain employment at the Royal Household were even rarer. He had considered ordering them to act immediately, but thought that to be very unwise. First, because the flap that had to be going on at the Palace, together with the additional security personnel accompanying the president, made any chance of their success most unlikely. Besides, the distraction of the fruit truck with a bomb would be out of the question at this short notice; and it would very likely be much less effective today, anyway.

Even tomorrow, he thought, might be too late. Additional background investigations were bound to be done in the wake of this damned reporter. And since the *Mirror* article had made such a great thing of the deficient screening process, the security services were bound to begin a re-examination of applications immediately. How far back they would go he didn't know, but the risk was great that his three associates would be discovered. To have them taken without completing their mission was unthinkable. To have them strike and miss might serve some purpose, but these were very valuable assets and not easily replaced.

He tapped his fingers on the top of his desk. He wondered if the sacrifice of one of them in a futile bombing would be useful. That was possible, but very unlikely. Besides, Nadeem had insisted that three was the minimum number to make a successful strike at such a heavily protected target. That could still be true.

Then the three simply had to be pulled out. Their identities could be changed quickly, and they could be kept in a safe place for at least a while. Mr. Kazan had always considered suicide bombers to be an unreliable group, at best, although he would never utter that sentiment to anyone. These three, having their end in sight, and suddenly being exposed, would be extremely likely to undergo an enormous psychological letdown, and therefore be much more prone to divulging information if questioned.

They had to leave. And, hopefully, in such a way that he would be able to utilize them again, at a later date, although probably only if they'd been properly reconstructed, preferably in the care of someone suitably devout. That was a matter for the future. He picked up his phone.

"They have to be gotten out, as soon as possible, but no later than this evening," he said to Nadeem. He listened briefly to the argument he'd expected. "This decision has been made at the very highest level," he said, "with great risk." The implication was that someone hiding from American bombers on the Afghan-Pakistan border had just spoken with him, and had run a risk of death to do so. This was not true, although it could have been, and it certainly produced the desired result. Mr. Kazan had the full confidence of his superiors, and knew it.

When the conversation was finished, he sat very still, composing himself. Years of effort, gone for nothing. He stood, abruptly. "Only nothing if you say so," he said to himself. "They are smart. Perhaps we could teach one of them to fly. . . ."

The planning to use the three bombers in another operation began at that moment.

Highgate
15:09 Greenwich Mean Time

While Jane took an enforced nap, Sue and I played Scrabble at the kitchen table and listened to the news on the tube in the living room. Lots of the coverage was about Thursdays playing of the World Cup finals in Rugby. New Zeeland and France were battling for third and fourth place. We assiduously avoided discussing the events that had led to Jane being injured. Well, I know I did, and Sue didn't bring it up.

Sue had leveraged Jane into the nap by promising that we'd go out for supper tonight. We weren't sure just where, and were sort of waiting for Vicky and her escort Carson to come back from school, when Alice called.

She told me that we were on for tonight, about 23:00.

"Tonight?"

"That's when we expect him home. He's taking the train. We need to do it this evening because there have been some schedule changes in the Department."

"Because of the footman thing?"

"Likely. We lose all eyes-on surveillance tomorrow, except for one team of two. We'll have two teams if we go for him tonight."

"Okay."

"Has Sarah Mitchell contacted you yet?"

"No, not a word."

"We shall contact her, then. I'm fairly certain that she'd try for tomorrow," said Alice. "Let me ring her up, and say that you have another appointment that might take most of the day tomorrow. Something medical with Jane. I'll suggest tonight."

"How're you gonna pull that off?" I wanted to hear this.

"She's got most of her information from his departmental secretary at the school," said Alice. "She's only been told that he will be back for class on Thursday, at ten forty-five am. We, on the other hand, know where he is. He needs to take the train in order to return here, and the scheduling would work out much more easily if he were to arrive tonight."

"Nice deduction," I said.

"He also told someone that he was going to return to London tonight." There was some amusement in her voice.

"Confirmation always helps."

"One of ours is actually on the train with him as we speak," she said, the lilt in her voice becoming more obvious. "They left at 14:10 and will arrive at approximately 19:24 at Euston Station. A ten minute taxi ride, and he's home."

"Cool. But that's cheating."

"Tisn't. That shall give Sarah Mitchell three hours to contact him, make the urgent appointment for an interview, and get us in there."

I thought that was going to be pretty close. "What if somebody talks to him before then?"

"It's taken care of. He has delivery of the *Times*, and they've disappeared. He'll receive no incoming calls, except from our Sarah Mitchell. And all outgoing calls will receive a busy signal."

"You can do that?"

"We can even fake his voice mail," she said.

"His computer?"

"Piece of cake," she said. "His server is down. No email, no net."

I decided to play the game. "He could always go to a pay phone. . . ."

"He'll be entirely to busy," she said.

"TV?"

"He actually doesn't own one," said Alice.

"Okay. But this interview business won't be a tip-off?"

"We can trust Sarah Mitchell to see to that," said Alice. "She can insinuate herself in anywhere."

"I believe that. Hey, while I've got you on the phone, is there some place nice to eat you'd recommend. We're taking Jane out for dinner tonight."

"She's well enough?"

"Oh, yeah. Sure. Fine."

"Well, if you'd like to dress a bit? That sort of thing?"

"Sure."

"Let us make a reservation for you. You three, plus Carson and Vicky?"

"Yep."

"I'll call you in ten minutes," she said. "I know the perfect place, and I can pick you up there for the interview."

MI5 Headquarters
Thames House
London
16:21 Greenwich Mean Time

"No, that's *not* the way it works," said the supervisor. "If your bloody shift ends at ten, you are done at ten. Not ten and then time to go home, or return to the office, or stow your gear or anything of the sort. Ten is bloody ten. If it takes half an hour to get to your check-in point, then leave at nine bloody thirty!"

"Sorry," said the agent.

"We've got so much overtime building up now. . . . No nonsense. Do you hear me? None. End of shift is when you've got yourself and your kit back to your hotel, or your office, or your bleeding bivouac. Not when you leave your assignment."

"Naturally."

"If you want triple time, with crumpets, emigrate and join the FBI."

"Got it." The agent started out the door. "Unless we're actually involved. . . ."

"Go away!"

In London that day, there were some 14,000 police and security personnel working the US presidential visit. Due to the large number of protestors, even the traffic wardens were very thin on the ground outside the central London area. The security personnel for the Underground were stretched due to the crowds of protestors taking the tubes to the various areas of the presidential itinerary. Law enforcement units in areas outside central London were operating under what the BBC called "minimum" staffing conditions. This was occurring even though leaves and vacations had been canceled, and various personnel were on extended shifts.

Among those so extended were Alice, who had begun her duty shift at two pm; and the two surveillance teams assigned to the Robert Northwood residence on Ashburnham Road, London. A detail that was left out of Alice's briefing due to the flurry of activity was that the surveillance pair known as the Blue team had come on duty at noon for their twelve-hour shift, two hours earlier than originally planned due to their presence now being required at eight am the next day in the vicinity of Number 10 Downing Street, when the President would visit the Prime Minister. In order to reinforce presence at the scene, several groups had been shifted with little notice. With the tightened rules, the two agents of the Blue team would find it necessary to leave their post at approximately eleven-thirty. This minor detail would be communicated to Alice via departmental email at approximately 7:40 PM. Due to events, Alice would not return to her desk after 7:15 PM.

The second team, the Green team, which was scheduled on at eight pm, would be available until sometime around seven-thirty the next morning. Alice's two team criteria would, therefore, only be in place for approximately thirty minutes after the meeting with Robert Northwood began.

Highgate
17:05 Greenwich Mean Time

Alice called back just after five. She apologized for the delay, saying that she had been very busy.

"I have reservations for all of you at a restaurant in Piccadilly Circus. Seven-thirty, at Criterion. It's one of the oldest and most beautiful restaurants in London. I think you'll truly enjoy it, especially Sue."

"Fantastic," I said, and meant it.

"If possible, I truly do recommend the duck," she said.

"Could you join us?"

After the slightest pause, she said, "Oh, no. I do have things to do."

"You know, Alice, it'd make your cover as solicitor work really well," I said. I'm at my best with broader hints. I thought she'd certainly earned it, and she was very good company.

I heard faint noises as she covered the phone. Then she said, "I'd be delighted, thank you."

I left Highgate to hightail it to our hotel, in order to put on the best stuff I'd packed. This turned out to be a shirt, slacks and a sport coat that Sue had insisted on as I packed in a hurry. I'd forgotten a tie, so stopped off at a men's store just outside the tube station. Five minutes later, and lighter by fifteen pounds sterling, I had a tie.

Just a couple of minutes after I got to the room, the phone rang. It was Sarah Mitchell, asking if meeting Professor Northwood at his place at eleven was all right with me. Good old Alice. I told Sarah Mitchell I was certain I'd be able to make it then, and was sorry about tomorrow not working for me. She said that was just fine, and we left it at that. She never asked about Jane, and why someone ambulatory would need more medical attention.

"I shall confirm with him, and be back with you."

"Okay, hey, I probably won't be here . . . but to make sure you can get me . . ." and I gave her my cell phone number.

She hustled me off the line, and I changed clothes. We all tend to forget little details when we get excited or in a hurry, or both. Like Sarah Mitchell not asking about why Jane needed to go to the doc. I thought Alice had taken that into account. I was really beginning to like our MI5 agent.

Everyone but Alice met at Piccadilly Circus at seven. We spent a few minutes watching Jane go through Tower Records. In fifteen minutes, she'd bought three CD's by groups I'd never heard of, and had stumped a clerk regarding another one.

We entered Criterion at about seven-twenty, and were greeted by Alice who was seated at a small table near the entrance.

"This way," she said, and we trooped toward the rear and were seated at our table.

The place was, as Sue said, "Truly gorgeous." Gold leaf on the ceiling, for example. Marble walls. Paintings and hangings. Real stuff. It was kind of like being wined and dined in a small, elegant museum.

"Established in 1870," said Alice.

"What style is this?" asked Sue.

"I have a friend who calls it a mixture of Imperial Persian and Glorious Victorian Pub," said Alice. "Before I forget, this is on our tab, so enjoy."

"Oh, no," said Sue. "Let us, really."

Sometimes. . . .

"I insist," said Alice. "It's already done."

I had a chance to check the prices on the menu as we ordered, and my quick math put the bill at about two-hundred forty pounds. That was around $430.00. I made a mental note to tell Sue that. That was without wine, which I seem to remember was about 45 pounds per bottle.

After we ordered, Alice asked me if Sarah Mitchell had gotten me at the hotel.

"You bet. Wanted to make sure eleven was good for me. She'll call me on my cell phone to confirm."

Alice smiled. "Brilliant. You know," she said, to Sue, "the pork is nearly as good as the duck. . . ."

The food was absolutely delicious, and I had a fine time, even though we had a job to do after supper.

Sarah Mitchell called at about nine. We were good to go.

Alice and I excused ourselves at about nine forty-five. Sue looked a little strained, and Jane really wanted to go along. Wiser heads prevailed. Mostly Sue's.

"You've done more than enough," she said to Jane. "As your father says, you won't do anyone any good if you're dead."

Much as I hate to be quoted, I wasn't about to disagree.

"Oh, Mom, it's not going to involve any danger at all, is it, Dad?"

"Probably not," I said. "But that's what I thought last time." I smiled at her. "I agree with Sue completely. You sit this one out."

While we had that conversation, Alice was on the phone. "Our car's outside," she said. "I do hate to rush off like this."

"Thank you so much for the lovely dinner," said Sue. "We're ready to leave, too, I think. This has just been so nice."

Alice and I were standing by this time. I glanced down at Carson. "Sure you don't want to come along?"

"It's okay," he said. "I'll escort the women safely home."

Outside, it was raining. I couldn't believe it, and said as much as we hurried to the car.

"It rains in London," said Alice, "much of the time."

"Only the second time since I've been here," I said. I held the door for her. It's just a habit, and she was gracious enough to duck in and not make me look silly.

Once inside, we turned immediately right onto Haymarket, one of the few street names in London that I recognized. After that I was lost.

"Now," said Alice. "Carl Houseman, this is Mark. You've met, I believe."

"You bet. Are you Blyth's Chuck or Dave?" I asked.

"He won't tell," said Mark. "Although I secretly yearn to be Dave."

"I just hope I'm Vera," said Alice. "Regardless of my hopes . . . we shall meet Sarah Mitchell around the corner from his place, on Burnaby Street. Just so you have some idea where you are."

"Oh, sure," I said. She could have given me the GPS coordinates, for all the good it would do me.

She opened her purse, and took out a map. "The three of us go to his flat about five before eleven. Here. There are two surveillance teams, with eyes on, here and here. Blue is parked on the street with a view to the rear of the place, where Burnaby ends. And Green is in a small room across the street from his flat, here. Both can hear everything that is said in his apartment. They will call me if anything is amiss."

"Okay . . ."

"Your role . . . you are simply trying to find out about anything Emma might have said to him, any sort of hint of someone after her. Remember that you don't know she's dead. But, then, he truly doesn't know that, so it shouldn't be a problem. Sarah Mitchell will try to pry all sorts of salacious information from him, and we just let her do that." She looked directly at me. "Does that work?"

"You bet."

"We let Sarah Mitchell play him out. For at least a bit. Would hearing anything about Emma be likely to make you angry?"

"Not that he'll be saying."

"Brilliant. Now, then, at some point we shall come clean with him." That brought a huge smile to her face. "Ought to be worth the admission fee. At that point, I would like you to keep Sarah Mitchell out of my way, if you would."

"Sure."

"We can't very well have him toddling off down the street. If she does anything foolish or unwise, you can legally assist me by, say, gently but forcibly restraining her."

"No marks?"

"Precisely. But do be firm. Blue and Green teams will be responding. They are Special Branch, and will be taking him into formal custody."

"Good."

"We truly do want to avoid uniformed involvement. The less fuss the better."

"Sounds good to me. If you'd happen to need a little help with Northwood, should I . . . ?"

"I consider that highly unlikely," said Alice.

"Well, I do, too," I said. "But just in case?"

"If I develop a migraine," she said, "you can hold him. That's fair."

"Cool."

"You are the main reason he has agreed to talk with us tonight. Sarah Mitchell has told him, quite truthfully, as much as she knows about you."

"Really?"

"Trust me. From the sound of his voice, I do believe he thinks this is a fine opportunity to reinforce his alibi."

"Okay." I smiled. "You certainly are resourceful."

"We hate to waste tax monies," she said.

Before we pulled up where we would be parking, we went by Professor Robert Northwood's apartment. It was a white building, three stories. Large windows that looked to be nearly floor to ceiling on the front face, with black framing. Two doors, separated by a window, with a short flight of steps leading up to them. That was about all I could see out the rain spattered window of the car.

"His is the top right. There seems to be a light on . . ."

"Yep." The curtains were opened, but all I could see was a white ceiling.

Alice looked at her watch as we went what I thought was north a long block, and then doubled back toward the apartment. It was just after ten.

"We'll sit at this point," said Alice, pointing to her map again. "We want to see if Sarah Mitchell brings anyone with her. She ought to be coming down this street," she said, as we turned left onto Burnaby again, pulled to the left curb, and stopped. I just couldn't get used to doing that. The left curb I mean. It felt really weird.

A more familiar feeling started in my stomach and diaphragm. It was the kind of tension that'll come when you're about to go on a warranted search kind of thing. Not fear, but excitement. It all comes from not wanting to screw up.

Unfortunately, adrenaline tends to slow down your perception of time passing. That was one hell of a long wait.

I'm pretty sure we all felt about the same, because we started one of those cop type conversations to kill time.

"You guys got any idea why they're doing this?" I asked.

"As in . . . ?" asked Mark.

"Taking Emma in the first place," I said. "Killing her. Why in the hell did they kill her, especially when they did?"

"I'm not certain," said Alice. "It was quite stupid, so I suspect it was a miscue or an outright mistake. That would explain why Northwood doesn't know of it."

"Okay. Sure. But what about their motives?"

"At least some of them are radical Islamists. From the files you gave us, you've dealt with the type before, I see."

"Entertaining file," said Mark. "I never would have guessed something like that could happen in rural . . . Iowa, isn't it?"

Bless him. "Yes, Iowa. I tell ya, nobody was more surprised than we were."

"You weren't working them prior to the incident, were you?" asked Alice.

"No. Hell, we didn't even know they were there."

"Let me give you some idea of what at least some of these participants are like. We think we may have a working ID on the one they call Imad. You've never heard of him. He's a friend of Northwood's. We think that this Imad has actually attended one of the terrorist training camps in the Middle East. It may have been bin Laden sponsored, but that isn't really essential. He's indoctrinated."

"And?"

"Basically he believes that killing anybody who gets in the way of jihad, or who's death will further the purpose of jihad, is absolutely respectable."

I'd never heard respectable used to describe a fanatic before. It sounded good.

"He believes," said Mark, "that the westerners have no right to exist. If you see one, you can take him or her captive. You can take their property. You can kill them. Non-Muslims have no stature."

"How's that go over with the Muslim community in general?"

"Here, in the UK? Not at all well," said Alice. "At least, not as far as I know. The Muslims I know think its radical foolishness, and that it has us painting them all with the same brush."

"That's about what we hear in the US," I said.

"On the other hand, we, here," she said, "are having a bit of a rough time with those members of the public who think that, because they are such intelligent, tasteful, highly motivated, and generally wonderful people, no terrorist would ever want to harm them. Especially after they find out how thoroughly nice they are."

"Come, let us reason together," I said, with a grin. "Yeah. That's always the case though, isn't it? I mean, I've gotten the same stuff regarding dope dealers, motorcycle gangs, street gangs . . . way before terrorism was a problem for us."

"I think you're probably right," said Alice, "although I must admit I've never had the pleasure of working as a street copper myself."

"Then trust me," I said. "Most people are like that. I knew a guy once, had a coin collection valued at more than a million dollars. He didn't think a burglar would ever harm him, because he intended to meet them, face to face, and talk with them."

"I suppose he was killed by a burglar," said Mark.

"Nope. His house burned down one night, though. Melted lots of the coins. He'd added a wood furnace to save money, and the chimney caught."

There was a silence. Then Alice started to laugh, deep and low. "You bastard," she said.

"Couldn't help it," I said, with a grin. "So, anyway, what are the reasonable Muslims doing about this?" I really was curious.

"As much as you or I would," she said. "If we weren't officials."

"Ah. Well, you really can't blame them. Like the shop owners in Chicago in the twenties and thirties? Pay the mob protection, because the cops can't protect you all that well most of the time. But you don't have to like it."

"That's adequate," she said.

"So how did our professor here get into this shit? He isn't even a Muslim."

"For a start, you have to realize that Northwood most likely didn't know he was dealing with someone quite as committed as this Imad. I think that's where things got away from him. I'm not at all sure he knows himself just how far this has gone."

"And Imad got the explosives?"

"From someone," said Alice. "I have no idea who."

"And Emma was grabbed off for . . . why? A stunt?"

"Frankly," said Alice, "there seems to be only one purpose, in the final analysis. She was taken to be killed, in order to establish their credentials. It's just that I tend to think that Northwood didn't quite realize that."

"Why did they let him in?"

"He's a non-Muslim Englishman," said Mark. "That's to broaden our focus, and dilute our concentration."

"You really think these guys are that smart?"

"No," said Alice. "Not in the least. But someone is. Somewhere."

Chapter 25

Ashburnham Road, London
22:50 Greenwich Mean Time

About ten minutes to eleven, a car drove past us, turned the corner, and the brake lights came on just before we lost sight of it.

"I believe that was our Sarah Mitchell," said Mark.

"It was," said Alice. "Let's just give her a bit, and then we'll walk in from here."

Mark's mobile phone rang.

"She's out . . . and standing by her car . . ." he chuckled. "Blue team says she's looking impatient. And . . . they think she's got someone else in her car."

"Good enough for us," said Alice, as she opened her door. "Let's go meet our man."

It was still kind of raining, but it had turned into more of a drizzle. Everything was nice and shiny, and the street lights were that yellowish kind they had in Highgate. Everything seemed to be okay until you looked at something that was supposed to be red and it had turned grey. Neat stuff.

Sarah Mitchell saw us as we rounded the corner. Alice, consummate actress she was, waived and said, in an excited voice, "Oh, here it is! We parked on the wrong street!"

Sarah Mitchell apparently had just low enough of an opinion of Alice to accept that without a second thought.

"So sorry about the horrible hour," she said.

"Fine with me," I said.

"It would be this door," said Sarah Mitchell. She turned and started up the steps.

Alice leaned over to me and whispered, "There's a cameraman in her car," as she passed. I didn't turn, but followed the two women into the building.

The stairs were varnished wood, and the light was provided by a chandelier that hung down into the stairwell from the third floor ceiling. It was more effective than I'd have thought, though the light wasn't hotel quality bright.

The stairs creaked just a little, and the dark wood banister was just a tad bit unsteady. A little glue, I thought, would fix that.

Since the stair wasn't carpeted, he had to have heard us coming from the second floor on. As we got to the third floor landing the only door opened, and there stood a man who just had to be Professor Robert Northwood.

"Ms. Mitchell . . ." he said, in a great, sophisticated English voice. He extended his hand, and she shook it. "And you must be . . . ?"

I could see his flicker up and down Alice's long body. "My name is Alice, and I represent Mr. Houseman."

They shook hands, and he gave her the two-handed version. He was trying to score just a little bit even now.

"And you must be Mr. Houseman," he said. We shook hands, too. I noticed he didn't give me the once over he'd given Alice. It was probably because he had to look up to meet my eye. "All the way from . . . Iowa, isn't it?"

His hand was firm, and dry. No sign of nerves. And I had to give him credit, he got the state right. So far, the Brits had done better than most East Coast citizens of the US, who tended to get Iowa, Ohio and Idaho all mixed up.

"Well, it's a small town," I said. "We try to look after our own."

"I'm sure," he said. "Won't you come in?"

It was a nice place, but unremarkable. I suspected he had a cleaning lady in once a week. There was a small couch, three stuffed chairs, and a large secretary kind of desk on one wall. A coffee-type table, and two end table with lights, and that was it in the living room. Just off to my right, there was another room that looked like a small library. Tall wooden shelves, filled with books, some hardbound, and the rest those big kind of paperbacks. Set back was the kitchen, which looked very modern and very neat. As soon as we walked in the door, we had to turn hard to the left, because the exterior wall was to the right, and about half of that was window.

"Great view," I said.

"Especially on such a rainy night," he said. "It adds an air of mystery about the place, don't you think?"

"Oh, indeed," said Alice.

The professor took the women's coats. I kept my sport coat on, and didn't have an outer coat. Well, it wasn't cold, and I hadn't expected rain.

"Do you have an umbrella?"

"No," I said. "Not with me. I left it at the hotel. It's hardly rained since I've been here."

"It *has* been unusual," said Sarah Mitchell.

"Please be seated," said Robert Northwood. "Would any of you care for some wine? Or, I've just made some fine Arabic coffee . . . Mazbuta. I add my own cardamom."

Both Alice and Sarah Mitchell chose the wine. I, and the professor, opted for the coffee.

Once we got the serving out of the way, and we were all seated, he said, "I've seen your article featuring Mr. Houseman, Sarah. Interesting. The messenger got it here an hour ago. Thank you."

"Certainly," said Sarah Mitchell.

That was sort of my cue. "Then you know how I found myself in the UK," I said. "There was also a bit of politics involved." I explained.

"How interesting."

"You sort of had to be there," I said.

"I do hope I can be of some service, but I'm not sure just how. . . ."

The way he said it, I knew that he was pretty wary, but in no way did he feel challenged. Good enough.

"Well," I said, "I know you know Emma. Reasonably well." I looked him right in the eye. He didn't flinch.

"Actually, quite well," he said. "We've had a bit of a fling. That's why I'm so concerned for her safety." He put his cup down, leaned forward, and played the sincere, confidential witness to the tee. "I shouldn't have told you that. There are some who feel that the faculty and the students should never fraternize. But, my God, Emma is thirty something, and I truly don't see that as being what they meant by faculty-student relationships. It isn't as if she were nineteen, after all."

If that was meant to gain our confidence, it seemed to work on Sarah Mitchell.

"Sure," I said. "No problem here with that. What I'd like to know is, well, you know, did she seem worried to you? Had there been any, well, threats? Did she say anything about some people following her?"

That was meant to throw him off the track. It worked.

"Oh, no. Not at all. She's never expressed any concerns of that sort. Never. She did feel some . . . well, I think concern is the right word here. Concern for how her flat mates might feel about the two of us. But that was all."

"Sure." I knew that, if he'd read the article, that he was very much aware that I was Jane's father. "Jane mentioned that you two had been seeing each other. I don't think she had any reservations over that. In fact, she said that you and Emma and Vicky and her had gone on some sort of tour together?"

"Oh, yes. Indeed. I have an interest in the tube system. Especially the old, and abandoned stations. We toured one. I thought that, the four of us being together, would ally some of Emma's doubts."

"Really?" said Alice. "How interesting."

He turned his all attention to her, and I do mean all. It was something to watch.

"Oh, yes. Fascinating stuff. Would you be interested in a tour? I can arrange it."

"That would be very special," said Alice.

"One other thing," I said. He looked back at me. With less interest, I might add.

"Of course."

"Good coffee," I said. He smiled. "I don't mean to suggest anything untoward, here," I said. I was getting fairly close to my "Aw, shucks," routine, and was being pretty careful myself. I didn't think that it had ever been used on him, frankly, and figured maybe a slightly modified version would do very well here.

"Yes?"

"Well, it's just that the bunch who have kidnapped her . . . their title is really close to the name of the group you chair . . . that Eidarous and Belmarsh thing?"

He stiffened. "And . . . ?"

"Well, I was wondering if you could give me some idea what that other group is like. I mean, I hear your group is more of a petitioning type of thing. Not kidnappers, like these others. So, I dunno, have there been any . . . well, contacts, between you and another group with almost the same name?"

When he looked at me this time, I swear I detected some condescension. "Oh, they're not the same at all. My group is purely political. There wouldn't be any contact, none at all. We wouldn't move in the same circles."

"Oh. I was afraid of that," I said. I tried to sound upbeat. Sometimes it's lots easier to convince somebody you're disappointed if you try to sound upbeat.

Alice's phone rang. She answered it, and then said, "Excuse me," and got up and walked over to the window. "Better now," she said into the phone.

"That's what I tried to tell them, too," said Sarah Mitchell.

"Pardon," said the professor.

"About the difference between the groups."

"Indeed," he said. "I'm so glad to hear you like the coffee," he said. "Would you care for some more?"

"Sure."

He got up and went into the kitchen. I watched his reflection in the window. He glanced at my reflection several times. To let him think I wasn't aware of him, I said, "I really do like this view."

In the small room across the street, the two-man team known as Green was watching, videotaping, and listening to the events in the target flat with minimal interest. Thus far, nothing that would seem to justify this particular effort was happening. Edward, the team leader, was just answering a call on his cell phone.

"Hullo?"

"It's Mike," said the familiar voice of the leader of the Blue team. "We're off."

"You're what?"

"Off, away, calling it a day."

"This is a prank?"

"No," said Mike, patiently. "You've got the memo, and we're scheduled for Number 10 tomorrow. I've just checked with the office, and they say to pack it in."

Edward was stunned. "You best talk with the Superintendent. They must have misunderstood."

"It was the Superintendent's office I called. They say we leave. Sorry, thought you knew that."

"My understanding was that we all worked our assigned shift. You've two hours left."

"Not so. We were called in two hours early due to the flap about the stealth footman. Thought you knew."

"Bloody hell. Right, then. We'll tell you all about it tomorrow."

Edward turned to his partner. "Blue's off for home, Danny. They were called in two hours early today."

"Truly?"

"Right. Well, then, we'd best cover both positions. You get on down to the rear of the place. I shall stay here."

"It's raining. Why don't I stay here, instead?" Danny was joking. He was the junior member of the team.

"Because of my exalted rank, you sot. Now off you go."

Edward looked back across the street. "It's not like there's a flurry of activity. Do you suppose we should ring her and tell her we've divided the posts?"

"It might break the rhythm for no reason," said Danny, putting on his coat. "Alice plays 'em well."

"True. Right, then. Enjoy your shower."

"More wine?" asked Robert Northwood.

"No, thank you," said Alice.

"Well, then," he said. "Is there any other way I can be of assistance?"

Sarah Mitchell spoke up. "Do you know if she's been sleeping with any of the other faculty?"

"Not that I'm aware of," he answered. "I do hope this isn't going to descend into the salacious." He said it with a smile.

"Oh, no," said Sarah Mitchell. "I was just wondering, would you happen to have a reproducible photo of you and her, together?"

"I fear I don't," he said.

He sounded pretty cocky to me. Apparently, he did to Alice, too, because she took off the gloves.

"Before we all get too comfy," she said, "I think there are a couple of bits of information you should know."

"Anything you can share will help us get her back," he said. I could gladly have strangled him at that point.

"First," said Alice, reaching into her purse, "My name is Alice Tennent. I work for the Government." She displayed her ID. "More specifically, MI5."

I don't know who was more surprised, Robert Northwood or Sarah Mitchell. Northwood was the only one who spoke, though.

"Are you here to kill me?"

No kidding. That's what he said. Alice never blinked.

"Certainly not," she said. "But I am authorized to tell you that Emma Schiller is dead."

While Sarah Mitchell recovered sufficiently to begin scribbling furiously, Robert Northwood's jaw dropped.

"No!"

"Indeed she is," said Alice. "Deputy Houseman identified her body."

"She's dead all right," I said. "No doubt in my mind."

"She can't be," said Northwood. "She can't be."

"I believe Hamza tried to contact you, but couldn't reach you," said Alice, delivering a second blow.

"This can't be," said Northwood, and looked at his watch. "It's Wednesday. The nineteenth."

"And she has to be kept alive until the twenty-first? I'm afraid someone changed the schedule," said Alice.

At this point, she'd given Northwood a near overload of information, all of it exceptionally bad for him. She backed off a bit, to prevent him going catatonic on her.

"It may have been a mistake," she said. "Your two little helpers are incredibly amateurish. It could well have been preventable."

Robert Northwood was looking a little green around the gills. "It's over, then?"

"Your part certainly is," said Alice.

"How did you find out?"

"Your associates tried to dispose of the body. It was found in the back of an automobile they were driving." She didn't say it was a chance thing.

"I need to see my solicitor," he said. He looked at his watch again. Because he did, I looked at mine. It was eleven twenty-five.

Northwood stood up, and moved generally toward the windows. Not nearly close enough to jump, and he wasn't the type, anyway. But close enough that he could see the other side of the street. He looked out, with his hands folded in front of him, and his head bent slightly down. He looked for all the world like he was praying. But I could see his eyes in the window, and he was looking out onto the street.

"Who are you expecting?" asked Alice.

"A young woman," he said. "No one you'd know." He paused, and then looked back into the room. "She happens to be my solicitor."

"Hanadi Tamish?" asked Alice.

Northwood sucked in a breath, and let it out with, "Of course. You tap phones, don't you."

Alice didn't say if she did that or not. "We'll need to talk with her, as well," she said.

Danny, the second member of the Green team, was examining his new post down on the wet street. He knew that Blue team had been parked in a car somewhere near here, but he couldn't for the life of him see how they'd been able to get a visual inside the Northwood flat. He'd walked back and forth three times, from the dead end to the intersection, and hadn't been able to see much more than a glimmer from the light in the kitchen.

He decided to walk up the alley way behind the building, to see if there was some better vantage point.

Mark, who had driven Alice and Carl Houseman to the Northwood residence, had been maintaining a distant surveillance, watching the western length of Burnaby Street in his rear view mirror, and the short eastern portion through his windshield. He had noticed a car leave the area, from the general location where he knew Blue team to be parked, but had simply thought it to be a local resident. Somewhat later, he saw a man come round the corner from Ashburnham Road, and walk east down Burnaby Street. The man flickered in and out of his view, but seemed to be walking aimlessly up and down. He picked up his cell phone, and called the number of the senior surveillance officer at the scene, Edward.

When Edward answered, Mark said, "I've got a man walking about near Blue team. Would you have them check it?"

Edward laughed. "That'd be my Danny."

"What the hell is he doing wandering about?"

"Blue have pulled out. They need to go sleep, as they're doing a bit at Number 10 tomorrow morning."

"They've gone?" Mark couldn't believe it.

"We've replaced 'em all with Danny," said Edward. "Not to worry. Are you listening to Alice?"

"I don't have the gear in this car," said Mark.

"She's identified herself, and our target passed a stone."

"What's he done?" asked Mark.

"Just looked out the window, and said something about expecting his solicitor."

Mark didn't like the sound of that. "I believe I'll go into the building," he said.

"Alice is quite capable. And she's got the American with her."

"Ah," said Mark, "well he's not much more than a local constable in a very rural area, really. And he's old. I'd prefer being closer, at least. I'll be in the building. I'll have my phone."

"I'll tell Danny," said Mark. "You do worry too much."

"You can't *ever* worry too much," said Mark, as he left his car.

Less than two minutes after Mark left his car, and while Danny was still exploring the alleyway in the rear of the Northwood flat, another car pulled up and parked some fifty feet behind the vehicle

Mark had just left. Hanadi emerged from the passenger side, and leaned in to address Imad.

"Find a way to let my parents . . ."

"Of course. You justify all faith in you. God go with you."

She then began walking westward on Burnaby Street, and had rounded the corner and was crossing Ashburnham Road on her way to Northwood's flat before she was picked up by Edward at his perch in the surveillance room.

By the time he'd dialed his mobile phone, and Alice had answered hers, Hanadi was already climbing the first flight of stairs to Robert Northwood's flat.

Imad left the car a few moments later, to follow Hanadi, and make certain that she completed her task. Anton slid over into the driver's seat.

"Wait at the corner of Damer Terrace," said Imad.

"Yes."

"If you hear nothing in the next few minutes, wait another fifteen. Then go to Clissold Park, and leave the car near Greenway Close. Do you have that?"

"Yes."

"If there is a serious problem, go to the Mosque, tell them you need a phone."

"Yes."

Imad walked away, and Anton headed the car toward Damer Terrace.

Alice's phone rang, and she moved in toward the kitchen to answer it. I stood, and moved to lean my hand on the end of the couch, between Northwood and the door. Just in case.

"You were sure it was her?" he asked me.

"Positive."

He was still having a hard time adjusting. "I just . . . well, I'd rather not believe it. But you were sure it was Emma?"

"Yep."

"I don't suppose it makes a difference, but I'd like you to know that I'm very sorry. Very sorry."

I looked him in the eye. "I don't care," I said.

He recoiled just a bit at that.

"I shouldn't have left before it was all resolved," he said, as much to himself as to me. Sarah Mitchell had now moved over toward the window, keeping her left side toward me. I could see in the reflection that she was making flicking motions with her right hand. Her cameraman was down on the street.

"You know," said Northwood, fairly loudly, "if it weren't for your president, this never would have happened."

That got Sarah Mitchell's attention, which it was supposed to do. Her head snapped around to us, and she stopped signaling the cameraman.

"You mean Iraq?" I had to ask.

"Of course. It's an injustice, an illegal war, an . . ."

"Put a sock in it," I said.

"The truth is hard to hear."

"Then wait until you hear about your friends," I said. "But don't waste your best excuse on me. Tell it to the courts. Maybe they'll buy it." I gave him what I thought was an insincere smile. "The Devil Bush made me kill her. I mean, it's pretty weak, but it's probably the best shot you've got."

Alice came back into the room. "A woman has entered the building seems to be on her way to this floor."

Northwood nodded. "As you said, Hanadi." He stared at Alice. "She may well end up representing me. I contacted her and told her that I would be more comfortable with her here."

"When did you do that?" Alice's brow was furrowed.

"When I thought this was a sincere interview," he said.

"What time was that?" asked Alice, knowing he wasn't supposed to be able to get anybody on his phone.

"I don't know . . . if you think it's important . . . I tried to call her when I got home, her line was busy . . . I went downstairs to Mrs. McGonagall's apartment to pick up my mail, we talked . . . and I called her from there. That would have been ten or so. You should know that, you've got my phone tapped. . . ." Then his face lit up. "I see. I see. You don't have Mrs. McGonagall's phone on your warrant, do you?"

Apparently London and Iowa had more in common than I would have thought.

"You will meet her at the door, and let her in," said Alice. "You will not attempt to dissuade her from entering. You will not attempt to tell her anything before I've identified myself to her. Do you understand?"

"Of course," he said. "You have my willing cooperation." When he said that, he looked over at Sarah Mitchell, to make sure she had that.

I was wondering just when we'd be getting rid of Sarah Mitchell, anyway. She had to have enough of a story by now, and things were going to get to the level of naming names pretty soon. I was sure Alice didn't want her to be around then.

"You and I," said Alice to Northwood, "will answer the door. I'll be over here. I can catch you before you go five paces. Carl, you and Ms. Mitchell stand in the kitchen, please. I want our guest in the room before she knows we're here."

We started to move the way we were told, although Sarah Mitchell was tending to hang back a little.

"After she is inside," said Alice, "I'm afraid you'll have to leave, Sarah. That's official, by the way."

"An order?" asked Sarah Mitchell.

"Indeed," said Alice.

Robert Northwood was still standing on the edge of denial. "You're really MI5?" He looked at Alice.

"Really, truly, and in every way, Mr. Northwood," she said. "Now come and answer the door. Nothing tricky. There are officers behind the building, and others across and in the street. Your cooperation will be duly noted."

"Yes," he said.

Sarah Mitchell was scribbling everything down. "Brilliant, just brilliant," she said, under her breath. It probably was something of an unanticipated scoop. She pulled her phone out of her pocket and speed dialed.

"Robbie?"

Whoever that was apparently answered.

"Get to the street, and get everything. There ought to be cops all over in a moment. I'm with MI5 up here. Yes, really. Get shots of the flat from the street. Hurry! Hurry!"

Alice hadn't mentioned Sarah Mitchell not making phone calls, and I really didn't see anything wrong with it. After all, we'd promised her a scoop of sorts, and it was turning out to be bigger than she could have dreamed.

There was a knock at the door, and Alice's cell phone rang at the same instant.

"Who's there?" asked Northwood, as if it were necessary. There was a soft response, and it sounded female, but I couldn't make out what she said.

"Yes," he said, and started to open the door.

At that point, Sarah Mitchell, I suppose to make sure she could be seen from the street in the photographs her partner was taking, began to move toward the windows. I don't know if the woman at the door saw her move or not.

"Welcome, Hanadi," said Robert Northwood. In the window, I saw a woman's reflection. She was fairly small, was in a dark grey raincoat, with a light grey scarf wrapped like Muslim women do, over her head. I watched her reflection as she looked at him, and saw her lower her head.

The blast blew him straight out onto the street three floors below. I know it did. I saw him go. It was the damndest thing.

Chapter 26

I sort of got my senses back, and pushed myself up out of the broken glass and pottery on the kitchen floor. There was thick plaster dust hanging in the air, and it made it really hard to see. I was disoriented anyway, and there was an enormous ringing in my ears. The living room lights weren't so much broken as they were gone. Most of the light was from the streetlight outside.

Half the wall where the door was mounted was just not there anymore. The door itself was stuck in the library wall, where it had apparently been blasted through the room. Alice was lying on the floor very near the entryway. She was on her left side, so she was facing me. She was covered with plaster dust, and some blood, and wasn't moving at all.

Through the plaster fog, I made out Sarah Mitchell, who'd been on her way to the window, laying near the far wall, very near to where the windows had been. She wasn't moving at all, either. There was no glass whatsoever remaining in the windows, nor any of the framing, and the cold, wet air was flowing in from the street.

I hadn't heard a thing in the way of an explosion. I mean, I must have heard something, but it must have just overwhelmed my senses. I sure as hell couldn't hear anything but a high-pitched ring now.

As far as I could tell the woman at the door had completely disappeared, but from the reddish and pink paste on the ceiling and what was left of the walls, I had a pretty good idea of where she'd gone. As I walked over debris toward Alice, I noticed in a sort of distant way that I could look right through where the wall had been, and see that the third floor landing had been pretty much destroyed, as well.

There was an acrid smell, and some hazy smoke mixed in with the plaster dust, but nothing seemed to be actually burning. I found that I didn't really care if there was a fire or not. I was just numb.

I got over to Alice as fast as I could, and nearly fell on her. I had reached my hand out to steady myself as I approached, and the plaster had given way and my arm went into the wall space. When I got my balance back, and knelt down, she seemed to be breathing all right, but there was no response to my saying her name.

"Well, you dumb shit," I said to myself, "she probably can't hear, either."

I reached down, and gently shook her shoulder. Her eyes flew open, but she didn't move. Idiotically, I grinned and waived my hand at her.

I became aware of some movement at the door, or where the door had been, and saw Mark and two men I didn't know trying to negotiate the ruined landing without falling through. They were only a few feet from me, but there was no way they were going to be able to cross that gap.

"Get an ambulance," I said. I saw their lips move, but couldn't hear a thing. "Alice . . . she needs an ambulance," I said again.

Mark picked up on my hearing problem right away, and nodded vigorously as he mouthed "OK."

While they dealt with whatever they had to do, I went over to where Sarah Mitchell was. She was moving, and was trying to sit up.

"Try not to move," I said, loudly.

She looked up and said something.

"What?"

I watched her lips very closely. It looked like she said, "Don't shout."

I concluded her hearing hadn't been as effected as mine.

I thought I'd sit down, but what little furniture was left in the room was either all busted up or upside down. I settled for leaning up against the wall.

Mark caught my attention by waving his hands. Somehow, he'd made it into the room despite the wreck of the third floor landing. I looked back over that way, and saw Alice sitting up. He mouthed and exaggerated "Don't move . . . I will check you . . ."

"How is she?" I asked.

Alice turned her head toward me, and looked bewildered. I suspected she couldn't hear, either. As I watched, she gently lay back down, and put her hands to her head.

"I'm fine," I said to Mark, trying not to shout in his face. "Just deaf." I put my hands to my ears, pressed, and pulled them away. No blood. "Temporary, maybe," I said. "Ringing. Can't hear over it." I think I must have been talking really loudly, as he stepped back and put his hands over his ears. "Sit down," he mouthed, and started kicking debris out of the way. "Here . . ." He stood one of the overturned chairs back to an upright position, right over by Alice. It looked pretty solid.

I sat. Very slowly and very carefully. Everything seemed to work all right, and there wasn't any pain. There was so much plaster dust, I couldn't even tell what color most of the room was. That, and the yellowish light from the street that was flooding into the living room, gave it all an unreal, movie set look. The library, with the lights still on, looked like it was in another, untouched world.

Mark was over by Sarah Mitchell, who was still struggling to sit up. She had a dazed, kind of stupid look that I think we all probably had about that time. She seemed to be saying something, but it was kind of hard to tell because I couldn't hear.

My gaze wandered a little, and I kind of stopped paying attention and started thinking of really weird things. I suddenly became very much aware of a burglary report I'd left on my desk back in Iowa. Unfinished. I could remember every detail of the pre-printed form, every box.

Then I started thinking of our local meat market. Weird. I sort of shook my head to clear it, and found myself looking at a hunk of meat. I focused, and it really was. The hips and one leg of somebody. I glanced hurriedly at Alice. She seemed intact. I remember saying, "Huh," to myself.

I looked back down at Alice. She looked pretty small, lying on the floor like that. I could see her breathing, but she kept moving her hands over her face and head. At about that point, I realized that my face was starting to tingle like crazy. It felt sort of like your foot does when it goes to sleep when you sit for too long. It was a strange feeling.

I felt absolutely useless, but knew enough not to move around. Mark had a tough enough job, and I realized somewhere in the back of my mind that blast victims don't always feel pain if they have severe internal damage. So I sat. I noticed that my sport coat, although pretty well intact, was absolutely light grey with all the dust. It was my only sport coat, and I figured it was probably ruined. Sue was gonna be pissed.

After that, things just got less and less important, and I don't remember a whole lot.

Chapter 27

B lyth stood in the street, gazing up at the curtains blowing through the empty windows on the third floor. There was glass and other debris all over the street, and the body of an unidentified male was under a rubberized yellow blanket. He assumed, based upon what he'd been told, that it was Robert Northwood, but he'd had a look and there was no way to tell at this point. The face bore a great similarity to an eggplant that had been stepped upon by a rather large horse.

The Emergency Services were using a scissors platform lift to re-move the survivors, and he watched as the last one was being lowered toward a waiting ambulance. He'd been told that it was Alice, that she appeared to be in fairly good condition but quite dazed, and that she was conscious. He'd seen Sarah Mitchell and Deputy Houseman lifted down and placed in ambulances, and had managed to talk briefly with the American. He'd seemed fine, although thoroughly covered with plaster dust, and quite unable to hear.

He'd asked Houseman what had happened, in an attempt to con-firm what Mark had told him.

"Lady came to the door," the American Deputy Sheriff had said, making an obvious effort to concentrate and speak in a normal tone of voice. "Smallish. Scarf on her head. I think it was her. Who blew up. If I'm too loud, it's because I can't hear much at all."

That confirmed what Mark had indicated.

The scissors lift stopped about twenty feet in the air, while some-one adjusted something. Then it continued its descent.

Alice, on a stretcher, was off-loaded, saw him, and managed a wave.

He walked quickly over to her. "You look a sight," he said, speaking slowly.

She smiled. "I'm fine," she said. "Really." Her voice sounded weak to him. "Can't hear much over the ringing. My face itches."

"I'll see you at the hospital." He watched them load her in the ambulance, and then turned around and collared Henry Morris, who was in charge of the post-blast assessment team.

"As soon as humanly possible, Henry," he said.

Henry Morris had been up to the scene, having crossed an aluminum plank that had been placed over the hole in the third floor landing. He'd returned via the same route, and had been waiting for the scissors lift to finish with the victims before commandeering it to take himself, his team, and their kit to the flat.

"Indeed. It looks quite a lot like a suicide bomber. Do you have a suspect, Adrian?"

"Female, possibly named Hanadi."

"Any DNA samples available? We have what appears to be a human head stuck through the ceiling plaster, some fifteen feet into the room. And part of a hip girdle on the floor. Other, smaller pieces are bound to turn up. A DNA sample would be good."

Blyth knew that suicide bombers, especially those wearing a harness of explosives around their body, had a tendency to have their heads shot straight into the air. Explosives acted three dimensionally, with as much force going inwards as out. The enormous, concentrated pressure of the blast waves from all sides meeting in the middle simply blew heads straight up. If the explosion was outside, they would be found a goodly distance from the scene. If inside, the ceiling usually stopped the head, although in less substantial structures, they had been known to be thrust into the spaces beneath the roof. Being intercepted by the ceiling certainly made them easier to locate, but it had the unfortunate side effect of making them much less recognizable.

"Special Branch are in the process of obtaining a warrant for her flat," said Blyth. "Hopefully, there will be something there."

"Good." Morris looked at the yellow blanket in the street. "The bomber seems to have gone off just at the door frame of the flat, really. Possibly outside the door, in fact. Quite a chunk out of the walls. All things being equal, I'd tend to believe that the chap under the blanket was right at the door, himself." He glanced up at the vacant window casings. "Assuming he's in the neighborhood of seventy kilograms . . . umm. Any idea what sort of explosive, Adrian?"

"You might start with Semtex," said Blyth. "Just a guess."

"Right. Then, I'd say several kilograms of the stuff." He looked wryly at Blyth. "Just a guess."

"Is that in keeping with female suicide bombers?"

"It would have to be, now, wouldn't it?" He smiled at Blyth. The two of them had known each other for many years. "Females tend to carry ten to fifteen kilos, really. Males tend to carry almost twice that. That's trends, only, you understand."

"Certainly. I've never quite understood why someone would do that."

Morris nodded in agreement. "Suicide bombers are psychologically difficult to predict . . . they're such a volatile lot."

Blyth looked at him with considerable disdain. "No humor, please. Continue."

"Yes. Shame, though, I do have more. Indeed. Well, then, according to my Israeli friends, those are typical weights. But forty kilograms would have taken out the facing wall, the roof, the rear wall, the flooring and . . . well, and generally made much more of a mess. Actually," he said, "if this one had gotten all the way inside, and had the foresight to close the bloody door, Adrian, we wouldn't be able to talk to any survivors."

"Really?"

"Indeed. I had a chance to talk to your Alice up there. She's quite dazed, but the paramedics can find no serious damage so far. Alice said that both she and the big American were partially shielded by the door as it was opened. Well," he corrected himself, "she actually said that the bomber was not seen because she was behind the door. The American was to her left. It opened inward, and to the left. From the hinge. Solid core. And a good thing."

"It's something to remember," said Blyth. "How close we come."

"The other woman, the first one down? She seems to have been thrown about. The medics thought she was the worst injured." He looked up at Blyth. "One of yours, too?"

"Not really," said Blyth.

"Ah. Well, then. One of them?"

"Not really that, either," said Blyth. "More of a neutral party."

"And the apparent innocent member of the public on the landing below," said Morris. "Quite a chunk of ceiling hit him."

"Who?"

"The chap on the stair. Looks to have been just at the landing, when the device detonated. Never knew what was happening, I'd guess."

"Do we know who he is?" asked Blyth.

"The constables are attending to that. He's on his way to hospital."

Guy's and St. Thomas's Hospital Complex
Central London
01:50

The doctor working on Sarah Mitchell ran beside her gurney toward surgery. He had ordered immediate X-rays as soon as the paramedic on her case told him she'd been in an explosion. Sarah Mitchell was talking, and seemed unusually calm. She complained of slight nausea, and a great lassitude. That was what worried him. She seemed to be shutting down as they talked.

BP had been low, respirations had been elevated, and she'd been very, very thirsty.

The X-rays revealed what was known as the white butterfly shape . . . her lungs had exploded at the time of the blast, the result of the enormous pressure wave. She might very well have had her mouth open at the time of the blast, although that wasn't absolutely necessary for the internal damage. Immediate surgery was the only possible course, but given the size of the white area, there was very little chance of her survival. The odds were also very good that there were many other internal injuries as well.

As they hurried her along, they'd intubated her, were administering oxygen, and three IV's were in her arms. Within fourteen minutes of being admitted, she was in surgery. Nineteen minutes later, she was dead.

02:10

They'd taken my sport coat, so I officially considered that a write-off. I had been X-rayed, questioned, scrutinized, probed, stripped and examined over every inch of my body. Now in a hospital gown, I found myself with an IV drip to ward off shock, a cannula under my nose, and a nurse washing my face and another irrigating my eyes.

The one swabbing my face kept saying, "Now, this may be a bit uncomfortable . . . how are we coming?"

I remember thinking, hey, I can hear! The ringing was still there, but it didn't quite drown out everything. It was a lot like trying to have a conversation standing next to a very busy street. "It's not uncomfortable at all," I said. "Can't feel a thing. Honest."

"Brilliant," she said. "I'll be applying ointment now . . . it should feel a bit cool to you. Not to worry."

Again, I told her I didn't feel a thing. In the meantime, I was looking at the other nurse from under water. I was just a little confused. I'd never had my eyes irrigated before, and it was taking a long time for me to realize that the under water effect was just the running water in my eyes.

The water stopped, and I was staring up at a bright light.

"Oh, fine," said a female voice. "Very good. Hullo. I'm Doctor Benton, and your eyes are just fine."

"Hi."

"Your face is a bit puffy, you've experienced flash burns, I'm afraid. Any discomfort?"

"Nope. None."

"The ointment will be cooling. They aren't bad, you understand. First degree."

"Okay."

"Your X-rays were just fine. How do you feel?"

"Okay, I guess. Numb . . . mostly mentally. But things are clearing up."

"I see," she said, as she made a note on a clipboard. "Well, brilliant. You were in a nasty explosion, I understand."

"You could say that."

"A gas main, they say."

"What?"

"A gas main or something . . . in the flat where you were." The doctor looked quite concerned. "You have a recollection of that?"

It took me a second. Then I got it. Gas main. Well, if it worked for the Brits, it was fine with me. "Okay. Yeah, I remember. Clear as a bell. Gas main, I said to myself."

The busy little movements in the room stopped.

"Indeed?" asked Dr. Benton. "You wouldn't be having me on would you?"

"No. Really, I remember it." I began to think I might have laid it on a little too thickly. You stand next to a bomb sometime, and see how well you do.

She looked at me without expression. "Higgins," she said, without turning around, "we'll need a look at his head. Within an hour?" I never heard Higgins answer, but I know that I was laying in a white tube a while later, and I suspect it was a CAT scan or something very much like it.

"Do you remember just who you were with?" asked Dr. Benton.

"No need for details now," said a familiar male voice. "Plenty of time for that." It was Blyth.

They must have given me a sedative, because I was getting sleepier and sleepier.

"How's Alice?" I asked.

"Very well," said Blyth. His voice faded.

05:31

I came around, and saw Sue sitting next to my bed. "Hey? How you doing?" I asked.

"Me! My God. How are *you*?"

"Well, fine, I guess." But as I talked, my face began to feel very tight. "Except for my face, maybe."

"You look like you have a very bad sunburn," she said.

"Ah. Sure. Thermal . . . thing. Can I have some water?"

I faded back out. The ringing in my ears was constant. It kind of helped me to sleep.

07:38

I was back and now I felt really good. Except for my face, which felt very hot and very tight. And the ringing in my ears.

Sue was still in her chair.

"Good morning," I said, and just about scared her to death.

She went out into the hall, to tell them I was awake, and then came back.

"You are so lucky," she said.

"You got that right."

"A natural gas explosion . . . good Lord, whoever would have thought?"

This time, I didn't need a hint. Natural gas it was. If that's what they wanted, it was good for me, but I'd had some experience with that in the US. The gas company was going to raise hell with some-body, and get a retraction. But that took time. "Quite a bang," I said. "How's everybody else?"

"Alice is getting along very well," said Sue. "I saw her about an hour ago, and she said to tell you hello. They tell me that you will be up and around in a few hours, but if you don't feel well enough, don't do it."

"Okay. But I feel good. I think. We'll see when I stand up."

"You wait for a nurse."

I thought about it. "Okay." I grinned. "How about a kiss?"

She leaned over and kissed me lightly. "Does that hurt?"

"Nope."

She kissed me again, and then stood back. "It looks like it would."

It was really weird. I got up with a nurse close by, went to the head after I persuaded her that she wasn't going to come in with me, felt very alert and rested, walked very carefully back to bed with her right there, sat down, laid down, and that's all I remember.

08:22

I was awakened by two doctors, who gave me a once-over that in-cluded peering into my eyes with a small light, asked if I'd had any head injuries in the recent past, and then decided that the best thing for me would be breakfast and a walk in the hall. They'd left, I'd gone to the head again without a nurse interfering, and was sitting on the edge of my bed, drinking a cup of coffee and telling Sue that I wasn't about to walk anywhere outside the room in a hospital gown, when Blyth came in.

"Very good to see you up and about," he said.

I'd gotten a look at my face in the mirror in the bathroom. "Well, at least up. I saw my face. I look a lot like a tomato," I said.

"That you do."

"How's Alice?"

"Absolutely fine, has what's apparently a mild concussion. She is bearing a strong resemblance to a tomato as well."

"And Sarah Mitchell?"

I could tell by the look on his face, even before he spoke. "She didn't make it, I'm afraid. Enormous internal damage. Just about got everything, they tell me. Painless, they said, but she was gone within an hour or two."

"Well, shit," I said. "That's awful. Hell, I thought I saw her talking to Mark . . ."

"Quite conscious, he said," said Blyth. "Apparently her systems were just shutting down from the moment of the explosion."

"Shit. . . . What about Northwood . . . I seem to remember him flying out the window."

"We'll talk about those details later. And, how are you getting along?" he asked Sue.

Great Portland Street
London
09:35 Greenwich Mean Time

A man well known to Mr. Kazan entered his shop, browsed, and when the other customer had left, approached the counter, and laid a paper bag on the counter, and left. In the bag, Mr. Kazan found a brand-new mobil phone. With it was a folded piece of paper, with the number of another cell phone.

Mr. Kazan went into the back room, closed the curtain, and using the cell phone, dialed the number.

Anton answered on the first ring.

"Why did you not know there were others with him?" asked Mr. Kazan.

"We had no way . . ."

"You had many ways," came the terse response.

"His phone was busy. Imad couldn't re-contact him, even on his computer. If he was on the telephone, he would very likely be by himself. It was reasonable."

"Except he was not alone," said Mr. Kazan. "So it was not reasonable. Who were those who were with him?"

"On the news, they only identify Northwood, and the Mitchell woman. The dead one. She worked for a newspaper. She is the one who interviewed the American?"

"I can read the papers. Who are the others? It says that there were two men and three women in the hospital. Who are they? Find out. And let me talk to Imad."

"One of them is Imad."

"What?"

"In hospital," said Anton. "Imad is one of them."

"*Imad? Our* Imad?"

"He was following her. He was to wait on the first floor, in case she failed to sacrifice herself. In case she came back down the stairs. He had her rigged with a phone detonator. He would set her off if she hesitated. But he had to be able to know where she was."

Mr. Kazan said nothing.

"He must have gone up too far. He was injured. . . ."

"He is at Guy's and St. Thomas's?"

"Yes. He is still there. I had someone from the mosque check that. The hospital . . . they will not divulge the nature of his injuries except to a relative. They do tell us that they are not critical."

"Do they know who he is?"

"How am I expected to know?"

"You will find out. You will be his relative."

"What name do I use?" He had no idea what Imad's true name was, and even less of an idea as to whether or not he'd used it.

"I will tell you within an hour. Stay where you are, and wait."

Mr. Kazan began what was essentially an exercise in resource conservation. The odds were, he knew, that Imad had been exposed and was either under arrest or close surveillance. There was a chance, though, that he was neither. If that were the case, it would be best to have him released from the hospital and in the company of friends. Mr. Kazan would check with an employee of the hospital, first to see what name Imad was registered under, and second, to see what possibility there might be to obtain his release. If there was a chance, he then would send an eminently expendable resource named Anton into the hospital to extricate Imad.

Mr. Kazan's route to becoming informed was circuitous, in keeping with sound procedure. He called a man, who called a man, who contacted a nurse at Guy's and St. Thomas's, who ascertained the information and began reversing the process. It took less than an hour. The nurse's information was accurate, but incomplete. Imad had been admitted under his real name. He had a cracked cervical vertebra, was suffering from a concussion, and was incommunicative. There was no information available regarding police interest. Since he was not talking with anyone, and was not cooperating in any way, he was being held pending notification of relatives.

Mr. Kazan was certain that police involvement would become more and more intense the longer it took to find Imad's "relatives." On the other hand, it did appear that a relative would be able to obtain his release. The sooner the better.

He called Anton.

Physicians Consultation Room
Guy's and St. Thomas's Hospital Complex
Central London
10:11 Greenwich Mean Time

"His name is Imad Imadhi, according to his identification. He won't talk to me at all," said Dr. Benton. "He does have a cracked C-5 vertebra, and a concussion. He could be released, but we have no way of being certain that we're communicating with him."

"What do you mean by that? Is he reluctant, or is it something relating to his injuries?" asked Trowbridge.

"It is definitely not amnesia," said Dr. Benton. "I suspect it is reluctance, for some reason. He appears to be Arabic. I thought it might be because I am a woman, but I had Dr. Givens try to talk to him, and he also got nowhere."

Blyth looked up from his notes. "Dr. Givens is male?"

"Yes. Sorry." She shook her head. "We have a counselor who is fluent in Arabic, but he gets no response at all. Judging from his reactions to things that we say, I'm certain the he *does* understand English."

Trowbridge looked at a receipt form. "All he had with him was his billfold, a large pocket knife, two keys for a door that is demonstrably not in that building, the ubiquitous cell phone, and a comb." He saw Dr. Benton's eyebrow raise.

"Were those the effects he had upon admission?" she asked.

"Done with a proper warrant," he said, pleasantly. "Properly served upon your administrator, who was most cooperative."

"Thank you," she said.

"He'll have it all back before he wakes up," said Trowbridge. "With a receipt that says we looked at his personal effects."

"Thank you, Doctor," said Blyth. "We'll just be another second, if you wouldn't mind telling them that the room is still occupied?"

Dr. Benton stood, and said, "I hope you can find who did this to him." She gave a tight lipped smile. "Not the gas company."

"I do as well," said Blyth.

As soon as she had left, Blyth said, "We're doing some things with his mobile phone numbers. I hope to have something fairly soon."

"He's an engineer," said Trowbridge. "Here on a visa. Works for a civil engineering firm in Cranford. Lives near there, on Hayes Road, Southall. We know nobody in Northwood's building knew him or knew why he would have been near the second-floor landing."

"Good. We have Northwood's laptop, or what's left of it. It was in the street. Hard drive seems intact, so we may have things," said Trowbridge.

"Since this Imad Imadhi does have the same first name as a possible conspirator in the Emma Schiller kidnapping, he may also have been the one who brought the bomber. Since the surveillance team isn't precisely sure how the bomber arrived," said Blyth, sarcastically, "it could well be him. But, however she got there, there's no vehicle unaccounted for in the vicinity. No cab, no limo service, had a fare there, you say?"

"None," said Trowbridge. "Perhaps she lived in the general neighborhood."

"We may have some information that says otherwise," said Blyth. "Should be going across your desk about now." Blyth stretched in his chair. "Long day. Well, then, my money's on the fact that our Mr. Imadhi knew someone who was killed. Either the Mitchell woman, or Northwood, or the bomber. I'd bet on two of the three." He dialed his cell phone. "Yes, Blyth here. Be a good man, and send an officer to the room of one Imad Imadhi . . . he's a patient here. Yes. One should do, he apparently had a bit of a broken neck. Just observe, for now. Yes. Good." He closed the phone.

"If he was her transportation, where's his car?"

"An excellent question. The ride certainly wasn't seen by Mitchell's cameraman. He was outside in the street when it happened."

"And he saw no one?"

"No. He's a photographer, wouldn't you think he would be aware? But, no. He turns out to be one of those who take wonderful photos, if someone points them at the subject and says to press the button. He saw lots of people. It was raining, he had the interior light on, reading a magazine. He can't identify any of them, just was aware they would pass fairly close. Just shapes in the rain. That's corroborated by the surveillance team, by the way. Actually," and he cleared his throat, "the way they ended up milling about, most of the people he saw were likely ours."

"The surveillance people, you mean?"

"Yes."

"I'm glad they were good for something," said Blyth. "Just to cheer you up, Henry Morris referred to suicide bombers as 'a volatile lot.'"

Trowbridge grinned. "I shall remember that."

"See to it you remember that it isn't funny. It's just an example of the dark humor you'd expect from someone who defused bombs for a living."

"Oh, indeed," said Trowbridge.

"But Mark says he saw the woman enter the building . . . he thinks she may have come from the west on Burnaby Street. That's a deduction, by the way. He first saw her near the corner, but had been looking up Ashburnham just before he saw her. It was an impression he got."

"But he watched her go in?"

"He did. Waited several seconds, and followed her. She stopped on the landing to the second floor, and that's when Mark turned around and walked to the first floor to make a call to Alice. Thought the woman might be aware he was following her, he said. At that point, a slender man of middle height entered the building, and started up the stairs. This Imadhi."

"No contact, though?" asked Blyth.

"No. Didn't even get a good look at him, he came in so quickly. Mark says that the blast occurred; he ran up the stair, had to jump over Imadhi on the second floor landing on his way to third. He says that our engineer was just sitting in the stairwell, covered with plaster."

"Struck on the head, wasn't he?"

"Apparently so. Yes. He was tended to by the first paramedic to go up the stair."

Blyth leafed through a small stack of papers. "And this is the paramedic . . . yes, who says that, and I'm quoting, 'the victim never uttered a word, although I spoke to him often. I did have the impression that he understood me . . . ,' end of quote. Stunned, do you suppose?"

"Don't know," said Trowbridge.

"Well, he doesn't appear to have said anything much at all since he's come in here. Sleeps a lot, I'm told. Although that's consistent with a concussion."

"It is," said Trowbridge, dryly.

"And it's also consistent with someone who doesn't wish to speak," said Blyth.

"Ah . . . indeed. Confidentially, that would be my guess. Of course, I suppose it could merely be that he doesn't understand English."

Blyth trumped with, "Or was rendered stone deaf by the explosion. Or he simply could have expired unnoticed." He started to laugh. "I tell you, this parrot's dead. . . ."

Trowbridge laughed.

"We'd best keep a guard on his room, then," said Blyth, after the tension-breaking moment had passed.

"This might be difficult to arrange . . . we're short now."

"I do hope," said Blyth, "that you remember to cancel your sub-scription to the *Mirror*."

"God forbid. It's our best source." He saw Blyth's startled look, and said, "The horoscopes."

"Right. As a favor, don't say that to the Americans. After the inci-dent with that bloody *Mirror* reporter, they're going to be . . . more in evidence. Since this lot were connected with the demand to meet with the president. . . ."

Guy's and St. Thomas's
London
13:02 Greenwich Mean Time

Sue had called Carson at the hotel, and he'd come over with a pair of sweatpants, a sweatshirt, socks and my tennis shoes. Then he'd gone to get the girls up at Highgate. I felt well dressed, and had taken my first walk with a nurse who didn't seem to me large enough to even break my fall, let alone keep me on my feet if I passed out. Not that I would do a thing like that, but it did seem to be on her mind. Sue went with us, up and down the hall three times. Lots of patients, and every one of them looked to be worse off than I was.

We looked in on Alice, whose room was being kept fairly dark by the drawn shades. She was sound asleep.

I was just done with lunch when Jane, Vicky and Carson came in. There was a nice feeling fuss about how I was doing from Jane and Vicky. I kept telling them that I was really just fine.

A nurse came in, and I found myself transferred to a three patient room in another wing. As she said, "Just until you're released this eve-ning."

That was just fine. Neither of my two roommates seemed too likely to strike up a conversation, although one of them had a cough that would have worried me if I thought I was going to spend the night. I figured since I was going to be out of the hospital by evening, then we could spend a couple of days between my being deposed and sightseeing, and that things concerning the kidnapping and murder of Emma had just about played their course.

Then Blyth and Trowbridge showed up.

After asking after Jane's and my health, they wanted to know if I felt well enough to have a talk with them. I thought they'd probably talked with the docs, or they wouldn't have asked.

"Sure. Be glad to."

Obviously, we weren't gong to talk here. They asked if I could meet them in a few minutes, and gave me directions to a consultation room.

My troops decided that, since I was out of the picture for the afternoon, they'd do a little sightseeing. Sue really wanted to see Westminster Abbey, and since it was just across the river, it seemed like a fine idea.

Once they were gone, I grabbed my billfold, intending to stop at a machine and get a Coke or the equivalent, and hied myself to where the directions directed me. Well, I thought I was right. Unfortunately, when I arrived there, it was a closed ward.

I asked, and the aide told me that I was at the wrong end of the complex. And a floor too high. Apparently I belonged in the North Wing.

I got off the elevator, and walked down a corridor, past a room with a bobby standing outside looking bored. I nodded to him, and he nodded back. Bored cops are a universal thing.

I started through a lobby, and saw a youngish man coming toward me who looked kind of familiar. I didn't think much of it, and crossed the lobby and went down another corridor. Wrong way again. I turned around, and headed back, and saw the same guy get just about to the room with the bobby, and turn smartly, and start coming toward me again. I grinned at him, thinking he was either lost or confused, too. He didn't grin back, but he looked even more familiar this time.

Well, why not? I'd just seen him a minute ago. Then, as he passed, I saw the flesh colored bandage on his forehead.

I stopped, turned, and watched him walk away. For all the world, I thought it might be the creep I'd smacked with my flashlight at Down Street station.

"Naw." I actually said that, and felt a little foolish. But I thought it just might be. So I followed him.

He was waiting for the elevator when I caught up with him. Dressed like I was, I think I looked more like a jogger than anything else. Well, with my girth, maybe more like a walker. With a sunburn.

In the elevator, I was right next to him, and he looked up at me. I was just about sure it was the creep. The way he looked at me, I thought I'd better give him a little distraction, so I flashed my best smile, pointed to my face, and said, "Sunburn."

He didn't say anything, and looked away instantly.

The elevator opened, and we were in the shop area. At least I was on familiar ground. He started walking toward the entrance at a pretty quick pace, and I managed to stay just about with him. As we went out the main entrance, I grabbed a nurse by the arm and said, "Call the cops."

She gave me a startled look and said "Wot?"

I didn't have time to stand around and talk, because he was getting ahead of me. I kept forging ahead, and saw him take a left to go by the fountain.

I turned after him, and thought I might be gaining a little. There was a man with an umbrella, hustling my way through the light rain, and I grabbed him by his umbrella hand as we passed.

"Call the police," I said. "It's important."

"I beg your pardon?"

"Gotta go, call the cops!"

We were on Westminster Bridge Road now, and heading for the bridge across the Thames. There was lots of car traffic, but not a cop car in sight.

As far as I'd seen, he hadn't looked back yet. That was a little disconcerting, because he was looking more and more normal to me as we moved toward the bridge. Was it the wrong guy?

I just stepped in front of the next oncoming person, a young woman in a raincoat and white shoes. Had to be a nurse.

"Nurse!"

She stopped.

"Call the cops. I've just come from the hospital. I'm following a suspect. Call the cops and tell them where you saw me. The name is Houseman."

Between the ringing in my ears, and the traffic sounds on the wet roadway, I saw her lips move, but couldn't make out what she said. I looked across the river, and my man was now another thirty yards ahead.

"Hurry!" I said, and started to jog. I really didn't care if he saw me now, I just wanted to grab him and find out for sure.

My lack of jurisdiction was really starting to bug me. What the hell was I going to do if I caught him? More importantly, what was I going to do if I caught him and I was wrong? Hell, I couldn't even make a citizen's arrest. I wasn't a fucking citizen.

I really didn't want to lose him, though.

We were on the bridge by now, heading toward Big Ben and the Houses of Parliament. I was at the first set of those double streetlights, and he was already at the second. Way ahead, but I was gaining. He did seem to be walking faster now. Probably not because he was nervous. Probably because it was raining.

My best guess is that the bridge is a little over 250 yards long. I was halfway, and he was now only about fifteen yards ahead. I was counting on finding cops near Big Ben. I was *really* counting on that. I don't know if it was the events of last night or what, but my legs were beginning to tire. I didn't know how far this guy was going to go, but I knew I wasn't going to be able to chase him a whole lot farther without either giving up, or of making a real effort and catching him before he knew I was behind him.

When he got to the end of the bridge, he stopped at the corner, waiting for the light to change. I came up on his right, a little behind, trying to look like I was just out jogging. By that time, he had reached in his pocket, pulled out a cell phone, and was dialing.

I got behind him, thought I had a few seconds, and looked down toward the cops that were on duty at Parliament. There were just two of 'em, I suppose because Bush was leaving London today, and wouldn't be anywhere near here. There were still a couple of anti-US banners and posters in the little park, but there were three people in plastic coats cleaning them up. I waived at the cops, trying to get their attention. No luck. I glanced back at the light, and thought it was about to change.

I turned back toward the two bobbies, made a funnel of my hands, and yelled, "Hey!"

Everybody looked at me but the cops. No shit. I guess it's true about us. I yelled again, and one of them looked up. I waived both arms, and motioned him toward us. I looked back, and the light had changed, and my quarry was about half way across the street.

It looked like he was heading toward the tube station. I had to do something, because I sure wasn't about to follow him down that way.

I ran across the street, against the light for about half way, and caught him just as he turned to his right and headed for the tube station entrance.

I grabbed him around the neck. It wasn't pretty, but he sure as hell stopped.

"We gotta talk," I said. "Now."

He was really squirmy, and I almost lost him as we sort of waltzed into the side of a building. He hit first.

"Hold still," I said. "You're under arrest."

I think that took him by surprise for just a second, and I got a better grip on his neck. As I did so, his right hand went into his pocket, and he kicked back with his left foot, getting me a good one on the shin.

For that, I just bent my knees, and let my weight do some of the work. I must have been nearly a hundred pounds heavier than he was, and six or seven inches taller. He bent at the waist, screamed in anger, and went to his knees. It must have hurt like hell when he hit the pavement, but I stayed on him. I was grabbing at his right arm, while he was kicking like crazy, and trying to head butt me by snapping his head back as hard as he could. He was pretty strong, and again, he just about got away. I kept catching his left elbow in my ribs, and he was really starting to piss me off.

As he wriggled, he was able to get his right hand out of his pocket, and I thought he was trying to hit me with his right fist. I just kind of leaned back on him, and he couldn't get his hand high enough to come back over his shoulder where it would do any good.

I was kind of aware that there were some people sort of gathering, some to watch, and some to just pause and move on. I looked up at them and yelled, "Just call the fucking cops, will you?"

He was really frantic now, and his struggles had moved us back toward the street. As we went, his and my right hand both ended up under him, and I felt something in his fist. I thought it was his cell phone.

Just then, there was a strong hand on my own right shoulder, and a very firm voice said, "Stop that!"

I glanced up and saw a constable in a yellow rain coat bent over us. He looked really mad.

"Watch him," I said. "Be careful, I think he's got something in his hand."

"Let him go!"

I didn't. I didn't, mainly because the constable didn't have him anywhere near under control. I did say, "Just a minute. . . ."

At that point, I caught a truncheon on the right elbow. I lost my grip, said something brilliant like "Ouch!" and started to lean back.

The man under me lashed out with his right, and I saw the knife blade pass in front of the constable's nose, missing him by about an inch.

I lost my balance, sat back hard, and kicked out with my left foot, catching my man in the back of the head.

"He's got a knife!" I said. A little late, maybe, but at least I got that much out.

The bobby smacked him right on the wrist, really hard, and the knife clattered to the street, and the man yelled something I didn't understand.

I don't know where all the other bobbies came from, but all of a sudden we were surrounded.

I found myself face down, being handcuffed behind my back, and saw my quarry getting the same treatment.

"Call Sergeant Trowbridge," I said. "Special Branch. Get him over here."

"Calm down," said a bobby.

"I yell because I can't hear very well," I said, pretty reasonably. "Get Trowbridge over here. He's at St. Thomas's hospital. Tell him Deputy Houseman needs to see him right away."

Okay, in his position, I suppose I wouldn't have done it, either. Instead, me and my man were placed in two separate squad cars, and were guarded while some things got straightened out. Let me tell you, those British squad cars are not large enough. I was sort of laying on my side, knees drawn up, getting more irritable by the second, when Trowbridge's face looked in the window. He saw me, grinned, and a few seconds later, the door was opened, and I was helped out.

"What on earth have you been up to?" he asked. "There must have been a half dozen calls received regarding you, in just the time since we were in your room."

"The man I was chasing," I said, as my handcuffs were removed, "I think is the guy who stabbed Jane."

"Really?"

"I got lost, when I was coming to see you. I went past a room guarded by a cop, and I saw that dude coming toward me. He looked kind of familiar. I was still lost, so I turned around, and saw him coming back toward me. I think he was headed toward the room with the cop on the door."

"Get him out, but leave him cuffed," said Trowbridge to one of the constables. "Are you sure?" he asked me.

I took a deep breath. "No. But I think so. He ought to have an injury on his head, in front. From where I hit him with my flashlight in the tube station."

I couldn't help noticing that the constable nearest me had a quizzical look on his face. He was the one who almost caught the knife blade in the face. "He didn't miss you by much," I said.

"That's right, sir," he said, calmly. "It was close."

As my suspect was escorted over, Blyth showed up with a senior officer in tow.

"How's our favorite American?"

I felt the knot on my elbow. "Sore, kind of." I pushed up my sleeve, and revealed a knot the size of a baseball on my right elbow.

Blyth looked aghast. "He got you a good one, didn't he?"

"He didn't," I said, grinning and pointing at the constable. "He did."

"Indeed?" said the senior man in uniform.

"Couldn't be helped," I said. "He didn't know who I was, and I was on top, and I wouldn't let go."

About that time, my suspect arrived. I looked at him closely. "It's him," I said.

He gave me a good look, and said, "I've never seen this man before in my life."

I pointed at the bandage on his forehead. "Take a look under that," I said to Trowbridge. "Should be half moon shaped. Kind of a cut."

Trowbridge reached out to lift up the bandage, and the man tried to bite his hand. The constable holding him twisted imperceptibly, saying "Here, here, we'll have none of that," and the man rose on his tiptoes.

Trowbridge reached out again, this time placing one hand firmly on top of the man's head, and lifted the bandage. Sure as hell, there was a half moon cut, still kind of swollen at the edges.

"Remember me now?" I asked. "The Underground station?"

He looked blank.

"You and my flashlight had a little collision? Remember?"

He did. He looked me with recognition, and said, "Too bad she didn't die."

He was close enough. I think that if I hadn't burned off the adrenaline in the scuffle, I probably would have hit him. But I didn't. I just said, "I don't think you could kill anybody who wasn't tied up, junior."

Guy's and St. Thomas's
London
15:12 Greenwich Mean Time

I had to go back into the hospital to get discharged. Blyth went with me, and while I was waiting, we visited Alice and told her what had happened. She was pleased, in a dopey sort of way. I figured we'd talk later.

Blyth and I got back to my room, and we had a short discussion, mostly to kill time.

"You handled that incident well," he said.

"Catching up to him?"

"No, not trying to kill him when he recognized you."

"Oh," I said. "Well, we don't need me in jail over here, too. I'm sure you'll come up with something. It would have felt good to strangle him, though. Very good."

"We'll do our best," he said. "If I get a chance, I'll see if I can arrange you seeing the recordings."

"Recordings?"

"We have surveillance cameras salted all over the city," he said. "You should have been picked up on at least two or three of them."

"No shit . . . I hadn't even thought about that."

"I'll see if I can obtain copies. Should make fantastic viewing back in Iowa."

"That would be really cool. . . ."

I looked at my watch. "My group ought to be showing up pretty soon. I'm surprised it's taken them this long."

"Westminster Abbey is a great, fascinating place," said Blyth.

"We can consider this case closed?" I watched a nurse go by, hoping she'd come in and let me go. No luck. "Officially, I mean."

"For all intents and purposes."

"I was afraid of that," I said. "Now I have to tell Jane that Emma's dead."

We sat in silence for a moment.

"Let me do that for you," said Blyth.

"I can do it."

"No, I insist. The least I can do."

I thought about it for a moment. "Okay. I'd appreciate that."

They let me go about five minutes after that. Blyth and I went down to the main lobby, where we waited about another fifteen minutes for the gang to show up. I didn't know how he was going to tell them there. Neither did he, apparently, because he didn't. Instead, he suggested he meet us at the girls' place in Highgate in an hour.

I told everybody about my little adventure as we walked across the bridge to the tube station. It was kind of fun, because I could stop at a particular place, and say things like, "And right here, I grabbed a nurse, and said . . ."

Jane was really excited, as we now had "one of 'em in the bag," as she put it.

"Now we can find Emma."

Back in Highgate, Blyth showed up as scheduled. After just a few seconds, he said, "I'm afraid I have some bad news."

There was instant silence.

"Emma Schiller," he said. "I'm very sorry to have to tell you that she's dead."

There was lots of commotion, of course. I think everybody had expected this, true, but still, it hit fairly hard. Jane and Vicky in particular. Regardless of the emotions, Jane pressed for details.

"I'm afraid I can't tell you much," said Blyth. "It's all still very secret. We do know that she was killed after the last tape. I can tell you that."

He was really adroit. He didn't say "after the last tape was made." By not saying that, the assumption on Jane's part was that she'd died after the last tape was *received*, not after it was made. That being the case, the wild goose chase at Down Street station wasn't revealed as such. I was very grateful for that.

He only gave us about three or four minutes, and then said to Jane, "Did you know that the man your father apprehended this afternoon was the one who had stabbed you?"

That got everybody's mind onto a different track for a moment, but not for much longer than that.

"Did she suffer?" persisted Jane.

"At this point, I can't say. I wouldn't think so, at least not much."

"Why do they hate us so?"

"It's the information age, really," said Blyth. "I don't think anyone appreciated the effects that such sudden, all-encompassing access to western society would have on some of the others."

"But to just kill people . . . ?" said Vicky. "I mean . . ."

"A fundamentalist segment," said Blyth, "who are enormously offended, feel hugely threatened, and who are fueled by fanatic followers . . ."

"Offended by what?"

"Different ideas."

"That's it? Just different ideas?" Jane was getting angry.

"Different ideas," said Blyth, "have accounted for the deaths of millions upon millions of people. I suspect it's second only to the great plagues, really."

"But . . . to pick somebody at random? Kidnap and kill at random?"

"She was an American," said Blyth. "That did have some influence on their choice."

"It could have been me or Jane?" asked Vicky. "Is that what you're saying?"

"It could have been, and easily," said Blyth.

"That's just not fair," said Jane. "Not fair for any of us."

Conversation stopped for a few seconds, and then Vicky said, "That wasn't a natural gas explosion, was it?"

Blyth surprised me by saying, "No. It was not."

"What was it?" asked Sue.

"It was a woman, a suicide bomber," he said.

"Why . . . ?"

"She was sent to kill the owner of the flat. You all know who he was. What you don't know about Robert Northwood is that he was also the man who originated the idea of kidnapping Emma Schiller. They wanted to stop him before he could talk with us."

A little lightbulb went on in my head. "The guy in St. Thomas's? The one with the cop at the door? Was that who the guy I chased was going to see?"

"You're entirely too good," said Blyth, "to be let out on your own. Yes, it was. He was a fellow conspirator. Injured in your same explosion, but on the second floor landing. On the way here, I was told that he was the backup plan."

"He was a bomber, too?" I asked.

"In a manner of speaking, yes. He was equipped with a mobile phone. They had rigged her with a phone detonator, as well as one that she could use herself. His intent was to wait a few moments, after he heard the door open. If he thought she was hesitating, or was not going to do it at all, his job was to set her off by dialing the number of the phone connected to the bomb." He smiled. "Unfortunately for him, he got too close, in order to hear her gain admittance."

"He set her off?"

"We don't think so. We believe he would have descended the stairs before dialing. What he didn't anticipate was that she'd self-detonate before she was completely through the door."

I was kind of surprised that they stayed with that natural gas explosion story, and even more surprised they got it to stick. Security Services were helped by the fact that England won the rugby match on Saturday. The World Cup, over Australia, and in overtime. The first time they'd ever won. Nobody talked about anything else, on TV or in the papers. November 22nd, 2003.

It was also the fortieth anniversary of the killing of JFK. Sue and I talked about that, remembering where we were on that day. Carson, Vicky and Jane hadn't even been born, then. It's hard to imagine that I would have ever thought of those as better times, but I did.